MW00513698

REPROBATE
WAYS

REPROBATE WAYS

THE UNVEILING OF ANN

PART II
OF THE WAYS TRILOGY

FELICIA BROOKINS

Tandem Light Press
950 Herrington Rd.
Suite C128
Lawrenceville, GA 30044

Copyright © 2022 by Felicia Brookins

All rights reserved. No part of this book may be reproduced, scanned, or transmitted in any printed, electronic, mechanical, including photocopying, recording, or any information storage and retrieval system, without permission in writing from the publisher. Please do not participate in or encourage piracy of copyrighted materials in violation of the author's rights.

Tandem Light Press paperback edition

ISBN: 978-1-7376438-1-4

PRINTED IN THE UNITED STATES OF AMERICA

This book is dedicated to the survivors and conquerors of generational trauma as well as those who have decided "it ends with me."

FOREWORD

For those who love a read that is entertaining, relatable, and full of lessons we can all benefit from then *Reprobate Ways* is just what you have been waiting on. Whether you have read award-winning author Felicia Brookins' book *Sister Nadeen's Ways* or are just being introduced to her popular character Sister Nadeen, you are going to enjoy how people who say they have faith have it tested in and out of their house of worship.

Reprobate Ways shows you can take the person out of the world but the world is still there—and sometimes it creeps right into your home. This is true for Sister Nadeen as well as some of those around her. Through the challenges they have to face not just the bad but also each other. Dark times emerge, but as Brookins has shown before, the light can shine again.

This is the kind of book that will make you laugh, make you reflect, and make you thankful for the thing we call forgiveness. Settle in and get ready to lose yourself in the pages. *Reprobate Ways* gives you everything you want in a fun read. Enjoy!

Cyrus Webb
Media Personality/Top 200 Amazon Reviewer

ACKNOWLEDGMENTS

I'd like to begin with acknowledging the power of Time. Time can heal wounds so they don't hurt as much as they did when they were inflicted. I appreciate that more than you know.

To my beautiful goddaughter, Brooklyne Edmond, who was born at a time when I needed her. Precious, sweet spirit, the most in my life. You, my darling, are beautiful and brilliant.

Next, the fabulous and supportive members of the Joy Book Club, these beautiful ladies were the first book club in Jackson, Mississippi to extend an invitation to me and Sister Nadeen Sim-mons to enter their joyous space and spill the tea. They have waited anxiously for Part II of this Trilogy and shared in the "sneak-peek" review of part of the manuscript for this book. I pray it doesn't disappoint.

Much love to the children who don't "feel" just how mentally and emotionally strong they really are because they are so smothered in the turmoil, they can't see how deep it really is and how far they have made it to the exit. Stay the course you will physically get out. Emotionally and mentally, you may never truly get away but always outrun it no matter how close the residue of your pain feels just keep going.

Hugs, Joy, and Laughter go out to the warm and embracing Ladies of the Circle of Color Book Club. They really brought my character to life all the way to the main character's attire during our book discussion. I love your energy and the Usher Uniform!

I want to thank the fans of my first book *Sister Nadeen's Ways*. You have been so patient yet you never let me forget for a moment that you were waiting. Thank you for your reviews, your financial support, and your excitement.

Married Couples, don't go to "work" in your marriage without putting on the "whole armor" of God, especially when your spouse seems to be your enemy or stumbling block. Marriage really is for "grown-folks" and that's not a number, that's spiritually, mentally, and emotionally. Build your wall, set the standard because trust if you leave a crack anywhere the battle will be great to restore things back the way they were.

And finally, last but definitely not least, this book would not be in your hands without the contributions and support of my family and friends—who show that love really is a verb.

"Congratulations! Counting it all JOY!"
— Leona Bishop,
JOY Book Club

"Great Series! Keep them coming!"
— Sherry Bouldin,
JOY Book Club

"Congratulations!"
— Deborah Cole,
JOY Book Club

"Heartfelt Congratulations to you, Felicia!"
— Keneasha Clark,
JOY Book Club

"Congratulations & Continued Success!"
— Kimberly R. Harris,
JOY Book Club

"Congratulations on Book Two Felicia!"
— Ruthie Sayles,
JOY Book Club

"Congratulations, Soror!"
— Carmen Gooden,
Zeta Phi Beta Sorority, Incorporated

"Congratulations, Soror!"
— Dorothy Cox,
Zeta Phi Beta Sorority, Incorporated
Alpha Delta Zeta Chapter Jackson, Mississippi

"Deserve is an understatement. Congrats, Soror!"
– Lynnice Higgins -Zeta Phi Beta Sorority,
Incorporated

"Congratulations, Soror!"
– Gerald McCarty -Zeta Phi Beta Sorority,
Incorporated

"Congratulations, Soror!"
– Pamela Odie Wright -Zeta Phi Beta Sorority, Incorporated

"Congratulations to my favorite Blu Author! Continued blessings, sister-in-law! Love ya, Your Denise."
– Lisa Brookins-Mercer

"Congratulations to you, my friend!"
– Elizabeth Edwards

"Felicia. Congratulations on Book Two! I anxiously await the experience.
– Gloria Brereton

"God's continued blessings on your success."
– Dana Davis-Chambliss

"Congratulations Classmate!"
– Jennifer Owens,
Meridian High School C/O 1984

"Congratulations BFF! Arise Queen Arise!"
– Author Thelma B. Cousin,
Forex Trader/Educator

"*Congratulations Sis in Law, Felicia Brookins, regarding your recently published book. We are all so very proud of you*"

– Ava Reaves

"*We celebrate you, friend!*"

– ROOSEVELT AND SHELIA GUY

"*Continue to hold His hand and watch doors you thought closed, Open! Much Love!*"

– GREGORY HALL-A PHI A-H. HAULER

"*Wishing you much SUCCESS Felicia!*"

– DOROTHY COX

"*Congratulations on another AMAZING book!*"

– JAKYRANEE PHILLIPS

1

PATSY SIMMONS ROLLED over into a beautiful Sunday morning with the sound of raindrops hitting against the new metal roof. Kenny had sent money to Nadeen from Miami to get it put on after she complained about everyone else in the neighborhood getting a decent roof over their heads except her. His new job was paying well and he had been able to send more money home. Money, he told Patsy, he would use to buy her a new car for graduation. She had been home from her International Ministries church trip with Deliverance Rock for about a week. It felt good, surprisingly enough, to be back home. During the eight weeks she'd been gone it seemed Ann and Josie had grown and changed.

Josie was more independent and though Ann was glad to see her, it seemed to Patsy, she had developed this nonchalant and secretive mannerism about her. She was acting as though she was hiding something. Patsy knew Ann pretty well and she could tell if things weren't right with her.

Ann had been sleeping in Kenny's old room since he moved to Miami. She'd transformed the room into a purple teenage paradise. It was full of life. Lamps with fuzzy trim, purple bean bag chairs, purple fairy lights with drapes, fuzzy purple pillows, and pictures of her and her friends on the walls. It was a different mood in the room now. Patsy looked forward to opening the door to the room and walking into an ethereal wonderland. Nadeen still seemed irritated. Patsy had walked upon her a few times sitting at the kitchen table with a frown on her face in deep thought.

Now that her hours had been cut at the nursing home, Kenny's income was mainly carrying the household and she was having to wait on him for money. She didn't like it but she had to accept it for the time being. He made sure she had enough for all of the household bills and savings, but he told her when it came to her shoes and clothes she would have to handle that since she had more than enough to him.

He always called on Sunday morning before they left for Sunday School. As Patsy crawled out of bed, she heard her mother's cell phone ring. "Ann, get that phone. I'm trying to get ready for Service anybody that knows me knows that's what I'm doing on a Sunday Morning!" Her mother said, irritated. Patsy and Ann both knew she'd already looked at her cell phone to know it was Kenny otherwise she wouldn't have allowed them to even pick it up. "It's daddy," Ann said excitedly.

"Well, he's your sperm donor, not mine, so you talk to him," Nadeen yelled from the bathroom.

"Hey, daddy. How are you?" Ann asked with a huge smile on her face.

"I'm still blessed even though I miss my family. Where your sisters? I already know your momma's in the mirror getting herself together in her pure white." He said letting out a slight laugh.

"Josie headed towards me right now. Patsy just getting up." Ann responded watching Josie wobble towards her. She reached down and lifted Josie onto the dresser. "It's your daddy Josie. You wanna talk to him?" She asked as Josie reached out for the phone.

"Daddy, Daddy," Josie said smiling as she clapped her hands together. She would be turning three years old soon.

"Hey, baby girl. You miss your daddy? Your daddy misses you." Kenny said. Josie just held the phone smiling as she listened to Kenny's voice. After a few minutes, Patsy came out of her bedroom. She saw Josie smiling, holding the phone.

"Josie, let me talk to daddy right quick please," Patsy asked reaching for the phone. Josie had a grip on it. Patsy tried to take the cell phone, but Josie wouldn't let it go. "No! No! Stop!" she yelled at Patsy as she pushed her back. Patsy hated to see her cry so she tricked her so that she could talk to Kenny. "Push the button, Josie. Push the button and talk to daddy." Patsy said as she held the phone back a little and pushed the speaker button.

"Hey, daddy," Patsy said happy to hear her daddy's voice.

"Hey, my international traveler I heard you were back home."

"Yep. Now when you coming home?" Patsy said tilting her head to the side a little bit as she looked down at the phone.

Kenny laughed as he always did and said, "As soon as the Lord releases me to. I got to stay out of his way and let him do what he needs to do for our family. I love you though, never doubt that," he always said with sincerity.

"Yeah. I know you do but we miss you. I hope God knows that and takes that into consideration while he's working things out for you."

"He knows baby. He knows. How's your momma?" He hesitantly asked. Patsy knew he wanted to talk to her but she also knew that Nadeen wasn't going to talk to him unless she wanted money. That was the only time she would talk to him, and it would be brief.

"I thought I heard her getting in the shower a few minutes ago. You know how long that and putting on her makeup can take." Patsy lied. She knew for a fact her mother had been sitting on her vanity stool in her bathroom doing her make-up because she'd peeped through her bedroom door on her way down the hall. "She usually just about done beating her face by now and about to take the rollers out of that beautiful hair of hers," Kenny said.

"Daddy who you been hanging around talking about somebody beating they face?" Ann asked with a grin. She and Patsy both laughed. "What you really doin' in Miami?" Patsy asked her daddy.

"Occupying that's all just occupying," Kenny responded. "Well, I have to be in the choir stands bright and early this morning. It's Men's Sunday. Reverend Mack referred me to a real good Bible-based church here in Miami. I'm really gonna miss them when God sends me back home but I'll serve whatever purpose I'm supposed to for the time I'm here. Tell Nadeen I called and I look to hear from her soon. Bye Josie. Bye girls."

They all said goodbye together in unison. Josie yelled into the phone. "Bye-Bye, Daddy." Kenny laughed and told her goodbye.

"Patsy! Come paint my toenails before we leave for church!" Nadeen yelled down the hall as she came out of her bathroom and sat on her bed with her back against her headboard. "Guess y'all let your daddy tell you some sweet lies this morning about why he ain't where he supposed to be."

Nobody answered, they knew better. She reached over to the nightstand and handed Patsy the bottle of pink punch nail polish. Patsy put Josie on the bed next to her. Josie liked to stick her fingers out so Patsy could put a little nail polish on them in between painting Nadeen's nails.

"Somebody up in Greater Trials got to teach that harlot Champagne Porter how to look and dress like a proper First Lady from head to toe. Reverend Craig just can't seem to get her in line. Our real First Lady, bless her soul, would never have worn some of the things that girl wears up in the house of the Lord. She better get that church attire right before the Lord come and get her while she in it and she be sliding into Hell with that skirt pushed up to her silicone butt. Ask me how I know," she said as she burst out laughing.

Patsy just shook her head in her mind. Her momma was always backsliding. Patsy thought how interesting it was that Nadeen still wore this color nail polish. After all, it was Kenny's favorite color. He always told her so.

"What did your sperm donor want this morning? If I had the money right now, I would divorce him. The Lord would be alright with it too cause he abandoned us. He left us after he claimed he loved us. You see Patsy? You see why I keep you out of them boy's faces? I'm trying to keep you from heartache and lies cause that is all a man got for you.

"The Word says put your trust in no man! Trust only in the Lord. You hear me girl?" Patsy couldn't help but to hear her as much as she wished she didn't.

"Yes, ma'am I hear you," Patsy responded.

"My daddy never walked out on my momma. Sure, they had their share of misunderstandings, but he never left us no matter what happened, and I know your grand momma was a handful back then. See my daddy knew what love was. He stayed for better or worse." She huffed. "Kenny claim he love me but he don't. He don't love me for better or worse."

Patsy wanted to respond so bad she had to bite her tongue. She knew better, to do so would be going into a territory called "Grown-Folks Business" and if you wanted to be crucified in Nadeen's house you just put your mouth in that. There wouldn't be a dentist in town that could repair all the teeth she'd knock out your mouth.

Ann was the victim of something similar a few years earlier. Ann was always different. She had something in her that just wouldn't let well enough alone when it came to her momma. Patsy recalled the incident between Ann and their momma that was forever a crucial life lesson for both of them about stepping off into "Grown-Folks Business."

It was a Wednesday night, right after Bible study. Nadeen came in singing and praising God. She had asked them where Kenny was. They told her he had gone out for a few minutes, said he would be right back. "He'll be right back alright. His 'right back' may be three to five hours from now and he won't even know how he got home. You can't believe what Kenny says. He talks a good talk but he ain't walking a good walk." She said as she headed down the hall to her room to change clothes.

Ann thought Nadeen was in her room, and she commented to Patsy, "If I was Kenny, I'd never stay home either. She acts like she don't want him here and the next minute she want to know his every move. Kenny grown. She ain't his momma." Ann whispered.

Patsy warned her then, "Ann you need to watch what you say. You know the rules around here, we are children and children stay in their place. Our place is not in their business. Okay? Just pray. Nothing else." Her big sister advised her. After the incident, Patsy later recalled she did hear what sounded like a door softly closing.

Later that night, Patsy cooked dinner. Nadeen ate with them up front but she didn't say much. When she finished, she told them to get ready for school the next day and ordered Ann to take her bath first while Patsy cleaned up the kitchen.

Ann got up and went to the back to run her bathwater. While she was removing the plates from the dinner table, Patsy could hear Nadeen through the walls moving things around in her closet or pushing a dresser around she didn't really think a lot of it. Ann went into the bathroom and had been in the tub for about ten minutes maybe when Nadeen tapped on the bathroom door. "I need to put something in the bathroom," Patsy remembered hearing her mother say. Patsy got a funny feeling in her stomach as soon as she heard her mother's tone of voice. It was something determined and dangerous in it.

The next sound was Nadeen slamming the bathroom door into the wall, a whistling sound in the air, and Ann screaming as things fell to the floor in the bathroom. Water was splashing loudly and Ann was screaming.

Patsy ran to the doorway of the bathroom and jumped back immediately. Nadeen was swirling a black extension cord through the air and it was hitting Ann's wet skin with a ferocity that would make a circus lion back all the way up. Ann was screaming at the top of her lungs. In between her cries she was shouting, "Yes ma'am!" as Nadeen beat her and taught her at the same time.

"You don't open your flip mouth about my business when it comes to your trifling daddy! Do you hear me! Do you hear me? I'm the wife I had to live with him and his sinful ways day in and day out. You don't comment on my business.

"If you got a problem over here you can go and stay with his ignorant momma and your Aunt Ernestine over there across them tracks."

"Patsy help me!" Ann was screaming as loud as she could. She locked eyes briefly with her big sister knowing she couldn't come to her rescue.

Patsy's heart broke in a million pieces as she looked at the pain on her sister's face and heard her screaming above Nadeen's voice. "You not the one that had to lay in her bed alone at night while he was out somewhere selling Christmas trees for crack instead of being here protecting us! I been your momma and his too cause his own momma didn't raise him right! I don't care about your screaming! I been screaming for years and ain't nobody come to my rescue!"

The agony on Ann's face was too much for Patsy. She felt weak in her knees and had to grab ahold of the wall to hold herself up as she ran away.

Josie ran up to her big sister and grabbed her pants leg. She put her face in her pants leg and started crying. Patsy grabbed her and ran upstairs. She turned on Josie's toy radio and stuck the earplugs in Josie's ears to calm her. She held her tight and rocked her. Nadeen beat Ann for an hour it seemed.

When Nadeen walked out of that bathroom, Ann was on the floor with her skin ripped open and shaking. The shower curtain was hanging from the shower rod by one clip. The rugs were soaked with water. Splatters of Ann's blood were on the bottom of the toilet and on the rugs. She looked like she'd crawled through barbed wire.

The extension cord hitting her wet skin left welts on her that would take a while to disappear. The marks laid open and bloody over the semi-faded razor blade cuts on Ann's thighs where she'd attempted to remove her hurt and pain many times.

Ann cried uncontrollably on the floor. Patsy put a towel over her little sister's naked body but she didn't say anything to her. She was too afraid Nadeen would do the same thing to her if she did.

"Girl, stop daydreaming and finish my feet," Nadeen said. That knocked Patsy back into reality with a few chill bumps on her back from the memory. "Did your daddy ask if we needed anything around here?".

"No. He asked how you were doing and talked about how much he was enjoying his new church Reverend Mack referred him to.".

"He don't need to put my name in his mouth. I apparently ain't his business no more so he can just ask about his children. When he walked out of my door, he walked out on us! Tell him that the next time he want to ask about me!" Nadeen said rolling her eyes and pursing her lips. "He had a good Christian woman but that ain't what he wanted. He wants to go out into the world and find him something unholy. He ain't foolin' me one bit talking about God sending him away from us so he can be out the way! Out the way of what? A lightning bolt before it strikes him in his throat for telling a lie?"

Patsy didn't want to hear the speech again on what a bad person her daddy was for leaving them and that money wasn't enough to make up for him shaming her before the entire church congregation. Patsy knew it was God's plan because she believed it was him who spoke to her the day Kenny drove off in his truck.

"I gotta get to the church in time to inspect the Ushers and make sure everything is in order before Pastor and his pet snake come into the Sanctuary. I ain't doin' it for her, I'm doin' it for him and in memory of my First Lady bless her heart. I hope she is resting in peace."

When they made it back from church service Nadeen was worn out. She sent Patsy to the kitchen to make lunch for them while she took a nap. Patsy knew what was expected of her even if Nadeen didn't say it. A few hours later, Nadeen came into the kitchen and lifted the pots. The collard greens, macaroni and cheese, and smothered fried pork chops had the kitchen lit up.

"Glad to see you learned something from your momma. This meal looks mighty good. You make some cornbread with this cause I got to have cornbread for this gravy." Nadeen said. "Yes ma'am. It's still in the oven. I just put some butter on top of it few minutes before you came up here." Patsy replied.

Patsy had covered all of her bases. "God is good. Yes, he is. I poured all I had out unto the Lord today and I need to be renewed. Ann you and Josie come on up here and eat this dinner your Sister cooked for us." Nadeen said tasting the gravy from the pork chops with her finger.

Just as Nadeen was about to take off her earrings her cell phone rang. "I declare can't even get a bite to eat before folks start calling. Let me gone get this over with so I can enjoy my meal." It was Sister Haymer. She was new to the church and had recently finished her new member's class so she could begin working with the usher board. She idolized Nadeen.

She thought she was so Holy Ghost filled and fire baptized that she hung on every word she said. "Well thank you, Sister Haymer. Thank you so much. I tell you it was nobody but the Holy Ghost did that thang today. Something got a hold of me and I know it was Jesus! I was so full of the spirit I still ain't come down." Nadeen said. Patsy rolled her eyes as she prepared her plate. Nadeen knew she was wrong for faking with them church folks the way she was doing.

"Amen! I receive it in the name of Jesus! Sister Haymer you done bless me today! I tell you. Well, I thank you for that word of encouragement. Remember I love you and I will be praying for you. Call me anytime. All right now. God bless you." Nadeen said slumping her shoulders and looking up at the ceiling.

As soon as the receiver was put down Nadeen started complaining, "Why did Pastor assign me to train her to be an usher? Every Sunday she in my face smiling with them dingy yellow teeth of hers. I can smell a Black and Mild all over her breath from one hundred yards away. She smoke the devil's cabbage too. I know cause Sister Reba told me, she also told me she got some STD from being out on the streets selling her old stale, stank-stank for a rock. I don't need no extra friends I got one and that's Jesus. He's the only one I need. Hallelujah!" Nadeen said as she waved her hand in the air.

The only one you had is resting with Jesus and with the way you talk about people you won't ever have another one, Patsy thought to herself. Patsy was so glad to have Sandra in her life. They were going to be best friends forever. Nothing could come between them but death and even then, Patsy believed whichever one of them was left on this earth would speak the name of the other one into the atmosphere to give their love for each other life.

She often wondered if her mother ever missed Dhmonique, her one and only true friend on the earth. Nadeen never talked about her it was as if she never existed.

*   *   *

Dhmonique had been Nadeen's best friend since high school. Patsy recalled hearing her mother tell Aunt Eva how She had no idea her friend wouldn't be alive for her to call her up and them just pick back up their friendship. Nadeen didn't think it was necessary to apologize to her best friend. Dhmonique knew her, she knew she had some funny ways, but Dhmonique had loved and accepted her just the way she was. In the past, whenever she'd gotten mad with Dhmonique they'd always done it the same way. Nadeen would call her up, say something funny to her and invite her to meet her at the Bratcher Coffeehouse. When they got there, she'd buy Dhmonique her favorite peppermint green tea and they'd just pick back up where they left off.

Nadeen told Eva she never imagined their last falling out wouldn't go the same way. Nadeen had just wanted to teach her best friend a lesson, give her time to see that she was the one that was wrong. She'd crossed the line. Dhmonique had to be taught that when you are a real friend you do what your friends need you to do regardless of any circumstances that may get in the way. You keep your word no matter what comes. It's almost like marriage.

She'd told Nadeen she'd be the Mistress of Ceremony for the Pastor's birthday celebration and that she'd mail out all of the invitations to the mega-churches in the area. She was also supposed to provide the decorations for the tables, but the Pastor had signed her up for the Advanced Ministry training for all the new ministry leader candidates. She'd found out later it would be that same weekend.

When Pastor Craig told Dhmonique the date of the training, she realized she was going to have to leave two days before the celebration. She'd asked Pastor Craig if there was another slot available and he'd told her it wasn't another until Summer of the next year and he needed her prepared before then. Dhmonique was excited about the opportunity to go.

When Dhmonique told Nadeen about it, she thought Nadeen would be happy for her. After all, she'd done this same training before she became the Head Usher and President of the prayer circle. Instead of Nadeen being happy for her, Nadeen got upset about her not being able to do what she said she would for Pastor Craig's big birthday celebration. She turned her back on Dhmonique and shut off all communication with her even at church.

Nadeen decided to show Dhmonique how she really felt about her choosing the ministry training over her word concerning the celebration. She distanced herself. She stopped taking Dhmonique's calls, ignored her text messages, and started going to places or events with other women of the church. They would laugh and talk about their weekend in front of Dhmonique. It didn't take Dhmonique long to realize what was going on. She'd been friends with her too long not to know.

Nadeen was just trying to remind Dhmonique of the rules of being a friend, rules she thought Dhmonique knew after all these years. Didn't the Bible say you chasten those whom you love? Well, she loved Dhmonique, but Dhmonique had chosen a trip over her promise, over their friendship, and that to Nadeen wasn't a true friend.

After about a month, Nadeen noticed Dhmonique wasn't attending services or any church functions. Nadeen thought she was just licking her wounds. Nadeen knew she'd hurt her deeply when she closed the door on their friendship, but reprimand never felt good.

One day a strange phone number showed up on Nadeen's caller ID. It was Shaun, Dhmonique's husband, calling her with a voice full of sorrow to tell Nadeen that Dhmonique had just passed from an aggressive infection she received due to a surgical procedure she'd had done on her kidneys a week earlier.

Nadeen went into a trance when she heard his words. Dhmonique was what? What surgery? What was wrong with Dhmonique? How long had Dhmonique had a problem with her kidneys? Why hadn't her husband called before? Nadeen offered her condolences and her help with the funeral. Dhmonique's husband exploded on her over the phone.

"You want to help? You should have wanted to fix this mess that you allowed the enemy to stir up between you and my wife! She died heartbroken because someone she loved like a blood sister closed the door of friendship in her face because she wasn't able to do something for her due to having an opportunity herself. An opportunity that if you had been as good of a friend to her as she was to you, would have made you happy for her but instead you were self-centered just like I kept trying to tell her you were. But no, she always made excuses for you!"

"What happened to you supporting her? Being happy for her? Being there for her when she needed something from you? All she wanted was your friendship and your understanding and you couldn't give those two simple things to her. She has been your only friend since high school and you treat her this way? What kind of Woman of God does that, Nadeen? Huh? Tell me that! What spirit tells you to treat someone like that?" He yelled at her.

"Now you can permanently stop speaking to her because I'm afraid she won't be attending the Pastor's birthday party or the new ministry leaders training! You happy now? She won't be going. Isn't that what you wanted in the first place? For her not to go and do something that was important to her? Well, you got what you wanted!"

Nadeen remembered feeling the force of hurt and anger behind his words coming through the phone.

"I need you to understand this is not my fault, Shaun. I had no control over her life or death." Nadeen remembered trying to explain to him.

"You want me to understand? You want me to understand what you had no control over yet when my wife told you she had no control over a date, you slammed the door in her face!"

Nadeen held the phone and softly cried. She didn't want him to hear her pain from his words and the news of her only friend dying. There'd been so much she wanted to tell Dhmonique once her punishment was done.

"Shaun, I was going to call Dhmonique in a few weeks so that we could work this out." She told him.

"No, you weren't. She'd been trying days before the surgery to get you to text or call her back so she could tell you what was going on with her but you never would. You just kept taking each day for granted that she'd be right there when you got good and ready but she's not. You gambled and lost this time!" Shaun said.

Nadeen had felt a little bit of regret in the deepest part of her belly. She managed to open her mouth and she tried again to express to Dhmonique's husband how heartbreaking the news was for her. "Shaun. I just want to be there for you and the children right now. Forgive me for waiting so long to fix this."

Shaun exploded, "Forgive you? Forgive you for breaking my wife's heart, treating her like she was some criminal or someone that had done some unforgivable violation to you? That's what really took her strength! Do you know that? Every day she cried to me, telling me how much she missed talking to you, how she couldn't believe that you had allowed the enemy's lies to split you all apart.

"She was only trying to do something to help her be a better person, to help her make some of her dreams come true and the only thing you cared about was what she didn't do for you. It didn't matter about anything she'd done or sacrificed before, just what she wasn't able to do for you this time!

"This one time, she wanted you to be as understanding of her dreams as you would have wanted her to be of yours, and instead of being there for her you turned your back and took for granted she'd be here when you turned back around but she's not. She's gone. Gone out of your life the way you wanted!"

Before Nadeen could respond, Shaun hung up the phone. When she told Kenny what had happened and what Shaun had said to her, he knew he couldn't tell her what he really thought, that Shaun had been right, and her entire conduct had been wrong. Instead, Kenny held her in his arms and let her cry it all out.

The day of the funeral, Nadeen was too ashamed to attend. She was worried about how Shaun would react. She asked Kenny to take flowers to the wake the night before on behalf of the family. When her church members asked her why she wasn't at her best friend's funeral, Nadeen told them she'd been in a deep depression because of Dhmonique's passing and the doctor had ordered her to remain at home out of concern the stress of seeing her friend laid in the ground would be way too much for her mentally and emotionally to bear.

She was the only true friend that Nadeen had. She'd been the only person other than Eva that knew her inside out and still accepted her. Nadeen truly hated that God called Dhmonique home before they could fix things between them, but she also believed she had every right to be upset with Dhmonique. She had planned to go to her and fix the problem like the Bible said but her and God's calendar were different. Dhmonique should have told her she was sick.

It was too late now. Her best friend was in eternity. Nadeen decided that she'd apologize to her when she met her there. She'd probably be at the pearly gates waiting on her.

A few months later Nadeen found out she was pregnant with Josie. She believed God had smiled down on her and given her joy for her ashes.

2

PATSY OPENED HER eyes. Dustin would be coming back home today. They'd kept in touch over the summer because Patsy still had the secret cell phone Sandra gave her. Sandra would keep minutes on it for her while she was gone because she knew how much Dustin and Patsy missed each other. She made extra money over the summer by watching two of the other kids in her neighborhood and she made sure her best friend could talk to her man whenever she wanted to. That was a real friend. Patsy promised her one day she would return the favor.

Dustin spent the Summer in Oxford, Maryland, a small charming town that his cousin's parents on his mother's side decided to settle in after working for the CIA for years. She couldn't wait to see him. She missed him so much. The things they talked about in whispers over the phone at night had her anticipating going back home to him and yet afraid. She was afraid because he was making her feel things that made her flesh want to take over where her Bible study had been. He had become bold in his conversations with her, talking about how much he wanted to be closer to her, to touch her in a way that would say much more than words.

Patsy always felt warm after talking to him, her heart would always beat faster because of the things he would say She day-dreamed about what it would be like with him.

She was so far into thinking about him that she didn't realize Josie had been pulling on her sleeve for a few minutes. "I want pancakes," Josie said as she tugged on her big sister's arm. "I want pancakes and juice," she demanded.

Patsy moved slowly from under the covers. She hated to release the things she was feeling in her body. "Okay, little bossy girl. I'll go make you some pancakes. Let's go clean up first." Patsy said picking her up. As she headed out the bedroom door, she could hear her mother's radio across the hall blasting *Holy Ghost 91.1*.

She was getting ready for her part-time shift at the nursing home.

"Come on, Josie. Let's go find Ann and make some pancakes. Josie jumped down and ran towards the stairs. It was too early for Patsy to chase after her so she let her go bouncing up the stairs looking like one big afro puffball. When she made it to the top, she stood there with a smile on her face looking down at Patsy.

"I ain't chasing you today Lil' Miss Roadrunner," Patsy said. "Ann? Ann you up here?" Patsy asked as she made it to the top of the stairs.

Ann came out of the bedroom door with her hair all over her face. It had grown down to her shoulders and was thick, wavy, and light brown.

"I was trying to get some sleep. What do you want?" She snapped at Patsy. "I want you to talk to me with some respect in your voice first of all, so you need to clean your attitude, and secondly I want to know if you want to eat pancakes with me and Josie." Patsy said, putting her hands on her hips as she spoke to Ann.

"Nah, I don't want none of your dry pancakes this morning. I was up late and I want to go back and finish my nap before your momma hear that I'm up and start calling my name one hundred times before she gets out the door." Ann said to her big sister.

"Dry? I got your dry, it's just like your attitude been since I got home. And furthermore, if you would go to bed at night instead of watching what sounds like some really nasty movies you might have a better disposition in the morning."

"Girl what are you talking about? You are having delusions. You must be missing your man cause you hearing imaginary sounds. I'm not in my room watching dirty movies at night." Ann countered.

"Well, it sounds like it. I have to put the pillow over my head sometimes cause I can hear it. You better not let your momma catch you watching them that's all I got to say about the situation." Patsy said as she reached out for Josie. "Come on, baby girl, let's go somewhere where the mood in the room is better."

"You need to get you some business, Chick. Worry about when that man of yours coming back with all that pent-up frustration cause you won't give him that sanctified kitty of yours." Ann said twirling her finger in a circle then pointing it at her big sister. Patsy stood there in complete shock, thinking in her head *What the Hell? Did my little sister just say that to me? I got to be dreaming.*

"Maybe you on drugs cause something has altered your mind thinking you can talk to me like that. I been wiping your behind since your momma brought you home don't get things twisted with me." Patsy said. Just as Ann headed towards her Nadeen yelled up the stairs. "Patsy! Come here!"

"We ain't done with this." She said pointing back at Ann as she headed to see what her mother wanted.

"Anytime you want to finish you know where to find me," Ann said. Patsy swooped Josie up and headed back down the stairs. She heard the door to Ann's bedroom slam just as she put her foot on the third step.

Patsy couldn't put her hands on it but something about Ann was making her uneasy. She had a sassiness about her talk now and she was always sneaking around on the phone. God would have to reveal it. In the meantime, she was going to make breakfast, clean up the house, watch a good movie, and wait to hear from Dustin. He promised to be back in town before the sun went down. She missed him. What was she going to do? He had waited a long time. Thinking about them spending time kissing, rubbing, and touching made her afraid to answer her own self concerning the next step for them. Patsy had to shake herself before Josie got blackened pancakes for breakfast.

Later when Patsy woke up from her nap it was after noon. She went to check on Josie and ran into Ann. She was on the phone laughing and softly talking to someone. Patsy knew that tone of voice wasn't for a girlfriend of hers. Ann had to be talking to a boy.

"When you get finished lying to some woman's son you need to make sure you got that kitchen in order before your momma gets home from work," Patsy told her.

Ann looked at her, rolled her eyes, then turned her back and walked away. "Okay. Keep being disrespectful. You gone get handled, Ann. I'm just about tired of your bipolar personality."

Patsy said on her way to the backyard with Josie. She slammed the door behind her before Ann could get in a nasty response. Patsy played with Josie for about an hour. She had really missed both of her sisters. It seemed like such a long time since she had seen them. It was good to be back home after the church mission trip even though it seemed like Ann's personality was the only thing that had changed.

"Come on, Josie. Let's check the mail." Patsy said. She scooped her little sister up, adjusted her on her hip, and walked towards the front of the house. Just as she stepped onto the driveway, her Aunt Eva pulled up with David. She rolled her car window down.

"Hey, Niece! How are you? Glad to see you back aren't we David? Eva said as she looked over at him. He winked his eye at Patsy and slowly shook his head. "I thought you would've called me and your Grandma by now to tell us all about the trip but I see you got some catching up to do with your sisters," her Aunt said.

"Your momma home today or she at work?" She asked.

"She at work right now probably be home in about another hour or two though," Patsy said. Eva got out of the car and gave her a big hug. "I'm glad to have my oldest niece back. This is your senior year and I'm ready to get it started. We're gonna have some fun this year just you wait and see. David and I was just talking about the big graduation party we're gonna throw for you with or without my sister's approval."

David walked slowly behind her chewing on a toothpick looking at her with his ugly grey eyes like a wolf circling his prey while he licked his lips. "Of course we are." He said.

"What new stuff did you learn niece?" Eva asked.

"Got you a new boyfriend while you was there?" David asked her with a smirk on his face. "I know about them young church boys pretending they altar boys in public but they 'nasty dogs' behind the church building." He grinned at Patsy. His grey eyes had a repulsive spark in them when he said it.

"David! Watch your mouth. That's my niece you talking to," Eva told him.

Patsy ignored him. She still had nothing for him. She hadn't forgotten what a "nasty dog" he'd been the night she stayed over with them for her birthday last year.

"Some folks you have to just walk away from. Save that breath for something important." Patsy said to her Aunt while looking at David. "You better leave her alone, David. You know whose blood running in her veins," Eva grinned and said.

"Her blood red, same as mine. That don't scare me none." David responded. "All y'all some disrespectful women, I swear," David said.

"Disrespectful? You came at me all wrong." Patsy frowned at him. Eva stepped between the two of them to block them.

"David, you been warned. Leave her alone and Patsy pull back. You still a child and I'm gonna need you to stay in your place even though David is acting like one too." Eva said with her hand planted in the center of David's chest.

"I'm a grown man, baby. I thought you knew," David said with a smirk on his face.

"Anyway," Eva said turning her back to David. "I need to talk to your momma. I guess I'll hang around in the car for a few minutes to see if I can catch her. I know how she is about anybody being in her house when she not home...even me or momma so I don't want no trouble for you. You just got back." Eva said. "Where Ann? She hasn't called me since you got back. The whole summer you were gone she was trying to get to my house every weekend."

Just as Patsy was about to answer her David stepped up. "I got to pay my water bill and I got to pay it now. All that sweet tea you had me drinking a few minutes ago has built up. I'm just gonna slip in, pay this bill and slip right back out. Unless you want me to be country and go out back and dump it on Nadeen's pretty little flower bed." He laughed.

"Go on! Hurry up. Don't you get in there dragging around and get caught. You bring down hell's fire on my nieces today it's going to be bad for you. You know how stir crazy my sister is."

David leaned over and kissed Eva on the jaw. "Maybe she needs to know what it's like to have a real man handle her." He said.

"Excuse me?" Patsy replied before she knew it. Eva touched her arm.

"Calm down, baby girl. David, get your ignorant talking behind in that bathroom."

David laughed. "No harm intended. Be right back, baby." He said as he hurried by them

Eva took Josie in her arms and kissed her. "Patsy. Ignore David. He's had a few too many beers. You girls talk to your daddy recently?" she asked.

"Yeah. We just talked to him yesterday." Patsy answered.

"Did he mention to you about coming back?" Eva asked.

"No. I asked him and he gave me the same old answer; he had to wait and stay out of God's way until God released him to come back." Patsy said.

"Well just between you and me, nobody else, he and I talk on a regular basis. He likes to keep up with you girls and he knows Nadeen won't talk to him unless she needs some money and even then she real cold with him. He told me he been having those thoughts again and he feeling this tug in his heart. He said he thinks God is preparing him to come back home. He said he been praying about it every night." Eva smiled and said.

Patsy's heart skipped a beat thinking about her daddy being back with them. "Aunt Eva that would be the best present ever if he came back home to us," Patsy said.

"Well, you get on one accord with him, honey, and y'all bother Jesus day and night until he stands up from that throne and come see about you," Eva said gently pinching Josie's face.

"What is taking David so long? He is as slow as molasses on a cold morning." Eva said, looking down at her cellphone. "David, come on here! I gotta go catch this sale before it gets too late and I need to check on my momma!" She yelled towards the front door. "Patsy, I didn't realize it was this late. I might have to come back later."

"Hold up, girl!" David said as he came out of the door straightening his shirt. I got in there and things got a little bit more complicated than I thought." He laughed. "Patsy. Glad to have you back home. You girls come by and see about your ole uncle David some time. Your Aunt so in love, she won't hardly let me out of her sight so I'll be around." He said laughingly as they both walked off.

"Remember what I said, Patsy. Send up them prayers and tell your momma to call me." Eva yelled back to her as she got in her car and backed out of their driveway. Josie waved goodbye until the car sped out of sight.

Patsy went into the house. Ann was in the doorway of the laundry room. Patsy looked at her. She seemed disheveled. "You feeling all right today?" Patsy asked Ann. "You look all crazy by the head. You must have slept hanging out the bed. What have you been doing to yourself?" Patsy asked as she looked at Ann in confusion.

"Patsy get off of me, please! I had to try my dress on that I got hemmed a few weeks ago."

"Ann Simmons, something strange is going on with you. I just know it is. I can't put my hands on it yet but I know it. You starting to act too much like your momma in some ways." Patsy said.

"You need to get your head checked. I'm no more acting like Nadeen than you are.

Now!" Ann responded as she stormed out of the kitchen fumbling with her hair.

"You just don't see it yet but I hope you do," Patsy said. "I got better things to do than argue with you." Patsy took Josie to the back and put in one of her favorite sing-a-long CDs and left to do her hair.

As soon as Patsy finished roller setting her hair, she heard the doorbell ring. Patsy looked out of the front window. It was Sandra. Patsy was glad to see her and Solomon. Patsy opened the door and gave her a great big hug.

"Hey, Bestie! How are you and the baby?" she asked.

Sandra smiled. "We're doing great, Patsy. I'm so glad you're home. I missed you so much. Talking on the phone ain't the same as seeing your face. My momma told me you were back. I figured you would have called me on that cellphone I gave you by now." Sandra said.

"Trust I was going to call you. I just been busy unpacking and readjusting to the chaos of home." Patsy said.

"Well, Reverend Craig must be jealous about you going on that mission trip with Deliverance Rock, 'cause now he says he's gonna send some of us next summer." Sandra said readjusting Solomon on her hip.

"You would love it my friend but what would you do about

Solomon?" Patsy asked kissing Solomon's little fingers. Patsy looked at Sandra's face. She seemed to be excited about the opportunity.

"He could stay with his daddy. Lavon and me will probably be married by then so I won't have a problem with a babysitter." Patsy looked surprised.

"Married? Sandra you sure you ready to get married? It seems like it's a lot of work. I thought you wanted to go to New York and be a fashion designer one day. Remember you use to talk about moving there and how you would draw some designs, buy a nice car once you blew up, and marry a rich, good-looking foreigner? You don't want that anymore?" Patsy asked.

"Well. New York would be nice but I won't go without Lavon. He's my baby's daddy I can't just leave him. I can't just go chasing some crazy dream I had and forget all about him." Sandra said.

"Sandra you gotta go get what God has for you. You giving up without even trying to reach it?" Patsy asked as she tickled Solomon on his side.

Sandra ran her fingers through Solomon's beautiful blondish red hair. "Patsy I gotta do what is best for me, Lavon, and our baby, leaving him here is not what is best. If I leave, Lavon would be heartbroken." Sandra said while twisting the baby's soft curls around her fingers.

"Sandra if you don't pursue your dreams one day you will wake up and be the one bitter and broken-hearted," Patsy told her. "Just because you ran into a delay doesn't mean you have to deny your future plans. Sure you got off track and you took a wrong turn but the turn has been taken, you've found your way back and you can keep moving forward you just got someone else along for the ride that's all." Patsy said.

"Patsy, can we talk about something else right now? I came to laugh with my best friend not get all serious with this Jesus stuff and my future. How's Dustin? You seen him yet or talked to him." Sandra asked.

That was just like Sandra, Patsy thought to herself. *Jumping all around to something else without finishing the first thing she started.* Patsy would let it die for right now but she would pick it back up later. She didn't want to see her friend stuck in this town married to someone she would hate for keeping her from her dreams years from now.

"He's supposed to be home today. As a matter of fact, shouldn't be much longer that his plane comes in." Patsy replied. "That sounds good. Well, what are you all gonna do once you graduate? You all still going to the same college together or is Dustin gonna hang around for a year or two? I'm not even asking if you leaving 'cause I've known that answer since grade school." Sandra laughed.

"We're going to college together. If God allows us to, we'll be moving into our dorms on Dove University campus next Fall. I'm so ready for us to go. We been talking about this for a long time." Patsy said smiling at the thought. "Well, that sounds great. How's your dad?" Sandra asked.

"He's doing fine. I talked to him yesterday."

"I hope he comes back soon. I like him he's a real cool guy." Sandra said.

"It would be nice to have him around especially if my momma knew how to act," Patsy said. "You asking for a Red Sea miracle on that Patsy, no disrespect intended towards your momma chile," Sandra said. They both laughed. "None taken, bestie." Patsy said.

"Well, we just stopped by to see you. I know how your mom freaks out if you let anybody in the house when she's not home so we won't stay any longer. By the way, tell Ann if she needs a ride to the clinic let me know. I can take her with me the next time." Sandra said.

"What? What clinic? Ann doesn't go to a clinic. Nadeen takes her to all of her appointments. Why would she be going to a clinic, Sandra?" Patsy asked, confused.

Sandra paused. She gave Patsy a look like she hated to bring it up. "Look, Patsy. Relax. I just saw her down there about six weeks ago and stopped to talk to her. She said she was there with a friend who had been scared to come by herself. Maybe her and Ralph have decided to take it to the next level?"

"If Momma finds out she been at some clinic the only next level she's gonna be taking is to the heavens. She better not be doing or planning anything like that with Ralph." Patsy said as she kissed Solomon's little fingers.

"Look, I love you. Glad to see you but I gotta go, this little man is ready to eat." Sandra said. She hugged Patsy's neck, adjusted Solomon on her hip again, and walked off.

The revealing of Ann Simmons had begun. Patsy knew there was something weird going on with her little sister and she knew that all things done in the dark would come to the light. She wouldn't give Ann the message. Instead, she would wait on God to expose what was going on. She already knew that if she asked Ann about being at the clinic and who her friend was, she wasn't going to get a straight answer.

Patsy did wonder about this friend of hers, however. Whoever she was they must have gotten really close since Patsy had gone on that International Ministries trip. She'd gone to make a positive difference in the lives of other people but it seems she'd made a negative impact in the life of her own sister.

A few minutes after Sandra and Solomon left, Nadeen came through the door.

"Landon, that Jordan Jackson is going to make me bust him over the head with a bedpan full of piss if he doesn't stay out of my face!" She said coming through the door. "One of us is going to have to leave that place and real soon." She said. "He cut my hours and put me on the worst wing in the center. I hope he knows God don't like ugly and he don't like it when the devil is playing with one of his children. He's going to get his just you wait and see." She said as she headed to her bedroom.

26

When she came out a few minutes later she was still venting to Landon on speaker. "I don't know what I gotta do to get Jordan Jackson to realize who he fooling with, but I am anointed and he best to leave me alone before I call down fire on him."

"Sis, look, I ain't no regular on Sunday mornings but even I know when Jesus got through with them folks in the temple disrespecting His house. He turned it out up in there and when he got through everybody had their minds right. They knew he wasn't playing. You gone have to do the same with Jordan Jackson." Landon said smacking his lips.

"You right Landon. I can't have him playing with my money. That's my tithing he foolin' with when he cuttin' my hours."

Landon laughed. "I hear you, Sis. One thing we don't play with is our money and our food. You put your hands on them two thangs you could end up somewhere you don't want to be."

Just then her phone beeped again displaying Pastor Craig's phone number. "Landon, I'll have to call you back this my Pastor calling and I really need to tell him about Jordan Jackson, it's a reason he's an ex-church member."

"Oops. Church mess. It makes the best mess. Well, call me when you're ready 'cause you know I'm all in for getting him all the way together especially after the way he did me a few weeks ago denying my vacation. I had that request put in two weeks before and he wait until the day before to tell me we short-staffed and he had to deny it. I was hot, you hear me? Steaming." Landon said emphasizing the 's' in the word steaming.

"Alright. I'll talk with you later." Nadeen said clicking over to Pastor Craig.

"Pastor Craig Thanks so much for calling me back. I really need some Godly advice from you."

"Of course, Sister. I'm always here to help. You need me to get my wife? She can give me a different point of view to consider if needed."

Nadeen strained to keep a smile in her voice, "No, Pastor don't bother her. I think you will do just fine."

"Alright then, Sister Nadeen, what can I help you with this evening?"

"Pastor Craig. I just don't know what to do about your ex-member, Jordan Jackson. He just keeps harassing me at work. He's still mad about what happened with that fundraising money earlier this summer. He best be glad you didn't have him arrested. He is making my workplace miserable. I have enough to deal with without including his drama. I think he blames me for not being there for him to complain to. He brought it on hisself and I was dealing with so much I didn't have time to hold his hand while he cried. My husband abandoned us and my oldest daughter was off on some church trip with another church. Only God knows what they taught her."

"Sister Simmons. I know this is troubling for you. I'm so sorry that he is causing you problems at work. Maybe I can try and bring him in for counseling if his new pastor doesn't mind." Reverend Craig said sympathetically. "I don't want him causing you all this frustration."

"Maybe you can talk to his new pastor and get him to stop this harassment," Nadeen said with the sound of frustration in her voice. "I hear he's an Elder at his new church. I would hate to think he's over the finances there, too." Nadeen paused to listen to the response on the other end of the line.

"Well, I'm not sure what exactly he is doing at his new church, but you know we have to forgive him and let him get back up again. Just because he fell down doesn't mean the Lord can't use him." Pastor Craig said.

"He need to be sat down until he changes his ways, Pastor. You are the only one I have to help me since my husband abandoned me." Nadeen said trying to sound desperate. "I'm afraid he might try to hurt me. I'm not one to start strife, you know that Pastor."

"I know, Sister Simmons. I tell you what. I'll inquire about him tomorrow at our annual check-up meeting. I'll explain the situation to his new Pastor and then I'll reach out to see if Brother Jackson wants to talk to me or him and I will let him know how much he is upsetting you," Pastor Craig responded.

"Well, thank you. I would appreciate that so much. The persecution of a good woman trying to stand for the ways of righteousness never seems to end. Jordan Jackson is being used as a tool by the enemy to try and make my life difficult but he won't prosper." Nadeen told her Pastor as she picked up her Bible to head back out the door.

"Well, I'm headed to the church for Intercessory Prayer now. I thank you for helping me."

"Remember to pray for Brother Jackson. He's still a child of God, too, you know? We all have fallen short." Pastor Craig reminded Nadeen.

"Pastor, Jordan Jackson is still falling. I'm just trying to get somebody to help him before he lands on a real sharp object. You be blessed now." Nadeen said and hung up the phone before her pastor could respond.

"Patsy. I'm headed to the church for prayer. I'll be home late," she said, dropping her cellphone in her purse. Patsy wondered if Jordan Jackson was on her mother's prayer list. After all, that's what a real saint would do.

3

DUSTIN CALLED THE house phone the next day. Patsy wondered why he hadn't attempted to call her yesterday when his plane landed. As soon as she heard his voice her heart started beating fast in her chest.

"Hey, there missionary girl how you been? I can't wait to see you. I know you're as beautiful as ever."

Patsy was smiling so hard her jaws hurt. "Hey, babe. I missed you too. Why didn't you call my cellphone, Dustin? You know nothing's changed around here."

"My sister said they got a board meeting or something at the church tonight. I know your momma is gonna be there till the gate closes. Anyway, didn't you say you missed me?"

"I did miss you," Patsy said feeling her face get warm.

"How much?" Dustin said in that low deep tone that made Patsy's leg shake a little bit.

"Enough to one day show you," Patsy said. Dustin was bringing out an entirely new person inside of her. He'd perked her interest in things she promised to wait for.

"I hope it can be soon, as much as I love you another day is way too long," Dustin said. "You trust me, don't you? You know I'd never hurt you, right?"

"Yes, I trust you. I know you wouldn't hurt me. Anyway, you know how much danger you would be in if you did."

Dustin laughed a deep slow laugh. His voice had gotten deeper over the summer and it traveled deep within her and landed in a spot past her navel. "Trust. I have seen the drama that comes from messing with you."

"Dustin, I love you too much to ever hurt you," Patsy said. She knew he was referring to what happened last year at school with Daphne's cousin, Eddie Porter, she'd bit him so hard through his shirt he had to have his nipple reattached. It was an ugly moment she never wanted to think about again. The only good thing about it was that her mother didn't kill her for getting suspended. Instead, she'd praised her for defending herself. Patsy wasn't sure to be relieved or confused by that.

"Well, that's good to know. Look. I gotta start unpacking all of this stuff and once I've done that, I'll call you back in about an hour."

"Sounds good, babe," Patsy said.

"Hey, and tell your sister to ease up on your cell phone line so I can talk to you. She must be in love or something. I tried to call you last night but every time I called, she told me she was on the phone to call back. After the third time, I just gave up."

"She didn't tell me you called. She knew I was waiting to hear from him. I gotta talk to her about that. She is really getting out of hand since I been back. Go unpack, baby. I'll talk to you later." Patsy said as she hung up the phone receiver.

As soon as she hung up the phone Ann grabbed it. "Patsy, can you give somebody else a chance to use the phone today please?" Ann said to her as she picked it up and started walking to the back.

"Who you calling that's so important anyway?" Patsy asked her. Ann seemed to be offended by her asking.

"Don't come back from over the waters getting all in my

business Patsy. I been handling it just fine without you in it." Ann said. "You not the only one with guy friends you know."

Patsy had just about had enough of Ann's funky attitude. What had taken over her in just a few weeks? Her talk was different, her mannerism was different and she had this nasty little sway in her hips now that made her walk different. Whatever it was taking over Ann, Patsy didn't like it.

"By the way, Dustin called you last night, but he never called back after I told him to," Ann said.

"That's not what he told me." Patsy said. "He said he did call back and you just kept telling him you were on the phone. That's my cellphone. I don't mind sharing it with you but you can't be blocking my calls."

Ann rolled her eyes. "There you go, believing what a man says. What your momma told you about that Big Sister? You in love too much to think Dustin won't tell you a lie? I hope not. I'm your blood forever remember? He's just a boyfriend. And last I remember, that is your bestie's cellphone not yours. You need to be worried about your momma finding out about that phone instead of worrying about when Dustin callin'," Ann said as she walked off with the house phone.

Since when did Ann agree with anything their mother said? Patsy knew it was official then: Ann was possessed. She had to be, the real Ann would never support anything coming out of Nadeen's mouth about a man or anything else, Patsy thought.

When Ann got off the phone, she came up front in her bra and panties. This wasn't unusual. They walked around like that a lot now that Kenny was gone. What was surprising was the type of bra and panties she had on.

The set was black and lacy. The bra was a push-up and the panties were low cut around her hips. Patsy couldn't believe what she was seeing. Where in the world had Ann gotten something like that? Had she been sneaking in Nadeen's underwear drawer? Patsy wondered. She knew it was about to be a verbal battle but she had to challenge Ann about her inappropriate attire.

"Girl, whose draws and bra you got on? 'Cause I know your momma ain't bought you nothing like that." Patsy said.

Ann ignored her and kept walking around at first.

"Ann. I know you hear me talking to you. You better stop and answer me or I'm going straight to your momma about that mess you got on." Patsy said. Ann turned around and looked at her.

"What's wrong with what I got on? I bought this myself with the money Kenny sent home for me. I'm a young woman. Don't be mad at me cause I got some lacey draws and you don't!" Ann said to her with her hands on her hips.

Patsy walked closer to you. "You expect me to believe Nadeen took you shopping for something like that? I know better than that and I also know she wouldn't let you go to a store like that with her or without her." Patsy said.

"You don't know what she would or wouldn't let me do this summer. You weren't here so how you think you know?" Ann said with an attitude while putting her hands on her hips.

"Girl, I will snatch that mess off your back if you don't take it down a notch!" Patsy yelled at Ann.

She had never done that before. Patsy felt bad inside but didn't let it show. "You better step back before you end up in the ER fooling with me, Patsy! I don't have to answer to you! You're not my momma though you act a lot like her!" Ann yelled.

"I told you I bought this myself. I like it and I'm going to wear it. You can tell Nadeen if you want to. I don't care. It's just underwear. Once again your words and actions don't click. You always talking about you love me but yet you turn around and throw me to the wolves." Ann said.

Patsy wanted to cry. What was happening to her baby sister? Who was this disrespectful female standing in front of her dressed like she was on a reality TV show?

"Ann, I do love you that is why I'm trying to figure out what's wrong with you? You weren't acting like this before I left. I wasn't gone that long. Who you hanging around that's got you acting so nasty?" Patsy asked.

Ann turned around and walked away from her. "I'm not hanging around anybody and I'm not acting nasty. You are acting nosey!" Ann said as she stomped off.

"What just happened?" Patsy asked out loud. She stood there feeling lost, dazed, and confused. Maybe it was her time of the month, Patsy thought. Ann could get cranky then but that still wouldn't explain the lacy underwear. Patsy was going to have to talk to Aunt Eva. Maybe she could talk to Ann and get to the bottom of what was making her act so crazy.

Later on that night, Patsy couldn't sleep. She'd drifted off for a few hours but woke back up. She was still thinking about what happened between her and Ann. She decided to go and talk to Ann if she was up. She just wanted them to be close again like they were just a few months ago before she left. She went upstairs and knocked on Ann's door. Ann didn't answer. She turned to go back and car headlights shined brightly into the room. She heard a car door slam. She looked out the side window and saw someone get out. The person ran across their grass and disappeared. Patsy wondered where they were going.

As she was about to knock on the door again, she thought she heard the sound of a window being shut in Ann's room. Patsy hoped no one was trying to break into the house by crawling up the side ladder to get in the window. She knocked on the door again.

"Ann? Ann, you okay in there?" She spoke through the door. It took a few minutes but Ann finally came to the door and opened it slightly. Patsy poked her head in the door a little and tried to look around.

"You okay in here, Ann?" Sounded like I heard someone open or close that side window. I saw somebody jump out a car and run across our yard a few minutes ago."

Ann looked like she had been deep in sleep. "I'm fine, Patsy. Stop babying me. I'm just tired. I was in a deep sleep when you woke me up," she said.

Patsy was staring at her face. The light of the moon was shining thru the shears over the window she could see just enough to see the lipstick on Ann.

"Why do you have on lipstick, Ann? If you were sleep why would you have on lipstick? You know Nadeen doesn't allow that," Patsy said.

Ann put her head down and let out a heavy sigh then she looked back up at her older sister. "I don't have on lipstick, Patsy. Go to bed, please." She said and closed the door in Patsy's face.

"And you still got on those stripper draws," Patsy said through the door.

That was it for Patsy. Aunt Eva was definitely getting a phone call tomorrow about Ann's behavior. Patsy was going to tell her everything including about the underwear. Ann was out of control and no one could tell her anything. Patsy couldn't tell Nadeen because she would stomp Ann into a grease spot on the kitchen floor. She couldn't tell Grandma Ruth because she might have a heart attack.

Kenny wouldn't know what to do so she couldn't tell him. He wasn't good with "female things" he would always say. His job was just to love them, feed them, clothe them and protect them and that was enough to keep him busy.

So there was no one left but Aunt Eva. She was cool and very laid back. She talked to them about everything from sex to tampons. She was the first one to show them a picture of a man's "cucumber" as she called it. She said a man's piece is just like a cucumber it comes in all types and sizes. Patsy recalled how funny her and Ann thought that was but to think Ann might be crossing the line wasn't funny now.

4

PATSY'S OPPORTUNITY TO talk to Ann came sooner than expected. It was a typical Friday night. They watched movies, reminisced about what Kenny would say about the movie, laughed about memories, and ate popcorn while fighting to keep Josie's hands out of the bowl. As the second movie went to commercial, Ann asked, "Patsy why did you change your mind and go on that missionary trip? You told me you wouldn't go since Kenny had already left us. You told me you were gonna stay here with me and Josie and help us get through this together but you didn't. You abandoned us just like Kenny did. You changed your mind and just left me and Josie here all alone. How can you say you love us and leave us like that?"

Ann sounded really hurt. Patsy wanted to take her, hold her, and tell her she was so sorry. That she never meant to hurt her by leaving and she had no idea it would affect her this way.

"Ann, I only went because Aunt Eva promised me she would come and get you and Josie while I was away. I had been waiting on this trip for the last three years and if I didn't go when I had the chance I wouldn't get it again. I would never have gone if I thought you would hate me for it." Patsy said.

"I was so hurt when Daddy left. I still believe it was because of what I did. I hurt him when I hit that boy in the face with that tray. I guess I opened up a wound for him and broke his heart. He just couldn't stand to look at me cause I acted like momma." Ann said as she began to cry.

"I could see the disappointment in his eyes that day. I know I hurt him but I didn't think he would leave me because of it. I begged him to stay and he left me anyway. He did just what Momma said all men do, they leave you." It pierced Patsy's soul to hear her little sister repeating the worldly advice of their mother.

"Ann, please don't let the enemy talk to you. He's lying to you about Kenny and me. We never left you. You were always there in our hearts. We never abandoned you. Kenny told you he had to go because God had to get him out of the way to fix things around here. I had to go because God gave me an opportunity to receive a blessing I had been asking him for.

"I had to trust God with you. I thought about staying. I thought I could keep things under control but you know what I had to accept? I'm not God. I can't keep anything under control. That's his job. He's got it. He doesn't need my help." Patsy told Ann.

"There wasn't a night I didn't pray for you and Josie or miss you but I had to let God be God. If He can't keep you then I surely can't. Why believe Him to be God if He can't do no more than we can? He brought me back didn't he and he's gonna bring Daddy back."

Ann looked up at her big sister with tears running down her face. "You sure about that? Cause he ain't back yet?"

Patsy looked her dead in her eyes with tears running down her face. She wanted to reach over and hug her sister. She was the one that fought in the home trenches with Nadeen to stay alive. It was a daily battle.

"Kenny escaped," Ann said. "Nadeen got a warrant out for him." They both laughed. It was a laugh they both needed.

"Keep the faith, Ann. We're going to make it. After all, the Word says that Jesus came to set the captive free. Believe that.".

"I'm trying to wait on him, Patsy, but it's been so long and I'm so tired. If he doesn't come soon, I'm going to just give up and give in. I'm already near the edge of a cliff," Ann wiped the tears from her cheeks.

Patsy squeezed Ann's hand. "Hold on to me, little sister. I'm holding on to God's hand so you hold on to mine. He got us both."

Ann put her head down and smiled. The warmth of her big sister's hand made her feel a small stream of hope spread through her body.

"Patsy?" Ann said.

"Yes?"

"I got something I need to tell you," Ann said.

"What is it?" Patsy asked. "You know you can tell me anything, anytime. Just like Kenny use to say to us. Tell me. I'll listen."

Ann released her hand, paused for a moment then said, "Not now. The time isn't right. When the time is right, I'll tell you." She whispered.

*   *   *

Ann laid down later that night feeling a little less burdened. She still felt convicted, sneaky, and ashamed but she felt just a little less heaviness in her soul.

She didn't know how to tell her Sister the terrible thing she'd gotten herself into but she was glad she was able to let her in just enough to know how much she needed her.

Now she had to figure out how to tell Patsy her "monster in the closet" secret. This one was scary and it was big. It fed off of the fact that every night while Patsy was gone Ann played the video in her mind of the day Kenny left.

She cried every night because he was gone and she truly believed her actions cost her a daddy and his love. In her mind, he was ashamed of her. In her mind, he left so that he wouldn't have to be around her and he gave Patsy permission to leave too, to teach Ann a lesson.

Her ways had cost her the people she loved. Her ways had pushed them both away. She'd believed that she'd bought this lesson at a price far more than she could afford to pay so she found a way to defer the payment.

These were the things that the enemy whispered in her ear every night. These were the things being planted in her mind and taking root in the soil of her heart. It fed her justification for what she let him do to her. She tried hard at first to fight it by cutting herself again. She did it until one night she saw Josie watching her. She didn't want her to do the same thing, so she turned to another form of relief that physically felt much better than the edge of a razor blade despite the fact that if her secret ever came out it would cut other people just as deep.

Kenny always told them God would fight their battles but it seemed like when she called on him to fight her battles he was nowhere around. He always seemed to be busy winning battles for someone else but never for her.

They wanted to leave her in the Lion's Den. Well, she would jump right in with the lion. She would make it hurt so good that if Kenny and Patsy ever found out, they'd know what it really felt like to be crushed by someone you loved.

They would feel guilt and regret for leaving her and giving her room to become this person she wouldn't have become if they'd stayed.

She felt heat come all over her when he was around her. When her touched her. He made her promise to never let anyone else touch her that way.

He'd keep spending time with her as long as she knew how to keep their business private. He told her she couldn't tell her sister anything about them or any of her friends, it would cost the both of them too much if she did.

He knew that her Aunt liked to go to the casino and that she would get back a little late after enjoying a day of gambling and drinking so she'd be "feeling mighty fine" and go fast asleep.

On those nights when he would come to visit her at her aunt's house, he would sneak in through the side door she left unlocked. Ann would wait for him. When he kissed her neck she felt an aching within her that she knew was sinful but was too good to stop.

She never thought she'd go this far with him. She was never attracted to him like that before but that changed when she believed she had been abandoned by her sister and her father. She didn't like him at first and he could tell it but he was determined to get what he wanted. His daddy had taught him to never give up on what you really wanted cause one day you will have it and he did, he had Ann, his own beautiful, desperate doll that he could play with whenever he wanted.

Ann was never shamed about what she did with him until she replayed in her mind what she believed God saw her doing. But even then, her flesh wouldn't let her repent. When she would go back home, she always felt like she was getting one over on her mother. She laughed to herself to think how Nadeen would pass out if she ever knew Ann had let some boy touch her in all the places he was not supposed to. Ann fell asleep dreaming about him.

*   *   *

The next day Eva came over. She wanted to know if they'd like to spend the rest of the week with her. Grandma Ruth was going to be stopping by and David had some new recipes he wanted to try on them and she didn't want to be his lab rat. Patsy was a little hesitant because she hadn't forgotten waking up and seeing David sitting next to her bed. She hadn't told anybody because she wasn't too fond of funerals and she'd had enough of hospitals and ICU. Before she could tell her to find out if it was okay with Nadeen, Ann jumped in all excited and said, "Yes. We want to come!" She seemed overly eager.

Eva laughed at her. "Ann, you always ready to come over. That Ralph boy must be wearing you down. I hear him out there on that front porch begging you to kiss him or let him hold your hand. You just like your momma; make it hard for a man." Eva said. Ann laughed.

Aunt Eva had no idea how easy it really was, she thought.

Patsy would have to go now. She didn't want Ann around David by herself. He might decide to try putting his hands on her and he would really have a tiger by the tail. She also needed to keep an eye on her and Ralph. She had a feeling they were doing something shady.

"Tell Nadeen to come on out that room," Eva said. "How long it take to change out of a work uniform? I be in such a hurry I come out of mine right in the living room."

"I don't have on nothing but my birthday suit."

The thought of it tickled Patsy and Ann. They laughed so loud it brought Nadeen out of her room.

"What is all this silly noise up front?" She looked up and saw her sister.

"Eva. What you want? Don't you need to be at home putting a pot on the stove or something?"

"Whatever, Nadeen. I came over here to get my nieces. I want some time to bond with my girls. I haven't spent quality time with Patsy since she got back from her trip and I want to hear all the details."

"You ought to be sick of your nieces as much as Ann and Josie stayed over there this summer. You and your momma worry me like they your children. They mine and they need to be home with me. I know how to properly supervise them. You liable to be out at the track or somewhere rollin' papers and let somebody come in there and put their hands on one of my daughters. Then you gonna have to call on the heavens to come down and save you." Nadeen said sternly to her sister.

Eva didn't flinch. "Nadeen, I done told you before I'm not scared of you. The devil and these kids the only one scared of you and you don't know nothing about what go on at my house so stop actin' like you do. I take good care of my nieces when they come over. We lock that house up tight as a jail cell and we have a good time with each other.

"Come on now. Let them go. Momma wants to see them too. All they ever do is go to school, come home, and look at these four walls. They too young and pretty for such a dull life. Anyway, Momma been having these funny tingling sensations in her arm and shortness of breath."

"It's called meanness, Eva. She feeling the effects of all that poison balled up inside of her she didn't get it all out when she had us at the house so now it's just hardening in her arteries. Can't nobody move it out but Jesus and she won't let him."

"For your own sake, I'm gonna let you make it and not tell your momma what you said about her.," Eva said. "You'd look real bad with a bald head due to her snatching all your hair out. Now let's just pack up my nieces so they can go have some real fun for a change." Eva said in a semi pleading tone of voice.

Nadeen started walking around looking. "Nobody opens that front door unless this house is clean and I mean that. If I have to go out and work they better keep my house clean. Cleanliness is next to Godliness, that's what your momma taught me." She said to Eva as she walked around inspecting the house.

"It looks okay. Not as good as I like it, but I guess it can get them a few days with you. I don't see why they like you so much. You stayed gone away from them so long when they were smaller, they ought to not want anything to do with you."

Patsy and Ann ignored that last statement and ran down the hall to pack. Josie already had a bag ready. They kept her extra clothes in her backpack to save time. When it came to Nadeen you had to move fast before she changed her mind. They were back up front in no time flat and ready to go. Patsy was holding Josie on her hip. Nadeen leaned over and kissed Josie on the jaw.

"You better take care of my baby," she told Eva with a look of warning in her brown eyes.

Eva turned to walk out the door. When she got to the porch and closed the door behind her she let it rip. "My Sister act like y'all going to Sodom and Gomorrah or something.

"My house is just as clean and holy as hers is and I make living in it a lot more fun. Come on, girls. Let's go get this party started!"

They threw their bags in the trunk of the car and hurried to get in the back seat.

"Hello, beautiful ladies." David smiled at them. "Looks like we're gonna be spending time together this weekend, so I'm gonna show you a real good time. Ann, you and Patsy ready for a real good time?"

Ann rolled down the back window of the car and let the breeze blow on her face. "I know I am," Ann said.

Patsy chose not to answer him. She looked up and saw him staring at her briefly thru the rearview mirror with those ugly grey eyes. Eva reached over the seat and handed Patsy her cell phone, "Here. Call your boyfriend. I'm pretty sure you haven't seen that handsome devil since you got back home."

Patsy laughed. "I talked to him. He's trying to get back in the swing of things. I'll see if he's got time for me."

"That Ralph boy sniffing Ann like a hound dog with a bird scent in his nose. What you been doin' with that boy Ann?" Eva asked.

"I ain't done nothing with him, Aunt Eva," Ann said. "He just likes me. He thinks I'm pretty."

"Well, every time I see him he asking about you and wanting to know when you coming back over," Eva said.

David looked back at Ann in the rearview mirror. "You better not be letting that boy get a taste of what you got girl. You let him even get close to that and you might lose something you can't get back." Ann cut her eyes at him.

Patsy whispered to her, "He needs to stay away from weed and your business."

5

THE HOUSE WAS lit up with music, laughter, and the smell of good food. Grandma Ruth was dancing the twist with Josie, Ann was dancing alone and Eva was showing David some nasty new dance move she learned from a choir member called "twerking." David was looking at her butt like he was hypnotized.

Patsy was on the front porch cuddling with Dustin. He felt as good as she remembered and smelled even better. He looked so good she wanted to lick his lips like a strawberry ice cream cone.

They both talked about how much they missed each other and couldn't wait to get back. The summer vacation gave Dustin some time to deal with his mother's death and help finalize some of her business. He told Patsy about the insurance policy his mother left him.

"My mom had a policy," Dustin said.

"Well, that doesn't surprise me. It surprises you?" Patsy asked.

"No. The surprise is the amount of the policy," Dustin said.

"Really? Well, how much is it for, a million dollars?" Patsy laughed and asked.

Dustin took her by the hand, looked her in the eye, and said, "As a matter of fact, it is."

Patsy stared at him for a few seconds trying to open her mouth. "What? You for real, Dustin? Your mom left you a policy for one million dollars?"

Dustin nodded his head yes. "It's for us, Patsy. Me and you to start our life. My sisters and brothers will get their cut but there will be plenty for us."

Patsy couldn't believe what she was hearing. Dustin was a teenage millionaire? She was gonna be married to a millionaire?

"Dustin, what are y'all gonna do with all of that money?"

"I'm still trying to figure it out. I mean momma gave us everything we ever needed without even touching it and we never missed anything."

"Well, I guess you got college tuition in the bag," Patsy said.

"Guess I do if I still decide to go."

Patsy looked at him as though she didn't understand the words that had just came out of his mouth. "What do you mean if you still decide to go? We been planning this ever since we been together Dustin. You know your mom wanted you to go to college and I thought you wanted to go too."

Dustin looked up into the sky as he spoke. "I did until she died. When she did, I felt like I was lost. I don't know what to do with my life now that she isn't in it. Everything I did, I did to make her happy. I wanted to make her proud of me and give her peace of mind. I never wanted to cause her any grief. Now she's gone and left me and I feel grief weighing me down.

"I'd burn that insurance policy up right now if I could have her back standing on that front porch." He said. "The trip this Summer helped a lot but I still miss her so much. I sleep in her bed just to remember her smell."

Patsy moved close to him and kissed him gently on his lips. "Dustin, I know you miss her but you can't give up. That money is to help you get everything you want out of life."

"I'm not changing my mind about marrying you one day and

us having our own little spot in the world. I'm still going to do that," Dustin pulled her closer.

"Well, that's the next step after our college degrees. College degrees then marriage certificates, in that order." Patsy said.

"No doubt, babe. No doubt. First, though, I want to make a donation to the church. My momma always wanted Greater Trials to have a kitchen to feed the homeless. I'm gonna get it done in her memory, call it 'Jessie's Place.'" Dustin said.

"Patsy!" Grandma Ruth yelled out the door. "You and that young man come in here and get some of this mystery dish David made. You can't live off kisses alone, honey." Patsy heard the whole house burst out laughing. She blushed and took Dustin by the hand.

"Come on. We can talk about this later on. Let's go check out this new invention David has. We might want to keep the pizza delivery number on speed dial just in case it turns out to be a taste bud disaster." They both laughed.

Everyone was around the table digging into all the food. David spilled red sauce all over his pants and had gone to change.

Patsy looked around for Ann. "Aunt Eva where is Ann?" she asked.

"She went to get the ice out of the freezer and some cups. You know she loves my punch. I forgot to turn the ice maker back on in the refrigerator so we gotta bust open a bag

A few minutes later Ann came back into the room dragging a large bag of ice. She must have had a time getting that bag of ice out the freezer because Patsy noticed her face looked flushed. Dustin jumped up to help her. "Why didn't you call for some help girl?" He asked. Ann looked worn out.

"I wasn't gonna let a bag of ice whip me. It was stuck down in there pretty good but I worked my way around it and finally got it to come loose. Just because I'm a girl doesn't mean I'm not strong as any man." She said.

"Alright, Lil' Miss Nadeen Simmons. We don't need no women wearing the pants in this house that's what we got men here for. Let them do the sweating and we do the petting." Eva said.

Patsy would always remember Ann's perfect smile and that sparkle in her eye as she laughed at her aunt's joke that night, it would be the last one for many years to come for on this night God would begin separating the wheat from the tare within their family upon his thrashing floor.

Sunday morning came quickly. Everyone got up moving slow. They'd danced way into the early morning hours forgetting that there was Sunday School and Worship Service to attend in this new day.

Eva was the first one up making coffee. She was grateful the Lord opened her eyes but if he wanted her to keep them open, she was gonna need a little help from a tin can. Grandma Ruth had the kitchen full of the smells of biscuits, sausage, and buttered rice.

Patsy woke up thinking about her and Dustin's conversation about college and his plans for the insurance money his mother left for them. She kept hearing him tell her he wasn't sure he wanted to go to college. If he wasn't sure about college then he may not be sure about them and that was a thought Patsy's heart just couldn't capture.

She never thought of her life without Dustin in it and she didn't want to.

"Patsy y'all get on in here and get this good country breakfast I made for you. I got a hangover to scare the devil from drinking this morning. Lord forgive me," Grandma Ruth said.

"We on the way!" Patsy yelled. She turned to her sisters. "Ann, you and Josie come on. You know what day it is and you know where we gotta be."

"Trust we know. Same thing every Sunday. When I get grown, I probably won't even go to church on Easter Sunday. I'm so tired of church folks," Ann said.

"Whatever. You probably gonna marry the Pastor," Patsy said running off towards the kitchen laughing.

"Y'all gobble that food down, get dressed, and get to that church. Eva, I don't want to hear Nadeen's mouth about these children being late. "Grandma Ruth said wrapping herself up a plate.

"I got them, Momma. Now go get ready yourself." Eva said as she sat a bowl of grits down in front of Josie. When it was time to leave, Patsy was surprised to see David going with them.

He was dressed in a nice navy business suit with a light blue shirt. It matched Aunt Eva's dress.

"David when you start going to church?" Patsy asked. Eva answered for him. "He started this morning. He made a promise to the Lord concerning a test he had to take for a new position at work and the Lord did his part." Eva said.

"It's a lot of things I done started doin' that might surprise y'all. Y'all don't know me. I'm turning over a new leaf girl. I got plans," David said as he winked at Patsy.

I doubt it, Patsy thought.

"You need to plan on getting to church on time. Come on, everybody out of this kitchen and in the car." Eva said.

Everybody piled out the house together. When they made it to the car Patsy glanced over at Ann. She was wearing a tight-fitting dress with Aunt Eva's pomegranate lipstick on her lips and heavy clear gloss.

"Girl, what have you got on your lips?" Patsy asked Ann." We must be dropping you off at another church this morning cause I know you ain't goin' up in Greater Trials MB Church where your momma is the Head Usher, with that lipstick on."

Eva looked in the rearview mirror straining to get a good look at Ann. Ann had already cut her eyes over at Patsy with straight hate. It was a good thing Josie's car seat was between them or they might tear that back seat up fighting.

"Now, Ann. You know your momma don't let you wear lipstick

yet. It's fine with me when you're over here but I'm not gonna fight in the church parking lot with my sister this morning about you and some lipstick," Eva said.

"I like it. I'm old enough to wear it. All the girls at my school do. I'm the only one that looks like an old lady," Ann said.

"It looks real pretty on you to me, Ann," David said.

"Thank you, Uncle David." Ann smiled and said.

"I bet that little boy is gonna like it too," David said.

"David. Stay out of this. You gonna cause a Homegoing Service up in Greater Trials today if you don't. Ann know her momma crazy." Eva said.

"Ann. That lipstick won't look so cute on a pair of busted lips," Eva said taking a napkin from her purse and handing it over to Patsy.

"Give this to your sister, put a little Vaseline on it and get that mess off of her lips before we get to church." Patsy took the napkin, pulled out the small tube of Vaseline she kept in her purse, put a small amount on it, and handed it to Ann. Ann gave Patsy a hard stare and snatched the napkin out of her hand.

She was pissed. She stared at Patsy for a good while as she began to remove the lipstick from her mouth. "I'm not a little girl anymore and I wish people would stop treating me like I am."

Eva was adjusting her rings on her fingers when she heard Ann's comment. She stopped and looked up. "What? What did you just say, little girl? You just getting buds big enough to put in an A cup good and still sprouting in certain places. You ain't a woman yet young or old and if you want to get there you better not try me or your momma this morning."

Ann popped her lips, rolled her eyes again, and let out a loud sigh.

"Stop the car!" Eva yelled. David looked over at her. "Eva stop trippin'. The girl just feelin' herself. She growing up trying to find herself, you know how you girls get once you get in junior high school and them boys get to lookin' at you." David said.

"David. What did I just tell you?" Eva said. Cutting him a look that said: You better shut up and do what I said.

"Why we gotta have some drama this Sunday morning?" David said as he pulled the car over to the side of the road. Eva got out of the car and before Ann realized what was going on, opened the door and snatched her out of the back seat.

She should have had her seat belt on, Patsy thought to herself. She didn't open her mouth. She was too scared. It was a good thing Josie had fallen off to sleep so she wouldn't see this.

Aunt Eva closed the car door and slammed Ann up against it. "Now I'm not sure if that Ralph boy got your nose or your legs wide open but whichever one it is, if you ever get an attitude with me like that again or talk sassy to me, I'll break your nose in five places do you hear me, niece? You better try Jesus, not me. I have never had to come at you like this. You must be on that same stuff my sister's on, acting up with me this morning." Eva said.

Patsy saw her Aunt's neck twitch and it reminded her of Nadeen right before she beat the daylights out of one of them. Ann couldn't get the words out cause Eva had the collar of her dress in her hands and she was holding it tightly in her grip.

When she finally did let Ann go, Ann gasped and started coughing.

"Now get in that back seat and shut up before I tell my sister just how grown her middle daughter thinks she is," Eva said. "You done made me spill out all my Holy Ghost this morning."

Ann got in the back seat of the car and put on her seat belt. She sniffled all the way to church. By the time they got there her eyes were red. David parked the car and everyone got out except Ann. Patsy tried to get her to come in with them but Ann said she wanted to be left alone.

Nadeen was inside the room next to the front church doors gathering up church fans. Josie saw her first and started running towards her calling "Momma!" Nadeen turned around and Josie ran up to her. She bent down and kissed her. She didn't pick her up because Patsy knew she couldn't chance that pristine white dress and gloves getting anything on them.

"Hey, Eva," Nadeen said. She looked back at Patsy. "Where's your sister?"

Patsy didn't want to lie in the church even if she was just in the vestibule. "She moving slow this morning. She still trying to unhook the seatbelt." Patsy said. That was a partial truth.

"Go out there and tell her I said get her behind in here now and get to that Sunday School Class." Nadeen barked. Eva reached over to get Josie. "Give her to me and go help your sister get herself together."

Patsy handed her Josie and turned to go back out the door to the parking lot.

When she opened the door to walk out to the parking lot, she saw David and Ann standing near the car. Ann had her head buried in his chest. He had his arms wrapped around her and was kissing her on her head. Patsy didn't like the way that looked. She rushed over to them.

Before she realized it, she grabbed David's arm. "Let my sister go. You don't need to have your arms around her like that! It looks weird." Patsy said.

David grinned and removed his arms from around Ann. "I was just trying to calm her little lady. Eva scared her pretty bad. She ain't never seen that side of her Aunt." He said.

Patsy grabbed Ann's hand. "Come on, Ann. We'll go through the side door to Sunday School so you can put some cold water on your face. You don't want Nadeen to see you looking like that and start asking questions."

Ann dragged behind Patsy and went in the bathroom to clean her face. "Ann, what's wrong with you? I never seen Aunt Eva get mad like that with you." Patsy said. "You need to get it together before you get ripped apart foolin' with Nadeen or Aunt Eva."

"I'm surprised Ralph even looks at me as ugly as I am compared to the other girls at my school," Ann said. "I'm just trying to feel normal."

"Ann, you are beautiful but if you don't get it together something ugly is gonna happen. You moving way too fast." Patsy said handing Ann a paper towel to wash her face with.

"I don't need Aunt Eva to tell me whether or not I'm a woman. I know I am. I been one for a while now," Ann said as she opened the bathroom door and walked out.

Patsy just stood in the doorway of the bathroom for a minute and watched Ann walk off down the hall towards her Sunday School Class. She was at a loss for words. What was Ann trying to say? A thought drifted across Patsy's mind but she brushed it away because Ann was her little sister. Her and Dustin hadn't even done "that" yet and that was what really made you a grown woman in Patsy's mind.

After service, Ralph walked Ann to the car. Nadeen was still inside the church folding up the sheets they'd laid out across the women who fainted in the spirit at the altar. He helped Ann transfer her bags from Eva's car to Nadeen's.

"Thank you for being so sweet, Ralph. You didn't have to help me. I got it." Ann said.

"I wanted to. You know I don't mind. See you at school tomorrow. Maybe we can have lunch together." Ralph said.

Ann shrugged her shoulders. "Maybe." She said and got in the car. Ralph stood there watching her put on her seatbelt.

Patsy walked up to him. "Boy, you got it bad. I don't why you like my little sister. She too moody for me," Patsy smiled at him and said.

"I like all her moods," Ralph said and walked back toward the church.

Aunt Eva and Grandma Ruth came over to the car. Eva lowered her head into the window and looked at Ann.

"Niece, I love you but I want to make sure you are clear on the fact that I won't tolerate that stunt again that you pulled in the car this morning. You've never acted like that."

"I guess maybe your daddy being gone has got you mixed up inside emotionally or it's the little bit of attention that Ralph boy is giving you, I don't know, but whatever it is you better get control of yourself," Eva said. "I still love you though."

Ann didn't even look up at her. Grandma Ruth was standing next to her. "Ann, I don't know what's wrong for sure but I might need to have a talk with your daddy about the way you acted this morning. Eva told me she almost had to yank your voice box out of your throat cause of how disrespectful you was actin'." She said. "We had such a good time this weekend don't you be acting ugly and spoil it. Do you hear me?"

This time Ann answered. "Yes, ma'am," she said in a low voice. Just as Grandma Ruth finished talking to her, Nadeen was coming up to the car.

"Okay, Momma. I'll talk to you later. I gotta get the girls home. I'm worn out today. So many women was falling out in that sanctuary I thought I was gonna have to start pulling off jackets and putting them over folks."

"Folks just faking. Fallin' out cause they neighbor did. I'm glad I'm not the one responsible for folding all them white sheets back up." Grandma Ruth said. "Bye, girls. I'll see you next week. I think your momma gotta go to her part-time sitter job with that old rich woman. Her daughter going on vacation and she need a sitter."

Patsy didn't know Nadeen had taken on another part-time job. She did know that her hours had been cut at the nursing home.

"I swear that momma of mine can't hold water in a gallon bucket. Nobody told her to go telling my business about a part-time job," Nadeen said as she drove off in the car. "If I wanted everybody at Greater Trials to know my business, I would've put it on the announcement board. She out there talking all loud in the church parking lot."

She was paranoid. She always thought somebody was trying to know what she was doin' so they could gossip about it.

"Ann, don't you and Patsy go telling Kenny my business you hear me?" She asked them both. She really didn't have to tell them this. They knew very well not to tell anybody anything about her or her business if they wanted all their body parts intact and in good working order.

They'd been home long enough to change clothes and sit down at the table when the doorbell rang.

"Now who is that ringing my bell this time of the day? A good Christian know folks just getting home and trying to relax after service. Whoever it is about to get the short version of 'get-the-you-know-what away from my door' greeting today."

Nadeen answered the door and the next thing Patsy heard was the voice of an angel floating from the front door.

"Well, Hello Pastor Craig. You and Champagne come right on in. What a nice surprise!"

"I hope First Lady and I not bothering you Sister," Pastor Craig said.

"Oh no. No, bother at all. We were just sitting down for some lunch. After a service like we had on today you know you got to restore yourself. Would you all like a bite to eat or something to drink? I got some peach tea in the refrigerator nice and cold," she said pleasantly.

"Well, Pastor and I might just take you up on a glass of peach tea. Your First Lady is a bit thirsty," Champagne Porter said. "The pastor and I on our way to the boat for some crab legs this afternoon and we don't want to spoil our appetites, do we baby?"

"No, First Lady we don't. So let's get this thing done." Pastor Craig said following Nadeen into the living room. Patsy knew Nadeen was grinding her teeth together right about now.

"Would you like a glass of tea, Pastor?" Patsy heard Nadeen ask. She laughed quietly to herself cause she could hear the tension towards Champagne in Nadeen's voice.

"Sure we would." Pastor Craig said as he and Champagne sat on the love seat sofa.

"Patsy! Patsy bring two glasses of peach tea in here for Pastor, please, and coasters too!" She yelled into the kitchen. Patsy noticed she didn't say for Pastor and First Lady. Nadeen wasn't ever going to acknowledge Champagne Porter as that.

Patsy couldn't wait to get those glasses in the living room. She wanted to see that fake smile on Nadeen's face and her effort not to curse Champagne out for even coming to her house with Pastor Craig. When she walked in, they were making small talk about the donation Pastor had received in the mail from a mystery person to fix up the church. Patsy figured it was probably from Dustin. She put the coasters and the peach tea on the table. Champagne smiled at her

"Sister Nadeen one of these for First Lady? I can't drink two." Reverend Craig asked. Nadeen forced a smile on her lips. "Of course Pastor, of course."

Patsy made sure to crack the door to the living room just a little on her way out so she and Ann could find out what this visit was about.

"Well, First Lady and I don't want to keep you so we gonna state our business and keep on going. I wanted to come by to tell you first of all that I spoke with Elder Jordan Jackson's new Pastor about your feelings and he spoke with him. He has assured his Pastor he is not singling you out at work and you not getting that supervisor position was nothing personal.

"He said it was a corporate office decision. He said he had to cut other folk's hours too just to make the budget. He says he hates the two of you can't seem to get along with him and his family being new to the area he would like to be friends in spite of what happened. He doesn't have any ill feelings toward the church or you. He still swears, however, that it wasn't what it looked like." Pastor Craig told her. Nadeen knew Jordan Jackson was lying about not harassing her at work, but she wasn't gonna debate it with Pastor.

She placed her hands in her lap, smiled, and said, "Well, Pastor I appreciate you talking to him and getting things straightened out between us. You know I can't stand confusion and strife in the church."

Pastor Craig smiled. "I know that, Sister. I also got some more good news to share with you since I'm here."

Nadeen smiled at him, "What's that Pastor?"

"Well, I have decided to give the new Usher, Sister Haymer, a try at being church secretary for a while. Take some of this load off of you."

Patsy almost fell out of her seat backward. Ann spit out her tea on her dress and looked at Patsy with her eyes open as wide as they could go. They both sat at the kitchen table waiting for the bomb that was about to explode in the room Reverend Craig was finally about to see the real Sister Simmons.

You don't fool with the Church Secretary position that had been Nadeen's position for seven years, as long as she'd been the Head Usher and now he was gonna just give it to someone else?

They waited for the cuss-a-thon to begin, the speaking of tongues like Reverend Craig had never seen before. If he wanted, Patsy and Ann could be the interpreters they knew every word she would use fluently.

They heard Nadeen clear her throat and prepared themselves for her next words. "Pastor. Did I do something wrong? I've had that position since you made me Head Usher. What is it? Please tell me. I'll go right in today and take care of it." She said in a humble tone.

Reverend Craig laughed softly. "Sister Nadeen, you have done a wonderful job as the church secretary over the last seven years but I wanted to give Sister Haymer an opportunity to get some work experience. You might not know it but she's real good with all that social media stuff. She was a lead technology supervisor a few years ago at her old job before she got caught up with them rocks. First

Lady and I just want to help her get some experience under her belt to help her get a good-paying job you understand? She missing out on her blessing not being able to pay her tithes and offering like everybody else."

"Well, I have a very precise and detailed system set up for each ministry and member. It may be a little too stressful for Sister Haymer considering what she been through and all. She might just do better collecting the information for right now. I'd be glad to give her a list to learn what information I need each month." Nadeen said.

"Well, no Sister. We don't want you to busy yourself with all that. You working two jobs already and I know you want to be here with your girls, especially with their daddy being away right now.

"Pastor she may not be able to understand what I have in place. I'd hate to get things mixed up when you were just trying to be considerate." Nadeen said slowly rubbing her hands together.

"You don't have to worry about Sister Haymer learning the current system you have in place, Sister Nadeen. She's gonna come in and set up a brand new and more efficient one. She's even gonna get us a webpage created."

"Won't that be something? Greater Trials getting their own website?" Champagne Porter pitched in.

Pastor Craig shook his head and smiled. "She's also gonna create us one of those Church Book pages like the mega-churches. I hear a lot of the other Pastor's talking about how much that has helped their congregation grow."

"Well, Pastor I'm sure you prayed over this before you made a decision and I ain't a woman to argue with the Man of God so I'll step down as the church secretary. I must say though I'm gonna miss doing work for the kingdom," Nadeen said fighting the urge to scream.

"Sister, you'll still be doing plenty of work for the kingdom. You're my Head Usher, you on the Mother Board, Director of the

Fundraising Committee, and President of the Praying Women's Circle. You got plenty to do for the Lord. This'll just give you more time to do it." He said gently.

"Well, honey, now that we had a chance to talk that over with Sister Nadeen we better be going and let her eat her Sunday lunch. You know them crab legs go fast at the boat." Champagne said as she patted her husband on his leg and stood to leave. As the door to the living room began to crack open, Ann and Patsy tried to look busy.

"Well, Pastor if you change your mind or she decides it's too much for her just give me a call. I'll step right back in like I never left," Nadeen said as she walked them to the door.

"Sister Nadeen, I thank you. See, I told First Lady if there is one member in my church that is full of the Holy Ghost for real, for real, it's my member, Sister Nadeen Simmons. I knew you wouldn't mind helping Sister Haymer to get on her feet. She's gonna be so glad to know you send your blessing in this new journey." Pastor Craig said as they walked out the door.

Champagne Porter turned to her with a big smirk on her face. "You be blessed now you hear?"

Nadeen envisioned herself choking her tongue out of her mouth at that very moment. Instead, she forced a smile on her face. "Pastor, you drive safe." She said looking past Champagne.

"I surely will. Thank you, Sister. See you next Sunday."

As soon as that door closed Nadeen headed to her bedroom.

She slammed the door shut and the next thing Patsy and Ann heard was her on the phone talking loud to Eva and she was cussing up a storm. "How could this Rahab, recovering crack addict come into my church and take my position I've had for seven years? God ain't pleased with this Eva! You hear me? God ain't pleased!" She shouted into the phone. "Seven years! I worked faithfully for him and along comes somebody fresh out of rehab working over the church business? Reverend Craig done lost his mind! I told you, Eva.

"She done put witchcraft on him. I always suspected it but today I know it's true!" Nadeen said pacing the floor back and forth.

Eva laughed, "You act like you don't know the power of the 'P,' Nadeen, and I ain't talking about prayer. You ain't seen the last of the things Champagne gone have done up in Greater Trials. Believe that.

Nadeen was steaming. "I'm not going to stand by and let the devil take my position away from me, Eva!

"Reverend Craig is blinded by a size D Bra Cup and a padded booty in a tight skirt but I'm not! I see the enemy at work here and I'm going to stop her just like I stopped Jordan Jackson. I got him out of Greater Trials and I'll get her out too!"

The rest of her conversation was too X-rated to repeat. Sister Simmons had been stripped of her church secretarial duties what could be worse than that? Everyone stayed to themselves walking on invisible eggshells the rest of the day. The enemy was in the house walking to and fro looking for someone to devour.

6

THE FIRST DAY of Patsy's senior year finally arrived. Ann was dragging a little bit cause she stayed up late.

"I think I'm gonna need a double power shot this morning," Ann said dragging out of the bed with her eyes closed.

"Well, you better do what you gotta do cause this is my senior year and starting today I'm already packing to get up out of here," Patsy said.

"You been packing since you realized your momma was a Bipolar Bible-toting, oil slanging, split tongue talking Saint," Ann said as she changed clothes.

They both laughed.

"Ann, come on now. Let's get it. We counting down this year, honey." Patsy said grabbing her sister's backpack.

Ann grabbed her backpack out of her sister's hands. "I got my own backpack thank you. Slow your roll, girl. That school ain't about to walk off from you." She told her older sister.

"But I'm about to walk off from it," Patsy responded. "Now let's go."

Ann took her time getting dressed.

"You been keeping those late-night phone sessions again I see.

You and Ralph must be getting serious when you need to be getting your sleep," Patsy said to her sister poking her in her arm.

Ann pushed her finger away. "Don't worry about me and Ralph. He has me an energy drink in his backpack for me every morning. That boy loves me."

"Ann you too young to know about love. Now let's get dressed and go. I'd love to get to school." Patsy said as she hurried and got dressed.

On their way out the door, Ann watched her sister walking in front of her and she felt scared. This was the year her sister would leave. The year she'd go away to college with Dustin in the fall. She'd probably never come back home. Ann couldn't blame her for that but she could blame her for forgetting that she was leaving two sisters behind. Two sisters who weren't ready to do home alone for the next few years with a mother who was more focused on her church image than her image in the eyes of her daughters.

This was why Ann had decided to cling to him instead of her big sister or her father. She knew that he would stay with her no matter what. The only way he would leave her would be them going together when it was her turn.

Ann was quiet on the bus. She was deep in thought about how her life was about to change forever. The first stop, as usual, was at Ann's school. Patsy looked out of the window and saw Ralph standing by the bus stop. Patsy waved at him and he waved back. Ann got up to leave, she didn't say goodbye.

"Bye, Ann. Have a good first day," Patsy said to her little sister. She loved her so much. She wanted her to be strong and to be happy. She watched her walk past Ralph without speaking to him and he started chasing after her. Poor Ralph. He reminded Patsy of Kenny chasing behind Nadeen just to get any sign of approval or love. *How sad to want love so bad you'd do almost anything to get it,* she thought.

When the bus arrived at her school, Dustin was there waiting for her just as he had always been since they became a couple—looking better, stronger, and edible. His broad shoulders, slim waist, bow legs, and big hands always made her look at him from the top to the bottom.

She knew one day she would see everything under his clothes and when that day came, they would be sealed to each other for life. She had to repent almost daily it seems from letting her mind wander. She tried to be serious about her vows of abstinence with Dustin. It was hard. Her mind said "wait" but her body said "give it to him." They promised each other they wouldn't seal the deal until their wedding night.

She came up to him and he kissed her on the lips.

"You taste good like chocolate and cinnamon." He smiled and said.

Patsy smiled back at him, "It's my new lip gloss. Aunt Eva snuck it to me,"

"Well tell her I like it."

Patsy blushed. "How was everything at home this morning?"

"It was pretty good actually. I hope it stays that way," she said as she wrapped her arms around his waist.

"Glad to hear that. Come on, let's get this senior year started so we can get out of here. I'm ready to see the world with you." Dustin said pulling her closer to him as they walked to class.

"I'm across the hall in physics first period. I'll meet you back here when the bell sounds to change classes, okay?" He asked.

"That's fine, babe. See you in a little bit," Patsy said.

When she stepped into her Introduction to Robotics class the only seat left was a seat next to Daphne Porter in the back. There was something different about her. She was dressed very conservatively and casually, not like before when everything was tight and had to show her cleavage. Everyone in the class was staring at Patsy as she went to sit next to Daphne. They all knew their history. Sandra had told Patsy that Daphne had gotten saved over the summer at a night service held at Greater Trials. A guest pastor had come out of the pulpit and went up to her and told her she'd been in his dreams. He'd seen her tormented and bound. Sandra said Daphne broke at that point and went down to the altar with the pastor and gave her life to Jesus. Daphne was full of all kinds of surprises this year. *Repentance and Robotics,* Patsy thought.

Patsy spoke to her as she sat down.

"Hey, Daphne."

Daphne gave her a slight smile and said, "Good Morning, Sister Patsy."

Patsy stared at her for a few seconds, *Sister Patsy?* Patsy wasn't ready for that. *She might be saved for real,* Patsy thought to herself. She no longer seemed to be the mean, bitter girl that harassed her because of Dustin. She seemed more peaceful and refined

Everyone in the classroom looked shocked. After class, Daphne walked off down the hall alone. *It's going to be a long year for her,* Patsy thought to herself. Her old friends weren't gonna fit in this new walk. She'd have to make some more.

Dustin told her once that Daphne was a pretty smart girl, she just didn't want to show it to her old crew. She always kept herself off of the honor roll by allowing herself one C or D in a class. Patsy wondered if her enrolling in the robotics class was her way of showing everyone she had truly changed. This new Daphne Porter was awkward to Patsy, it was going to take a while to get used to it. Patsy would proceed with caution, watching, listening, and waiting just in case Daphne's newfound salvation was more emotional than spiritual.

She was known for persecuting Patsy and pursuing after Dustin so Patsy knew she wasn't the only one that might not be fully convinced Daphne had changed.

On her way to her next class, she ran into Sandra.

"Hey, girlfriend. What's goin' on?"

"Sandra, where you been? I didn't see you at the bus stop this morning and you didn't come by the house to walk with me and Ann." Patsy said.

Sandra smiled and walked briskly with her to her next class. "Solomon was sick this morning so Lavon and I took him to the doctor. It seems he doesn't like this new formula and it doesn't like him.

"It got him so locked up I had to take him to see Nurse Russell at the clinic. She had to perform some weird procedure to get him to release his bowels. He was screaming like somebody set him on fire. I didn't get any sleep last night he just cried and cried." She told Patsy.

"I tried reaching Lavon last night so we could take him but he never answered his phone, it kept going to his voicemail. Sometimes he acts like he's disconnected from me and Solomon."

"Maybe you should ask him what's going on."

Sandra looked down at her finger at the promise ring Lavon had given her last year. "I did. He told me to worry about the baby not him."

"Guys can be jerks sometimes. Anyway, is Solomon better now?" Patsy asked.

"Yeah. As soon as Nurse Russell finished with him, he was smiling and laughing again. Guess I better leave him on his old formula and try to keep momma from feeding him cornbread and collard green liquor. He's as fat as a Thanksgiving Turkey. He needs to go on Weight Watchers." Sandra laughed and said.

"Well, I hope he doesn't get sick anymore. This is our senior year and we are not missing graduation because he got a tummy ache. You gotta cross that stage with me Sandra, you hear me?"

"Yes, Momma. I hear you." Sandra said looking Patsy directly in the eye. "You think Lavon would cheat on me, Patsy?"

"Girl, no. He loves you and that baby. He just being a donkeylike guys do sometimes."

"I hope that's it. My heart would break if I found out he was." Sandra said with her eyes getting misty.

Patsy reached out and hugged her friend. "Trust he isn't. Focus on graduating, girl. That's the only other thing you need to be concerned about."

"You right. I'm trippin'. Thanks, best-friend. Love you."

"I love you, too. Now get to class. You smell like baby puke." Patsy said as she headed to her next class.

The first day of school went by fast before Patsy knew it Dustin was walking her back to the bus. "You got your acceptance letter to Dove University yet?" She asked him. Patsy had already gotten an email confirmation from the university letting her know they'd received her application.

"No," Dustin said.

"Well, you better follow up with them. I hate to be on campus without you. No distractions and no delays Dustin."

Dustin bent down and kissed her gently on her lips. "Never that, baby. Wherever you go, I'm gonna be there."

"You better," Patsy said as she turned and boarded the bus. When the bus got to Ann's school. She was standing near the curb blowing bubbles with her gum. Ralph was standing next to her. She was looking straight ahead at the bus. When it stopped, Ralph waited for her to board. She boarded the bus and sat next to Patsy.

"How was the first day of your senior year, Patsy?" Ann asked completely ignoring Ralph who sat in the seat across from her. Patsy felt so bad for him. Ann controlled his heart. She decided when he could love her and when he couldn't. She was playing a game with him and she had written the rules.

"It was great. I even got a class with Daphne Porter and had to sit next to her." Patsy told Ann.

Ann looked shocked. "For real? You sat by her? Ms. Side-piece International? I can't believe that!" She laughed.

"Hey, Patsy. How you doin'?" Ralph leaned forward and asked hoping Ann would at least look at him.

"I'm doing good. How about you, Ralph?" Patsy responded back to him. She felt awkward between him and Ann.

"Ann, I need you to answer the phone when I call you tonight. I want to talk to you about something," Ralph said.

"I might," Ann said.

"You see what I have to deal with, Patsy? She has my heart and she's just dragging it in the mud." Ralph said sadly.

"I don't recall asking you for it," Ann responded.

"But you got it," Ralph said and sat back in his seat. He was quiet the rest of the ride. When it came to dragging a man by the nose, Ann apparently had skills like her momma. Patsy had to admire that about her little sister.

"Talk to you later tonight," Ralph said as the bus slowed down to drop Patsy and Ann off at their stop.

"Do what you want to," Ann said to him as she headed to the front door of the bus. She never even looked back.

"You give that boy too much grief for your narrow butt," Patsy told Ann as she walked down the bus steps behind her.

"I learned it from my momma," Ann laughed and said.

"I sure hate it. Just remember he ain't Kenny. One day he's gonna get tired of you playing with him and he's gonna stop chasing you." Patsy said.

"A dog will always chase a firetruck, darling. That's what Aunt Eva says."

"Yeah, and everything gets old," Patsy said.

"Trust me. Ralph ain't going nowhere. I told you before, we got this. You just handle yours." Ann said.

"That's what your momma thought too but where her man at now?" Patsy said and put her earplugs in her ear. Ann rolled her eyes at her sister and looked straight ahead for the rest of the walk home.

As they got closer to home, they could see Josie out in the front yard. She was playing with what looked like her tea set. She had someone sitting at the table with her pretending to drink. As they walked closer, they saw it was their neighbor, Mrs. Wilson.

"Hey, Mrs. Wilson how you doin'?" Ann asked popping her gum.

"I'm doing just fine. I'm watching Josie for your momma until she comes back. She had to run over to the church to pick up some things. I heard how Reverend Craig got a new secretary for the church after your momma done worked in that office for seven years."

Patsy didn't feel comfortable talking too much about Nadeen's business. She could feel her eyes on her even when she wasn't around.

"Yes, ma'am. Well, I'll take Josie on in from here. Ann and I got homework to finish and Josie is probably ready for a snack. Thanks for watching her," Patsy said as she picked Josie up from the tiny table.

"You girls know you welcome anytime. By the way, you heard from your daddy lately? I heard from that girl Sara that went to his old church that he doin' real good at that job in Miami." Mrs. Wilson said.

Really? Patsy thought to herself. *Kenny been talking to Sara from his old church?* Patsy remembered her. She was the one that always looked at him like she was a love-sick puppy. She was always bringing him something to eat or checking up on him after church on Sunday when he and Nadeen were separated.

Nadeen didn't seem to want him but nobody else was gonna take what was hers and Kenny Simmons was hers to do with and treat the way she pleased.

"Yes, ma'am we talked to him. Well, thanks again, and have a nice evening," Patsy replied trying to quickly get in the house.

She didn't need to give out any more details than that. This thing could get complicated and she didn't want her name mentioned in any conversation pertaining to Nadeen and Kenny. Speaking of taking what was Nadeen's, Patsy hoped Sister Haymer wasn't at that church office when Nadeen got there. If she was, she better make sure Reverend Craig was there with her because if he wasn't she might get a revelation right there in the church office about the Head Usher.

Patsy made Josie a peanut butter and banana sandwich then sat down to complete her homework. By the time she finished, Nadeen had made it back home. She walked through the door with a large box.

"Patsy, go out there and bring that other box in for me." Nadeen commanded. Patsy knew not to hesitate.

"She won't walk around spreading her peacock feathers at Greater Trials off of my hard work and my supplies. If it's her office now let her get her own files, her own trays, and her own office supplies. She can also create her own announcements and church directory." Nadeen said, setting the box on the table.

"If my First Lady was still alive she would have never let this happen. She knew how hard I worked and how faithful I was to that position. Now Reverend Craig want to put me out and let somebody off the street come in and rise up to glory off of my hard work. Not while I'm still livin' and breathin'." She said a matter-of-factly.

Patsy listened to Nadeen rant around the house for about an hour before Sister Cullum, one of the Sisters of the Praying Circle, called to check on her. Nadeen put the cell phone down on the counter and just let her talk on speaker as she went about unpacking her office supplies.

"Sister Nadeen, I am so sorry to hear about what happened up at the church." She said. Nadeen just kept unpacking.

"I know you always been there for Pastor to do whatever was needed to further the Kingdom. I pray you're going to be all right, sugah."

"Sister Cullum, I appreciate your concern and your prayers. I'm doing just fine. God got this." Nadeen responded as she sat and continued to take her color coordinated office supplies out of the box.

"We gone miss those nice church bulletins of yours. I'm sure the new girl will do fine though, and you gone be there to help her if she need it." Sister Cullum said. "What's her name again?"

Nadeen stopped for a minute and looked down at her phone. She had to remember this was a church member on her phone. "Sister Cullum. I got to go catch this other call looks like it's my husband. Thanks for checking on me though," Nadeen said as she quickly hung up the phone.

"She is one messy member. If I could go through that phone and reach her, I'd staple her lips together. If one more person calls me talking about what they glad I'm willing to do they gone cause me to act like my momma and I don't want to have to do that," Nadeen said as she slammed the stapler down next to her box.

7

IT HAD BEEN about a month since Reverend Craig replaced Nadeen as church secretary but she was still mad about it, and every time Reverend Craig thanked Sister Haymer for some new social media site she put Greater Trials on or some new database she created it made Nadeen even madder. She told Eva one day if Reverend Craig didn't come from under this spell Champagne Porter had put on him, she just might move her membership to Deliverance Rock and join over there. She was sure Reverend Mack would love to have all her many gifts and talents to bless his ministry. Patsy wondered what Reverend and First Lady Mack would think about that. She knew Kenny would be perplexed by the very fact that Nadeen even entertained the idea.

Nadeen wasn't gonna be happy until she found out what she believed to be the real reason that Reverend Craig took her position away. She just didn't believe it was his idea. On the night of the church Focusing on Fellowship Festival, Nadeen found out the real reason for her removal.

Kenny called just before they were leaving out for the festival. Nadeen didn't recognize the number he was calling from and she answered the phone.

"Hey, Nadeen. It's Kenny." He said surprised to hear her voice.

"Me and the kids are heading out for the Fellowship Festival. You'll have to call them back later," Nadeen said trying to rush off the phone.

"Okay. I'm not gonna hold you up. Look, I'm sorry to hear your pastor let his new wife pull your position from you but you know, blood is thicker than water sometimes; even in church." His last statement got her attention.

"First of all, how do you even know about that?" Nadeen asked.

"A friend of mine up here has an Aunt that goes to your church," Kenny said.

"And what do you mean blood is thicker than water even in church?"

"Nadeen now I know that you know by now that Sister Haymer is Champagne Porter's first cousin. They momma's are blood sisters." Kenny said. "Reverend Craig is the one that got her off the streets and put her in rehab. I regret to say it, but I was there the night he came up in the crack house and took her out.

"She had called Champagne and told her she was scared she was dying and to come get her quick. Champagne and Reverend Craig both came in there and got her."

Nadeen just held the phone and stared into space. She was speechless for the first time. She was in such disbelief she was too far gone to even talk about him being at the crack house in the first place.

"Well, at least somebody around me finally let the truth out. I should have known Champagne Porter had something to do with this. She got Reverend Craig all messed up in the head. Well, I'm going to address this tonight." Nadeen said. She hung the phone up on Kenny without even saying goodbye.

"Girls, come on. We gotta get to the Fellowship Festival right now." Patsy and Ann were already dressed so they just grabbed Josie and followed their mom out the door. She was focused on something.

She shook her head as she was driving and said, "Lord have Mercy." At least one hundred times before they made it to the church.

Nadeen got out of the car with a weird smile on her face. Patsy knew that meant she was up to something she just hoped it didn't involve embarrassing her or Ann. When they walked into the festival, everybody was busy bobbing for apples, eating sweet potato pie, and dancing.

She spotted Reverend Craig and headed straight for him. "Good evening Reverend how are you?" She asked.

Reverend Craig shoved the remainder of the potato pie in his mouth and chewed as fast as he could before answering.

"Why I'm doin' just fine Sister Nadeen. How about you?" He said wiping the pie crumbs off of his mouth. Nadeen smiled back at him.

"I'm blessed and highly favored of the Lord. How is your wife?" She asked sweetly.

"The First Lady is doin' just fine. She over there dressed up as a scarecrow. See her over there? "He asked as he pointed in Champagne's direction. "She sure is a cute little thing. God been mighty good to me Sister. I mean mighty good."

"Pastor, I want to talk to you real quick about the street ministry. I know you been looking for someone to get that started and now that I don't have to come in on Saturday mornings for administrative duties I was wondering if you would let me organize it.

"I can gather up some of the women of the Praying Circle along with a few of the ushers and we can go out and pass out the church tracks in the community."

Reverend Craig seemed to like that idea. "You know, Sister Nadeen, I think that would be a great idea.

"We can have a different group of members to go out each month. It would be nice for the first group to be our praying women and our ushers. I tell you, Sister Nadeen, you always thinking of ways to help others." He smiled.

"See? I told you God had a reason for moving you as church secretary it was so you could get the street ministry started. I'll leave it in your hands. Let me know by the end of the month how it goes. I want a full report and hopefully an increase in membership."

That's it? Patsy thought. *That's her way of settling it? She's gonna kick off the street ministry?* Patsy thought to herself.

Patsy decided to keep watching this thing play out because this wasn't the normal way Nadeen played the game when it came to her church and her pastor. She saw David and Aunt Eva sitting at a table a few feet away. She grabbed Ann and went to talk to them. Eva saw a strawberry Jell-o-cake and jumped up to go get a piece just as they got there.

"Babies, you wait right here for your Aunt. I'll be right back. I gotta get a piece of that cake before it's all gone." She said.

David looked over at them with a glaze in his eyes. Patsy hated his eyes. They were full of evil to her. He licked his lips.

"What you sweet lil' pumpkins up to tonight? You ain't got no little boys running around here to go bobbing for apples for you?" He laughed as he slurred the words out of his mouth.

Neither Ann nor Patsy answered him. Patsy spotted Sandra and Lavon and waved Sandra over. She came over grinning with black marker on her teeth and a straw hat on her head.

"Hey, y'all. What you just sitting around here for? Get up and have some fun." She said. "I saw your momma over there talking to Reverend Craig. That's good, in spite of what he did."

"Ann how you feeling? The doctor give you something for those bad migraine headaches you been having?" She asked.

Ann looked up at her like she wanted to shove straw in her mouth. Patsy looked over at Ann and then at Sandra. "What migraine headaches you talking about Sandra?"

"Sandra, you need to put a piece of cake in that big mouth of yours," Ann said as she frowned at Sandra.

Sandra looked hurt. "I was just trying to check up on you. You better be glad you my best friend's sister." Sandra said turning to Lavon. "Come on. Let's go before I hurt this little girl." Sandra said turning to walk away.

"San, you and Ann been friends too long for some drama. You know the girl going through with her daddy being gone, ease up on her. You need to squash whatever it is going on with you two." Lavon said.

Sandra turned towards him. "Why it gotta be me with the problem? You saw how she was acting. I was just concerned about her. Since when you care so much about Ann?" Sandra asked taking Solomon out of his arms.

"It's not even like that. I care about the fact that you seem to forget that she going through some things just like you did when your momma was out in these streets instead of at home with you." Lavon said.

"Lavon, you about to cross the line. Just do us both a favor and stay out of this. That's the best thing for everybody, okay? Stay out of this. Ann is doing some shady stuff you have no idea so stay out of it before you end up with your face cracked trying to protect her."

"I'm going to the car. Drama ain't my game." Lavon said walking off from Sandra and Solomon.

"I can't tell," Sandra said and headed off with Solomon in the opposite direction.

Patsy watched them walk away. She could tell they were arguing. She looked back at her sister. "Ann, you were wrong to snap at Sandra like that she just asked a simple question and since when you go to the doctor on your own about anything and when would you find the time?" Patsy asked.

"Patsy, I ain't your man. You don't question me. You question Dustin!" She said and stormed off. David laughed slowly.

"That ole Ann starting to act more and more like her momma every day. Wonder what or who done got a hold of her?" He said and took another sip of whatever was in the cup making his eyes get tighter and tighter.

Patsy didn't respond to him. Instead, she got up and went to find Sandra. She found her over by the baby pumpkins drawing on one for her son, Solomon, who was looking more and more like Lavon every day.

"Hey, Sandra. Everything okay with you and Lavon? It looked like the two of you were kinda goin at each other." Patsy asked.

"He just giving his opinion where it's not wanted that's all. He been acting different over the last few months. "I guess being a dad is a lot for him, but he will be all right cause he gone be one for the rest of his life with or without me." Ann said as she turned her pumpkin around and started drawing on it.

"I hope y'all work that out," Patsy said. "And by the way, what is this about Ann being at the doctor for migraine headaches?"

Sandra stopped drawing on the pumpkin and hesitated before she spoke. "Patsy, I gotta learn when to shut my mouth. I never should have said anything to her no matter who was around," Sandra said.

"What do you mean? Will you please just make it plain and tell me what's going on with Ann?" Patsy pleaded.

"The other day when I was late getting to school because I had to take Lil Solomon to the clinic, I saw Ann there again. At first, I thought I was mistaken so I went up to her and got a good look. It was her. I was surprised to see her cause the only girls that come to the clinic on that day are girls who are getting birth control or waited too late for birth control. You know what I mean?" Sandra asked her raising her eyebrow.

Patsy wasn't comprehending what Sandra was saying because this was her little sister she was talking about.

"Sandra, you sure it was Ann? Did you talk to her?" Patsy asked trying to interpret what she was hearing.

"Yeah, I talked to her. She looked surprised to see me and told me not to mention it to you. I just forgot. She said she'd been having bad migraine headaches and couldn't function good in class so she came to the clinic to see if the doctor could give her something.

"She said she would have told your momma but she never believes her when she tells her she not feeling good so she just decided to come with her friend and get checked out. She might have been there with her friend but that pink clear bag she had in her hand is for birth control. They supposed to keep you from getting pregnant so I guess they can stop migraines too."

"So what are you saying, Sandra? You think that birth control was for her?" Patsy asked in disbelief. "You know Ann is not having sex. How would she get to do something like that? Her and Ralph still playing games with each other. They haven't gone that far. They must have been her friend's. She just didn't want you to mention it to me or Nadeen so we wouldn't get the wrong idea," Patsy said.

Sandra looked down and started drawing back on the pumpkin. "You probably right, Patsy. I'm sure that's what it was. We both know Ann wouldn't get involved with Ralph like that. Not knowing how crazy your momma is if you don't mind me saying." Sandra said.

Patsy was still trying to process and rationalize in her head what Sandra had just told her so she didn't respond. Lavon came up to them and picked up Solomon.

"What's up, Patsy?" He asked as he looked over at Ann.

"Hopefully nothing. Sandra, I'll give you a call tonight." Patsy said and walked away. Her head was spinning. She went and sat down with her aunt for the rest of the night as she replayed in her mind what Sandra had just told her.

* * *

Wednesday night, a few nights after the church festival, Nadeen met with the Sisters of the Praying Circle and her usher board members. She told them about the great opportunity the pastor had given them to go out and do work for the Kingdom in the community. Everyone was excited. Nadeen set up a chart with everyone's assigned partner and everyone's assigned street location.

She chose Sister Haymer and Mrs. Wilson to go out with her. She told them they would meet at the church on that upcoming Saturday morning around 10:00 am and go out for about an hour each Saturday of that month.

"Sister Haymer, I know it's gonna be a big sacrifice for you to do this and your secretarial duties too, so if it's too much just let me know. Everybody can't multi-task like I do," Nadeen said sarcastically.

"Sister Nadeen if you can do it, I can too. You are my spiritual mentor and I want to help Pastor and First Lady in any way I can. I really appreciate them and you for giving me this opportunity at the church,"

"I try to do whatever I can to promote the ministry," Nadeen replied

"Well, you do a great job. One day I hope to be just like you." Sister Haymer said with a big grin on her face.

Nadeen smirked a little bit. "I hear you. I'll see you on this upcoming Saturday. I'm looking forward to it."

"I am too." Sister Haymer said as she packed up her notepad full of meeting notes.

Before the week was out, Sister Haymer would know the true meaning of "Hell hath no fury like a woman scorned."

That Saturday morning everyone met at the church and got into their groups.

Later on, when nosey church members would ask Mrs. Wilson what happened that day, she always told the same story. Nadeen drove Sister Haymer and Mrs. Wilson to their location. When they got out of the car, they saw young men and women walking up and down the street begging for money. Sister Haymer, according to Mrs. Wilson, seemed to tense up immediately and walked slower than the rest of them.

When they got to this one particular abandoned building with the smell of urine and excrement reeking from it, Sister Haymer froze, Mrs. Wilson said. Nadeen tried to comfort her by telling her not to be afraid to enter into the Lion's Den to bring souls to the Kingdom. She told her she wasn't going alone; she had them and Jesus with her.

Mrs. Wilson said she watched people going in and out of the building and wondered what was going on. When they stepped in they smelled this weird odor she couldn't explain. People were doing something with what seemed like baking soda and they were shooting needles in their arms. They tried to minister to them but they were so far out of it she didn't think they got through to them. She said they spent an entire hour in there.

Nadeen took great care to help Sister Haymer minister to the people. She took her to each one and stood by her while she tried to pray with them and talk to them about Jesus and his delivering power but Sister Haymer seemed to have trouble focusing. She was sweating and licking her lips.

"Sister Haymer, you sure you up to this? It's okay if you're not, sometimes we take on more than we can handle," Sister Nadeen said squeezing her shoulders.

Sister Haymer was looking like she was about to faint. "I got this, Sister Nadeen. I'm not going to disappoint you and Pastor. I got it." She said holding on to Nadeen's arm.

"Maybe you better let me finish up in here and you go on back outside. I'm more experienced at handling things like this. I shouldn't have started you at this level." Nadeen said. "You still a baby when it comes to Kingdom business."

"Maybe you right, Sister Nadeen. I better step out and get some air. I'll be right back." Sister Haymer said.

When they finally made it outside, Mrs. Wilson said Sister Haymer threw up on the sidewalk. Nadeen said it was just her nerves. Being that close to all that evilness in one place was too overwhelming for her but she told her she did good for her first time and she just had to finish the month out.

"Sister Haymer, what would that look like, the Pastor's new right hand in the church dropping out of the street ministry?" Sister Nadeen asked. "You are the church secretary, you are the voice of Greater Trials, this type of ministry is exactly where you're needed," Nadeen told her.

"I didn't realize this was going to be a part of the position, Sister Nadeen, but I got it. I'm the church secretary, I have to communicate with the congregation and the community." Sister Haymer said.

Mrs. Wilson said Nadeen dropped Sister Haymer off in the church parking lot so she could go and prepare for the programs for Sunday service and by the next Saturday, they were taking her back to rehab due to a drug overdose.

Somebody found her in the back of the same building she'd gone into with Nadeen to minister, with a needle stuck in her arm babbling something about "A righteous man falleth seven times and raiseth back up again." Sister Haymer would fall more than seven times after this before she got back up again.

In the meantime, Sister Nadeen told everyone that she felt it was only right to take on the responsibility of being church secretary again since it was her idea for them to go to the crack house in the first place. If she had known Sister Haymer wasn't prayed up enough to go back into the very crack house she came out of, she never would have taken her there. When the story got back to Patsy, she stood in complete awe of her mother's skill to stick the knife in and hide her hand.

*　*　*

A month later, Nadeen found herself having to go back into battle with her ex-church member, Jordan Jackson. She was going back into the enemy's camp and take back what belonged to her: her dignity and her full-time supervisor position she'd worked so hard to try and get.

That was the beginning of the whole mess. Jordan Jackson had come into her territory and tried to be in charge and no man was going to run her she had to teach him. He was mad with her for getting him shamed out of his financial officer position at Greater Trials. She'd done what she had to do to protect the integrity of her church's finances.

When the collection was taken up for Pastor's anniversary, Nadeen made sure he had the collection plate that held the pastor's anniversary donations. She also sat with him and the other committee members when they counted it in the back. When they got ready to put the money in the safe, Nadeen handed Jordan Jackson the key and they all watched him lock it up.

What they didn't see was Nadeen's extra key on her key chain. While the financial board members were busy counting Sunday School offerings next door, Nadeen slipped back into the office and removed the money. She placed it in the pocket of Jordan Jackson's coat pocket which he'd left laid across a chair, with the keys to the safe that he still had.

When the financial officers sent Jordan Jackson back to get the anniversary donation to present to Pastor Craig it was gone. What happened next sealed Jordan Jackson's fate at Greater Trials MB Church. Pastor Craig called an emergency meeting.

"Anybody know what happened to the money?" He asked. Everyone shook their heads no. He looked at Nadeen.

"Sister Nadeen, you have anything to offer?"

"Well, Pastor, I'm not one to point fingers or stir up mess, but the last person to handle the funds was Brother Jordan so you'd have to ask him." She looked over at him.

"Brother Jordan where is the money?" Reverend Craig asked.

"Pastor, the money was in your safe. That's where I left it." Jordan said.

"Well son, I believe in miracles but I don't think that money grew legs, unlocked that safe, and walked out." Reverend Craig said.

"Well, I didn't sprout legs and walk out with it either." Brother Jordan said. "I don't appreciate the accusations. I'm leaving." He got up from his chair. He grabbed his suit coat and as he did the keys to the safe and the money hit the floor.

Everyone in the room gasped.

"Brother Jordan! Tell me it isn't true. Pastor trusted you. I trusted you." Nadeen said.

"I didn't put this here. I don't know how it got here!" Brother Jordan declared. Reverend Craig stood up from his desk.

"Brother Jordan, because I know you have a family, I won't press charges if you just leave the money, leave the church and never come back. We will put this all behind us."

"But I didn't do this." Brother Jordan pleaded looking around the room.

Reverend Craig pointed to security. "Escort him out please and if he is ever seen on this property again have him arrested."

The security guards dragged Brother Jordan out screaming and kicking that he didn't do it.

"Sister Nadeen, you are to be the only person with keys to the safe from now on and no one is to touch the safe but you. Is that clear?" Pastor Craig asked handing over the keys to Nadeen

"Crystal, Pastor," Nadeen said with a smile on her face and the keys firmly in her hands.

What Nadeen didn't realize was that she'd also have to fight Brother Jordan in the workplace. Coming into her church wasn't enough. He ended up getting a job at Garden of Peace Nursing home as an HR Assistant. Rumor had it that he was rolling around in the sheets with the HR Director. She was an older woman, recently widowed, and she loved the attention. Nadeen was livid. She recalled the day she got the call, the day her mind began turning on how she would break Jordan Jackson for good.

She had gotten in the tub and turned on the Jacuzzi. The feel of the jet sprays and the smell of almond butter flakes relaxed her. She must have dozed off because the next thing she knew the phone was ringing. She always kept it with her, even in the bathroom just in case Pastor Craig called and needed something. She saw that it was someone from Garden of Peace nursing home. She answered the phone.

"Hello?" The voice on the other end sounded familiar.

It was The HR Director. Nadeen wondered why she was calling. "Hi, Ms. Boudreaux How are you? I was just getting ready to come in. Everything okay?" Nadeen asked. The voice sounded like she had difficulty getting her words out.

"Hi, Nadeen. Yes, everything is fine. Since I consider you to be a friend of mine here at Garden of Peace, I wanted to personally call you and let you know I have decided to retire as HR Director. Since my husband passed, I just don't have the same joy in working like I did before." She told Nadeen.

"But no worries, I have found the perfect candidate to replace me. I think you and he went to the same church at one time, his name is Jordan Jackson, and he will be coming on as the new HR Director and will be making the final decision on the new Day Shift Supervisor. I know you were very interested in the position so I wanted to be decent and out of respect for the number of years you and I have known each other and let you hear the news from me first instead of the gossip mill. I know how you hate work mess." She said.

Nadeen started to feel her mouth go dry. She was starting to not hear clearly. She almost dropped the phone to the floor. She had to get herself together. She wouldn't let the enemy cause her to grovel like a desperate and scared woman.

"Well, I appreciate your thoughtfulness. I will miss you. Hate to see you leave before the final decision is made," Nadeen said.

"I will miss you too, Nadeen. You know how everything works

around here I see no problem in you getting the position. I've already talked to Jordan, I mean Mr. Jackson, about your interest and your qualifications."

"Thank you. Well, I better get moving if I want to make it in on time. You take care of yourself, Ms. Boudreaux, and thanks again for calling me."

Nadeen knew Jordan Jackson was going to try and get even with her now for what she did to him at Greater Trials. One thing she wasn't gonna do was kiss his flat, black behind to get that supervisor position.

Nadeen laid down on the bed with the towel half wrapped around her and let the feel of the cool ceiling fan take her away to a place where she could digest all the things just said to her and develop a plan to become the new Day Shift Supervisor. Just as the wheels of her mind started turning real good, her co-worker, Landon called. Landon was an acquired taste for her that she was still not quite comfortable with but he was interesting and up for drama any time, and that was just what she needed now.

"Hey, Landon. To what do I owe this pleasure darling?" Nadeen asked him.

"Hey, Love. I was just calling to check in on you. I heard that Jordan Jackson's undercover lover gave him the HR position and he's gonna be selecting the new Day Shift Supervisor. I know how hard you been working for that," Landon said popping his lips after almost every sentence.

"And do you also know I'm not about to let him pass over me for that position?" Nadeen asked in a matter-of-fact tone of voice.

"Honey, if it were me, I wouldn't either. You need to raise all kinds of hell about that if they do give it to somebody else."

"That's not going to happen if I can help it," Nadeen said.

"Well Sis, I know you a praying woman and all but after what went down with you and him up in that church you might need to send for the Angel Gabriel to talk to him on your behalf," Landon said chuckling afterward.

"No need. I got my wheels turning about a plan. You have to deal with people like that from a bottom-of-the-barrel mentality and I can go there if need be. I just need a little motivation to come up with one."

"I got all the motivation you need, sugah. You know I don't like him anyway. He wants to turn his nose down at me in front of everybody at work but when they not around he watching this Tootsie Roll bounce and he know it. Old closet freak. What we gone do to get him up outta there?" Landon asked eagerly.

It took them three days to come up with the perfect plan. Nadeen believed there was no way it could fail.

The day she and Landon put their plan in motion, Nadeen was moving all over the place at work full of energy and anticipation. She'd volunteered for overtime so that they could pull it off without a full staff present to notice either her or Landon not on their usual floors.

Nadeen had requested a meeting with Jordan after her shift ended. He was more than happy to accommodate her request. She'd slipped into his office ten minutes before her late-night shift ended, standing in the shadows of his office in a sheer, cinnamon red, one-piece nightie with a matching garter belt, black fishnets, and her hair hanging down around her shoulders. When he stepped into his office and closed the door, she stepped out of the shadows and whispered his name, "Jordan." Jordan Jackson turned around and nearly lost his breath.

She was enticing. He started towards her to grab her but she told him to take it slow. She told him she had one more surprise for him but he needed to turn back around, slowly undress and close his eyes. He eagerly agreed.

She stepped back into the shadows and Landon stepped up behind him, wearing a long lace front wig and no shirt on as Nadeen prepared her cellphone video camera to start rolling.

"Turn around slowly, Jordan. Don't open your eyes just yet."

Nadeen said from the shadows. Jordan was grinning and full of expectation. He eagerly did what she asked.

"I knew you wanted this. You tried to cover it up cause you got a image at the church to uphold, I understand." Jordan Jackson said.

"Well, you know a real lady has to maintain her image at all times," Nadeen said from the shadows.

"I get it but you about to have to make it up to me on this nice wooden desk cause it cost me a few weeks on the couch at home for that little stunt," Jordan said with his eyes closed and a huge grin on his face.

"Oooh, baby I'm about to make it unforgettable," Nadeen said. "Come get this. You know you can have it."

"That's what I been waiting to hear," he said.

As he turned towards her voice Landon steadied himself, Nadeen pushed the video button on her phone and Landon ran up, grabbed Jordan Jackson by the lips, begin kissing him passionately. Jordan was returning the kiss just as passionately and the camera captured it all.

"That was a good kiss, lover," Landon said rubbing his hand down Jordan Jackson's chest. "You ready to put me on that big desk of yours?"

Jordan heard the bass in the voice and opened his eyes. He was shocked when he saw Landon standing in front of him butt naked. "What the whole hell is this? What are you doing Landon?" He staggered backward, looking around the room.

"Baby, I thought you wanted to video it this time? You said the next time you wanted to do something risky. This is it!" Landon said, jumping up and down while clapping his hands together.

Before Jordan Jackson could respond, Landon stepped back into the shadows and Nadeen stepped out.

"This is your final lesson in playing games with me," Nadeen told him. "Landon has just secured my new promotion as the Day

Shift Supervisor before you go and oh, yes, you will go. This video I just shot on my phone will make sure of that."

Jordan Jackson fell to his knees and looked up to her. "How could you do this? How could you be so full of evil, such a bitch from Hell that you would try to destroy me like this? I thought you were better than this!" Jordan Jackson said looking desperately into Nadeen's eyes for some speck of compassion. He found none.

Nadeen just stepped up to him and threw his clothes in his face.

"We won't miss you when you're gone." She told him as she turned to go sit on the couch in his office. Jordan started putting on his pants and shirt.

"Nadeen, you wouldn't. You wouldn't do such an ungodly thing to me." He cried out.

"You wouldn't post such a lie. You tricked me. This was a trap!" He shouted at her. Nadeen turned around and smirked at him, put her hands on her hips, and looked him in the eye as she spoke slowly.

"Your lust for me and apparently young boys was the trap. Now, type up that recommendation for Day Shift Supervisor if you want this video to go away."

It was a magnificent moment. Nadeen knew she was good at handling those who trespassed against her but she realized she had gone into an entirely different realm of necessary vengeance with what she and Landon had just done to Jordan Jackson.

She and Landon congratulated each other on a well-executed plan on their way out of the office that night. "Landon. You are the best. Not only can you slay a mean sew-in, but you can also act. You got him, baby! He was petrified! All I can remember is him turning around in his draws as you grabbed his face and stuck your tongue down his throat. I had that video camera rolling! He never knew what hit him. That's what he gets for lusting after things he's not supposed to have like me, my job, and my church position.

"When that video hits social media tomorrow he won't have anything."

Landon looked at her with a smirk on his face. "You really want to post it to social media?"

"Yes! I want the entire world to know what he did. I don't get on that mess but I hear the folks at church talking about all of the ratchedness that goes on. It sounds like the perfect place for it." Nadeen said seriously. "Can you handle posting the video?"

"Of course. I love some hot tea, honey! Especially when it's me serving it. I'll post it later on tonight in return for one small favor." Landon said with a grin on his face. "You hook me up with a new schedule when you get the position."

"Consider it done," Nadeen said shaking hands with Landon.

"Well send it right over to my phone and I will make it do what it do, baby." Landon said winking at Nadeen.

Nadeen looked down at her phone and sent the video. "Delivered." She smirked and said. "Be sure to cover your tracks."

"Of course, fake social media account, untraceable IP address and all. I was born for this type of drama. One day I'm gonna get my degree and work for the FBI. Believe that!" Landon said letting out a hearty laugh.

"He thought he was going to make me beg by holding that position over my head, now it's his turn to reap what he sowed. It's biblical. Biblical principles being applied to his life. I promised him I wouldn't post the video but I didn't say anything about you not posting it!" she cackled as she went to her car.

When he got to work the next morning, everyone was whispering and laughing behind Jordan Jackson's back. He was called to the Executive Manager's Office before he had time to turn his computer on.

"They asked him to leave the premises immediately due to the sensitivity of a certain video going viral on social media involving him and an individual they had not yet been able to identify, putting him and the nursing home in an unfavorable light.

Landon called Nadeen right after it happened and gave her all the details. She was overjoyed to hear about the final disgrace of Jordan Jackson.

"Landon spill it, honey. Tell me everything that happened up there this morning." She giggled.

"It's hot today, Sis, let me tell you! Well, he got called to the Executive Manager's office so you already know that wasn't gonna be good. When he came out, they had his white box already packed and waiting for him at the front desk. I just happened to be standing there when he came out you know."

"What did he say to you?" Nadeen asked laughing the whole time.

He was too shocked and ashamed to say much of anything, so I just asked him, "Well JJ whatever is the problem? You look like a cat sucked your tongue this morning. He reached out to grab me, honey, but that big security guard got to him first. He almost slung him to the floor. He was crying and slobbing, 'She told me she wasn't going to post it! She gave me her word! I thought she was a Woman of God'."

"Did he really now?" Nadeen asked. "See therein lays the problem: folks mistake saved folks for doormats bet he found out today. So what else happened?"

"He was looking pitiful at me, and asked me how could you let her do something like this to me? She has destroyed me. You and her both! She is a witch! I just told him you know I'm the last person to speak on what somebody is or isn't. I just walked over to the front door and held it open for the security guard as he pushed him and his box out the door. He landed on the ground." Landon said.

Nadeen laughed out loud. "That's better than landing his behind in jail where he really needs to be."

"Right, right, next I threw him a kiss and said, sorry to see you go lover as I put on some extra cherry lip balm honey. My mouth was dry from watching all that action unfold." Landon said as he smacked his lips together. "It was indeed my pleasure to see him outside them doors looking perplexed."

"Guess he knows not to try me now. You would think he'd learned his lesson from our little run-in at church, but I guess his greed for me and money blinded him. Well, that's him and his wife's problem now, not mine. Thanks for the update darling. I should be getting my notification about the supervisor position any day now."

"Just remember your boy when you start." Landon chimed in.

"How could I forget you? You helped me get what is rightfully mine. I will reward you indeed." Nadeen said as she wrapped up her conversation with Landon.

* * *

The next day after the incident Nadeen was in one of the best moods she'd experienced in a very long time. It didn't take long for her phone to start ringing off of the hook with calls from coworkers about what happened. *Touch not my anointed. Do my prophet no harm,* was the scripture that ran through her mind.

She had her pink satin robe on and her hair was hanging loosely down her back. Eva called her after viewing the video. "Nadeen. By the looks of this video blowing up on social media, it looks like somebody did you a favor and got rid of Jordan Jackson for you didn't they?"

"Eva, honey won't he do it? Yes, he will. It was hilarious! You could have bought Jordan Jackson for a penny! My co-worker, Landon, and I got him real good chile!"

"You and Landon set this man up?" Eva asked in surprise. "You and your co-worker are going to be without jobs when the Nursing home finds out what y'all did to that poor man. I ain't feeling sorry for him cause God knows he deserves it but what about his poor wife?" Eva said pretending to be empathetic

"He should have been worried about his wife before he tried to take food off my table. He stood there looking like a sick mule. I showed him the video and he started begging and pleading for me not to post it. He told me to ask for what I wanted and he'd give it to me.

"Well, that was all I needed to hear I told him I wanted a promotion recommendation sent to corporate that night to give me the Day Shift Supervisor position. I watched him type it up and email it to them. He was dripping sweat the entire time he was typing it." Nadeen said with a big hearty laugh.

Eva congratulated her on the execution of her plan then she yanked her chain, "Sister that sounds like vindication to me."

Nadeen responded, "It's not vindication, it's victory. I have the victory because no weapon formed against me shall prosper, especially if it's a man weak in his flesh. It made Adam weak in the garden and it's still doing the same thing today. Girl, let me go. I got to go read my daily meditation."

* * *

A few months later, Ann and Patsy were talking about all the events coming up at school on the way home. Ann was hoping she could go to the school dance for Homecoming.

"Patsy, do you realize our whole life has been home and school?" She said. "I mean, think about it. Other than an occasional sleepover at Grandma Ruth's or Aunt Eva's...and a few trips to the ER when Nadeen flips out."

Patsy laughed at that even though she knew Ann was right.

"You speaking the truth Ann. We been homebodies all our lives." Patsy said.

"I really want to go to this dance. I don't need to go with a boy I just want to go and hang out with my friends from the basketball team. They all hype about getting a chance to wear formals," Ann said.

"Well, Nadeen has been a little bit better these last few months since she shamed Jordan Jackson out of town and put Sister Haymer in drug rehab. I guess if you fast and pray, and don't piss her off she just might agree to let you go," Patsy said.

"I guess I won't be going then 'cause your momma snaps if I breathe. She irritates me so bad with her crazy ways. I'm so tired of her being a B—"

Patsy stopped Ann before she got the rest of the word out. "Ann! However crazy your momma may be you are out of line to call her out of her name like that. God is not pleased with that and you can shorten your own life speaking like that about her. I know it's hard living with her and even harder to understand her but we got to pray for her deliverance. That's all we can do—pray and wait for God to move." Patsy said.

"So how God feel about her calling me, you, and Kenny out of our names? Huh, Patsy? How you think God feels about that? She crying in church on Sunday and cussin' like a gangsta rapper Monday thru Saturday. Girl, it's something wrong with your momma." Ann said.

Patsy laughed. "Oh, she just *my* momma now huh?"

"Yep. You can have her all to yourself." Ann said.

When they made it home Grandma Ruth was there. She was sipping something out of a coffee cup that smelled like whiskey and maple syrup. "Hey, babies. Come give your favorite Grandma a hug. I missed you girls." She said extending one arm out while holding Josie with the other.

Ann leaned in and kissed her on the jaw. Josie pushed her back and grabbed for her grandmother's cup to put it up to her mouth.

"Josie must like that a lot," Ann said as she stepped back and gave Patsy room to step up. Patsy hugged her grandmother.

"Grandma, momma ain't gonna like you giving Josie whatever's in that cup," Patsy said.

"She don't like a lot of things but none of them keep me up at night. Anyway, this just a little coffee to help keep the worms away. I gave it to the both of y'all and you turned out just fine," Grandma Ruth said.

"You girls need to start packing up your bags. You got to stay with me for a few days. Your momma gotta supervise double shifts at the nursing home. She wanted this position now she got it and all that come with it."

Ann and Patsy looked at each other at the same time. God had worked out a way for Ann to go to that dance and Nadeen didn't even have to know.

"Now ain't God good?" Patsy whispered to her sister.

"You need to get them bags together. Nadeen already left and she said she didn't want y'all here for a minute unsupervised." She breathed warm, sweet, whiskey in their faces. They knew Nadeen didn't like alcohol in the house but they also knew she wasn't gonna tell their Grandma what to do even in "her house," as she liked to call it when she was cussing Kenny out.

When they got in the car, Ann told her grandmother about the Homecoming dance.

"Grandma, they got a Homecoming Dance at my school this Friday night. This my last year at that school. I'd like to go and hang out with my friends." Ann said.

"I think you should go. You too young to be stuck up in the house all the time. If your momma doesn't loosen the ropes now when you cut them loose you'll be like a wild horse with that thang of yours," Grandma Ruth said.

"Grandma!" Patsy said.

"Patsy!" Grandma Ruth responded back. "The same goes for you. Y'all stay so locked up it'll be easy for a man to trick you out of your business then the next thing you know you got a broken leg that takes nine months to heal."

"I just want to go to a school dance that's all," Ann said.

"And I'm gonna let you go. How about that?" Grandma Ruth asked.

Ann jumped up and down with excitement. "Yes! I promise not to get into any trouble. Thank you, Grandma." Ann said.

"You welcome baby. You make good grades in school and you

take more punishment than a child should living in that house so why not let you enjoy yourself sometimes?" Grandma Ruth said.

"What you gonna tell Momma?" Patsy asked.

"Probably to mind her business and stay out of mine." Grandma Ruth said. "I do what I want to do in my house with my grandbabies."

Nadeen called later that evening. "Momma, don't let them be all up and down the street over there." She told her. "You get some granddaughters and you get all brand new when it comes to the way things are supposed to be done with girls."

"Sweetie, you the one acting brand new shooting off at the mouth with me. I'm the same ole momma you once knew don't forget that. You trying to keep them locked up is the problem." She told her daughter.

"Ann got a dance coming up and I'm going to let her go. Things have changed since you was coming up, Nadeen. Let this girl go with her big sister and have a good time." Grandma Ruth said.

"And if that good time goes bad whose gonna be stuck dealing with that, Momma?" Nadeen asked.

"The same person who caused it to be created. You. Now goodbye." Grandma Ruth said to Nadeen and hung up the phone,

"Your momma gave me a list of do's and don't's for you girls but she forgot that you in my house and we do things the way I say," she told the girls.

Dustin came over later. He and Patsy sat on the porch and talked. "So how long you think it's going to be before you hear back from Dove University? What dorm are you thinking about choosing once you get your acceptance letter?" Patsy asked. "I want to stay in the dorm with the kitchen in the suite and a bus that can take you to class." Dustin didn't say anything for a minute then he took a deep breath and released.

"Patsy. I hadn't sent mine in yet. I put it in my new car and forgot about it. It slipped under my car seat and I just recently found it."

Patsy was stunned. "What do you mean you didn't mail it yet? I asked you about it a few weeks ago you said you mailed it." She said looking at him in disbelief. "You lied to me?"

"No. I did fill it out and I meant to mail it, but I just forgot," Dustin said. "Anyway, I'm still trying to decide if that's what I want to do. Some days I'm sure and other days I'm just tired of school and ready to get it over with. I need a mental break. You know I still have trouble dealing with my mom being dead. Just knowing she won't see me graduate tears me up inside."

Patsy wanted to finish this fight but when he said that and those beautiful green eyes filled up with water she couldn't, she just pulled him to her chest and held him as he cried. She kissed his face.

"Baby, I understand. I really do. I don't mean to pressure you. I'm sorry. I know you'll take care of it," she told him.

"We would still be together even if you went to college and I didn't. You don't really have to go anyway. I got enough money for us to get married soon as we graduate, and build us a house," Dustin said.

"I want my college degree, Dustin. I would be the first one to get a college degree in our immediate family. I mean my mom and dad got pretty good jobs without them, but things are different now than when they were growing up and I want to be able to teach on a college level one day." Patsy said squeezing her fingers in between his.

"You can still do all those things without leaving and I'll be right by your side," Dustin said.

"I love you with all of my heart, Dustin, but I have to go. If I don't, you won't have a good life with me. I'd be full of bitterness and regret. We might become my parents and I don't want that." Patsy said.

"We could never be like them," Dustin said.

"You promised me we would start a new life together," Patsy said.

"I told you I haven't completely made up my mind yet but whether I go away to Dove University with you or not, my love for you will not ever change. We got dreams to make come true, remember?" He asked her.

"Yes. I remember the question is do you?" Patsy asked. "I don't want to be making plans by myself."

Dustin reached over and kissed her. "I'm right with you."

Patsy was melting fast from his kiss. He started sucking on the side of her neck and pulled her closer. She could feel him pressing against her. One thing she had never told him was that the feel of him was intimidating. No wonder the girls were so crazy about him.

His breathing got heavier and his movements against her got rougher as he pressed against her. He moved her hand towards his zipper. "Just touch it, baby. Just touch it again that's all. We won't do anything else. I love you. I promise I do." Dustin whispered in her ear.

He led Patsy's hand down to his zipper and placed her hand on him as he undid his belt. He was hard as a brick. "Dustin. No. My grandmother might catch us. I can't." Patsy said snatching back her hand in between her own heavy breathing. She tried pushing him away though she wanted him closer. The sound of her Grandma's voice broke the spell.

"Patsy it's time for you and your young man to come on in this house! It's getting dark. The night air ain't good for you. It's something poisonous about being out in it too late!" She yelled.

Dustin laid back and kept his eyes closed. "I want you so bad. Don't let it scare you. I promise to respect you and I promise to take it nice and slow. We almost married anyway. Let's just go on and put it in motion." Dustin put his belt back in the loop and tried to adjust himself. It was hard for Patsy not to stare as he did.

"I can't yet, Dustin. I'm not ready. Guess we better go back in before she comes out here and screams seeing that." Patsy said pointing at the hump in the front of his pants. They both laughed.

"Yeah, cause I don't need your grandma wanting to get with me and you don't."

Patsy hit him on the shoulder and they both laughed. She gave him a few more minutes to get back to normal and then they got up from the front porch and walked in.

"Grandma where Ann?" Patsy asked.

"She back there laying down. She said she was tired and wanted to go to bed early. She near about talked my ear off about that dance she going to. I told her she better act civilized. I'd hate to have to handle her momma cause she didn't know how to act at that dance. She better be a young lady. You make sure of that Patsy, you hear me?" Grandma Ruth asked her. "Yes, Grandma. I hear you." She answered.

"Well, I probably better be heading home. It's getting late. Thanks for everything." Dustin said lifting his hand up at Grandma Ruth.

"You come back anytime you want son, as long as I'm here." Grandma Ruth said.

Dustin laughed slightly. "Thank you, ma'am."

Patsy rolled her eyes and walked him to the front door.

"Don't forget about our plans, Dustin," Patsy said as she looked him directly in his eyes to let him know she was serious.

Dustin kissed her at the door. "I won't, babe. I won't forget anything about us." Then he turned around and walked down the sidewalk in front of the house where he'd parked. Patsy wondered how much longer his love for her would be enough to keep him from getting the relief he needed, from someone else. And then there was the fact that he really did kind of lie to her. She decided to try and step over that given the reason. She knew he was still dealing with a new life without his mother.

The next night was Ann's Homecoming Dance. Aunt Eva came over and brought her everything she thought she might need, A beautiful teal-colored sleeveless dress with a sheer diamond overlay, sugar-frosted lipstick, eyeshadow, makeup, and matching teardrop-shaped earrings. Ann's eyes sparkled as she looked at the gifts laid out on the bed.

"Aunt Eva everything is so pretty." She said as she touched the dress. Her Aunt smiled.

"Nothing but the best for my niece."

"I wish Ralph had a driver's license so he could come over and pick you up. That would be the real treat of the night. He's gonna be there, right?" Aunt Eva asked.

"He wasn't sure when we talked last night. His parents are out on a date so he might come if it's not too late when they get back."

"Well, you are going to be looking too good not to walk up in there with somebody on your arm." Aunt Eva said slightly pinching her niece on her jaw. "Take your Uncle David. I'll clean him up real good for you."

"Uncle David too old to go with me," Ann said. "What about Patsy going with me?"

"Girl I know you love your big sister but she is not going to walk through those doors on your arm. Where they do that at?" Eva asked putting her hands on her hip and tilting her head at her niece.

"Ann, I promise to look like a million dollars and be so cool nobody will notice," David said walking towards her with a little swag just before he spun around one time. "I'm a Pimp, you better ask your aunt."

Eva giggled and lightly pushed him in the chest," You more like a blimp."

Ann laughed. "That's a good one, Aunt Eva. Well, David, I guess you can escort me in, as long as you don't try to dance with me. Hopefully Ralph will be there for that."

"Girl, you don't know what you missing. Me and your Aunt always turn the club out but if that's how you want it, so be it." David said.

Eva pointed at the door, "David get out of here so I can get her ready. Momma, you probably need to call Nadeen and remind her about this dance."

Grandma Ruth called Nadeen "Just wanted to remind you about Ann's dance tonight. I told her she could stay until it's over."

"You shouldn't make decisions about my daughter without my approval," Nadeen replied in a firm tone.

"Remember that the next time a caseworker wants to take your daughter." Grandma Ruth responded back.

Nadeen got quiet for a moment. "I have to go. I'm working," she said, lowering her voice before hanging up. Nadeen knew she couldn't stand up to her mother, she didn't have the skill set.

Ann went to her Homecoming Dance escorted by David and trailed by Patsy. Patsy sat in the back of the gym all night eating cake and peanuts while she watched the disco lights bounce off of a million silver stars on the ceiling. She managed to get one glance of Ann on the dance floor. It was nice to see her little sister having fun. She was so beautiful.

Patsy must have fallen asleep because the next thing she knew, Ralph was tapping her on her shoulder. "Wake up old lady. You let Cinderella get away." He said.

Patsy was still a little out of it so she didn't get his meaning. "What Ralph?" She said groggily.

"You let my princess get away. Where is she?" He asked her. Had she been asleep that long? Patsy looked around. It was dark on the dance floor except for the DJ's red light flashing.

"She was on the dance floor with you what happened?" Patsy asked in a panic.

"I just went to the bathroom. It was a long line, maybe she got bored and went outside." Ralph said looking around.

Patsy stared out onto the dark dance floor looking for Ann. "I'll find her. She has a habit of disappearing lately." Patsy said as she headed outside. Ralph followed out the door behind her.

She saw David in the distance sitting in the car smoking a black and mild cigar. As she headed across the parking lot to him, Lavon pulled up in front of her with his car window rolled down. Patsy jumped back startled as he started talking to her.

"What's up, Patsy? You a little too old for this crowd, aren't you?" He grinned at her and asked as he leaned back in his car seat.

"Lavon what are you doin' here? You too old to be riding through yourself. You got plenty to keep you busy already." Patsy said as she looked around the parking lot for her sister.

"Hey, I got to have my space sometimes too. I was just cruising through chill out."

"Lavon I ain't got time for this Q &A session I'm trying to find Ann and go home."

Lavon turned to his right and pointed. "Oh, I just passed her back there. She was on her way up here."

"Well, let me get on back to my responsibilities. See you around Patsy…and you ain't got to tell your girl every time you see me out without her. We straight. No worries." Lavon said as he started driving off.

Patsy started walking briskly back toward David's car. When she made it to him, she reached through his rolled down window and shook his arm.

"Hey. You let Ann out of your sight? You were supposed to be her chaperone too where is she?" Patsy asked, about to go in panic mode thinking about what Nadeen would do if Ann was kidnapped or something. She always said that was another reason she didn't like them out at night: too many perverts.

"Relax, Patsy. She's fine. She was out here with her friends from school earlier. I think she told me she was going to the bathroom and to wake you up," she said.

"You were cutting quite a few logs over in that corner." He laughed.

Patsy felt someone tap her on her back. She turned around to see Ann standing there looking a little disheveled. Her face was flushed and her hair looked a little out of place. It looked like she'd knocked off all the pretty little diamond sequin off of the top of her dress.

"Hey, Patsy." She smiled. "I was just looking for you. I was gonna wake you up so we could leave."

"Where'd you go, girl? I was looking for you." Ralph said.

"First of all, you are not my daddy, Ralph. Secondly, I told you before you walked off that I had to go talk to my friends and I'd be back. You the one that was out of place so don't start asking me questions." Ann said to him.

"Oh, now you want to act different on me? You call me when you get yourself together." Ralph said and walked off.

David smirked. "Ann, you remind me of somebody I know."

Patsy ignored him and tore into her little sister.

"Ann! Did you lose your mind out there under them fake stars in the gym?" Patsy yelled. "What you did was not cool! You scared me to death. I thought you had been kidnapped or something! David out here chilling like he don't even care. Aunt Eva said he was triflin'!" Patsy yelled.

David raised up from his car seat as he put out his cigar.

"Hold up, little girl! This a grown man you talking to! You need to get back in your place and you need to get there quick before I put you in it! I ain't your daddy! A woman can't talk to me like she wear the pants. I wear these! Now get in this car so I can take you home before I take off my belt and teach you a lesson!"

Ann went around to the passenger side of the car and got in the front seat. She slammed the door. "Patsy get in the car! Why you got to go and spoil my night? I had such a good time, now here you go actin' like your momma! I swear when I leave this crazy family I ain't never coming back!"

Patsy was so mad she wanted to shake Ann's teeth out of her mouth and spit rusty nails into David's body. *Who did he think he was talking to?* She wished he would put his hands on her. She would tear into him so fast he would think a jaguar attacked him.

David stepped out of the car and approached her.

"Patsy, look. I know you was worried about your Sister but you see she's just fine. Nobody kidnapped her. She in one piece. She's goin' back home the same way she left. Now get your crazy behind in this car before I have to call your Aunt and tell her how you showin' out. Come on now. I ain't got all night. I got to get up early in the morning."

Patsy got in the car but she didn't want to. She didn't talk the entire trip home. David and Ann laughed and talked the whole ride.

"Ann that little boy is really crazy about you," David said. "I barely got two dances in with you. What you really been doin' that's got that boy so in love?" He said patting Ann on her leg.

David made Patsy feel creepy. She hadn't forgotten what he tried to do to her during the sleepover at Aunt Eva's last year.

Grandma Ruth was still up when they got home. David pulled into the driveway and let them out. "Guess I better walk you two in. I'd never hear the end of it from Momma Ruth if I didn't." He said, putting out his cigarette with his shoe.

When they came in, Grandma Ruth was peeling pears for a pear preserve she was going to make tomorrow.

"Well, Cinderella how did the dance go?" She asked as Ann and David came in behind Patsy.

"Ann had a real good time," Patsy said. "She just disappeared into the crowd."

"It was the best time I ever had," Ann said spinning around in her dress.

"It probably was. It's the first time your momma let you go any further than the mailbox." Grandma Ruth said.

"Y'all kill me with that," David laughed and said. "I'm out. Talk to you tomorrow."

"Let me go take this dress off. Thanks for everything, Grandma. I'll never forget it." Ann said leaning over and kissing her grandmother on her jaw. Grandma Ruth smiled.

"It was my pleasure. You deserve some joy sometimes, not always pain."

Patsy felt the tears coming to her eyes. Her grandmother was right. Patsy had plenty more to say about Ann's night but when her grandmother said that her throat closed up and something punched her in her stomach. It was the truth and it was a hard blow. Patsy decided to drop it.

"I'm sleepy. My job is done so I'm going to bed too, Grandma." Patsy said leaning over and hugging her grandmother's neck.

"You a big sister, Patsy. Your job is never done while on this earth." Grandma Ruth said patting Patsy on her back.

"You probably right," Patsy said and headed down the hall towards the bedroom. She decided she'd mention to Sandra that she'd seen Lavon.

8

ANN DIDN'T SPEAK to Patsy at all the next morning. She cleaned up and went to sit out in the sunroom. Josie followed her and sat in her lap. Ann stroked her hair while she pretended to be asleep. Grandma Ruth said she had to run an errand and would be back in about an hour.

"Girls you know that nobody gets in this house if they don't have a bed in this house, right?" She said on her way out.

"Yes, ma'am!" Ann and Patsy both yelled behind her. When she left Patsy tried to ease the tension between her and Ann.

"Ann, you want a sandwich or something?" She asked her.

"All I want is for you to leave me alone," Ann said as she leaned her head back on the couch and closed her eyes.

"Since you obviously must be on drugs talking like that to me, I'm gone let you make it this morning. You still mad about last night but you might as well get glad cause I had a right to be upset with you. I'm the one that would have to take those blows from your momma if something happened to you think about that with your selfish acting ways. Now put that in your crack pipe and smoke on it." Patsy said and stormed out of the room.

Dustin called not long after her fight with Ann. Patsy told

him about the fight between her and Ann earlier that morning. He seemed really surprised.

"Maybe Ralph is doing something to make her like that," Patsy said.

"Sandra did say she saw her at the clinic a few times."

"Sounds like you need to get Sandra in on this. Doesn't she have a cousin that goes to that same school? He can probably find out." He said.

"That's what I plan to do. Maybe she can also find out who this girl is that Ann says she went to the clinic with a few times. I haven't heard Ann mention having any really close friend that she would risk the wrath of Nadeen for." Patsy said. "And by the way, Lavon was at the dance too."

"At the dance?" Dustin asked sounding surprised. "You gotta have that wrong, Patsy."

"I mostly certainly do not. I talked to him. He said he was just riding through. Why he riding through a junior high dance is weird to me. Sandra said he has been acting a little different."

"You gonna tell her you saw him?"

"You already know the answer to that. She's my best friend. Of course I'm tellin' it."

"He was just driving through, Patsy. Don't get your girl to having crazy thoughts now."

"I don't know what he was really doing but I know he wasn't home with his baby Momma where he needed to be and I'm telling her," Patsy said in a matter-of-fact tone of voice.

"Chill girl, I was just trying to keep you from making it a big deal. Sounds like I need to let you go recover from last night. Let's try this again in a few hours." Dustin said softly.

"I'm sorry, baby. I didn't mean to come across like that. Forgive me?" Patsy asked sweetly. She missed him, the last thing she wanted was to fight with him.

"We good. Look I'm heading out to my mom's gravesite. I'll

call you later." Before Patsy could answer he hung up. He was still having a hard time with his mother being gone; she could hear it in his voice.

When Patsy finished talking to Dustin, she decided to call Sandra. Lavon answered the phone like he lived there.

"Hey, Patsy. What's up? You still kickin' it on your momma free weekend? Sandra told me she was working that double shift this weekend. I know you and Dustin are loving that." He said laughing in the phone. "She keep doing that shift you and Dustin gonna mess around and seal the deal."

Patsy wasn't really up to small talk so she went straight to her reason for calling.

"Hey, Lavon. I really need to talk to Sandra right quick can you get her for me?" She asked.

"Okay sure. She was just drying off the baby. He made a mess this morning after eating all that baby food junk. He gets that messy eating from his momma." He said laughing as he called Sandra to the phone. "And don't be trying to tell your best girl my business either. I was just passing through last night."

"Uh-huh, whatever. Go get her please."

Sandra came to the phone sounding a little out of breath. "Hey, girl. What's going on with you?" She asked.

"Hey Sandra, don't you have a cousin that goes to Ann's school?"

"Yep. Why?" Sandra asked.

"I need to know if your cousin can find out who this boy is that's got Ann losing her mind or this girl she sneaking to the health department with," Patsy asked. "Last night we got into a little argument at the dance and it almost got a little physical between us, now you know Ann has never come at me. That's the devil for real."

"Maybe her friend is influencing her. I didn't see the girl either time I went to the doctor though. Ann was sitting there by herself both times. She told me she was holding the girl's bag. Like I said before my friend, the only thing in them bags is condoms and pills.

I found out about that lunch bag a little too late." Sandra laughed and said. "She must be pretty close for Ann to risk y'all momma beating her out of her skin for skipping school and being at the clinic."

"See that's the same thing I thought," Patsy said. "I gotta find this girl or what her and Ralph are really up to. If I find out her and Ralph been sneaking around this whole time, I'm going to hurt the both of them."

"Don't worry about it. I'll get my cousin 'Boogie Man' to check into it for you." Sandra said.

"Boogie Man? Why is he called Boogie Man?" Patsy asked.

Sandra laughed. "Cause that boy is so ugly it's scary. He look like an accident walking around looking for a place to happen. My aunt said she got drunk one night at the club and rolled up on the first thang with a pretty smile, nice cologne, and a roll of money. Turned out the next morning he was a 'swamp monster' that had been abundantly blessed in certain ways and my aunt had a hard time letting him go until her belly got big then he took that joystick somewhere else and left her with the consequences and they wasn't cute." Sandra laughed so hard she almost choked.

Patsy laughed herself. "She said that about her own child?" Patsy asked.

"Girl, she say it's best to tell the truth and shame the devil. Anyway, Boogie Man knows he's ugly but I hear he got that 'good-good' like his ole ugly daddy so things might work out for him." They both laughed at that.

It felt good to Patsy to laugh till her stomach hurt after all the tension in the house from last night. "Thanks, Sandra, and kiss Solomon for me."

"I'll do it. Lavon is getting him dressed for me right now. He is a pretty good dad overall." Sandra said with a smile in her voice that Patsy visualized. She decided she'd wait to mention that she'd seen

Lavon riding through the dance scoping out little girls. They were upperclassmen he knew better than even coming that way.

She hung up the phone trying to figure out a way to break the ice with Ann. She really did love her and nothing like this had ever happened between them.

She saw Ann playing with Josie's fingers and tickling her. Patsy thought this would be a good time to talk to her. She walked up to Ann but she never lifted her head or stopped playing with Josie. "Ann, look. I know last night was bad but I forgive you and I know whatever is bothering you must be pretty bad for you to have acted the way you did with me. I love you and you know you can tell me anything." Patsy said looking in Ann's face for a reaction.

Ann gave her a look like, "Did you really just say that to me?"

"Why are you looking at me like that? I'm trying to let you know I'm here for you and I forgive you." Patsy told her.

Ann looked her straight in her eye. "I could care less if you forgive me. You ain't Jesus. What you forgiving me for? You were the one in the wrong. I need to be deciding if I want to forgive you for trying to be my momma instead of my big sister. Leave me alone. I don't want to talk about this with you anymore."

Patsy just stood there in disbelief. Whatever spirit this was it was strong and it was trying to split them up. She didn't have the energy to fight with this demon today. She went to her grandmother's living room and begin looking through her family Bible. It was a huge book with names and pictures as far back as the 1930s. Grandma Ruth had every wedding, funeral, and birth in that book that you wanted to know about and she was pretty good about keeping up with the dates. She had a copy of her marriage license folded up in the front of it and a picture of their Grandpa.

He had a big smile on his face with a cute little girl standing next to him. He had his arms around her wrist. Patsy looked closer at the girl then she saw a familiar curve of her upper lip. It was Grandma Ruth. *She looked a lot like Josie,* Patsy thought to herself.

She flipped through more pages of pictures, obituaries, and newspaper clippings.

"Patsy! Patsy where you at girl?" She heard her grandmother yell through the house. Patsy jumped up and ran to the door of the living room. Just as she stepped out, she bumped into her grandmother.

"What are you doin' in there?" She asked her.

Patsy studied her face and tone a minute to try to figure out how to answer her. She couldn't tell if she was upset with her or just asking a general question. She walked up to Patsy and pushed her hair gently back into place.

"You hiding from your sisters?" She asked. "I use to do that with mine. It was so many of us in that little house we made each other crazy as a jack-rabbit."

"I was looking for a scripture to read."

Her grandmother patted her on the shoulder and pointed towards the Bible. "Well, that's the place to find it."

"Grandma, why is our momma so mean?" Patsy asked. She was feeling a little tired in her soul after fighting with Ann and she just wanted some peace. Her grandmother looked at her, surprised.

"Why you asking me about your momma? She ain't been under my roof since the day your daddy married her. She done got some nasty ways since that time. I don't know what foul spirit got ahold of her. Sometimes she reminds me of my own momma. She was a 'Bible beast'." Grandma Ruth said as she looked down at her hands.

She began nervously rubbing them. "Your great grandmother, Gerthie, would beat me and quote the scripture at the same time. She was hard on us girls but even worse on the boys. My daddy left us when I was five years old. She was a Bible-toting ball of bitterness after that. She literally ran my big brothers off with the degrading way she treated them.

She would stand in a chair and beat them cause they were too tall for her to reach. She would dare them to move. Each one left home the day after they graduated or turned eighteen.

They moved to San Diego with my daddy. Daddy was too scared to stay down south. He said he had nightmares of waking up with momma standing over him holding a Bible in one hand and a hatchet in the other. She'd promised him she would find him, cut him up and bury him in the church cemetery cause that was the closest he would get to God for leaving us like he did." Grandma Ruth said.

"Your momma reminds me of her so much. That's why I have to keep her in check when she around me. I won't let her run my house with that nasty spirit of hers."

Patsy noticed the sweat on her grandmother's hands as she talked about her own daughter.

"Grandma, I'm sorry for asking. I didn't mean to upset you. I just wanted to know what made our momma act the way she does. She doesn't love anybody. Not even us." Patsy said. Her grandmother looked up at her and touched her hand.

"She does love you. She loves you so much she doesn't know how to express it. I guess she's bound by something." Grandma Ruth said. "Just pray for her, Patsy. One day she might wake up. Your great-grandmother did on her dying bed."

After that statement, she got up and walked out without another word. She was quiet the remainder of the day. She seemed to be in deep thought.

Patsy woke up the next morning to the song, "This Little Light of Mine" blasting on the radio. Sun shining and biscuits baking. Grandma Ruth had the kitchen lit up and Patsy was ready to eat. She looked over and saw Josie lying next to her. She kissed her on the nose and shook her to wake up.

"Come on, baby girl. Let's go get a biscuit." Josie tried to say it back to her, but it came out sounding like "biz kiz." That made Patsy smile. She took Josie with her to the bathroom to clean up. Grandma Ruth was putting out plates when she came into the kitchen.

Ann surprisingly was up and she was helping her set the table. "It's about time you sleepy heads got up. Me and Ann been up for hours. We had a good walk around the block this morning and she helped me cook this wonderful breakfast you got in front of you." Grandma Ruth said wiping flour from her apron. They finished the Sunday breakfast Ann helped cook and hurried out the door.

Sunday school was just getting started by the time they made it to Greater Trials. Patsy dropped Josie off in her class. She wouldn't see her again until the end of service. They put all the babies in one room after Sunday School. Usually, Ann usually walked with Patsy to their classes since they were next door but this morning she just kept walking.

She didn't even give Josie a kiss like she usually did. Patsy was really worried about her baby sister. How could someone change so much in just a few short months? Jesus was going to have to hurry up and fix whatever in Ann that was broken. After all, he was the Savior, not her, she couldn't make it right but she knew the God who heard her prayers could.

She never lost her faith in prayer. Prayer was the one thing keeping her sane.

"The Boogie-Man is gonna get you!" she heard a voice yell as a hand hit her lightly in the back of her head. She knew the laugh behind it.

It was Sandra. She was smiling and wrapping her arm under hers.

"Come on here, girl, before my cousin pops up and kidnaps you." She said as she pulled Patsy by her arm.

Patsy laughed at that, "Why would he do that?" She asked. Sandra walked fast almost dragging her along. "'Cause I told him I needed him to do a little investigating for me on Ann. He said he would do it if I could get you to go to their last school dance for football season with him. I told him, 'Boy! Patsy old enough to be your momma! She can't go to no dance with you.'" Sandra laughed. "He said he thinks you are finer than a line on a piece of paper."

They both laughed down the hall at that and before Patsy realized she and Sandra were standing at the front of their own Sunday School door.

They tried to straighten up before opening the door. Sister Clay didn't play that actin' rebellious as she called it in her classroom, she always told them.

"You need to respect God's time and be on time."

When Sandra was pregnant, Sister Clay stayed on her all the time about "detours to her destiny" and how she should have her butt whipped letting some nappy-headed boy get her off track like that. Sandra would just blow real hard and answer, "Yes, ma'am." To try and keep it moving.

She didn't argue with Sister Clay because she was too happy to be accepted. After having to ask her mother's old church congregation to forgive her for getting pregnant, she didn't feel wanted there so she started coming to Greater Trials.

"Glad you little angels without wings could make it to Sunday School this morning." Sister Clay said to them sarcastically as they came through the door trying to keep a straight face.

"If the Jubilee train was coming today you would have missed it. I've told the both of you, especially you Sandra, you need to get it together and stop being late for your destiny. You out there in that hall playing around and you gonna miss something you need in life. Now sit down in my class and open that Sunday School book right now."

They both knew better than to "talk back" as Sister Clay would say so they both sat down and did as they were told. If you got labeled in Sister Clay's Sunday School class, you were put on an invisible list of children to watch and that list was reported to Nadeen. You could look around at any minute and see the ushers watching you with an eye that dared you to move or even breathe. It was too much pressure, and for Patsy, she knew the drama would continue at home if she embarrassed her mother in front of her church family.

Before Sunday School class was over, David stuck his head in the door, he was holding the offering plate. Patsy didn't feel safe around him even in the house of God. He gave Sister Clay that old fake smile of his as he leaned in to hand her the plate.

"Good Morning, Sister Clay. Just dropping off the offering basket. I'll come back through before class is over and pick it up. Amen."

Patsy looked at him acting like he was Holy Ghost-filled. She bet he'd lit up a pack of cigarettes and drunk a little communion wine before he came around collecting offering. He looked over at Sandra and Patsy.

"Good Morning ladies. Y'all pay attention now," he said as he backed out the door and closed it.

Patsy had to repent right then for the terrible things she was thinking about him in God's house. It was something about David that just made her envision a grey-eyed devil with a pitchfork and a tail no matter how dressed up he got on Sunday mornings. Why was Aunt Eva with him in the first place? She had to see he was no good for her and that he was a pervert.

Maybe she just liked helping strays. She had, after all, met him when he was down on his luck, she'd told Patsy. She cleaned him up, got him back focused, and now she was reaping the fruits of her labor she said. He cleaned up pretty good, she believed, and that big check on Friday made him look even better to her.

Patsy didn't care if he had money bags hanging around his waist, he was bad news. Patsy was thinking about all the reasons why her Aunt shouldn't be with David when the bell rang to end Sunday School.

On her way out, Sister Clay stopped her, "Patsy, I hope to get a chance to let you share your ministry trip with the class. I know your mother is so proud of you."

Patsy bit her tongue. "Yes, ma'am. Thank you." Patsy said. She looked around for Sandra. She was probably chasing Lavon to the sanctuary by now.

Patsy walked out of her classroom door and saw Ann talking to David. It looked like he was saying something really serious to her and Ann's body language didn't look like she was happy to hear it. Patsy hoped Ann had not snapped out on David. She was acting so crazy lately; no telling what she might do or say.

Before Patsy could get close to them to find out what was going on, David walked away. As he passed Patsy, he had a disturbed look on his face.

"You need to tell your little sister to stay in her place." He said with a scowl

What had Ann said or done now? Patsy thought. When she got to Ann, she spoke very carefully because she could see something was wrong.

"Ann you okay? Did David say something crazy to you? 'Cause if he did you know all I got to do is tell Momma or Aunt Eva and they will set him straight. You know Momma don't like him anyway." Patsy said.

Ann looked directly into her eyes. "David is just being a jerk. He better be glad I decided not to tell Aunt Eva how he was all up in First Lady Champagne's face a few minutes ago instead of picking up that Sunday School Offering."

Patsy looked surprised. "What you mean all up in her face?" she asked Ann.

"He just seemed to be mighty close in her face when they came out of the church office so I asked him about it. I just wanted to know what was going on." Ann said.

"Girl, have you lost your mind?" Patsy asked before she realized it

"If your momma finds out you ran up on that grown man like that, she is going to drag you out of this parking lot and you might not make it home before she beats the black off of you. You know how she is about us getting in grown folks business. Anyway, he is a member of the church, he's gonna run into First

Lady Champagne. Ann, you need to relax. Something got you all bent up and you need to straighten it before Nadeen straightens it for you." Patsy said

"Patsy I know what I saw. David ain't gonna tell Momma nothing. He enjoy living too much." She said and headed towards the stairs to the sanctuary.

Patsy watched her walk off with that nasty little sway in her hips she'd picked up since Patsy had been gone. She really had been invaded by a spirit. Patsy didn't know exactly which one it was, but she had just about had enough of it. Kenny needed to come back home real soon. His baby girl was turning into something not even he would realize. Whatever sanctuary he was in this morning, Patsy hoped he was praying.

9

IT WAS A beautiful autumn morning. The leaves on the trees were softly falling to the ground. The smell of smoke from the fireplace made Kenny want to jump in his truck and drive for miles. He missed his girls this morning just like every morning. He was a little late getting up this Sunday morning so he would have to call them when he got back home from church. He got in his truck and turned on the radio. Every day he got in his truck he played that scene in his head: Ann on the ground on her knees, screaming and crying for him to come back. Patsy standing next to her with tears running down her face. That's why he called every week—he never wanted them to believe he had abandoned them, that he was gone and never coming back because of them.

How did he explain to his girls that his heart was breaking in a million pieces as he saw them torn up with tears because of his actions? How did he find the strength to pull out of his driveway with his baby girl on the ground begging her daddy to stay? It tore him up, too. It had ripped every tear from his body, and they poured down his face as he turned the corner leaving his home and his family. He never saw Nadeen's face.

He saw her form in the screen door but he never saw her eyes as he left. He didn't have to. He knew. He knew they were full of venom for him. He remembered how they stared at him with just a little more hate than usual when he told her that he had to leave for just a little while, but he would be back a better man. A better man for her and for his girls.

When did she start changing like the seasons? It seemed they quickly went from love and happiness to hate and despair. Maybe eighteen was too young for them to marry but they were in love, and he wanted to get Nadeen out of that house before she hurt herself or someone else. It seemed to start two years after they were married, when Patsy was born, the first few months were great but then she began to change.

It was like one night he went to sleep next to his high school sweetheart and woke up the next day to a raging vixen. It broke his heart every time she cursed him, hit him, or belittled him behind closed doors or in front of his kids. He hurt so bad inside he turned to the only thing he thought would give him some relief. He turned to something he thought he could control—alcohol and drugs—but just like Nadeen, they'd turned on him and begin telling him what to do and when to do it.

When Nadeen tore into him, he tore into them. They never said a word back to him and he liked that. They allowed him to use them, abuse them, and take as much as he needed to make him feel better inside. When he hung out with his buddies on the streets and in the clubs, he had a good time that always had a bad ending. He tried to stay focused on the good time he was having but his mind kept sneaking back to the last fight, the last words, the last hit and he had to drink or smoke more to hold back the tears or bash the memory.

His sister and the rest of his family never understood why he stayed. His own mother seemed not to get it and Kenny found that the hardest to understand because of all she'd been through in her own life.

They stopped coming over to the house a long time ago. Nadeen and his family were like oil and water. At first, he believed it was just the way a mother and daughter-in-law acted, leaving the son/husband in the middle to referee the fights.

Kenny begin to notice whenever his sister, mother, or other family members were at a family gathering and said something about how nice the house looked or how well they seemed to be doing Nadeen would be quick to point out that it was her hard work and Jesus that made it all come together.

She would never speak kindly to him in front of them. She was always short and seemed irritated by doing the smallest thing for him. He remembered like it was yesterday. The final straw that caused his sister, Ernestine, and his mother to swear they'd never come back unless it was a repast dinner for Nadeen, it happened a few years ago on his thirty-third birthday.

He invited them over to celebrate with him earlier that day and told Nadeen they were coming just as he was leaving to go pick up the cake. She wasn't happy about it, but it was too late to change it. She felt they could not control their children or their mouths and she really didn't want his ungrateful sister or his mother sitting at her dinner table.

Kenny, for the sake of peace, let her get all of her frustrations out before he left to go pick up the cake. By doing that, he hoped she would have let out enough steam to be the nice, Christian wife he saw in action on the Sundays when her pastor came over for dinner.

She was a picture of domestic holiness on those visits. He was amazed at her ability to love, nurture, and serve during those visits.

Kenny's mother, sister, and cousins all arrived at the same time. They came in and struggled out a smile and a hug for Nadeen. Everyone was sitting around the table enjoying the food and the fellowship as much as possible when Ernestine asked for Patsy to get up and fix her a to-go plate so she and his mother could have something for later on that evening.

Nadeen heard her and gave Patsy a look that told her not to move. Ernestine noticed that Patsy hadn't gotten out of the chair yet and Kenny noticed the look Nadeen gave Patsy. He started wishing right then that he had a glass of anything dark brown with no ice and a couple of joints.

Ernestine challenged Patsy and Nadeen almost jumped across the table at her.

"Girl! Did you hear what I said? Get up and fix some plates for me and your Grandma. You young and energetic. You move slower than me and momma go on now!" She snapped at Patsy.

Patsy looked at her momma and then at her daddy. Before Kenny could address it, Nadeen turned toward Kenny's sister and pointed her finger.

"Who you think you talking to Ernestine? You ain't carried that one not one day and you don't feed and clothe her! I tell her what to do. This is my house and I'm the Queen in it! You hear me?" She yelled at her sister-in-law across the table.

"Well, it looks like Kenny needs to find him another Queen of his castle cause you got to be the sorriest I have ever seen raising these disrespectful children!" Ernestine snapped back at her.

"Son, you need to get your wife in check. You go out and work too hard every day to have to deal with disrespectful children and a disrespectful scripture quoting wife," his mother said, pursuing her lips as she tilted her head slightly to the right.

This made Nadeen stand up at the table. She knocked over about ten glasses and some ice cream. "Disrespectful?" Nadeen shouted. "You sitting at my table, eating my food, in my house telling your son to get me in check. You the one about to get checked! Again! This is my house. My children do what I say and your son better do it, too!" Nadeen yelled at her.

"You think your son put all this in this house well he didn't! He spends all his money out in the streets barely has enough to keep the lights on around here or even put food on the table. If it was not for me going out every evening busting my butt at the nursing home for old ladies like you, we would be living in a box. No! My daughter ain't fixin' you or your lookin' like a man-faced daughter a plate!" She yelled at his mother.

"Son, you gonna let her speak to me and your sister like that in your house? All your family up in here and this how she act? I told you not to marry her from the jump, didn't I? I told you she come from a crazy momma and would drive you to the hospital or the morgue. Didn't I warn you about her?" She yelled at Kenny.

Kenny tried to interject but before he could get a word out Ernestine was up and coming around the table towards Nadeen. "We don't need your food and we don't need to come back to your house. Come on, everybody. Let's leave before I have to hurt this woman in *her* house! Talking crazy to my Momma! I will drag you up in this—"

"Come try it!" Nadeen yelled at Ernestine, cutting her off mid-sentence as she lunged towards her sister-in-law. Ernestine grabbed Nadeen by her pearl necklace, just as Kenny made it around the table to his wife, Nadeen landed her fork into his sister's hand. Blood went running down her hand as she let out a horrific scream and squatted to the floor. Nadeen's eyes were blazing with anger.

"Now! You got what you came for! I love the Lord but he equipped me to slay demons!" Nadeen yelled at Ernestine. Kenny's mother was running to her daughter's side screaming

"Oh, Lord Jesus! Kenny this nut done stabbed your sister!"

"Nadeen! Nadeen stop!" Kenny said as he grabbed his wife and pulled her away from the table.

"You should have told your sister to stop! I bet she stop now!" Nadeen yelled back.

"Please calm down, baby," Kenny said as he pushed her down the hall to her bedroom. Everyone else at the table stood in shock looking at Ernestine moaning beneath the kitchen table.

Patsy and Ann were more embarrassed than shocked. They

watched as their Aunt Ernestine's hand bled all over the kitchen table and the floor. Kenny's mother pulled the fork out of her daughter's hand, wrapped it with a dish towel, grabbed Ernestine's things, and headed out the door with a promise.

"Kenny you can best believe we won't ever come back unless it's the day of her funeral! Trust and believe that!"

The rest of Kenny's family rushed out behind her, too scared to speak.

"Get control of your house, Kenny! Get control fast! One day she's gonna kill you if you don't. Then your blood will be on them pretty white usher gloves of hers! There is an exception to every rule just remember that. I know what I taught you but sometimes you gotta adjust to your surroundings." His mother yelled. She dragged Ernestine out of the front door crying, screaming, and cussing. Her words tore his heart in half.

He knew he was now standing between two families he loved and he didn't know how to make peace between them. He also knew that a man leaves his mother and father and cleaves to his wife. He didn't understand Nadeen, but he had married her for better or worse but he never expected so much worse.

Since that birthday party, his family never stepped foot back into his home. The last time he saw Ernestine was at the hospital in ICU after Nadeen shot him. He was glad to see her but hated it had to be at such a bad time. His mother couldn't take it, so she didn't come to the hospital. Ernestine told him she was home praying and crying that God would keep him alive and set him free from his wife. Nobody seemed to understand that he loved his wife. He loved her and his girls despite the problems.

He knew his daughters were afraid and he needed them to see him alive and well to keep them from going into a deep depression. They were so young to deal with so much. He wanted them to have peace. That's why he went back home and that's why he moved away from them. God started speaking to him about leaving the first night he came home from the hospital but he just ignored his voice and from that point on he got no rest.

By the time he left, he knew only God could put him back in his rightful place as the head of the household. Only God could put Nadeen back beside him instead of in front of him. He had to get out of God's way and let him work all the logistics out of how to get Nadeen off of the tower and back on praying ground. All while preparing Kenny to truly love and protect her as Jesus loved the church and even died for it. Kenny spent many nights talking and repenting to God about his failures at keeping the enemy out of his home.

He made promises to God that he planned on keeping when it came to him being a better man and a better child of God. He wanted to fight the enemy himself, but God had to remind him the battle was not his. He needed him to step back

He was so busy thinking about how God was gonna fix it that he got to the church before he realized it. When he pulled up to the parking lot, he saw Sister Sara outside. Sara was a past member of Deliverance Rock his church back home, she would come over to his apartment when he was separated from Nadeen and help make sure he had enough food to eat and if he needed any help fixing things up. He appreciated her acts of charity and was surprised when Pastor Mack called him and told him she was moving to Miami and her family would appreciate if he would help her get settled.

She would make someone a nice wife one day, he thought. She was such a sweet young lady.

"Hey, Brother Kenny." She said with a big smile on her face. "Good to see you on such a beautiful Sunday morning. I just got here myself. I had to put some finishing touches on my blueberry cobbler this morning." Kenny hadn't had a blueberry cobbler since he got out of the hospital. His momma sent it over by a church member. It was one of his favorites. He'd asked Nadeen to learn how to make it for him but she said baking wasn't her thing and if he wanted one so bad go get his momma to bake it since she always wanted his feet parked at her dinner table. So that was the last time he asked.

"A blueberry cobbler, huh?" He said as he walked towards the front door of the church. "Sounds like a mighty fine dinner you got planned for yourself, Sister Sara. How you liking Miami?"

"Oh, I love it. I'm so glad that I moved. It has everything I'm looking for here. It's going to be my promised land, I do believe." She walked beside him into the sanctuary. It was a little awkward to Kenny because they looked almost like a couple.

Kenny found a seat on the pew close to the pulpit. Sister Sara slid next to him and sat down. Kenny tried to make small talk with her until service began, which seemed to be the longest fifteen minutes of his life.

"Have you joined the Single's Ministry yet, Sister Sara?"

She smiled at him, "No, Brother Kenny I have not. I'm not interested in the Single's Ministry. I believe my Boaz is looking for me and I don't want no misunderstanding when he realizes he's found me. If I got some other man in my face when he finally notices me, he may mistake it for me being already spoken for and I don't want that. God sent me here, I do believe because my Boaz is here."

Kenny smiled back at her. "Well, I hope he opens his eyes soon and sees you before somebody else tries to steal you and your blueberry cobbler."

Sara laughed. "Oh, don't worry. I won't let that happen. I got my eye on him. He just doesn't know it yet. He'll notice me. God is already working that out. He knows the desire of my heart and I believe he'll give it to me." Just as she patted his hands, the choir director stepped to the pulpit and asked the congregation to lift up their hands to Jesus. The service was about to begin.

This church had been recommended to Kenny by Pastor and

First Lady Mack and Kenny knew they wouldn't have sent him there if it wasn't a real Bible-based church with a leader who was serious about his walk with God and his assignment for God's people. Kenny loved the fact that he let the Holy Ghost have his way in the service. They never passed out programs.

Kenny's stomach was growling by the time service was over but he was so full of joy deep down inside he just pushed past it. He decided he would just make a sandwich when he got home and call the girls. On his way out the door, Sara grabbed him by the arm.

"Brother Kenny, you got lunch plans?"

Kenny sort of laughed. "Kinda. I plan on making me a sandwich, watching a little television, and calling my girls back home."

Sister Sara playfully put her hands on her hips. "Brother Kenny. A sandwich on a Sunday? After such a wonderful service a man should have a good hearty meal to replace all that he poured out unto the Lord and you did some pouring out, Brother."

Kenny laughed slightly. "You know you right, but I just didn't have time to put something together in that ole crockpot last night. I'm gonna have to do better next Sunday."

"I would love to have some company for lunch," Sara said. "I'm all alone in this big city except for my church member which I'm so grateful to God to have here with me. I would love it if you fellowshipped with me over some steak and potatoes, green bean casserole, cornbread muffins, sweet tea, and blueberry cobbler."

Kenny felt his stomach kick at the mention of her menu. "Sister Sara, why'd you cook so much food?" He asked.

"It's a habit. You remember how my momma would always cook enough for visitors on Sunday and we'd bring you a huge plate. She believes that you never know who may be stopping by and it's nothing like a good warm meal with a Brother or Sister in Christ."

"Well thank you for the invite, Sister Sara. I guess I can wait on that sandwich until later on tonight. My stomach seems to be real excited about that menu."

"Come on then. Let's go fellowship over some good home cooking. After all, I need to practice serving my husband his plate," she said.

Kenny had such a great time fellowshipping with Sister Sara it was almost five o'clock when he realized how long he had stayed.

"Sister Sara, I have truly enjoyed the meal and the fellowship but I better be getting on back to my side of town now. My girls are probably wondering why I haven't called yet. Make sure you tell your mother I said hello when you talk to her today and let her know I'm here to help you when you need it."

"Brother Kenny, you don't have to be in a hurry to leave. I ain't got nothing to do the rest of the day but read over some clinical notes. I decided to go to night school now that I finished nursing school and work on becoming a Nurse Practitioner."

Kenny was impressed with Sister Sara. When her Boaz finally found her, he would have one smart, good cooking, God-fearing woman on his hands.

"Sister Sara that is such good news. I'm happy for you. I know you're going to be successful but I better move along and check on my girls. It's been hard on them since I moved out here." He said.

"Let me make you a plate to take with you then. I can't possibly eat all this food myself this week." She said as she got up off of the couch. She piled the food on a plate.

"Sister, you gave me enough food for a week," Kenny said.

"You don't have to be a week coming back for more though. You welcome at my table anytime you want to be here," Sara smiled at him and said.

Kenny thought if he didn't know better this young girl might be flirting a little bit.

"No, I wouldn't want to be a bother you got school and pretty soon you'll probably have young men knocking your door down," Kenny said.

"I don't answer just any knock brother Kenny," Sara said seductively.

Kenny reached out and gave her a quick hug. "Bless you for your kindness, Sister. See you next Sunday," he said and waved goodbye to her as he rushed out the door.

As he was putting his key in his car door a thought crossed his mind. *Don't get yourself in any trouble with this young girl. You're married. Don't give her the wrong impression.* Kenny brushed it off and got in the car. Where did that come from? Sister Sara was just that, a Sister. As he opened the door to his apartment his phone was ringing, he recognized the number. It was Sara. He was just about to answer it when he heard a soft voice say, "Not now. No distractions. It's time to humble yourself and talk to God." Kenny looked at his phone again and headed to his prayer closest, he felt a strong need to go prostrate before the Lord. He needed strength to keep moving in God's Will. Sister Sara's blueberry cobbler couldn't do that no matter how good it made him feel deep down inside.

10

"I PROMISE I love you. I know you are scared but you know I wouldn't hurt you. It would be different with you, Patsy. Believe me." Dustin said into the phone.

Patsy felted pushed against a wall but it was a wall she wanted to be against as long as it was Dustin pressing against her. "I know. I been thinking about it. I'm scared Dustin. I'm scared of you and I'm scared of God. He said we are supposed to wait until we are married and what if I get pregnant as punishment the way Sandra did?" Patsy asked him.

"I respect what you saying about God and his Will but I have to tell you my struggle too. I would never be with anyone else but I really want to be with you. I would make sure you didn't get pregnant." Patsy could hear the loud beating of her heart just with him talking in her ear through the phone. Kissing was getting old with Dustin. She knew it the night he put her hand on him. She felt the heat through his pants. She didn't know what he thought she was going to do with that thing and she was too scared to find out. Yet, she wanted to know. She was so mixed up.

Patsy thought she heard a door close. She jumped up off of the bed. "I gotta go. I think my mom is heading this way." She whispered.

"No problem. Call me back if you can." Patsy hung up the cell phone she had gotten from Sandra and hid it in her backpack.

She could hear Nadeen's voice. It sounded like she was on the phone. "I know he been so good to me, Sister! He been keeping me and my babies. I just wanna be used by God!" She shouted.

Patsy put her earplugs in and listened to the music on her laptop. She closed her eyes and begin to see Dustin's face. Her mind drifted to them being on her grandmother's porch a few weeks ago. She was so wrapped up in kissing him and the feel of her hand being pressed between his legs. She probably would have given it up if they hadn't been on that porch. He made it hard to resist the temptation.

What am I going to do about Dustin? She thought to herself. *He's been patient with me and I know it's hard for him since he's use to being with other girls. It's hard for me too, God. I like the way he makes me feel. I'm a little scared but I want him to stay with me. I don't want to lose him. And I don't want you to be mad at me. Help me. Help us."* She prayed.

All of a sudden she heard the bedroom door slam against the wall. She jumped and opened her eyes. It was Josie.

"Little girl, what you want bustin' down my door like that?" Josie stood at the door looking at her with something that looked like Vaseline smeared all over her face and in her hair. Patsy jumped off the bed and headed towards her. Josie turned and ran down the hall laughing.

"Josie! Josie come here you little greasy baby doll!" Josie was giggling as she ran as fast as her thick little chocolate legs would let her go. She got to the edge of the carpet and fell on her belly.

"What is going on out here?" Nadeen asked opening her bedroom door. Patsy held Josie around her belly as she struggled to get down. She turned to show her mother. "Josie found the Vaseline." She told her.

"Aren't you and Ann suppose to be watching her? What were

the two of you doing while this mess was being created?" Nadeen asked looking at Patsy then at Josie squirming.

"I was working on some Algebra. I think Ann might be sleep." Patsy lied and said. She could feel her heart beat increasing.

"You got ten minutes to get her cleaned up or she won't be the only squirming do you hear me?" Nadeen asked giving Patsy a stern look.

"Yes, ma'am. I was taking her to the bathroom." Patsy said as meek as possible. Nadeen stared at her a few more minutes then closed her bedroom door.

Patsy swooped her up. "Little girl you starting trouble for me. How did you get into this Vaseline? Ann was supposed to be watching you up there. Come on here let me go rub you down and get this off of you."

Josie wiggled in her arms and started whining. "Oh, you gonna get it off. You can just stop squirming. I'm not going to get beat down cause you decided you wanted to use up a whole jar of Vaseline. By the way, where did you put it?"

Josie looked in her eyes but didn't make a sound. A few more steps and Patsy got the answer. Her barefoot landed down on the plastic jar.

"Ouch!" Patsy yelled as her foot went down on the plastic jar and cracked it, slightly twisting her ankle. "Darn it, Josie. You need your greasy butt whipped." She told her baby sister. Knowing full well she couldn't spank her.

She was her baby. She had taken care of her and Ann since they came home from the hospital. They were her babies. She went to the bathroom, put Josie under her armpit, grabbed a towel, put hot water on it, and headed back to her bedroom as Josie kicked her legs trying to get free of her big sister.

It took Patsy an hour to clean Josie up, get the gobs of Vaseline out of her hair, comb it again, and put her on clean clothes. It must have worn Josie out because as soon as Patsy had finished, she was fast asleep. Patsy covered her with a blanket and tip-toed out of the room to find Ann.

Patsy climbed up the stairs to Ann's room. She called her name as she put her hand on the doorknob to open it. The knob didn't turn, it was locked. *Now, there are nothing but girls in this house,* Patsy thought to herself. Why does Ann keep locking her bedroom door? She knew Nadeen didn't like that.

She always told them they had no privacy in her house. They want privacy they needed to get their own house but until then she could walk into any room at any time that she paid for. Patsy knocked on the door. She thought she heard some movement then a bump.

"Ann! Ann you all right in there? Why you all locked up in here instead of watching Josie? She has greased herself down with a whole jar of Vaseline. I should have made you clean it up." She said thru the door. Ann didn't answer. Patsy was about to knock again when she slowly opened the bedroom door. Ann gave Patsy a look like she was irritated.

"Patsy, what do you want? I was really deep in my sleep and you come knocking on my door like the house on fire." She said rubbing her eyes. Patsy pushed the door open further and tried to look around.

"How you let Josie end up looking like a can of Crisco?" Patsy asked. "She could have gotten into worse and then what? You gotta do better, Ann. The last time someone wasn't watching her she almost died." Patsy said.

"Don't start going off the deep end with me about Josie. I accidentally fell asleep while she was in here playing, I guess." Ann said. Patsy titled her head. "You been sleeping a whole lot lately and you locking doors around here. What's up with that?"

"You my momma now? You think you get to question me? You better go on with that Patsy." Ann said as she began closing her bedroom door.

"Where I'm gonna go is to your momma about your behavior if you don't snap out of it," Patsy replied.

"Why you trippin'? She okay. Nothing major happened to her and as they say. 'You do what you feel you gotta do'." Ann said.

"I might as well. Seems like that's how you doin' it these days little sister." Patsy said as she looked Ann up and down. Just as she looked down at her purple-painted toenails she noticed something on the floor at her feet.

"Look. I'm gonna go back to sleep. Let Josie sleep with you tonight. I ain't up to her kicking me in my navel all night tonight." She said trying to close the door in her big sister's face.

Patsy put her hand on the door to stop it from shutting.

"Ann is that a cigarette on your floor?" She asked never taking her eyes off of the object on the floor. Ann turned her head in the direction of Patsy's eyes and looked. She was quiet for a minute then she turned back to Patsy.

"What? A cigarette? Why would I have a cigarette, Patsy, and where would I get it?" She asked. "See what I mean? You are over-reacting. Probably a pencil that fell out of my backpack. You never seen a white pencil before?" Ann asked. "Let me go back to sleep please and stop being so full of drama." She said as she started closing the door in Patsy's face.

Patsy knew that was a cigarette. She had focused too hard on it to make sure. It wasn't a pencil. It was a cigarette. Was Ann smoking now? Was she really losing her mind enough to do it in Nadeen's house?

Patsy didn't know for sure what was going on with Ann but she wished God would go ahead and reveal it to her so she could help her. As she walked away from the door, she heard Ann say, "Damn!" that really shocked her senses. Ann cussing now? What was going on in this house? It seemed that Kenny left and something bigger and even more evil moved in and was holding Ann hostage.

11

SANDRA WAS RUNNING to get out the door this morning. She had something hot off the press to tell Patsy and she couldn't hold it much longer. Lavon was taking his time coming to pick up the baby and take him to the daycare. Just as she was about to text him for the tenth time, she heard his car horn blowing outside. She gathered up the baby. Told her mom goodbye and grabbed the baby carrier.

"Hey, can you just drop him off without me this morning? I'm gonna ride the bus I got to talk to Patsy it's really important. It's about Ann." She told Lavon as she locked Solomon into his car seat. "I'll meet you at school by the lockers after first period." She kissed him and turned to walk off down the street then she turned back around to him. "Actually, give me a ride to Patsy's street then I'll meet her the rest of the way."

"What's goin' on with Ann?" He asked, frowning. "You can ride with me and tell me what's goin' on. She in some trouble?"

"This some hot tea just for my girl, Patsy. I can't spill it to you Lavon." Sandra said buckling her seat beat. "Just drop me off and I will see you at school."

Sandra had gotten a tip on her investigation of why Ann was

acting so strange and she needed to drop it before she passed out from excitement.

Lavon dropped her off a corner from Patsy's house. Just as she got out of the car, she saw Ann and Patsy heading up the street.

Sandra met them halfway. "Hey, Sandra. What brings you this way this morning?" Patsy asked.

Ann managed to get out a low "Hey, Sandra." But other than that, she just chewed her gum and kept slowly walking.

"I just wanted to ride the school bus with my friend this morning." She said.

"Well, isn't that nice of you? But you know I understand now that you got the baby you can't be waiting around on a bus. I understand, we good." Patsy said.

When they boarded the bus, Sandra sat close to the back and motioned for Patsy to follow her. Ann sat further up front. Ralph sat next to her trying to make conversation. Sandra pushed in close to her on the bus seat and whispered.

"I talked to my cousin Boogie-Man. The one that goes to Ann's school." Sandra said. Patsy looked at her. Now she knew why Sandra rode the bus this morning: she had some news and Patsy knew she was about to bust to tell it. "He called me real late last night so I couldn't call you. I figured you were sleep anyway." Patsy wanted her to get past all of this unnecessary chatter and tell her what her cousin found out.

"What did he tell you? Does he know why Ann been acting so crazy lately and doing crazy stuff?" Patsy asked.

Sandra was smiling so big her lips seemed to touch her ear lobes. The bus came to a quick stop in front of Ann's school. Patsy looked up. Ann was walking off the bus with Ralph behind her. Patsy hoped Ann would turn around so she could at least wave goodbye to her but she didn't she just joined her circle of friends. Patsy missed her little sister so much.

"Okay. listen," Sandra said. "My cousin, Boogie-man, is friends with one of Ann's buddies in her circle. She told him Ann got a boy-friend and it ain't nobody that attends their school. She told him Ann went to the health department with her for her annual check-up and made an appointment herself for Family Planning." Sandra said. Patsy wanted to speak but she couldn't find the words. In her mind, she was asking Sandra a thousand questions but in reality, she was hearing her and not understanding what she was saying.

"Your little sister is on birth control pills. She been messing with him since the summer when you and your dad left the girl told Boogie-man. He must be at the church or something cause he apparently got a car. He has been to the school to bring her lunch and even pretended to be related to her and checked her out of school for a few hours." Sandra said with a satisfied grin on her face. She had delivered as promised.

Patsy sat in that bus seat stunned. She was numb from her face down. The only thing moving was her racing heart and her nervous stomach.

"I hated it to be something to find but at least now you can sit her down and talk to her. You need to tell her how messed up things can get when you step out of God's plan for your life. Tell her just look at me. I got to re-arrange all my plans now since I'm a mom. I mean, I believe I'm gonna get where God wants me to be it's just gonna have to be a slightly different route and an hour or two late." Sandra said. "Patsy, you okay?" Sandra asked. "You asked me to find out and I did."

"No, Sandra, I'm not okay. You just got through telling me my sister is on the pill and she is sneaking around with some older guy who she might have met at church and he has her skipping school. She really has lost her mind, cause she done forgot who her momma is and just how crazy she really can be.

"This guy got her mind messed up bad for her to take risks like that. I'm gonna need a few days to process through this. I got to find the right way to come at her about this. She just started the eighth grade and she is doing all this crazy stuff. Nadeen is going to blow the house up if this gets out." Patsy said as the bus came to a stop in the school parking lot.

"What color is his car? What kind is it? Did the girl say?"

Sandra was looking out the bus window and fixing her skirt as Lavon was pulling up. she was more focused on him.

"What? Oh yeah, I asked Boogie, he said she thought it was silver or platinum. He always picks her up on the side of the building from what she said Ann tells her. For one minute I was like silver? Wait a minute, my man got a silver car, but we both know that's way out the ballpark." Sandra said laughing.

"Girl, Lavon is like a big brother to me and Ann. He would never approach her like that." Patsy said. Just then the bus driver opened the doors.

"I know. I was just joking. Okay, gotta go catch up with him. Talk later." Sandra said standing up and stepping into the aisle "It's gonna work out, Patsy. Once you sit her down and talk to her, she will come back to her senses." Sandra said.

I hope so, Patsy thought to herself. "Here I was thinking her and Ralph was sneaking around and it's a whole other person or both."

"Ann might have Ralph on backup," Sandra said heading towards the front of the bus. "Later, Bestie."

Patsy couldn't pay attention in class all day. She just kept seeing Ann's face and thinking about what Sandra told her.

Why hadn't God stopped this? He parted the Red Sea, and he raised the dead, but he couldn't keep Ann from opening her legs for not one but possibly two guys? The bell for the end of the last class of the day didn't ring soon enough. Patsy ran out the room and made it to the bus stop before anybody else. When the bus made it to Ann's school, Ann seemed to be in a better mood. She was laughing and talking with Ralph.

Maybe Sandra's cousin had gotten her information mixed up,

maybe it was just Ralph. *When could Ann meet anybody else?* Patsy thought.

When they made it home, Eva was there with David. He was lurking around outside on the porch smoking. Patsy hated to walk past him. Every time she saw him she felt ashamed and uncomfortable. He had this look on his face when they passed like he was thinking something dirty. Patsy hoped he wouldn't speak to her.

"Hey ladies. How was school today?" He asked. Looking at them with those wolf-grey eyes of his. Patsy kept it real short with him as she rushed to get past him and through the front door.

"Fine." She replied.

Ann took her time coming in but she didn't speak to him. Nadeen and Aunt Eva were fussing about something but Aunt Eva cut it off when she saw them.

"Well, there are my other two favorite nieces. Come give me a hug." She said as she stretched out her arms. She gave them both a big kiss then she pushed them back a little bit.

"You girls must have passed your Uncle David out there. Your clothes smell like that stinky cigarette of his. I've told him if he is gonna work in the Lord's house, he needs to start dropping those bad habits."

"What bad habits you need to drop?" Nadeen said to her sister. Eva shot her a nasty look.

"You go first, dear sister. When you put all yours down at the church altar, I'll be right behind you. Until then, you just pull the plank out of your own eye." Eva rolled her eyes and said as she tilted her neck towards her sister for emphasis.

"It's way past time for you and your pet lizard to go home, Eva." Nadeen snapped back.

"At least I got one to crawl up next to me at night. Where yours at? Oh yeah, that's right. You ran him off. Wonder who he curled up in bed next to now?" Eva shot back with a look of satisfaction on her face.

"You must have forgotten whose house you in? You way out of place. You delivered your momma's package now walk out before you get drug out," Nadeen said.

Eva smirked and turned to leave, "I told momma I didn't want to bring that food over here cause you might be in a rattlesnake of a mood! I told her bring it herself. No wonder Kenny took off. I don't blame him!" Aunt Eva said. "Your nasty ways is why your husband gone and Dhmonique, the closest person you ever had as a friend is sleeping in her grave because of your nasty, hypocritical ways!" Eva shouted.

Nadeen screamed at her. "You keep Dhmonique's name out of your nasty mouth! Do you hear me? You don't know anything about me and Dhmonique!"

Eva knew she had stabbed her sister in her heart mentioning Dhmonique. She had hit her most vulnerable spot.

"I didn't mean that one, Nadeen. I know that was too low for even your nastiness. I'm out. Call your momma about that casserole." Eva said as she hurried out the door.

Nadeen slammed the front door behind her. Patsy and Ann could see Eva had hit a very sensitive spot in their mother. They chose to ease away.

Nadeen's head started spinning. She felt the tears start to form in her eyes and her heart beating rapidly. Eva had punched the air out of her with that last remark. Every day Nadeen thought about her best friend, missed her but she couldn't show it. To show that would be saying she was responsible for her only friend's demise and she wasn't. The feeling of guilt rose up in her and she ran to her room to cry behind the door. Her bedroom was her sanctuary, her safe place.

"It's not my fault, Father. You got your own calendar of when we suppose to come home. You decided to take her home. I had no control over your decision," Nadeen said as she put her face in her pillow and cried.

✳   ✳   ✳

When Patsy finished her homework later that night, she decided to go and try to talk to Ann again. She hated this new person her sister had become. She was nasty and bitter like a young version of their mother and having one of those spirits in her space was enough for Patsy. She found Ann laying on the couch upstairs. She looked deep in thought. Patsy took a deep breath and stepped into what felt like an arena to talk to Ann.

"Hey, Ann. I gotta talk to you about something." Patsy said. Ann stared at her a few minutes before she moved her legs so Patsy could sit next to her. She sat up and straightened her hair.

"What now? "Ann asked. "I'm trying to relax after all that homework I just did. That geometry class got my head hurting."

Patsy was careful in the way she spoke to her.

"Ann, I love you. I love you and I missed you every day while I was gone on that mission trip. I know now that I should have stayed at home because ministry begins at home. I'm sorry for leaving you here to deal with Momma with Kenny being gone. I may have left you physically but I carried you and Josie every day in my heart. If I hurt you by leaving please forgive me." Patsy said to her little sister.

Ann looked at her with tears welling in her eyes and they slowly began to drip down from her thick black bottom eyelashes. She just looked at her big sister for a few moments and then she responded.

"You don't know how much you and Daddy leaving me at the same time hurt me. I was all alone. Do you hear me, Patsy? I was all alone. Nadeen was mad at Kenny for leaving and for him paying for you to leave. She cussed me and she hit me every day about something and every time she did, she reminded me how I was going to grow up to be a sorry excuse for a human just like him. Y'all left me in this mess and you knew how hard it was." Ann was crying harder now as the tears ran under her neck.

Patsy's heart ached as she saw the hurt and the pain in her little sister's eyes. Tears she had caused. She leaned over and held her in her arms. Ann laid her head on her big sister's shoulder and cried loudly onto it. They seemed to sit in that moment forever but when it was done, Patsy believed a heavy weight came off of her little sister.

When she let her go. Ann started talking. "I been angry for so long. I've done something that is too shameful to tell and all because I was hurt and angry. I did something I couldn't believe at first I was doing and then it began to feel good and it replaced my hurt. It made me vengeful instead. I been doing things I thought were to hurt you and Kenny but it's really hurt me." She told Patsy.

Patsy grabbed her sister's hand. "I know Ann. I heard that you've gotten involved with someone and that you might be taking birth control pills which to me would mean you must be having sex with this guy. Is that true? Are you having sex?" Patsy asked.

Ann put both of her hands over her face and nodded her head yes. "I only did it at first out of anger. I knew it would hurt Kenny if he knew it and I knew you would be disappointed, but I blamed you both because if you hadn't left me, I wouldn't have gotten involved with this guy.

"He came around and listened to me and he did things to me that made me feel good. I forgot about you and Kenny for a while. I replaced my anger with guilt and that made me feel even worse. I been so ashamed I couldn't even confess it to Jesus and know if I told him, he would forgive me but I'm too ashamed to tell him." Ann said beginning to cry again.

"Ann there is nothing you can tell God that he doesn't already know. He knows how much you were hurting. He has seen everything we been through. He'll forgive you. If you will ask him and stop what you are doing with this guy or guys. He'll forgive you and you can start all over again. Don't let the enemy whisper in your ear anymore. He doesn't love you, Ann. I love you. Kenny loves you. Most of all Jesus loves you." Patsy said as tenderly as possible.

"I have messed up so bad Patsy," Ann said.

"Ann lots of girls have had sex before marriage. It's not going to stop God from loving you or hearing your prayers. I know it isn't easy. I'm learning that more and more the longer Dustin and I date." Patsy told her sister.

"This is bigger than being worried about God loving me and forgiving me. It's about the violation I've done but I know he loves me and I know it is going to be hard for everyone to accept what we have done but I needed love so bad. I couldn't even love Josie and she didn't do anything to me. She's just a baby." Ann said holding her head down.

"Everything is going to be better when Daddy comes back. God is going to send him back to get all this mess in line including your momma and her nasty ways." Patsy said.

"She your momma too. Don't give all that craziness just to me." Ann jokingly said to her sister. This made them both laugh for a minute. Patsy stood up

"It's gonna work out. I promise. You'll get stronger and walk away from this boy just watch and see."

Ann nodded her head in agreement but in her heart, she knew this wasn't going to end well and it wasn't going to be okay. She was confused and mixed-up doing things she knew she shouldn't be doing with somebody she knew she wasn't supposed to be doing them with.

Patsy reached over to hug her little sister and Ann roughly pushed her back. The next thing Patsy knew Ann was vomiting everywhere. Patsy jumped up and ran to get the garbage can. She shoved it under her. Ann reached for the can and at the same time managed to projectile the vomit onto Patsy's leg.

"Ugggh! Ann, what is wrong with you?" Ann kept throwing up and Patsy stood watching in amazement out of her reach.

"Who is that?" She heard her mother yell from downstairs. Patsy heard her feet coming up the stairs. Ann fell to the floor like a limp rag doll.

"Get me a towel please," Ann whispered. Patsy headed down the stairs to get her a warm towel. On her way, she passed her mother going up the stairs with a shocked look on her face.

"What is going on up here? Sounds like somebody up here throwing their guts up!"

"I'm sick," Ann said sounding weak.

"You better get well real quick and get this mess up. I swear. I can't keep anything nice in this house. If it ain't you destroying it then it's your daddy." Nadeen said to Ann as she headed back down the stairs.

Patsy heard her fussing at Ann as she headed back up the stairs with a warm towel and a glass of ginger ale. That always made the stomach settle. She waited until her mother had finished lashing out at Ann instead of helping her before she came fully into the room and gave Ann a towel to clean herself up.

Ann took the towel out of her hand and weakly said, "Thank you. I'm so glad to have you back home." Patsy managed to smile. "I'm glad to be back home with you and Josie."

"Let me clean this mess up. I haven't had to do this since you were a baby."

"Get out of here girl. I got this. Go on. I'm fine. I must be getting ready to have my period. You know how that is sometimes when it gets close. I'm gonna clean up and lay down for a few minutes." Ann said in a weak voice.

"Okay. I'm gonna go get Josie and get my stuff ready for school tomorrow." Patsy said. She was glad she and Ann were talking better. God was moving in some areas of her life.

"Patsy! Patsy come here!" Nadeen yelled from her room. Patsy went into her bedroom and there was Josie brushing her mother's hair and smiling.

Patsy stood at the end of Nadeen's bed. "Yes ma'am?" She said humbly.

"What's going on with your sister?" She asked her with a look on her face like Patsy was keeping a secret. "She been acting real strange over the last few weeks I can't quite put my finger on it, but she got something going on with her and it ain't of God.

"I can feel that it's not. Whatever it is, it's going to get her in a world of trouble around here. She been getting a little beside herself I done just about met my fed-up point with her. I know you all talk to each other, you sisters. Now you gonna tell me what is going on with her or do I have to find out at her expense? If I gotta get it out of her she won't like it." Nadeen said threateningly.

Patsy felt a chill run down her spine and her stomach did something it hadn't done in a long time now, it balled up. Patsy didn't know what to tell Nadeen but she knew she better speak fast.

"You hear me talking to you, girl!" Nadeen snapped at her. Patsy was beginning to feel sick in her stomach now.

"She said she is about to have her monthly visitor and it made her sick," Patsy told her mother.

Nadeen looked at her again the way she had a few minutes earlier when she saw Ann hanging over on the floor after throwing her guts up. "Well, whatever it is you better talk to her and remind her that her momma hasn't changed.

"I got to keep everything together around here since your daddy abandoned us and I don't have the time nor the strength to deal with disobedience and disrespect in my house and when I sense it, I will stomp it out, you got that?" Nadeen asked.

Patsy knew to answer quickly." Yes ma'am."

"Now make sure you give her my message cause it's my last warning. I got a feeling she's gonna make me put the rod of correction on her back real soon. Now take Josie out of here."

Later that night, Ann came back and got in the bed with Patsy and Josie. Patsy didn't say anything to her she just smiled to herself and softly said, "Thank you, Jesus." Under her breath. A few hours later, Nadeen bust into the room and flipped on the light.

"Ann? Ann wake up!" Ann rose up from the bed with a confused look on her face. Patsy was trying to focus her eyes on Nadeen's hands in case she needed to move out of her way fast. She was standing in the doorway talking to Ann.

"I'm taking you to the doctor. Something just told me to take you to the doctor. I'm gonna call tomorrow morning and make you an appointment. You hear me?

Ann was so crazy with sleep, she just answered her, "Yes ma'am" and her head fell back down on her pillow. Nadeen cut the light off and slammed the bedroom door as she walked back out. Patsy slept in alert mode the remainder of the night, scared Nadeen might come back swinging those three twisted branches that brought so much pain.

12

NADEEN CALLED DR. Rivers early the next morning. She scheduled Ann for a check-up that coming Friday. When Grandma Ruth called Nadeen told her she had gotten a message out of nowhere to take Ann to the doctor.

"Nah that wasn't out of nowhere. That's a message from the Holy Spirit believe that. I pray it's nothing serious." Grandma Ruth said.

"Probably something changing in her body. These girls these days eating all this junk food with hormones in it no telling." Nadeen said. "The voice I heard was so strange though that it sent a chill over me."

"You should have taken her when she first started into womanhood and I even told you that she should have been on some pills." Grandma Ruth said.

"I will not put my daughter on birth control pills! I'm not going to give her an excuse to go out and lay up. I'm surprised at you, Momma. You wouldn't have ever done that for me or Eva."

"Girl, you better wake up! Lessie Jean granddaughter twelve years old and got twins from sneaking around. She was letting them boys in through her bedroom window at night. They will do anything for these boy's attention."

"My girls fear me, Momma. I don't have to worry about that." Nadeen said.

"Yeah, but they don't fear these little boys musty tally-whackers. Now get your head out of your butt crack and get them both to the health department. You hear me?" Grandma Ruth said.

"Momma, I gotta go call Kenny and make sure his insurance still active. We haven't been to the doctor in a minute and I don't want to get in that office and have to pay out of my pocket. I'll call you later."

"That's fine, just remember what I said and keep your doors bolted." Grandma Ruth said as she hung up the phone.

*　　*　　*

As they headed down the street to the bus stop, Patsy talked to Ann. "You feeling better this morning, Ann?"

"A little bit. I don't really have an appetite though. I just had big glass of ginger ale that helped some," Ann told her sister.

"Momma gonna make you that doctor's appointment. Funny how she said a voice told her to do it." Patsy told Ann.

Ann seemed nonchalant about it. "That's her money. She want to use it up for no reason let her. I don't need to see a doctor. Just because I got sick on the stomach. You know I get to feelin' some kinda way when it gets ready to come on. I don't know why she trippin' talking about 'something' told her to make me a doctor appointment. That is crazy." Ann said. They both laughed.

When they made it back home later that day, Nadeen was sitting at the kitchen table with the phone in one hand and Josie in the other. "You all are just in time. I was just about to call Kenny and tell him to put some money in my account for this doctor's appointment. If I gotta take his daughter he gotta pay for it." She said. She found Kenny's cellphone number and called putting the phone on speaker. It rang a few times and just as she was about to hang the phone up a female voice answered.

"Hello?" the voice softly said. Nadeen pulled back and looked strangely at the phone. "I must have dialed the wrong number. Excuse me." Nadeen said and hung up the phone. "Let me try his house number." She carefully dialed the number again.

"Hello. The Simmons residence. Who's calling?" The female voice said again. Patsy looked at Ann and Ann looked at Patsy. Everybody seemed to be frozen in time. Nadeen had the phone in her lap looking at it with a frown on her face.

"Hello? Who is this?" the female voice asked again.

"This is Mrs. Simmons. May I speak to my husband please?" Nadeen asked, emphasizing "Mrs."

Oh, he your husband now? Patsy thought to herself. She and Ann must have been thinking the same thing the way they looked at each other at the same time. There was a brief moment of silence and then the voice spoke.

"Oh, hi. This is Sara, Kenny's church member. If you hold on a minute I'll be glad to get him for you. He's outside bringing some things in from my car." Nadeen looked at them and didn't say a word but you could see and feel the heat rising in her face.

"Hey, baby," Kenny answered sounding a little out of breath. She answered him slowly so that he could get the message in her tone without her having to say it with his company present.

"It seems you are busy taking care of more important business so maybe the girls and I need to call back when you have time for us."

"No. I'm not too busy to talk. I'm surprised to hear from you. Is everything okay with you and the girls?" He asked. "That was my church member, Sara, from back home. She was just stopping by to bring me the books for our Sunday School Class. She just caught the phone for me." He said without Nadeen even asking because he knew that Nadeen was hot about it just by the tone of her voice.

"You're a grown man, Kenny. What you do is between you and God. As I recall, you two supposed to be so close lately. Anyway, I called to make sure you still had your children on your insurance. I gotta take Ann to the doctor this Friday. I don't want any surprises, or should I say any more surprises." She said.

Kenny caught that meaning real quick.

"All of you are still covered on my insurance policy," Kenny responded.

"Well, it's good to know some things haven't changed. The girls and I have had enough of that lately. I'll let you get back to more important things." She said.

"Bringing in Sunday School books is not more important than talking to you and the girls Nadeen. Why Ann going to the doctor what's wrong? Something happen to her?" He asked.

"Nothing but the fact that she's growing up Kenny. Girls' bodies start changing at her age. She just need a wellness check-up that's all. If you had time you would call her and find out for yourself." Nadeen replied.

"I do call, Nadeen. We both know you answer the phone when you want to. Can I talk to the girls?" He asked. Nadeen wasn't having it. She didn't appreciate Sara answering his phone and she wanted him to know it.

"They busy right now. Call back when your company is gone if that's not too late and make sure you put some money in my account tomorrow to cover your daughter's co-pay."

Before Kenny could respond Nadeen hung up the phone.

"Like I told y'all before, God ain't had nothing to do with Kenny Simmons abandoning us. He got a whole different agenda." Patsy and Ann both knew not to answer.

Nadeen got up from the table, went to her room, and turned her gospel music up as high as it would go. This meant she was in an unholy mood and it was best to leave her alone.

*   *   *

Kenny was going to have to wait a few days before he called back. He knew Nadeen was cussin' mad. Sara hadn't meant any harm by answering the phone. She was just being helpful.

"Kenny, everything okay at home?" Sara asked. Her voice sure was nice and sweet. Soft like a summer breeze.

"Yes, Sister everything is fine. My daughter Ann just gotta go have herself a check-up. She's growing up you know becoming a young lady and her body is changing. I leave all that up to Nadeen to handle. I just make sure she has medical coverage." He said.

Sara laughed. He was such a fine, handsome, and God-fearing man. *How could his wife let such a blessing of a man get away?* Sara thought to herself. Well, Pastor Mack always said if you didn't take care of the blessings God gave you then he would give them to someone else and Sara believed she was that someone else.

This whole thing had to be a set up by God. Only God would have fixed it where she was able to get a job in the same city as Kenny. God knew her heart and he had answered her desire to have him in her life as more than a friend. She knew the very first time she met him back home at Deliverance Rock that he was special, he stole her heart when she saw him humble himself before the Lord at the altar. Her heart melted at the sight of him bent down in agony crying out the name of the Lord. She knew then he was her Boaz.

"Kenny that macaroni and cheese would taste mighty good right now. If you ready I'll make us a plate of it and we can watch the service from last Sunday together. I'm so glad to have a friendly face to keep me company in this big city." Sara said.

Kenny smiled. Sarah sure was sweet but she was going to have to be kept at a distance. It was what was best for the both of them.

1 3

IT WAS A long night for Nadeen. She tossed, turned, and cussed all through the night. If she could have gotten her hands on Kenny Simmons, she would have busted his head to the white meat trying to play her for a fool. She knew better than this girl being a "friend." She answered his phone. What kind of female friend answers the phone of a married man and what married man would let her? Kenny was trying to get back at her for going to the arms of Brother Ryan that's what he was doing.

He made her go into the arms of Brother Ryan. He pushed her and pushed her until her flesh won out. She was a good Christian woman. She never meant to be side-tracked by Brother Ryan but at the time Kenny had given the devil an opening and he came right in and sat on down in the form of a prayer partner.

He had offered her shelter from the emotional storm Kenny always managed to stir up inside of her. He would hold her in his arms and comfort her. He would pray with her and encourage her with the scriptures. Somehow his lips managed to meet hers after she came to him complaining about Kenny being out all night. She was seeking an ear to hear and arms to understand. She found it in him. She was too tired to fight. He woke her body up and made her feel a joy and happiness she had not felt in a few years.

God knew she deserved to be happy. He knew Kenny had not been the husband he was supposed to be. Brother Ryan was supposed to be her new beginning, he just didn't have the faith to follow through with her and go into a new promise land so he looked back and turned all of their dreams into salt, he got afraid and turned back to what was familiar to him and left Nadeen standing with a broken husband and a broken home. She still had not been able to forgive him for turning back but she would continue forward alone if necessary.

She decided that she would give Kenny the chance to redeem himself in her eyes. After all, it was because of his actions that she'd committed her actions. She remembered he had told her he forgave her and she told him he needed to be forgiving himself for driving her to the point she needed someone to do his job. A few weeks later, Ann had to stand her ground at school and the next thing Nadeen knew he'd packed his bags and left.

He left his girls, his home, and his wife—all the things he told her he loved—and now it seemed that he was going to leave their marriage. He had allowed another woman to answer his phone and speak to her, this said to her that he was trying to get back at her for what she had done. How could he have been so disrespectful? How could he have played with her and God by pretending he was going to change? This was one of those times she wished she had Dhmonique around to tell her what just happened. Dhmonique kept her confidence and allowed her to be herself.

*   *   *

Patsy and Ann eased out of the door headed to school the next morning. They knew Nadeen had been tossing and turning all night. She confused them. She didn't seem to want Kenny yet she was mad because she thought somebody else did. It was crazy to them. Nadeen was crazy to them. Just before they made it to their bus stop Patsy gave Ann a warning.

"Ann, you need to be on your best behavior these next couple of days. Your momma is on fire about that lady answering your daddy's phone yesterday," Patsy said.

"Oh, when stuff go down he my daddy, huh?" Ann said.

"Girl, stop. You know what I'm saying. Heed the warning, okay?" Patsy said trying to keep a serious look on her face.

"Patsy. I have a mind and a voice and I need to be allowed to use them. I'm so tired of being on lockdown for doing nothing. I'm young and should be out having fun like all my other friends. But instead, I have to tiptoe 24/7 so she won't come close to killing me when she's upset," she said. "It's Daddy she really mad at but she taking it out on us."

As the bus pulled up for them to board, Patsy said to her, "That's true but if you keep on trying your momma, you gone be forever young six and a half feet under."

Ann turned up her lip at Patsy's comment. "Whatever. Anywhere is better than being in that house." She said as she sat down next to her.

Her comment saddened Patsy. She was always afraid that the next time Ann got a desire to cut herself would be her last. The only good thing Patsy could say about this mystery guy she was fooling with was that whatever he was doing, it had distracted Ann from cutting her body to ribbons, and for that small thing, Patsy was grateful.

When they made it home after school, Nadeen was gone. Mrs. Wilson was sitting on her front porch with Josie in her lap eating what looked like gumbo.

"Girls, your momma went to the church to type up the programs for service on Sunday. She ask me to watch your sister till you got home." She said as she dipped the spoon back in the bowl and brought it up to Josie's open mouth. Josie was so busy eating; she didn't pay them any attention.

Ann reached out to take her from Mrs. Wilson and the smell of the food hit her nose. As she turned to walk down the stairs her foot hit the first step and Ann projectile vomited across the steps and Mrs. Wilson's potted plants. She quickly put Josie on the ground. Mrs. Wilson jumped up screaming.

"Oh, my Lord!"

Ann went to her knees and kept throwing up on all fours. Mrs. Wilson ran in the house and got a towel for Ann to wipe her face. Ann looked up at her and thanked her for the towel. She had vomit all over her clothes.

"Baby what is wrong with you?" Mrs. Wilson asked looking worried. "You got a stomach bug or something?" She asked. "You better get to the doctor soon. Your momma told me she set an appointment for you on this Friday but the way you throwing up I don't think you gonna make it. I'm gonna call her and see if she can take you to see the doctor today." Mrs. Wilson said turning to go back inside.

Ann jumped up and ran behind Mrs. Wilson. "No! No, Mrs. Wilson don't do that! Please." She begged. "She already gonna be mad about me messing up your pretty flowers and my school clothes."

Mrs. Wilson looked pitifully at Ann. "Well, baby you got something bad going on inside of you the way you was throwing your guts up on my front steps."

"I think I just ate too many burritos at school today. I was having a stomach ache before we got over here but I thought I would make it home before it got worse. That's all it was, I promise." Ann said pleadingly.

Mrs. Wilson stared at her for a minute then she decided not to call Nadeen at the church. "You need to go right home and settle your stomach." Mrs. Wilson said.

"I'm going," Ann said as she tried to wipe her clothes clean. Patsy took Josie by the hand and walked across the street staring at Ann.

"This the second time you did that Ann. If you got some type of virus me and Josie don't want to get it. You should've gone to the doctor like yesterday the way you just dumped your guts in Mrs. Wilson's yard." Patsy said.

Ann ignored her and went in the house. She headed straight to the shower. When she came out, she went to bed for the rest of the night.

When Nadeen made it home she came through the door calling Ann's name. "Ann? Ann where are you!" She yelled on her way up the stairs to Ann's room. She flung the door open to see Ann laying under the covers.

Ann looked up from her pillow at her mother standing in the doorway.

"Girl, what is wrong with you? You got a flu bug or something? Mrs. Wilson told me you messed her porch up this afternoon when you got home. I need to get you to a doctor fast cause I don't want you giving that mess to Josie. My baby girl been through enough already in her little life. I don't want her back up at that hospital with tubes coming out of her nose," Nadeen said as she stood in the doorway gripping the doorknob.

"I think I got food poisoning from lunch. I been feeling bad all day," Ann said putting her hand over her stomach.

"If you felt bad why didn't you call your grandmother or Aunt to come and get you? Why you go the whole day then get here and shame me in front of our neighbors?" Nadeen asked.

"It wasn't that bad until I smelled that junk Mrs. Wilson had in her cup. It smelled like a swamp," Ann said as she frowned remembering the smell.

"Probably some alligator or possum she cooked up for her husband. That man hunts every tail but his wife's yet she drinks his dirty bathwater. I hope she wasn't giving that to my baby." Nadeen said.

"Every drop," Ann said and laughed softly.

Just then Nadeen's cell phone buzzed. "I hope this isn't work. I just got home."

She pulled out her cell phone and started checking her messages. After the very first one, she looked up at Ann, "Looks like we gonna have to reschedule your check-up. The nurse left me a message that the doctor had to schedule a patient for a procedure this Friday morning. I gotta call her and set a new date."

Ann looked relieved a bit. "I won't need an appointment. I'll be fine. I just need to lay down for a minute. I don't have any homework tonight." She told Nadeen who turned and headed back down the hall quickly.

"You don't get to decide that, Ann Simmons. I do. I'm the momma. What I say go and I say you goin'." Nadeen said as she turned around and looked down the stairs.

"Patsy, I don't smell any food cooking in that kitchen why is that?

"I made grill cheese sandwiches today," Patsy said. Me and Josie already ate. Ann was too sick. You want me to fix you one?" She asked humbly.

"No. I don't. I had a nice, juicy steak courtesy of the Men's Outreach Ministry tonight. I was on my way out the door and one of the Brothers begged me to go, said he had just gotten engaged and he wanted to get some advice from an older and wiser woman other than his mother. He said he could tell I had that." Nadeen said with a smile on her face.

"See when you a God-fearing Woman, everybody can see it except the ungodly husband you married to." She said as she scrolled through her cell phone messages.

The next sound Patsy heard was the doorbell.

"Somebody at the door." She yelled up the stairs to her mother.

"They don't need to be. I just got home. I'm tired and I don't want no uninvited company. See who it is and tell them I'm in the shower." Nadeen said heading to her bedroom to lock the door and hide out.

Patsy went to the front door; it was her Aunt Eva and Grandma

Ruth. Aunt Eva and her Momma must have made up after Aunt Eva hurt her feelings bringing up Dhmonique.

"Hey, baby. How you?" Her Grandma Ruth said walking up in the house and kissing her on her jaw. Eva walked in slowly behind her.

"I'm good," Patsy replied hugging her grandmother. "Hey, Aunt Eva."

"Hey, Niece," Eva said

"Where your momma at? Me and your aunt wanted to come through and check on y'all since we was on this side of town." Grandma Ruth said as she walked past her looking down the hall towards Nadeen's bedroom.

"She upstairs with Ann," Patsy said.

"Doing what?" Eva asked.

"She had a little issue in Mrs. Wilson yard today," Patsy said

"An issue? What kind of issue?" Eva asked.

"She been having stomach problems lately," Patsy said. Eva and her grandmother both looked at each other as they sat at the kitchen table.

"Nadeen! Nadeen come here." Grandma Ruth yelled. "I know you hear me and your sister up in here."

A few minutes later Nadeen appeared in the hallway with a ledger and calculator in her hand. She didn't even look at Eva.

"Momma, what you need? I just got home. I need to work on something for Pastor and I'm about to get ready for work tomorrow." She said folding her hands as she let out a sigh. Something told Patsy to walk off and she did just that.

"I didn't ask you about what you were doing, chile, I came to see about my grandbabies. You made that appointment for Ann yet? We saw Mrs. Wilson outside she told us about what happened today." Grandma Ruth said. She didn't want to bring any trouble to Patsy for mentioning it to them.

"I wish everybody would stay out of me and my children's business," Nadeen said.

"You got a hemorrhoid up your butt or something girl? You switching around here like you irritated."

"Momma, I got things to do before I lay down for the night," Nadeen said heading to the kitchen table to sit down. "I need to balance the church financial records, so I don't have time to visit with you and your daughter," Nadeen said as she sat down with her hands in her lap.

"Really? Me and my daughter, huh? She not your blood too?" Grandma Ruth said looking at Nadeen as she pointed back at Eva. Nadeen didn't respond.

Grandma Ruth stood up from her chair and walked over to Nadeen. She looked at the top of her head.

"I know you hear me talking to you. I asked you a question. You sitting here talking about doing work for your Pastor but Kenny can't get you to fix him a hot bowl of piss if he wanted it. If you don't want us to come in your house just say it. We can do just like your husband and leave," she said to Nadeen.

Unfortunately, right at that minute. Josie came running down the hall screaming and crying with Patsy behind her. Nadeen ignored her mother standing next to her and looked at her soon-to-be-victim of the rage boiling inside of her.

She slammed her hand down on the table so hard the calculator she was using fell to the floor. "Patsy! What is wrong with her?" She yelled.

"She sleepy and she's mean. I had to pop her legs cause she came up to me and bit my thigh."

"You did what?" Nadeen asked sitting back in her chair while she tilted her head. "I know you didn't put your hands on nothing that came out of my womb up in my house. Who you think you are? You got some children? I'm that child's momma. She do what I say and I'm the only one that can put my hands on her is that clear?" She screamed at her oldest daughter releasing the anger she meant for her mother.

"Yes ma'am," Patsy said as she picked up Josie and rocked her to make her stop crying.

"I know you ain't trippin' about a little pop on the leg as much as you be swinging blows up in here, from the children to your husband," Eva looked over at her sister and said.

Nadeen stood up at that comment, pushed the kitchen table back, and pointed at the front door. "Eva you and Momma better walk out my door right now before I do something I might regret up in here," Nadeen said, placing her hand on the knife that was wrapped neatly in the napkin on the kitchen table.

Grandma Ruth saw her and snatched her wrist with the knife in it. Her sudden move startled Nadeen and Patsy too. Patsy froze. Grandma Ruth pushed Nadeen away from the table and slammed her up against the kitchen wall. She got directly up in her face and pointed towards Patsy first then Eva.

"Now that one standing in that hallway may be yours but the one over here that you think you about to raise your hand to, she mine. Do you understand that? She came out of my womb and before I allow you or anybody else to put a hand on her I will personally see to it that you lose that hand. Is that clear?"

"I'm tired of you thinking you run everything and everyone from the church to the household around here. I'm tired of you beating on my grandchildren and my son-in-law like you some lunatic yielding a whip. You drop that knife right now or I will bust all of your teeth out of your mouth with it and you won't be able to smile in Pastor Craig's face next Sunday."

Patsy saw the tears pooling in her mother's eyes and slowly backed out of the room. Eva was standing with a smirk on her face.

"Drop that knife before I make you eat it!" Grandma Ruth said putting her nails into Nadeen's wrist.

Nadeen slowly released the knife and cut her eyes over at Eva. She was full of hate at that very moment. Hate and shame. She remembered the many times she had been in this same situation growing up and the many times she had taken the abuse from her mother, abuse she believed was meant for somebody else that had pissed her off way before she made it home to them.

Nadeen did something next she knew she shouldn't have but she believed she had to for the sake of keeping her house in order. She leaned towards her mother and pushed her back.

"Momma get off of me! This is my house, not yours! I run this! I'm a grown woman. You and Eva both get out my house right now!"

Her mother looked at her in disbelief. "Lord have mercy!" Eva said as she started towards them to grab her mother. Patsy came running back up the hallway. Eva put her hand on her mother's shoulder and Ruth pushed it away she shoved Nadeen to the ground.

"Don't do it Momma! Don't do it with these babies in this house." Eva begged as she tried to pull her mother back.

"Get off me Eva! This heifer done met her match today." Grandma Ruth said pushing Eva's hand off of her shoulder.

Before anybody knew what was happening, she started stomping her. Nadeen balled up like a child and started screaming.

"What's going on?" Ann said as she ran into the kitchen. She couldn't believe what she saw, her grandmother was over her mother stomping her. Ann froze in fear watching the scene unfold.

"I should have stomped the hell out of you a long time ago and you wouldn't be causing so much up in this house right now! I should have beat the devil out of you but your daddy kept getting in the way. He kept stopping me from straightening you out the way I really needed to and now we got a psycho for a church usher, a momma, and a wife!" Grandma Ruth yelled as she stomped her daughter.

It took Patsy and Eva to pull her away from Nadeen. She was as strong as a mule pulling a plow. "Grandma! Grandma, please stop! Stop! You hurting Momma!" Patsy yelled. She pulled with all the strength she had, to get her off of her mother.

"Momma! Momma come on! Come on and let's go! We didn't come over here for this. You and Nadeen both done acted up in front of these girls enough today," Eva said out of breath from trying to get her and her foot away from Nadeen.

"I should have done it long before now. If I had then maybe my son-in-law would still be here and my granddaughters wouldn't be so afraid all the time." Grandma Ruth was breathing hard and her foot was in the air about to strike Nadeen one more time when Eva finally got some distance between her foot and Nadeen's stomach.

Patsy looked at her mother on the floor halfway under her kitchen table whimpering. Grandma Ruth glanced at her grand-daughters and started to the door still breathing hard and trying to fix her dress.

"Eva, grab my purse off that table, and let's go! That heifer done made me come up in here and regress back to my old ways! Kenny should have straightened her a long time ago. I'm tired of her beating on my grandbabies and now she think she gone jump up in my face? The day she do it again will be the day Satan come to town with a tank top on." She said as Eva pushed her out the front door.

Eva glanced at her nieces. "Come get this door. Lord Jesus. Y'all go see about my crazy sister. She done officially lost her mind today coming up against momma."

Patsy stooped down to the floor and whispered. "Momma, you want me to help you up?" She knew her mother was embarrassed and hurt. Patsy had never seen her this way.

"No. Just go to your room and leave me alone. I can get up on my own. I'm fine just get away from me," Nadeen moaned.

Patsy turned towards Ann; she was standing there smiling.

As wrong as it might have been, for those few minutes, Ann felt avenged for all the times her mother abused her out of her anger for Kenny and left her crying on the floor. She felt good that her Grandmother had put her mother in check in her own house. It *was* wrong, but for the moment Ann felt it was right and long overdue.

Patsy shook her head and softly whispered to her sister "Ann. You wrong." Ann walked past her sister on her way back upstairs. "I'm just expressing myself the way you want to." She whispered back.

14

NOT A SOUND was heard the next morning. Everybody tip-toed around the house. Nadeen was in a rattlesnake mood when she went to her room last night and this was the kind of environment when bad things happen. Eva had called later that night and tried to apologize to her but she told her she didn't want to hear it and slammed the phone down. Patsy left Josie asleep in their bed while her and Ann got ready for school. They even skipped breakfast.

They were a distance away from the house before they even brought it up.

"Ooooh wait until Kenny hears about yesterday. He is gonna really need a drink. I can't believe Grandma snapped like that." Ann said with a look of excitement in her eye.

"Well, Daddy said Grandma had another side to her and I guess we saw it. Really we been seeing it. It's in your momma." Patsy said to Ann.

"That ain't all in her today," Ann said. "She got Grandma footprint in her navel this morning." She and Patsy both knew it wasn't funny but they both laughed.

"Lord please forgive us," Patsy said. The bus pulled up and they boarded. Ann went straight to the back and sat down next to Ralph.

Patsy was confused. One day she didn't want him breathing on her and the next day she all up under him

Ann sat down next to him, smiled, and said, "Good morning. You got room for me?" in a sweet, flirtatious voice. Ralph could barely stop smiling long enough to stutter his reply out of his mouth.

Patsy sat behind them puzzled. *What was Ann up to?* Surely she had not just woken up one morning and decided to forgive and forget, not after the hard time she had been giving Ralph. She was reminding Patsy of the way Nadeen acted when she wanted something from Kenny. She knew how to smile at him, show a little cleavage, wear her hair down the way he liked, and act real sweet just like Ann was doing now with Ralph.

When the bus stopped at their school, Ralph got up behind Ann, turned to Patsy, and said,

"My momma told me prayer changes things." He walked off the bus smiling and following Ann's every move. He even took her books for her.

Patsy told Dustin about it when she saw him later that morning. "I guess my sister has let Ralph back in her good graces." Patsy told him.

"Why? What happened?" Dustin asked as he walked her class with his arm around her. "She was being extra sweet to him on the bus this morning. And just like my daddy does when my momma shows him a little momentary kindness, he just ate it up."

Dustin laughed, "Well you might be watching a storm forming, stay woke with that."

"I know right." Patsy answered.

"Like mother, like daughter. Sometimes yet they are oil and water."

Sandra called Patsy a few days later on the cell phone she kept secretly. "Hey, Patsy. What's up?" She asked.

Patsy knew when she heard that question, Sandra was about to tell her some gossip or about to get into something she didn't need to. Patsy braced herself.

"Nothing in my life. What's up with you?" Patsy asked.

"I'm just lovin' my boo and our sweet little baby boy." She said. "Hey. I saw Ann the other day when I went to pick up my cousin from school, you know my cousin Boogie-Man, remember him?" Sandra asked.

Patsy remembered. He was the one that told Sandra Ann was skipping some classes with some guy. "Yeah, I remember him. Why?" Patsy asked.

"I was just asking. How your Sister doin'?" Sandra asked.

Patsy wondered where this was going. "She fine. Why you ask?" Patsy asked Sandra.

"She must not be playing basketball anymore?" Sandra asked.

"Yeah, she still plays. You know she not practicing right now. She been sick off and on." Patsy said. Sandra just kind of hummed in the phone.

"Nadeen must be feeding y'all real good over there. Ann look like she done picked up some weight. You noticed that?" Sandra asked. Patsy just wanted her to get to the point. What did she want?

"No Sandra. I haven't noticed. She looks the same to me. Why you asking about Ann anyway?" Patsy asked, irritated. Sandra must have picked up on it. She cut the conversation short.

"Just checkin' on her. She like my little sister too, you know. Look. I gotta go. My baby need his diaper changed. I'll call you later or see you at school tomorrow." Sandra said, immediately hanging the phone up.

Patsy didn't feel right about this conversation, it wasn't over. She knew her friend. There was something on her mind and she wanted to get it out.

* * *

At the end of the week, Ann and Patsy were sitting in the room they use to share together until Ann decided she needed more space and started staying in what they nick-named Kenny's prison cell upstairs. Ann pulled out a beautiful platinum, diamond solitaire ring, Patsy heard herself gasp.

"Ann where did you get that ring? It's beautiful."

Ann was smiling really big as she put it on her finger and looked at it from different angles. "Ralph gave it to me. You know he was helping his brother cut yards over the summer and he saved up his money. He said he wanted to show me how much he loves me. His brother bought it for him from a pawn shop but I don't care it's beautiful. I don't think it's the real deal but that's okay." Ann said.

The ring glittered brightly as the light hit it.

"Ann how you gonna hide that from Nadeen? You know she's not playing when she says she'll break our necks if she finds out we call ourselves having a boyfriend. Why do you think I keep Dustin locked down? If Nadeen finds out about Ralph and that ring you gonna have to leave the state. You play with the skin on your behind too much for me, little sister."

"Stop hatin' on my ring. I can't help Dustin hasn't bought yours yet. You two been together forever and now he got that money from his momma burial insurance and you still just wearing a necklace," Ann said.

Patsy wanted to choke her then.

"Anyway. It's just a promise ring."

Patsy looked her little sister straight in her excited little brown eyes and said to her, "At your age, the only man's promises you need to be accepting and believing is the promises of Jesus Christ."

Ann put her hands on her hips and twisted her neck. "Your attitude is real unholy, Patsy. Real unholy. Ralph put a ring on it, now when is your man gonna do the same?"

"Ann, this is not about which one of us has a ring. This is about keeping your neck from being broken if Nadeen finds that ring or finds out about Ralph. You having sex with Ralph?" Patsy asked.

Ann looked at her in disbelief. "Why you all up in my business like that big sister? If I am, I'm not going to be giving you the details. That's private. What you and Dustin doin' other than sweatin' over each other and trying to stay hydrated." Ann laughed.

Your ring is cute and I'm glad for you, but you better be careful that's all I'm saying. You remind me of Nadeen with Kenny when she wants something from him. Once she gets it, she kicks him to the curb. You better not be playing with that boy, Ann. He seems to really like you." Patsy told her sister.

Ann got up off the bed, put the ring in her pocket.

"I got this Patsy." She said as she walked out the bedroom door. Josie just sat on the bed looking at Patsy like, "What was that all about?"

Sunday rolled back around fast. Kenny called as he usually did on Sunday mornings. He didn't talk long.

"Hey, baby. I just wanted to talk to you girls to tell you I love you and check on Ann. She feeling better?" He asked.

"A little," Patsy said. "That's good. I been dreaming about her every night this week. She keeps tossing and turning in my dreams saying she's sorry. Eva is in my dream too on her knees with blood coming out of her eyes. It's crazy." Kenny said.

Ann yanked the phone from her. "Hey, Daddy. What's up?"

"I'm headed out for church just checking in with you all. Let me know how your doctor's appointment goes. I can send you some money if you need a prescription filled or something just let me know," Kenny said.

"Okay. We gotta go now we'll call you later." Ann said and hung up the phone.

Patsy just walked out the room. It was too early. She didn't have the energy for Ann this morning.

Patsy wanted to get back to Deliverance Rock Church and have some real praise and worship with Pastor Mack instead of the disco song festival at Greater Trials. Reverend Craig had changed a lot of things in the church since his first wife died.

She loved the old school praise and worship songs, but First Lady Champagne Porter liked to have music she could twist to and pop her fingers. The choir sounded more like the club than the church. They appealed to the flesh instead of your faults in Patsy's opinion. She missed the songs that made you want to lay it all at the altar. The music that made you ashamed for whatever you'd done or said before you got to church on Sunday morning. Patsy didn't believe any strongholds could be broken in Greater Trials. But no matter how bad she didn't want to go, that is where she was headed every Sunday.

It was First Sunday. They couldn't be late. Nadeen wanted everyone in place on time. She helped distribute the communion and she took that seriously. No talking or laughing when you approached her for your juice and your wafer.

Once a woman was laughing when she got to Nadeen for communion. Nadeen stood and covered the container with the communion wafers and juice with her spotless white gloves. She looked at the woman like she wanted to slap her and wouldn't move until the woman stopped snickering and asked Nadeen to forgive her.

Nadeen cut her a nasty look, removed her gloved hand from the communion bowl and allowed the woman to take communion. No one else said a word during communion after that. When they pulled up to the parking lot Nadeen passed everybody a dollar, kissed Josie on the jaw, and told everybody to get out.

They dropped Josie off in the nursery and headed to their different classes. Ralph was standing next to the door opening of Ann's class smiling as she walked up. He spoke to Patsy and went in behind Ann. Patsy saw him sit next to Ann. *Looking at her from the side she did look a little thick*, Patsy thought to herself. On her way to her room, she saw Nadeen walking fast. She was counting tithe envelopes to take back upstairs and put in the sanctuary. A woman came walking past them both at a quick pace and bumped into Nadeen. The tithe envelopes fell to the ground.

The woman apologized and bent down to pick them up. Nadeen never moved. She stood there and waited. Patsy could see the muscles in Nadeen's jaw tighten. The woman quickly picked up the envelopes and gave them neatly back to her.

"I'm so sorry about that. I was trying to get back upstairs to wait on my sister. She coming to fellowship with me today." She said. She glanced at the tag on Nadeen's dress. She extended her hand to Nadeen but Nadeen just smiled and held the tithe envelopes tighter.

"Hi. You must be Brother Kenny's wife. My name's Marjorie. I'm Sara's aunt. She friends with your husband, they use to go to Deliverance Rock together when he was here and looks like they done bumped into each other again in Miami." She smiled more broadly.

Patsy started to squeeze by the lady. She could see the heat coming from Nadeen's face.

"He is such a good man and has been such a help to my niece. She speaks so highly of him. I was worried about her moving out there at first but when Pastor Mack said Kenny was there working and he got him in touch with her I knew she would be all right. He told me you went to church here. I'll have to tell him I met you."

She paused a minute, Nadeen answered. "Be blessed."

"You too, Sister." The woman said and walked off. God knew the best place for that conversation to take place. Patsy thought to herself.

Nadeen looked Patsy in the eye. She didn't have to say a word. Patsy already knew by the look on her face she didn't appreciate what she'd just heard.

Patsy couldn't focus in Sunday School after the encounter in the hallway with Nadeen and Sara's aunt. She told her teacher she had to go to the restroom and ran out the door. She headed down the hallway towards Ann's classroom. As she got closer to the Pastor's study, she thought she heard loud voices. Two males and a woman. The door opened and David walked out. He looked mad.

He glanced at her and kept walking past her. Usually, he had something nasty or flirtatious to say. Patsy slowed down as she neared the Pastor's door to his study. She heard First Lady Champagne screaming, "You worrying about the wrong thing when it comes to me and Brother David. He was doing a little harmless flirting that's all. You did far worse or have you forgotten?" Patsy heard Champagne ask Pastor Craig.

"Champagne you know my love for my first wife had been long gone when I met you. It was just a matter of time before I left her. Her getting sick just caused things to take place another way. It was God's will. That has nothing to do with what I'm asking you about." Pastor Craig said sounding like he was exasperated.

"I know you and your sister didn't grow up with a man in your house so you might have some self-esteem issues but just know I got enough love for you. There ain't no need for you to even entertain another man's compliment." Pastor Craig told his wife. "I can be a husband to you and a father figure to Daphne. I can tell she needs one."

Champagne titled her head back and laughed. "Can you now? You can tell she needs a Father figure? Well while you getting revelations why don't you tell me who her daddy is? Can you tell me that? Since she needs one so bad where is the one that she should have had in her life?" Champagne yelled at her husband.

"If she doesn't know, why do you think I would? This conversation has gotten way out of hand. I need to prepare for my sermon this morning not argue with my wife about things that don't matter." Pastor Craig said searching his desk for his glasses and his sermon.

"It's you! Since you wanna pretend you don't know who her daddy is and you seem to think she needs him so bad, go be it."

"Champagne, this has gone too far. You letting the enemy use you now. It's crossing over into disrespect and what I won't have is my wife disrespecting me. You need to go and get yourself together and let me do the same."

"Disrespect? Disrespect is what you did to my momma and daddy's relationship. You think I'm kidding with you? I'm not. You're my sister Daphne's daddy! You jack-leg, sneaky, hypocritical dog in heat! You hiding behind a preacher's robe rubbing up between the legs of other women in your congregation just like you did with me!"

Pastor Craig felt his mouth go dry and his chest started to tighten. "Baby what are you talking about? What's gotten into you?" He asked his wife.

Patsy froze. What was Champagne saying to Reverend Craig? She was talking crazy. Patsy tried to move her feet but she couldn't.

"Years ago you took advantage of my momma in this church on the floor of this very office! She was engaged to my daddy but you just had to have her! You wouldn't stop till you filled her belly with a baby and then you disappeared! You changed your phone number and you changed her life! My daddy left her standing at the altar in her wedding dress! Did you know that? She'd finally got up the nerve to tell him that the baby she was carrying wasn't his, he told her he had enough love for the both of them and it didn't matter but on their wedding date he couldn't do it. He just couldn't marry her knowing she'd been with someone else. My mother told me they were each other's first. They'd been together since high school.

You used her until you knocked her up and then you thought you could slither back to your happy life with your first wife. You made my momma an outcast in our family! Nobody wanted her around when they found out she was pregnant by another man. My grandmomma was too ashamed to tell anybody that my momma said she didn't know who Daphne's daddy was, but she did know!

"You never even knew who I was did you? You laid with me every night not even recognizing my face, but I never forgot yours. I remember all the times you came over when my daddy was away working offshore. I remember you bribing me with your church peppermints to keep me quiet and send me to my room so you could 'talk' with my mother.

"You made her keep a dirty secret. You never once came to see Daphne. You walked away as though she was going to disappear. She has no ideas you are her father but all of that changes today! Today I tell my baby sister who her daddy is and I tell his congregation!" Champagne Porter said with a wicked smirk on her face and her arms folded in satisfaction.

Patsy heard Pastor Craig moan, "Oh my God! No! No, you can't it will destroy me! This can't be true. She can't be mine. You can't be...I'm up for Church Bishop next year you can't do this to me!" Pastor Craig said putting his hand on his chest.

"Oh, but I can, she is, and I will dear husband," Champagne said as she picked up her purse to walk out of his office. "I'm headed to the pulpit to make the announcement right after I tell my poor sister her long lost, dead-beat daddy has been found and by the way, you be sure to get her CashApp tag, because you owe her a lot of back child support." Champagne said as she laughed at the look of horror on her husband's face.

The next thing Patsy heard was things falling onto the floor with a loud thump then she heard Pastor Craig say "Champagne, baby, baby you can't do this to me! You my wife! I never meant to hurt anybody! I risked my marriage to be with you! I'm sorry. Don't do this to me. You'll destroy us!"

"There was never an *us* Pastor! There was just me and my desire to do what my mother couldn't do, and that was to expose you for the wolf you are! I care nothing about destroying you. You destroyed mine, my sister's, and my mother's life. My daddy left us when he left her. You see this letter? This letter is to you from my momma!

She wrote it the last few weeks of her life. She gave it to me and told me to give it to you when she passed. She must have known I was going to read it! She had to know that!" Champagne screamed. "This letter says that Daphne is your daughter. My mother hated that you didn't want to claim her or my sister after she lost so much. She was too ashamed to tell her momma it was her own Pastor that was impregnating her and had cost her my daddy's love.

"She lived her life afraid of going to hell for being seduced by a preacher that was more on fire for her than he was for the gospel!"

Pastor Craig's voice thundered in his office. "Why are you doing this Champagne? Who put you up to this!" He yelled falling back against the wall and crashing to the floor

"You took my momma's dignity and her chance at having a marriage of her own!" Champagne screamed. "And today I'm going to take everything that my mother should have had! After all, I already got your last name."

Patsy heard a thump against the wall, then she heard Pastor Craig groan like a wounded animal. Champagne slung the door open. She met Patsy's eyes and Patsy saw hate. She ran past her and started hollering "Somebody help me! It's Pastor! He's having a heart attack! My husband is having a heart attack!"

The doors of the Sunday School classroom flew open people started running towards the Pastor's Study. Patsy just stood still. It felt like she was in a horror movie. Nadeen was the first one down the stairs from the sanctuary. "Pastor! Oh, sweet Jesus, Pastor! Pastor you okay!" She yelled running towards the Pastor's Study.

People were knocking each other over trying to get down the stairs. David went in and started CPR on him until the ambulance arrived. When the EMTs got to Pastor Craig, he was no longer breathing. They put him on a stretcher, covered his face, and rolled him out past his congregation. Champagne Porter put on a performance worthy of an Academy Award. She screamed with tears running down her face.

"Baby please wake up! Wake up don't you leave me now. I can't go on without you. I love you. Please get up!" She cried as the church members tried to hold her to keep her from running behind the stretcher that carried her deceased husband.

Patsy felt like she was about to faint. Ann got sick and threw up in a corner. Nadeen grabbed Josie out of the nursery and with tears running down her eyes told Ann and Patsy to go to the car and take Josie with them. Everyone stood around in shock. Everyone that is but Daphne. Patsy passed Daphne and looked into her eyes.

"Something happened to my Sister's husband?" She asked with a blank look on her face. Patsy couldn't take it anymore she ran to the car. She needed a fresh wind.

Nadeen just cried and called on the name of Jesus all the way home while her cellphone kept blowing up. When they walked through the door, the house phone was ringing off the hook. Nadeen instructed no one was to answer it. The answering machine came on and it was Grandma Ruth. She sounded upset and told Nadeen to call her soon as she made it in. Eva had left a message asking her where she was.

Nadeen went to her room and closed the door. Patsy, Ann, and Josie all went to their room and sat on the bed. Patsy just stared at the carpet in disbelief. She was trying to put everything together in her mind. This just had to be a dream. She was hoping God would wake her up. This felt too real to deal with. Ann just laid down on the bed and rocked Josie. She didn't know what to say either.

Patsy felt the cell phone in her purse vibrating. She pulled it out and it was Dustin. She answered softly. He sounded excited.

"Patsy? You okay? What happened at the church this morning? I heard there was an ambulance there and people at the church were coming out crying. What's going on? Somebody done made Nadeen set it off up in there about communion?" He asked nervously laughing.

Patsy couldn't even laugh. "Pastor had a massive heart attack in his study this morning." She said. She just didn't have the strength or mental clarity to say much more.

"What?" Dustin asked. "He had a heart attack, Dustin. I just told you." Patsy said. She was a little irritated and just wanted some quiet to think this whole thing out. Dustin could tell she was not okay so he decided to end the conversation for now.

"You sound pretty upset. I'll give you a couple of hours to calm down and then check back on you. Is that okay?" He asked.

Patsy hung up the phone not sure if she said yes or not. They must have slept for hours. When they awoke, it was dark outside. Nadeen was up front talking to someone. Patsy's throat was dry and it seemed closed up. She had to get something to drink. She knew Nadeen wouldn't like the interruption so she decided to say the water was for Josie and she would make sure she shared with her so she wouldn't be guilty of lying.

When she made it to the kitchen it was full of the members of the Praying Circle. They were all discussing what a wonderful Pastor Reverend Craig had been and how he was probably in heaven right now getting fitted for his wings. They believed he was a good man. He wasn't perfect but he was a good preacher. He sure knew how to bring that Word. There wasn't ever going to be another preacher anointed like him. Everyone was wiping tears and saying "Amen." Patsy eased in so she wouldn't disturb them during their teary-eyed reflections.

Nadeen looked up at her with an irritated look on her face. She mouthed to her that Josie needed some water. Her face softened.

Patsy's stomach was growling but she knew not to stay any longer than it took to take the bottled water out of the refrigerator. When she made it to the back, the phone rang, Nadeen told her to get it. Patsy went to the back and answered. It was Kenny. He sounded a little worried.

"Little girl, what is going on down there?" He asked. "I heard

Reverend Craig died during service. Say he was preaching the Word and just fell dead from a heart attack."

Who went and twisted this around already? Patsy thought to herself. "That's not what happened, Daddy." She told Kenny. "He was in his study talking to First Lady Champagne and he fell dead from a heart attack."

She wanted to tell Kenny the rest. She wanted him to know she was standing at the door and she heard everything. She wanted to tell him that he had a heart attack after finding out that his fine, new wife was about to tell the entire congregation that skanky, Daphne Porter was his love child and her momma had been his unsanctified secret side-piece at one time. No wonder Daphne was so loose with her goodies. She was just like her daddy passing his penis around town like a collection plate.

She wanted to tell it but was too ashamed. She was ashamed for Reverend Craig and ashamed for herself so she just gave him the basic version of what happened.

"How is Nadeen? I been calling her cell, but I guess she cut it off. I know she loved that man. She was mad about him marrying Champagne Porter but she would do anything for him. She holding it down okay?"

Patsy really didn't want to talk about Nadeen but she knew she had to answer him or he would not stop asking. After all, he was a man in love with a woman who did not love him so he was thirsty for anything to do with her.

"She's not doing so good but her Sisters from the Praying Circle are up front with her right now."

"I kinda figured as much." He said sadly. "Tell her I called to check on her. If she wants to, she can give me a call back."

Now surely he knew that was not going to happen, Patsy thought to herself.

"Okay, I'll tell her," Patsy said.

"Patsy? Can I talk to Ann?" Kenny asked. "I been having some troubling dreams about her, but I keep praying no harm come to her, I don't want harm to come to any of you. I love you."

"We love you too, Daddy. I'll go get her." Patsy said and put the phone down to go upstairs and get Ann. She was sitting on her bed staring out of her window.

"Kenny on the phone. He said he been having bad dreams about you so he wants to talk to you." Ann looked at her funny but she went to the phone.

"Hey, Daddy," Ann said.

"Hey, baby. You doing okay? You been in my dreams a lot. You okay, you need anything?" He asked.

"Just for you to come back home," Ann said in a sad tone.

"I'm getting closer every day, baby girl. I promise you that." Kenny said.

"Yeah, I know. You tell me that every time."

"And I mean it every time," Kenny said. "Look, you need anything you call me, okay? Don't get yourself caught up in any trouble or go to hurting yourself. You call your daddy before you do that. You hear me?" Kenny asked with a slight sternness in his voice.

"Yes, Daddy I hear you. I'm not in any trouble and I'm not hurting myself. I'm just real tired." Ann said.

"Well, okay. I'll let you go take a nap but remember what I said. I love you, Ann. Don't you ever doubt that," he told her.

"Sure. Okay, Daddy." Ann said. "I gotta go."

She put the phone back on the receiver and told Patsy, "I really need him to come back home. I don't know how much more I can stay in this house without him."

"Ann, he sounds really concerned about you getting into some trouble," Patsy said.

"He too late for that," Ann said and walked off.

*　　*　　*

Greater Trials and their Pastor was the main topic of conversation the next day at school. People that Patsy had never spoken to were coming up to her asking her questions about what happened.

Champagne picked Daphne up from school every day that week. She wore dark shades but Patsy could feel her looking at her. Looking at her because she knew. She knew her nasty, little secret that caused Reverend Craig to have that heart attack. It was her spirit of vengeance and hate that killed him and she also knew that Patsy couldn't prove it nor tell it because that would mean she hadn't been where she was supposed to be. That would be embarrassing to Nadeen. Patsy knew better than to do that.

Reverend Craig's funeral was held on a Saturday. Greater Trials was packed. Guests were even sitting in the choir stands. A guest pastor of a megachurch in Meridian, Mississippi, eulogized him. First Lady Champagne was surrounded by ushers and church fans. She had to be restrained three times from turning over the casket she was rocking it so hard. Church members testified about all the good things he'd done for them and how he was such a man of valor in the community.

His deceased wife's sister got up and told the congregation she believed her sister welcomed him into heaven with open arms. Patsy glanced over at Champagne then and saw her with a smirk on her face at that.

Before the final procession, First Lady Champagne placed a single red rose on his chest and went into the pulpit to address the congregation. She told them though it was hard for her she wanted to try to be a strong wife for him in death as she had been in life and she was sure that he was exactly where he belonged now. Patsy wondered if anybody else realized there were no tears on her face behind the handkerchief she carried. She walked out behind his casket in her six-inch black, red bottom heels holding Daphne's hand escorted by clergy from all over the world.

She buried him in a gold-toned casket carried by a horse and carriage. He had on a crème-colored suit tailor-made to fit, and his Bible was in his glove-covered hands.

As she walked out the church doors no one at the Homegoing Service, knew she was about to be walking onto a plane headed for the Bahamas a week later with all of her husband's money from his savings account, which included the $500,000 he'd collected from his first wife's policy, her secret lover, and a pending check for another million from a policy that she asked her deceased husband to take out a month before they got married.

She left the decision of a new pastor for the church on hold until she returned from a proper period of mourning. Only her little sister Daphne, who was staying with family members, knew how to reach her. The church board was frantic. They wanted to get a new shepherd to cover the flock, but they had to get her vote because it was written in the agreement between them and Pastor Craig many years ago that if he passed his widow would have the majority vote in who would head up the church after he was gone.

15

NADEEN WAS IN a daze for the rest of the month. Grandma Ruth said they all needed to sit down to a home-cooked meal together and try and appreciate the gift of life God had given them so she had everyone come over. Nadeen didn't want to go but she knew the backlash that would come if she didn't, so she picked up a cake and took it to Eva's house.

Eva had the blues playing and she was swaying to the music in the kitchen as she made gravy for the homemade mashed potatoes. Grandma Ruth was drinking something in a teacup and singing. They seemed to be having a real good time. When Grandma Ruth saw them come through the door, her smile spread across her face.

She put the cup on the table and reached out for them. She never made eye contact with Nadeen. Things were better but not the best. They never talked about what happened, they just kept moving forward as though it had just been a stick in the road or something they stepped over and kept going.

"Well here come my babies. It's about time you showed up. I thought it was going to be time for dessert by the time y'all got over here. Come give me some sugah." She said as Patsy sat Josie in her grandmother's lap. She kissed her and gave each one of them a kiss on the jaw.

Nadeen walked past her and gave a quick, "Hey momma." As she went to put the cake down on the counter.

Eva turned around from beating her potatoes and asked, "Nadeen you about to come out of that funk you been in since pastor died? You been looking like you lost your own husband."

"The way she catered to him I thought he was," Grandma Ruth said.

Nadeen rolled her eyes at her mother but she didn't respond.

"Champagne Porter missing so we can't get a vote on who the new pastor is gonna be. Every time you ask her little sister, Daphne, she gives the same old answer, 'She just needs a little time. She'll be back soon.' I hear they looking out of state for a new pastor. David said they got about six candidates they looking at but they can't make a final selection until First Lady Champagne comes out of mourning from whatever dark corner she's in." Eva said.

Grandma Ruth laughed at that, "She ain't mourning in no dark corner. She somewhere in plain sight spending that old foolish pastor's money. You see you reap what you sow. He played around with that girl behind his first wife back and let her trick him into marriage a few weeks after she died and now, she done put him in the ground and left town. Follow the money trail, you'll find her." Grandma Ruth said.

They both looked at Nadeen then, waiting to get a reaction out of her. It didn't take long.

"You two should repent for the things you saying about that man. He is gone to be with the Lord. It isn't right to talk about the dead like that. Eva he your pastor, too, so why you scandalizing his name?"

"If the truth cause a scandal, so be it, Nadeen. Jesus didn't come to make peace with sin, he came to shake it up. Anyway, all I said was that they need to find his widow so we can move along with the business of the church. Your momma is the one stirring up mess. Now say something to her." Eva said.

Grandma Ruth sipped from her cup and said, "Hmmm. I wish she would. I been knowing that Reverend Craig a long time and I know what I'm talking about. Don't get hurt taking up for something you really don't know about girl," She said looking at Nadeen from behind the rim of her coffee cup. Nadeen walked over to the cake she brought and started cutting it up. "Girls you go on to the back room and find something to read or watch on television. You don't need to be hanging around being entertained by grown folk's conversation." Nadeen said. Patsy was glad to leave the room and she was sure Ann wasn't too far behind her. Grandma would give up Josie when she was ready.

"Speaking of a man, where is mine?" Eva asked. "He suppose to be out there working on building me a 'she shed' for me to entertain in. His company sent him off for training a few weeks ago and he came back just as lazy. He says he worn out from that new position at work. One day he's gonna be the Regional Manager. I'm hanging around for that paycheck!" Eva said.

Just as she finished talking David walked in.

"Hey Ladies. You got that food about ready? I'm starving. A man can work up a real appetite around here foolin' with Eva." He said with a grin on his face.

Aunt Eva smiled back at him and told him to go take a shower she would have the food on the table by the time he showered and shaved.

"He got a new job?" Nadeen asked. "No. He got the same job but they promoted him to a supervisor after his training. It seems like they might be getting ready to move him up again and you know we could use that money."

"He look different to me when he got back." Grandma Ruth said. "I think he been up to some devilment."

Eva looked at Grandma Ruth and said, "You really don't need

to think when you drinking that coffee. It just makes the words coming out of your mouth sound more confusing." She said as she opened the oven to put in her casserole.

"You the one confused." Grandma Ruth said. "Sometimes I think you act more like your daddy's people than mine. They could be looking right at something and not know what they looking at."

"Momma. You not gonna spoil my good mood or my good food with that mess. Just enjoy all of us being here together. I miss my brother-in-law. If he was here it would be perfect." Eva said.

"I'm sure he somewhere eating a good dinner prepared by his girlfriend, Sara," Nadeen said.

Grandma Ruth let out a short laugh at that. "Well, men will park their shoes under another woman's table when the stuff they being served at home is always cold." She said as she took another sip of what was in her cup.

Nadeen cut her a look that said she wanted to knock her out that chair but she knew better.

"And another thing, you need to put Ann on a diet. She looking a little thick to me. What you been feeding that girl? She too young and pretty to be round here lookin' like Miss Piggy." Grandma Ruth said.

"Girls, come on up here so we can eat," Nadeen ignored her mother's comment. Patsy came up to the dinner table.

"Momma my casserole ain't ready yet." Eva said.

"We can eat that salad I made first. We got plenty of time to taste everything up in here today." Grandma Ruth said as she straightened out the table mats. "Patsy help your Aunt set this table."

"Where Ann? Tell her to come on. I'm not gonna say it again." Nadeen asked looking over at Patsy.

"I guess she laying down in the back. I ain't seen her." Patsy said as she took the plates and utensils from her aunt to set up the dinner table.

"Ann! Ann, you come on up here and help in this kitchen." Her grandmother yelled.

Ann came up the hall a few minutes later.

"Girl, where you been? You taking naps like an old lady. I don't sleep that much." Her grandmother said. Ann sounded a little out of breath when she spoke.

"I was just out back talking to a girl from my school," Ann said as she leaned against the wall.

"I ain't never seen no girl from your school come over here," her grandmother said.

"She and I just realized that we went to the same school. She takes different classes from me. I was telling her you were my grandmother. We just got to talking and I didn't realize how long I'd been out there." Ann said swiping the hair out of her face.

Grandma Ruth studied her face a few minutes like she wasn't sure that was the truth. "If you say so, Ann. Come on up here and help with this table so we can eat." She said, following Ann with her eyes.

When dinner was finished, Ann and Patsy started to the kitchen to clean up. Patsy heard Ann softly say her name, then Ann grabbed her shirt and fainted on the kitchen floor. Patsy screamed.

"Momma! Momma Ann fainted!" She screamed. Everybody came running into the kitchen.

"Get back! Get back and bring me that smelling salt out the cabinet, Eva!" Grandma Ruth said pushing for everyone to move away from Ann.

Eva swore that old-fashioned stuff didn't work no more but as soon as Grandma Ruth put it under her nose, Ann sat straight up.

"Girl, what's wrong with you?" Grandma Ruth asked her. Ann looked dazed. She couldn't talk. David reached down and pulled her up off of the floor. Eva walked her to the kitchen table and sat her down.

"Nadeen, you need to hurry up and get this girl to the doctor," Eva said handing her a glass of water.

Nadeen just stood back looking at her. Grandma Ruth tilted Ann's head back slightly. She was looking at her face and her neck then she said.

"Nadeen. You better start paying attention to your child instead of walking around in a funk over your Pastor." She said looking Ann squarely in the eye.

"You know what I mean don't you, Ann?" Her grandmother whispered. Ann just looked deep into her eyes. Knowing, that her grandmother could see what she thought was secret.

"Come on girls let's go home. Ann, I'm taking you to the doctor as a walk-in tomorrow. I can't wait two more weeks. We gotta get there early because they close early on Saturday's and I don't want to wait too long to get this exam done." Nadeen said.

"Where you gonna find a doctor to see her on a Saturday?" Eva asked.

"Dr. Rivers works at the clinic some Saturdays. She'll let me bring her in. All I have to do is call. She and I have a good relationship." Nadeen said as she started packing up plates and Patsy started putting on Josie's coat. Patsy hated to be leaving so soon. She enjoyed being away from home. Her Aunt's house, other than David, was a nice place to be and she always had a good time.

Ann rested on the back seat and never said a word all the way home. Nadeen called the clinic and left a message for Dr. Rivers telling them she was going to bring Ann in tomorrow as a walk-in.

Ann was quiet the rest of the night. Patsy hoped she didn't have cancer or something. What if her little sister had a terminal illness? Tomorrow morning they would know for sure. They would find out what it was and hopefully, the doctor would write a prescription that would fix it.

Nadeen woke Ann up at 6:00 am the next morning and told Ann to get ready quickly, she wanted to get there as soon as the staff walked through the door.

"Ann, I got a lot to do this morning for the guest pastor

tomorrow and making sure he has what he needs for breakfast and for his sermon. Let's get to this doctor, get this prescription or shot, and keep it movin'." Nadeen said.

Dr. Rivers got them in five minutes after they arrived in the office. The first scheduled appointment was not until 7:30 am and since the doctor was a member of Greater Trials, she didn't mind making an exception for Nadeen.

Nadeen sat down and immediately started telling her Ann's symptoms.

"Dr. Rivers some kind of nasty bug has gotten ahold of my daughter. She has been feeling bad for the last few weeks and throwing up everything she sees just about," Nadeen said. "Yesterday she fainted at a family dinner."

Dr. Rivers looked at Ann. She noticed she was holding her head down the entire time.

"Ann, what's goin' on with you?" Dr. Rivers asked. Ann looked up at her. There was something in her eyes that made Dr. Rivers feel sorry for her.

"I don't know for sure," Ann said hunching up her shoulders.

"Well, your mom brought you to me for us to find out and that is exactly what we are gonna do. Let me get the nurse in here to find out what we got causing all this havoc." Dr. Rivers said as she smiled and patted Ann on her knee.

Dr. Rivers checked her heart rate and blood pressure and then laid her back on the stretcher. She had Ann pull up her shirt and pressed down on her navel and around it.

"Ann, how have you been feeling the last couple of weeks?" The doctor asked as she continued to push on Ann's stomach.

Ann could hardly speak, her throat was dry, "I was okay till a few weeks ago. I think I ate something spoiled at school," she said speaking in a low, soft voice.

"Your mother says you been throwing up and been kinda sluggish lately. Is that true?"

"I guess," Ann whispered. The doctor shook her head in agreement as she pulled Ann's shirt back down and smoothed it out over her belly.

"Well, the first thing I want to do is to get a urine sample, then we will do an ultrasound to make sure everything is working the way it is supposed to." Dr. Rivers said reaching for the plastic cup.

"Ann, take this and step over there into the bathroom. Put it in the little door once you are done and we will get you back for an ultrasound." Ann took the cup and went to the bathroom.

"Dr. Rivers, you think it's something that serious that she needs an ultrasound?" Nadeen asked. "That's a pretty expensive test for a stomach bug."

"Nadeen, you know I am very thorough. I make sure I cover all bases before I give out a diagnosis. Ann will get that same quality care. I do the same things with all my patients."

"Yes, you do. I'm not here to tell you how to do your job. I know how that is, I deal with it at the church all the time. Reverend Craig use to just let me get them folks right on together and keep it moving so I'm gonna get out of your way before you do the same to me." Nadeen said. They both laughed as Ann came back into the room.

Dr. Rivers stepped to the door of the exam room and called for her nurse. "Nurse Grant can you please escort our patient down the hall to have an ultrasound done and then bring her back to us?"

"Of course I will." Nurse Grant said as she smiled at Ann. "Come with me, young lady. We are gonna find out what's going on with you." Ann followed her down the hall to the radiography room.

"Ann should be back in about fifteen minutes." Dr. Rivers advised Nadeen. "Sister Simmons, you know when we gonna get our new Pastor?"

"Can't quite say right now. We all waiting on Champagne to come back and let us know her final decision." Nadeen smiled and said. "Dr. Rivers, I really appreciate you letting us come in at the last minute especially on a Saturday. I know that's your golfing day."

Dr. Rivers smiled, "Yes. That's why I only come in for a few hours. It's part of me giving back to the community. Working moms really appreciate it."

The nurse brought Ann back in a few minutes later.

"Well, Ann while we are waiting on your ultrasound results let me ask you about your cycle. You been having any problems with it?"

"No. I haven't had any problems with it. I take medicine if I cramp too bad and I usually sleep a lot because I don't have much energy but nothing else." Ann told Dr. Rivers while twisting the ends of her shirt around her fingers.

"When was your last cycle?" Dr. Rivers asked

Ann put her head down and kept twisting the ends of her shirt. "I don't quite remember the exact date. I usually write it in my calendar but I haven't been feeling too good lately so I guess I forgot." Ann said avoiding looking at Dr. Rivers.

"Well, that's probably the problem anyway, Dr. Rivers. Her cramps have probably intensified as she has gotten older. I know mine got worse the older I got when I was in high school. Guess Ann did get something from me after all." Nadeen said

Just then Nurse Grant opened the door and stepped in. "Dr. Rivers here are the results of both tests," she said as she passed her the envelope. She looked into Ann's face and then glanced at Nadeen as she began opening the envelope, it took her a few minutes to read the test results then she looked up at Ann and smiled. "I know your mom is really concerned about you, so I am going to go ahead and let you both know what's goin' on. Is that okay with you Ann?"

Ann nodded her head yes as she looked down at her shoes while grasping onto the sides of the examination table.

Nadeen let out a slight laugh, "She has no choice but for it to be okay. I took out time from my busy day to come down here and make a bill because of her not making healthy choices in what she picks up in that school cafeteria. I have told her before all that junk food she eats at school was going to catch up with her and here we are." Nadeen said folding her hands in front of her.

"Well, Ann it seems you've been very dehydrated lately and you seem to have a slight urinary tract infection. I recommend plenty of water and cranberry juice. I'm also going to give you something for nausea." Nadeen started to gather her purse when the doctor handed the slip of paper to her.

"Sister Simmons, you'll need to get this prenatal vitamin prescription filled immediately. Ann looks to be about fourteen weeks pregnant." Ann gasped and the contents of Nadeen's purse spilled all over the floor. Ann started shaking her head.

"What? Pregnant? I can't be. I can't be pregnant." She said with her head in her hands hiding the shock on her face. Nadeen looked at Ann and then back at the doctor.

"Excuse me? She what? Doctor, with all due respect you must have picked up the wrong test results! My daughter is not allowed to date or have a boyfriend so I know she can't be pregnant! I raised my daughters to keep their hands up in praise and their skirts down in obedience to the Word of God so I know your nurse has picked up the wrong test results. You better get her in here right now and get this straight. This kind of mistake can cause all kinds of confusion." Nadeen told the doctor.

"Sister Simmons, I know how difficult this is for you both but your daughter is pregnant and she probably already knew it before you brought her in here today." Dr. Rivers said bending down to help her pick up the items that had fallen from her purse.

Nadeen was in complete disbelief. She looked so helpless. She grabbed Ann's wrist.

"Ann! Ann, you tell this doctor you don't even have a boyfriend! How you gonna be pregnant? Tell her you are not that kind of girl.

You been raised to be a young lady. I taught you and Patsy better than to let some boy trick you out of your most precious gift. Ann, you know to keep your virginity until you get married. Tell this woman before I have to go off up in here!" Nadeen yelled at her.

Ann couldn't speak—she was praying. Praying that God would just open up the floor and allow her to be sucked up. Where was Patsy? She needed her big sister right now.

The doctor handed Nadeen the prescription for the prenatal vitamins, gave her a hug, and said. "It's going to be fine. She isn't the first young lady this has happened to."

Ann didn't want the doctor to leave her alone with her mother. She knew she would be in danger. Nadeen was bent down picking up a bottle of blessed oil. She was crying, something in itself that seemed strange to Ann. This whole moment seemed unreal.

"I know damn well you ain't pregnant Ann. I know you ain't been opening your legs for some boy! How could that happen? She misdiagnosed you that's all. We going to Eva's doctor as soon as we leave here." Nadeen said. "I hate to say it but this is some bullshit! God forgive me for saying it but I had to."

Ann eased off the table. She couldn't get her thoughts together. Nurse Grant came in and gave her a pamphlet on becoming a new mother and breastfeeding. Nadeen threw it in the trashcan.

"We don't need that!" She told the nurse. The nurse looked at her.

"I understand this is very difficult for you but your daughter is pregnant. We ran the test twice to make certain. She is going to have a baby in a few months and you both must come to terms with that." She said before she walked back out the door. "Call us if you need anything."

"I need you to get out this room. That's what I need right now." Nadeen said as she continued picking up the items from her purse off the floor. Ann was so petrified she didn't think not to turn her back to her mother. As she buttoned up her shirt, she felt something slam into the side of her head. She fell forward into the cabinet in front of her with silver sparks in front of her eyes. She stumbled and turned to see Nadeen holding a silver pan in her hand. She came down on Ann's head again.

"You know better, Ann! How could you embarrass me so! I brought you up in the church! How could you do this? You hardly developed yourself!" She yelled as she slammed the pan down on Ann's head each time she spoke. Ann screamed for help.

"Who is the daddy, Ann? Who were you so stupid for that you did something so shameful? Your life is ruined. Ruined!" Nadeen yelled bringing the pan back down on Ann's head again.

"You trying to be like Patsy's friend? I should have stopped you from being around the two of them anyway." Nadeen said wiping the tears from her face. "I'm going to put a stop to Patsy dealing with that girl right now today!"

The nurse and the doctor came rushing back in and pulled the silver pan from Nadeen while Dr. Rivers tried to restrain her. The doctor pulled Nadeen into her arms and held her. "Please. Please don't tell the other church members." She cried. "I just can't handle the shame. It's too much to bear. Lord Jesus! It's just too much to bear."

Nurse Grant took Ann out of the office and sat her in the waiting room. She spoke softly to her." Your mother is hurting right now. Give her some time. She needs time to accept this pregnancy. Time and prayer will get your family through this." She said to Ann then she walked out of the waiting room.

Ann was afraid to ride home with Nadeen. She asked to use the phone at the front desk and called her Aunt Eva. "Your momma already called. I told her I was on my way. No way I'm going to let you ride home with her considering the state of mind she's in right now. Ann, you have hurt her deep. She's broken. I can hear it. She is broken and ashamed."

Ann felt worse hearing those words. "I know. I never meant for it to happen. I just needed someone to be with me and make me feel loved. Patsy was gone. Kenny was gone. I felt so alone. I'm so sorry. I was taking my pills. I didn't think I would get pregnant." She said.

"Well, you apparently missed some days or nights. My God, Ann, you are gonna send your momma to a mental hospital with this. The church gossip mill is gonna be going full speed when this gets out. I'm on my way just stay there and try to stay out of her way," Eva said.

When Ann hung up the phone Nadeen came out of the office. Her eyes were bloodshot and swollen from so much crying. She couldn't even look at Ann. She walked by her and said, "Your Aunt is going to have to come and get you. I can't deal with this right now. I can't wrap my mind around the thought of you parading around my home with your belly swollen like you are a grown, married woman.

"You should be ashamed, Ann Simmons. Wait till I tell Kenny. This his fault, too. If he had been the man I needed him to be in our home instead of being out in the street nursing a whiskey bottle and a pipe, he might not be getting ready to nurse a baby out of wedlock. A bastard. That's what that child is gonna be Ann. A bastard just like its granddaddy." She said as she walked out the door.

Ann didn't say anything. She didn't even look at her mother. She knew she devastated her. She also knew it wouldn't be long before her mother asked about the father of the baby. What were they going to do then? They were going to have to both deal with the consequences. It was not about to get easier for Ann it was about to get worse. She had finally released one hurtful secret; she didn't know how or when the final one would come out.

The ride to Aunt Eva's house seemed so long. Ann wondered if Patsy knew yet. She could see Patsy's face looking at her like she had antennas on her head asking her, "For real Ann? You pregnant for real? See that's why I keep fighting to keep mine. I'm too scared of what he got and what it could give me. I don't want no baby." She could just hear it.

"Baby girl, you got to come out of dreamland now," Eva said. "No more daydreaming for you. You got a baby coming that is going to need food, shelter, clothes, and love and those things are real not make-believe. You have dropped a bomb on your momma and you got to pick up the pieces from the fallout." Ann knew she had messed up bad.

Her boyfriend had told her he had it all under control. He had used a condom every time the first few times then her friends told her she should get on birth control pills so she sneaked off to the clinic with them a few times not expecting to see Sandra there. She prayed Sandra would keep her secret but of course she didn't. Ann had to avoid telling her sister by pushing her away with distance and anger. Well, there would be no more secrets, it was eventually all going to come out and everyone around her was going to be hurt.

Ann thought about all her friends at school and how people were going to be staring at her and gossiping about her. Gossiping about her and Ralph and what they thought they knew.

When they made it to Eva's house, Grandma Ruth was standing at the front door. Ann walked past her with her head down and went to the back guest room. Grandma Ruth came back a few minutes later.

"One thing about sin done in the dark, baby, it always manifest itself in the light. Ann, I knew you were pregnant when I looked at you yesterday but I knew it was not my place to break that to your momma. That's why I wanted her to go ahead and take you to the doctor. I taught you at an early age, keep your skirt down and your legs closed. I see you decided to take rods instead of wisdom." She said shaking her head at her granddaughter.

"It was a mistake, Grandma. I never meant for it to happen." She said and the tears started falling again. Grandma Ruth sat on the bed and put her arms around her shoulder.

"Baby, bumping into somebody is a mistake. Buying egg salad from the gas station is a mistake. Getting pregnant is a consequence. All actions have consequences. You didn't mistakenly lay down with this boy. You did it on purpose. You did it because you wanted to. You thought your only consequence was to feel good but it's about to be this baby. Now you gotta grow up mentally and prepare to deal with it. You and this little boy that helped you make it."

Ann didn't feel like talking. She just listened. She realized that her actions were going to change the lives of her entire family forever.

* * *

Patsy called to talk to Ann but her Grandmother wouldn't let her.

"Patsy your sister needs a minute. She just had her entire life side-tracked by her disobedience and her hot tail. Give her some time to deal with this. Give us all some time. Call her back in a few days." She told Patsy.

"I'll just see her at church tomorrow," Patsy told her Grandma. There was a brief dead space then Grandma Ruth answered. "She won't be there Sunday. She won't be there for a couple of Sundays." She told Patsy just before she hung up the phone. Patsy just held the phone in her hand. The depth of what Ann had done seemed to really hit her at that moment with her Grandmother's words.

Monday came and Patsy couldn't stand it any longer. She had to talk to her little sister. She knew that Ann needed her even if she might act like she didn't. She waited till she got to school and called on the cell phone she secretly got from Sandra. She was in complete disbelief that her little sister was going to have a real, live baby. Ann had given her most precious gift away. She had to talk to Ann to let her know that if she was truly sorry, she could repent and God would forgive her.

When she called, David answered the phone. Patsy didn't feel like dealing with his foolishness right now so she changed her voice when she asked for Ann. Ann came to the phone sounding like she was exhausted. She hadn't slept much last night.

"Hello?" She answered. Patsy wanted to reach out and hug her the moment she heard her voice.

"Hey, Ann. How you doing?" Patsy asked.

"I don't know right now. I'm kinda crazy since the doctor said I was pregnant. I can't believe it. I'm in the eighth grade and I'm gonna be a momma. I can't believe it." She told Patsy.

"Me either. Ann, I told you to get yourself together and stop sneaking around now it's all about to come out." Patsy said. "This makes me even more afraid of giving it up to Dustin. He might get carried away and get me pregnant too. I would just die if that happened."

Ann was silent on the phone. Again, she didn't really know what to say. It was mind-blowing to her and the thought of how much worse it was going to get made her head hurt.

"Patsy, just pray for me don't give me a sermon. I know it was wrong. I know what the Bible says. I know I stepped out of God's Will and I know what I gotta do to get it right." Ann said. Patsy was glad to hear that.

"When you gonna tell Daddy?" Patsy asked Ann.

"I don't know yet. I will though unless Nadeen tells him before I can." Ann said. Then came the question that Ann knew was going to be next on everybody's mind.

"You told Ralph you pregnant? I know he the daddy." Patsy asked.

"I'll talk to him tonight." Ann said." I want him to hear it from me not anybody else. Look. I don't feel good right now. I have to talk to you later." Ann said and just hung up without even saying goodbye.

Ralph had a conversation with Ann Simmons later on that night that changed him forever. He was young, but he was also in love and he would do anything for her. He would step up to the plate and tell his family and hers that they had made a big mistake but they would take responsibility for it. He had heard from Ann how crazy acting her mother was so he was going to need his own mother to go and talk to her with him.

If Ann didn't really believe he loved her before, she would believe it today as he stepped up to the plate and owned this baby. He only asked that she put the promise ring on her finger that he had given her. There was no reason to hide it now.

When he saw Ann at school the next day, she had the ring on. She came up to him and put her arm in his. She was going to need to lean on him heavily for the next couple of months. When Ralph got ready to talk to Nadeen he agreed with Ann that he should do it at church with his mom present.

The conversation took place the following Sunday in the church parking lot just like they wanted. Ann didn't like the idea of being at Nadeen's house when she met Ralph, especially with the bomb that had exploded.

Eva parked her car next to Nadeen's so when Ralph saw them standing together, he came up and introduced himself. His mother stood by his side.

"Nice to meet you, Mrs. Simmons," Ralph said extending his hand. Nadeen didn't shake his hand. Ralph's mother stepped in.

"Ma'am, I can tell you are upset about this but as you can see my son is a gentleman and as the father of this child, he will do the right thing." She said.

"I'm not happy about this pregnancy so him doing the right thing isn't going to change that he did the wrong thing by tricking my daughter," Nadeen said.

Ralph's mother took a deep breath and made one step closer to Nadeen.

"I'm not happy either but what you not about to do, Mrs. Head Usher, is make it seem like my son tricked your daughter into doing something that she didn't want to do willingly. Remember it takes two people to make a baby." She said.

"You might want to step back and give me a little air, darling. I'm not one to be played with whether we on the church parking lot or in a grocery store parking lot." Nadeen said putting up her hand to signal for Ralph's mother to move back.

Eva stepped in. She knew this was about to turn for the worse.

"Let's end this right now. This is about accepting what has happened and helping these two foolish, hot-in-the-pants children to prepare for the biggest change in their lives. There won't be any additional drama here today." Eva said placing her hand on Nadeen's wrist.

"Momma, let's go. I don't want to upset Ann." Ralph said as he pulled his mother back.

"You right son. We should go. Looks like you done tied yourself into a deal with the devil in this family but that ain't that little girl's fault." Ralph's mother said. "Come on. We'll be in touch when you need us, Ann." She said as she walked away with her son.

"I can see now this is only going to get worse. Ann, you have opened up the pit." Nadeen said. Ann looked hurt but she just replied with a meek, "Yes ma'am."

"And another thing. I would appreciate it if you all would keep her away from this church It is so shameful to see a child with child. I raised her according to the Word of God and the only thing she got to show for it is a decision she will regret for the rest of her life. She has shamed this family and who is left to deal with the gossip and the stares?" Nadeen asked.

"Your daddy sure isn't here to deal with it. No. He's off somewhere courting somebody twenty years his junior. He don't care." She said as she turned and walked back into the church.

"Come on, baby, get in the car." Eva told Ann. "I'll go by your momma's house for the rest of your things later this afternoon. Your momma is a little touched in the head. She quick to put them scriptures on somebody else but she don't use them herself." Eva said. Ann started walking around to the passenger side of her aunt's car.

Patsy walked with her and whispered, "You could have just told me, Ann. No more secrets about you and Ralph now." Patsy said.

Ann opened the car door and got in with the window down. She looked out the window at Patsy and said, "You still don't get it, do you. I don't tell you everything. I stopped doing that when you left me and it's hard to change." She said as she closed the car door.

Patsy was speechless. She thought she had gotten her little sister back again but maybe she was wrong. Eva backed the car out and told Patsy she would see her later when she came by the house.

Patsy prayed right there in the parking lot.

"God please don't let her hurt herself." She knew this kind of stress could push Ann to cutting herself again and this time she'd be risking two lives.

* * *

By the time Nadeen came back out of the church with Josie, the sun had gone down on the Greater Trials parking lot Patsy didn't say a word to her mother. She could see the strain on her face. Her image was now scarred she didn't know how to handle it.

Eva came by the house late that night. Patsy cracked the door open so she could hear what she and Nadeen were talking about. Patsy heard Nadeen say "No, ma'am. I will not have her in my house with her stomach all blowed up carrying some boy's baby. She can go and stay with him and his momma. She can't come here, Eva. I can't deal with seeing that. I just can't do it. You say you love your niece so much you keep her. You the one ran up to the doctor's office to get her the day we found out, now you keep her."

"Nadeen I can't keep her. David found out tonight about her being pregnant and he is just as bad as you, talking about he don't want to watch her blow up every day with some little boy's baby growing inside of her. He says he ain't comfortable seeing that. He says she should have been woman enough to put herself on some pills and prevented all this. Now he says she got to go deal with it somewhere else." Eva said.

"Well, it seems to me he is close to giving you an ultimatum Eva. You gonna choose your foolish niece or your foolish man. You say you love her so much so choose. Funny how that changes when it comes to your man. Anyway, how he gonna tell you she gotta leave when the both of y'all shacking up? You playing wife with him every night. How is it any different from what Ann did?" Nadeen asked

"Nadeen I'm grown! I do what I want to in my own house and I got a God that knows all about me. I'm growing every day but I'm not perfect. Not like you!" She said. The next noise Patsy heard was the slamming of the front door. Every time they got to talking it always ended with loud voices and slamming doors.

How could Aunt Eva turn her back on Ann at a time like this? Patsy thought to herself. Was she really that in love with David that she would put Ann out to make it on her own? One thing was for certain, as long as Ann was pregnant, she was not coming back in Nadeen's house and why hadn't Kenny called yet?

She was trying to give Nadeen or Ann a chance to tell him first but they were taking too long. He needed to know no matter how bad it was. He wouldn't react like Nadeen about it. He would be more understanding. He might even send for Ann to come and stay with him until she had the baby.

Kenny knew what it was like to fall from Nadeen's good grace and have to struggle to get back up. Ann, just like Kenny, would be climbing a long time to get back there.

16

ANN MOVED IN with her grandma on a Friday night. She had
gone home early from school because she wasn't feeling well. She
caught a ride with Ralph's mom since she was already there to take
him to a job interview. She was determined that Ralph was going
to be a responsible father. He had chosen this road and now he was
going to have to walk it. She would be behind him but he would
have to face the obstacles he'd created.

When Ann got to her Aunt Eva's house Grandma Ruth was
sitting out on the front porch. She gave Ann a big hug when she
came up on the porch.

"Well little girl. You filling out more and more every day." She
said. "I came by to move you over to my place. Eva got too much
going on over here on the weekends for a little girl in your condi-
tion to be hanging around. David and his strange friends coming
in and out all times of the night. I know they working on their
walk with the Lord but they still got a lot of things to be delivered
from and you don't want them spirits jumping off onto you. You
can tell that little boy to come by my house if he want to see you."
She said to Ann.

Ann was tired of feeling like she was being passed around but she knew not to say anything after what she was putting her family through.

"Okay, Grandma. Just let me go pack my stuff and tell Aunt Eva bye." Ann said.

"I already got your stuff. We packed it up earlier but you can go tell your aunt goodbye." Grandma Ruth said. Ann walked in the house and saw David sitting on the couch smoking a cigarette and rubbing on Eva's leg. He was saying something to her that made her laugh. When David saw her he stopped and just looked at her.

"Aunt Eva, Grandma Ruth gonna move me over to her house so I can have more room and give you and David some privacy." She said.

Eva got up off of the couch and came to give her a hug. David just looked straight ahead and kept smoking his cigarette.

"Baby, we gonna miss you around here but your Grandma knows a lot more about taking care of pregnant women and babies than me or David." She said laughingly.

She kissed Ann on her forehead. "Call me or your Uncle David if you need us to get anything for you, and don't worry we'll be coming by to see about you. Won't we David?" She asked. David just nodded his head yes and kept on smoking his cigarette and looking ahead. Eva walked Ann out to the car.

As soon as Ann walked into Grandma Ruth's house, she heard the phone ringing. Grandma Ruth was pulling her luggage with wheels so she told Ann to catch the phone for her.

Ann answered and a familiar voice on the other end said, "Hey little girl. How you doing? I hear you done broke your leg." The voice said. She knew the voice. It was Kenny.

She had been waiting for what seemed like months to get the courage to call him and tell him she was pregnant. It was so hard to say the words. It just did not seem like her name and that sentence went together. Now that someone had already told him she was grateful. Grateful that she wouldn't have to say it to him herself. Ann spoke low because she was ashamed having to talk about it.

"Yes, sir. I didn't do it on purpose."

"Baby, I know you didn't mean to get pregnant. You and that boy barely know what you was doin'." Kenny told her. "Don't you let this stress you out okay? I don't want you hurting yourself. You know what I'm talking about?" He asked her.

Ann knew what he meant. She was fighting the urge even at that moment. "I won't daddy. I promise." She told him.

"We might fall from your momma's grace, but never God's, okay? You just remember that." Kenny said. "I guess God was preparing me with all these dreams I been having about you. It's going to be okay. God got plenty of mercy for us both"

"Thank you, Daddy. Well, I guess I won't keep asking the same old question. I already know the answer so I'll ask a new one." Ann said.

"You can ask me anything," Kenny said.

"Why?" Ann asked her daddy

"Why what? Why did I leave? I told you baby God told me I had to. It wasn't anything Nadeen, you or your sisters did. It was what God told me to do."

"I don't want to know why you left I want to know why you didn't stop her, why you didn't stop what Momma was doin' to you and still doin' to us?" Ann said. Kenny could hear the emotion in her voice.

The question stunned Kenny. His throat became dry and he couldn't seem to answer his middle child. It took the wind out of him. After a brief silence, he answered her.

"Ann, I tried. I tried talking to her about the way she treated you and Patsy. I may have deserved her anger but not the two of you. She wouldn't listen to me so I hoped by me moving out of God's way, that she would listen to him. I'm so sorry I didn't do what you needed to make you feel protected."

He could hear her crying over the phone.

Ann was tired, emotional, and ashamed.

"I'm sorry too, Daddy." Ann said putting the phone down without saying goodbye.

She went to her room to cry. She cried because her daddy was gone. She cried because her virginity was gone and most of all she cried because the pain she had caused was not over yet.

* * *

The following Sunday, the members of Nadeen's Prayer Circle group were hugging her and telling her they were praying for her and for Ann. Somehow the word had gotten out at the church that Ann was pregnant. Nadeen wanted to just disappear into the carpet on the floor. How embarrassing to have the Head Usher, Praying Circle President, and Church Secretary's daughter pregnant out of wedlock.

Nadeen forced a smile and thanked each Sister for their kind words and support but in her mind, she was stomping mad.

Who had opened their filthy mouth and told the congregation about Ann? She already knew that once some of the praying Sisters got a hold of that it was going to spread. For some reason, Sara's aunt came up to her and hugged her.

"Sister Simmons, I'm so sorry to hear about your daughter's situation. My niece, Sara, told me she was pregnant. She said Kenny was taking it kinda hard but he was praying his way through it." She said.

It took all Nadeen had not to shoot through the sanctuary roof. In her mind, she was stomping and screaming. How dare Kenny tell his raggedy girlfriend their personal family business? Who was she to open her mouth and tell somebody about her daughter's situation? *Kenny better get his side piece in line before she had to do it,* Nadeen thought to herself.

"My family and I would like to handle this privately if you don't mind. Please refrain from coming up in my face again about my private business." She told Sara's aunt and walked off leaving her standing there with her mouth wide open.

The guest Pastor ended church services early and Nadeen was glad. She was at her car and gone before the benediction was complete. She would be back on Wednesday night for Bible study and the special business session they wanted everyone to attend.

Nadeen went straight into the house and picked up the phone to call Kenny. She laid her religion down on the kitchen table, poured herself a large glass of orange juice, and proceeded to cuss him out on his answering machine since he didn't answer his cellphone. She also told him to let his sidepiece know she was not welcome in her or her daughter's business.

*　　*　　*

Sara had stopped by his apartment prior to leaving for work that afternoon to drop off dinner for him. They'd exchanged keys with each other in case of an emergency and sometimes she would just leave him lunch or dinner in the refrigerator with a note. When she walked in, she saw his answering machine blinking. She clicked play out of curiosity.

She listened to Nadeen leave her scathing voicemail message on the answering machine and then she erased it. After all, it was just a matter of time before she would be permanently erased from his life forever. She didn't know how to treat her blessings. Sara was going to gladly show her. She had to laugh when she heard Nadeen refer to her as Kenny's side piece. She didn't know just how right she was. Sara was going to be right by his side now and when he put the divorce papers in the mail to her.

*　　*　　*

Nadeen went to Wednesday night Bible study expecting it to be a regular Bible study. The other ministers had been taking turns teaching every Wednesday night since Reverend Craig died. They were trying to keep Greater Trials moving forward until First Lady Champagne returned to settle the decision on a new pastor

Nadeen stepped into the meeting room and noticed everyone hugging a woman in a tight teal-colored dress with hair down to her butt. She was wearing six-inch gold heels. Nadeen wondered who it was. As she got closer, she saw the woman turn to the side. She heard her laugh and her mouth went dry. It was Champagne Porter! She had finally come back.

After leaving them in limbo for a month she had finally returned to tie up the business of selecting a new pastor for the church. She turned and saw Nadeen. She stepped out of the circle and extended her arms out to Nadeen to give her a hug.

"Sister Simmons, I'm so glad to see you. I heard how you been helping to keep things moving smoothly here at the church. My husband always said he could depend on you to handle church business." She said as she quickly hugged Nadeen and stepped back. "I also heard the stork is coming to your house real soon. Somebody on the Mother Board told me your daughter Ann has gone and got herself in the way of a grown woman. That's too bad because I think my husband was considering her to represent our youth this year at the convention before he died. Now we gotta look for somebody else. We don't want to give our young innocent girls the wrong idea about things like that. You understand, don't you?" Champagne asked with a fake smile on her face.

The cuss words were oozing in between Nadeen's teeth and she was straining to hold them back.

"Champagne, I understand your concern, but you just focus on wrapping up Pastor's business cause I got mine," Nadeen said and walked out of the room before she had to clean that pretty hardwood floor with Champagne's fresh, Brazilian human hair weave.

"Hey, sis-in-law," David said almost bumping into her on his way to the board room. Nadeen didn't bother to answer him. "I know you got a lot on your mind right now with Ann getting herself knocked up like that but you might want to go back in there. We got some serious business to discuss and we need you to take them minutes," David said.

"First of all, I'm not your sister-in-law and I will go back in that room when I get good and ready. You run Eva, not me." Nadeen snapped at him.

David just shook his head. "You and Eva got some serious issues from way back when it comes to men." He said and walked past Nadeen into the board room.

Nadeen made them wait a good fifteen minutes before she came back ready to take notes. When she came back, David stood up.

"Okay gentleman, these women have had us waiting long enough. Let's get down to business. We been without a shepherd way too long." Nadeen wondered who'd put him in charge of anything up in her sanctuary.

He catered to First Lady Champagne all night long. If she needed to blow her nose, he was right there to do it for her. He acted like a groupie. It was a sad sight. Nadeen made a note to make sure she told Eva how her man was treating Reverend Craig's widow. When it came time for the business session to elect a new pastor, each candidate's name and resume was read aloud and passed along to First Lady Champagne to select the top three.

Nadeen thought she recognized one of the last names but was pretty sure it wasn't him. It had to be somebody else. They wrapped up the final selection and asked First Lady to present her choice at the next scheduled district meeting. Nadeen was glad to know that things were about to get back in order at Greater Trials, from the pulpit to the First Lady.

* * *

Champagne had stayed away as long as she could without causing the congregation to send out the FBI to find her. She had given her little sister, Daphne, just enough information to share with the congregation to give them the impression she was somewhere in deep mourning and attempting to heal after the death of a faithful husband.

She had decided while on her travels from the Bahamas to the Mediterranean to come back, elect a new pastor and then leave town again with Daphne. Their work was done. She had gotten revenge not only for what Daphne's daddy, her husband, had done to their mother mentally, emotionally, and spiritually but also for her and Daphne. He took away her daddy and Daphne's right to have a father in her life. For that, he had to pay and as the big sister, Daphne's protector, Champagne knew it was expected of her to handle it and handle it she had done till death once again finalized things for her and Daphne.

Their mother held the dreadful secret of who Daphne's father was until she was on her death bed. She told Champagne to make sure she watched over Daphne and not let her get caught up by a wolf in the church dressed in sheep's clothing. People always wondered why her mother was so messy and so full of a fighting spirit. If they had only known it was the wounded spirit of a young woman abandoned at the altar by the man she loved and who loved her but couldn't get over the soul growing inside of her womb.

She was beguiled by a goat disguised as a sheep with a Bible in one hand and religious hypocrisy in the other.

Her pregnancy caused her isolation even by the Man of God who told her she had to bear this cross alone just as Jesus had. Champagne smiled as she played the whole scene in his study that Sunday back in her head. Her husband would rather die than have his congregation know just how long he'd been in these streets going into houses of silly women. This time he'd walked into a trap perfectly designed.

She had avenged her mother and it felt good. Her mother had not been strong enough to do it, but Champagne had.

She played back the look of horror and disbelief in her husband's eyes when she said the words, "Daphne is your daughter, and I am about to go and tell your whole congregation. You are her deadbeat daddy." He had looked at the yellowed DNA test and grasped his chest as his knees gave way under him. She hoped he felt the pain in his heart that her mother had carried for years. She had one more gift for Greater Trials, one she thought would cause Sister Nadeen Simmons to be stripped down to her lily-white cotton panties Champagne was pretty sure she wore under that usher uniform. Champagne recalled how she always looked at her like she smelled bad.

For now, she would hold that card just a few days longer. Right now, she needed to call her lover and see how bad he'd missed her. She hated to have sent him back home so soon but how else would he explain to his woman what he was doing away from home more than a week. Champagne had enjoyed his comfort during her supposed mourning period as well as those of a few others as she traveled around the world. Just knowing she would be seeing him when she returned home sent chills over her entire body.

*　*　*

When Nadeen made it home from church later that night, she was surprised not to have a message from Kenny yet. She had straightened him out pretty good about putting their family business out in the street the way he did. He usually would have called by now begging her to listen to his explanation. He had no right to tell anyone about this situation, especially that fake sanctified church girl who was just trying to get in between the sheets with him.

The more she thought about Ann being pregnant the more her blood pressure rose. How could her daughter sneak around with some nasty little boy and get herself pregnant? When did she find time to do it? Where did she do it? Surely she didn't have the nerve to bring him into her home and violate it that way. Nadeen felt the side of her temples throbbing just thinking about Ann fornicating in her home.

How could Ann have done something so opposite of the example she set for them? What about Patsy? She was the oldest. Could she have convinced Ann to do this? Was she doing it? If she was, who with? She didn't need Kenny to handle this, but it would have been a good idea to have him help her keep a close eye on her girls.

Now because he was off somewhere playing with a love-sick church member, his middle baby girl was about to have a living, breathing consequence of disobedience.

This was all his fault. All his fault for leaving. If he thought she would break down under the pressure of a teenage daughter pregnant and unwed he was wrong. She was a strong, Christian woman, strong like her momma raised her to be.

Nadeen had taken all the arrows from the enemy she could handle for one day. She decided to go to bed early and start all over again in the morning with a new determination. Patsy had taken care of Josie and dinner. She was glad to have one daughter who hadn't shamed her good name all over Greater Trials.

The morning came quickly for Nadeen. She hadn't slept well the night before. She kept having this dream of walking in a river. The river had two different types of water, one was clear and crisp like a glass of cold water and the other side was foggy and looked like it was bubbling. Whenever she tried to cross to the cool side a wave would come between the two sides and knock her down.

She was calling for help but every time she did the wave came and knocked her back down. A voice kept telling her to crawl; to crawl or die. She didn't understand the dream but when she woke up her legs hurt like she had been kicking. The sheets were all over the bed. She hadn't had a bad dream like that since her best friend Dhmonique died. It had haunted her for weeks. She decided to take a quick shower and go in to work early.

17

"SANDRA, YOU AND Lavon, and the baby should come over to my Grandma Ruth's house tomorrow for the birthday dinner celebration in memory of my great grandmother, Gerthie, I invited Dustin and Ann invited Ralph. Grandma said they could come. She said she especially wants to talk to Ralph." Patsy said trying to talk low as she packed her and Josie's bags.

"Bless Ralph's heart he got more courage than me. I wouldn't want to have to be the one to sit down and talk to your grand-momma after knocking up her granddaughter, that's almost as bad as having to face the wrath of your momma."

Patsy laughed. "I know right."

"Anyway, is this the party where your grandmother bust her pants out in the backyard a few years ago showing everybody how to drop it to the floor"? Sandra asked while trying not to laugh too loud.

Patsy laughed with her "Yes, girl! You remember that? My momma was so shame she just went in the house for the rest of the night. We had a good time."

"Good to see y'all having that again I know the last year or so been kinda rough for your family my friend. Let me check with Lavon we just might stop by."

"Good. My grandma won't mind. She hasn't seen Solomon."

"That's right she hasn't. I been busy with him and school so I don't get to do a lot anymore you know that but that is reason enough to come. I have to sneak Solomon out the house cause my momma fussed about him coming here but now she won't put him down. He is rotten." Sandra laughed and said.

"Well, his Auntie Patsy looking forward to him coming. See you tomorrow around five."

"Sure will. Later bestie," Sandra said just as Solomon started crying in the background.

"Go feed my nephew," Patsy said and hug up the phone.

"Girls, come on out of there! We got some baking to do!" She heard her Aunt Eva yell down the hall. She'd gotten there to pick them up quicker than Patsy thought. She was usually late.

"Nadeen, what time you coming over to momma's tomorrow?" Patsy heard her aunt ask.

"I don't recall telling you that I was," Nadeen said sarcastically.

"Oh, that's what we doin' today? If I didn't know you as good as I, do I'd swear you need Kenny or somebody to knock the edge off." Eva shot back at her sister.

"What you not gone do today Eva is cause my blood pressure to go up. Get your nieces and go on to mommas. I got to get some rest tomorrow I have been working none stop. Just tell Momma to send me a plate. Patsy get on up here!"

"Well, it's what you wanted remember? You and Landon shamed poor Brother Jordan right into recommending you for that position so now you gotta stand up in it like the woman you say you are. I told you before nothing good comes from vengeance." Eva said.

"Nothing good comes out of your mouth." Nadeen shot back. "No please exit out the door you just came in. My temples are starting to throb."

Patsy grabbed the remaining items on the bed and threw them

in the suitcase. "Come on Josie, before your momma changes her mind," Patsy said as she threw open the door. She stepped out the door and must have swung the suitcase without realizing it. The suitcase hit Josie in the face. She let out a loud scream.

"Oh, my Lord! What is wrong with my baby?" Nadeen yelled as she and Eva ran down the hall. Patsy dropped the suitcase and picked Josie up, she was trying to comfort her and make sure she hadn't broken her nose or cut her face. She bore enough scars from the Drano incident.

"Give me my baby!" Nadeen yelled at Patsy as she pushed her against the wall. Patsy's head hit the wall hard and she tasted the blood from her tongue.

"Nadeen she alright. She just a little scared. She ain't bleeding nowhere." Eva said to try and calm her sister down.

"What did you do, girl?" Nadeen turned and yelled at Patsy as she was examining Josie's mouth and face.

"I accidentally hit her with the suitcase. I didn't realize how close she was behind me." She told her mother. Her body was tense waiting for a blow to her face.

Patsy must not have heard the supposed tone in which she answered her mother.

"Oh, you getting aggravated or frustrated now?" Nadeen asked her. "You been gone a few weeks with them folks from Kenny church and you think you can come back in here with attitude?"

Before Patsy could respond, Nadeen reached down and took off her shoe. She hit Patsy in her face so fast and so hard Patsy was still trying to put together what she had just been hit with as the sparks danced before her eyes. Her face was aching and the inside of her mouth was torn and bleeding.

"Who do you think you talking to, girl? It's been a minute since I tore into you but don't think I don't remember how! You better wash your face and cleanup that nasty attitude." Nadeen said putting the shoe up to Patsy's face.

"Nadeen. You crazy as a bat drinking moonshine! You about to drop Josie and break poor Patsy's jaw for nothing. Don't go spoiling our special day just because your man ain't home for you to kick him around." Eva said as she pulled the shoe from Nadeen's hand.

"Give me this baby and please leave Patsy alone so we can go. I got to get to the store for your momma's evaporated milk."

Nadeen stepped back from her daughter while still staring at her to let her know she wasn't playing with her. She handed Josie to Eva.

"See that's why your sister wobbling around here with her belly swollen. She got beside herself and thought I had took my foot off her neck so she snuck around and got herself tricked by some boy. I still got a leather belt for her back don't think I don't!" She said. Patsy couldn't respond even if she wanted to her jaw hurt too bad.

Nadeen turned to face her sister. "And as for you Eva, I could care less if Kenny was home or not. I don't need him to be here with me. He where he want to be so let him stay! You take care of your household and I'll take care of mine!"

"I'm not doing it with you today Mrs. Beelzebub. I don't see why Pastor Craig didn't sit you down long before he died. I guess he was too busy looking under Champagne's dress instead of looking at what he had working the front door of the Sanctuary You really need to be ministered to instead of ineffectively ministering to other folks. If you keep being the doorkeeper folks gone be dirty coming in and dirty coming out with what you got on you."

"I got boldness on me, honey. Just because I don't allow unholy spirits to get comfortable in my house doesn't mean I need to be ministered to. It means I'm not one to be played with when it comes to living holy. You should try it sometime when you not busy playing house with David." Nadeen shot back at her sister.

Eva bit her bottom lip, "Patsy, let's go before the police have to come to your house to get me off of your momma. Can anybody ever have a good day with you Nadeen?" Eva asked as she turned and walked away, leaving Nadeen standing in the hall. When they made it to the car, she looked at the slight bruise on her niece's face.

"Patsy, you okay?" She asked gently turning her face.

Patsy nodded her head yes as she tried to keep the tears that had filled up in her eyes from falling down her face. Patsy couldn't talk. Her jaw was hurting so bad. How much longer was the Lord going to sit by and watch Nadeen mistreat them? Had Kenny and God both left the scene?

When they got in the car Eva tried to make Patsy feel better. "Patsy, your momma got demons inside of her she ain't even responsible for and she done had them so long she don't even know they inside of her. We both do. She just chooses to deal with them by hurting her family. I choose to ignore mine and party them away when they try to come visit."

The rest of the ride was pretty quiet other than Eva talking about David and the turkey legs he was suppose to be at the house smoking.

"I hate she messed up your jaw baby. David is putting those turkey legs in the smoker and they are gonna be delicious! I hope he's already got them wrapped and on the grill. He left out early this morning going to check on a sick aunt he said." Eva told her as she tried to drive and light her cigarette at the same time.

"I'll let your grandmomma take a closer look at you when we get there okay?" Eva said as she blew the smoke from the cigar towards the window. Patsy just shook her head in agreement.

When they made it to Grandma Ruth's house Ann was sitting out on the porch. She was leaned back in the chair with her belly looking like a gumball. Now that she wasn't hiding it Patsy wondered how she never noticed Ann's stomach before?

Patsy got out of the car and looked at her with amazement. Her little sister really was going to have a baby? Ann seemed to rock a little trying to get up out of the chair. When she got up to the porch, Ann looked straight into her big sister's eyes and she could tell something was wrong. She knew that look too well.

She knew the sadness. She saw the bruise on her jaw. Her heart sunk deep within her belly. She was glad she wasn't home. She'd been reading up on how babies can feel things in the womb. She didn't want to have her child being born depressed because of her internalizing the drama that took place at home.

"Hey, Patsy," Ann said. Patsy put her hand on her jaw and struggled to speak. "Hey Ann." No other words needed to be spoken between the two of them because they both knew. Ann reached out and gave her sister a hug. She kissed Josie on the forehead and carried her in the house.

"Is that my oldest grandbaby coming through the door to help her grandmomma with this party?" Grandma Ruth said as they walked through the door.

She reached out for Patsy when she came into the kitchen, she hugged her then pushed her back and looked at her face.

"What door knob did you slam into girl?" She asked turning Patsy's jaw so she could get a good look at the bruise.

"It's called the heel of Nadeen's shoe. Don't ask no more questions and spoil our celebration." Eva said to her mother as she put her car keys in her purse.

"My. My. My. What am I gonna do about that crazy daughter of mine and her crazy ways?" Grandma Ruth asked.

"Eva go get that ice pack out the refrigerator. Patsy, you go take two of those blue pills by my bedside, put that ice pack on your jaw and rest a spell. Eva and I got these pies. We'll save the peaches for you to do the deep-dish peach pie later tonight. Ann get your sister a glass of water."

Patsy went to lay down in the guest bedroom. Ann followed with a glass of water and the ice pack.

"What small thing did you or didn't you do to get that bruise on your face?" She asked as she sat down on the bed and handed Patsy the glass of water.

"You know the usual, the mysterious attitude or tone in my

voice. I accidentally hit Josie in the face with my bag. I guess it scared her and you know your Momma loves her baby girl. She thought I hurt her and I tried to explain I didn't mean to do it. I didn't know she was behind me." Patsy explained as she picked up the pills on the nightstand and took them.

"Yeah, she love her for now. Let's see how that love working out for our little sister in a few years." Ann responded taking the glass of water from her sister and handing her the ice pack.

"One day, Patsy. One day we won't have to be treated like we don't matter. The day I leave her house is the last time I will ever step in her house or God's. I'm done with church. Everybody in there pretending. Pastor Craig was too scared to call folks out for the wrong they was doing cause he was doing it too. I know I ain't got much room to talk but at least I'm not pretending with God," Ann said looking down as she softly rubbed her stomach.

Patsy knew she was right. "Maybe she'll change." She said as she held the ice pack firmly against her jaw.

Ann looked at her and rolled her eyes, "And maybe I got a bad case of gas. Look, I'm gonna go back up front and help Grandma. I'll come back and check on you later."

She slowly closed the door as she left. She tried not to think about her sister's face because when she did, she started scratching her leg and if she dwelled on it too long she'd find a nice, sharp razorblade to ease her pain.

When Patsy got up it was midnight. She'd slept through the pain. She enjoyed the quietness of the house. It was relaxing. She found the peaches in the freezer and without a soul to talk to, she made the best deep dish peach pie that she ever had. She kneaded all of her tears, hopes, and desires for a better life in that pie crust dough.

When the rest of the house woke up, they stepped into a kitchen with a beautiful table setting all ready for the birthday celebration dinner. Patsy had even decorated the glasses by making fans out of the napkins.

Grandma Ruth was so pleased she clapped her hands and said "Praise God for my grandbabies. They are such a blessing in my old age. Your great grandmother would have loved this." She hugged Patsy and was careful to kiss her on the side of her jaw that wasn't bruised.

"It's beautiful, big sister," Ann told her sister. She just wanted to see her smile.

"Thank you. It's no big deal." Patsy said touching the napkins.

"I guess that ice pack and pain pills helped."

"Fixed me right up, grandma," Patsy replied, forcing a smile.

"I'm surprised your momma doesn't have a few ice packs herself as many 'accidents' as she have with you girls and your daddy." Grandma Ruth said as she walked off. Well, we better get a little breakfast in our bellies and finish getting things ready for the party. When I'm gone you won't have to do this anymore. It's just my way of respecting the vessel that gave me life. No matter her ways she was my mother and God has directed me to honor her. You girls remember that okay?" Grandma Ruth said opening up the refrigerator to find something for breakfast.

Neither Ann nor Patsy responded right away. Grandma Ruth peeped at them from behind the refrigerator door. "I said you girls remember that."

"Yes, ma'am," Patsy and Ann both said in unison.

* * *

Eva arrived with balloons a few hours later, she looked a little bothered.

"Momma, David been over here yet?" She asked.

"No, he hasn't. You tell him I don't wait for no man. He was supposed to smoke these turkey legs for us last night and just like a man he didn't come through. I don't understand why you attract to men like that. Your daddy showed you what a reliable man looked like and you can't seem to pick' em to save your soul." Grandma Ruth told her daughter.

"Momma, David had to go check on his aunt yesterday. she isn't doin' well. I think she got cancer. He left the house before I did again this morning. He said he was headed back over there."

"I ain't never heard him mention no aunt being sick." Grandma Ruth said.

"That doesn't mean he doesn't have one," Eva said placing the balloons around the kitchen.

"You been over there with him?" Grandma Ruth asked.

"No. He told me he didn't want to have to pop a cap in one of his cousins about saying something out the way to me. He says those his real daddy's folks and they, not the kind he like to deal with so he didn't want me being around them." Eva said.

Her mother stared at her. "If that's what you want to believe. A man and his excuses always got a skirt with a big booty behind 'em." Ruth told her daughter.

"Not today, Momma." Eva responded." You and my sister won't give a good man a chance I swear. Every one of them ain't bad."

"Again, if that's what you want to believe." Her mother responded. "By the way, what time is my other daughter getting over here? The one that likes to put her mark on folks."

"She say she need a day to rest cause she been working so much. She said you can send her a plate." Eva told her mother.

"Did she? She trying to run me now? I'll think about it but I won't make no promises. It ain't a job that's keeping Nadeen away, it's the shame of being the topic of church gossip for a change instead of helping to spread it" Grandma Ruth said glancing over at Ann.

Ann pretended not to hear her.

"Grandma, I invited Sandra and Lavon to come over too. She said she wanted you to see the baby." Patsy chimed in. She'd almost forgotten to mention it to her grandmother after what happened yesterday.

"Babies having babies. You girls just gotta find out the hard way that fifteen minutes of sweat ain't love but anyway I'm looking forward to seeing her and that baby. Girls, you go get dressed. We gonna get this party started. I know you want to look cute for them little boys." Ann and Patsy smiled and went to change.

A few hours later Ralph and Dustin arrived. They came up at the same time. Dustin rang the doorbell. Patsy went to the door. She could see the expression on his face when he spotted the bruise. He held her face in his hands and kissed her gently on the lips.

"Y'all better stop that. That leads to the stomach mumps." Ann laughed from behind Patsy.

"Not here." Patsy said. "Come on in Dustin. We still cooking some stuff." Patsy muffled as she took him into the kitchen. Ralph stepped up and kissed Ann on her jaw.

"Everything okay with you and the baby?" Ralph asked touching Ann's stomach. She smiled at him.

"We good. Just hungry all the time…like now. Come on in. I'm ready to eat." She said taking him by the hand. Ralph followed her in like a puppy.

When they all entered the kitchen Grandma Ruth and Eva were wrapping turkey legs. They both looked up at her and Ralph.

"We got company, I see." Grandma Ruth said looking up as she rolled up the turkey. "You the person responsible for my granddaughter being at my house for the next few months?" She asked Ralph. Ralph didn't quite know how to answer.

"Momma, you getting nice in your old age. That had been me or Nadeen you'd have already cussed him right back out that door and sent us with him probably," Eva said taking the turkey leg from her mother and placing it in a pan.

"Let me just make it plain for you, young man. You that baby's daddy?" Eva asked. Ralph put his head down as he held Ann's hand.

"Yes, ma'am. And I'm gonna be with Ann through all of this because she didn't do it by herself, that's what my momma said."

Grandma Ruth stopped and looked at Ralph. "She had to tell

you that? Surely you knew it. You and Ann got yourselves a big responsibility son. I'm sure your parents already told you that."

"It's just me and my mom. My parents separated." Ralph said squeezing Ann's hand tighter. "I'm going to do what is right."

"That's good. We all gonna be all right in a minute, we a little disappointed right now, but it won't last long. Once we see that baby's sweet face, we'll forget all about that disappointment." Grandma Ruth said wiping her hands on her apron.

"Can I get some cake or a sandwich or something we starving," Ann said rubbing her stomach.

"Look over there on the oven it should be something. Ralph, you go on and get you something too. We gone talk again real soon." Grandma Ruth said pointing to the oven with a half-wrapped turkey leg in her hand. "Young man, you and Patsy go out back and get that homemade ice cream started. Patsy knows what to do." She said looking at Dustin.

Dustin laughed slightly. "Yes ma'am." He said as he headed towards the back door with Patsy following behind.

When they'd gotten down the back steps out of hearing distance Dustin brought up Patsy's face. "You want to talk about that bruise or maybe I should ask can you talk?"

Patsy barely opened her mouth and let out a soft "No."

"Is your mom coming over today? I don't want any problems for you. I know your grandmother said we could come over and all, but I don't want no police cars or ambulances showing up today." Dustin said. Patsy just shook her head no.

Dustin touched her arm and turned her to him. "Things are going to get better for us in a few months. Just believe that okay?"

"I believe it." Patsy said. "Now let's get this ice cream done before my grandmother throws a fit." She said pouring the salt into the bucket.

When they walked back into the house Grandma Ruth was headed out the back door. carrying the turkey legs in a pan.

"Somebody come hold this door open for me. I'm about to drop these turkey legs in this smoker so we can eat. I don't wait around for no man. I never had to when your granddaddy was living and I won't do it now. You girls better take notes." She told her granddaughters. Ralph and David both went to hold the door open for her.

"Look like you boys might work out after all." She told them as she backed out the door.

Just then, David walked in. Eva had been standing at the front door looking out, she had seen him get out of a car, but it wasn't his. She went back to the kitchen table and sat down so she wouldn't look desperate. He walked into the house grinning. Eva noticed he didn't have on the same clothes he'd left in that morning. His cologne lit up the kitchen. Her mother glanced over at her as she came back in.

"David, whose car did you just get out of, and where you been? You changed clothes and everything. You knew we were waiting on you to smoke these turkey legs for momma." Eva said. Crossing her leg and shaking it to keep from slapping the taste out of his mouth.

David threw up his hands and stepped back. "You asking me five hundred questions. I had some business I needed to take care of. I didn't have time to call you. If you gotta know, I got called into work after I left my aunt. I had to fix a system problem, that takes time Eva! You know I got trained to work on those machines. I got to give them folks they money back by using what I learned and I'm trying to get another promotion." He said. "I couldn't get a signal on my phone so I couldn't call you."

"Whose car was that? Where is your car?" Eva asked tapping her fork on the table.

"My car stopped on me on the highway on my way here and I had to push it into the parking lot over at that hotel on Hwy 44. Just so happened our church member was on her way to the casino and saw me walking. She was nice enough to pick me up and drop me off." He said.

"A church member?" Eva asked. "What church member got a

crème-colored Lexus at Greater Trials? As soon as she said that, Ann and Patsy both looked at each other with knowing in their eyes.

"Eva you better start doing a better job of checking your surroundings." Her mother said.

"Did you forget that Pastor Craig bought a fancy crème colored Lexus for First Lady, Champagne, she just got back into town recently remember?"

Eva looked at David with confusion on her face. "How is it Champagne Porter came about picking you up?" David's grey eye's flashed in anger.

"I just told you my car broke down on the way here! She saw me walking.

I had already gone back home and changed. I was driving fast as I could to get here. Do you even care that I was walking the highway?" David asked Eva. "The woman was nice enough to go out of her way to bring me here so I could be questioned like a child instead of the grown man that I am!" David said as he turned to walk back out the door.

"Man. If I knew this was what I had waiting for me I would have stayed where I was."

"You come back here!" Eva yelled as she picked the electric knife up off the table and threw it at the back of his head. Fortunately, it missed his head and landed on the floor in the doorway. David turned around and looked at her.

"This whole family is straight crazy! I don't blame Kenny for leaving. I'm about to do the same myself!" He said as headed for the door. Ann got up and went to pick up the knife. She tried to bend over to get it. David yelled at her.

"Ann, you know you ain't got no business bending down like that. Let your crazy aunt pick it up she threw it." He said to Ann.

"You're not that girl's daddy! You don't raise your voice at her!" Eva yelled back at him. David took out his cigarette and headed out the front door.

"You don't know whose daddy I am!" He said and slammed the door behind him. Ralph went to pick the knife up off the floor.

Patsy just put her head down. She was so tired of being ashamed. She wouldn't be surprised if Dustin changed his mind about marrying her. Dustin reached over and rubbed her back. It was a sign to her that it was okay. He understood and he still loved her.

"Let me go get this nut to come in here. We all starving in here waiting on him and he actin' a fool!" Eva said. When she came back in the door with David they were holding hands and he was telling her, "You know I love you, crazy girl." It looked to Patsy as though Ann rolled her eyes when he said that. She was probably tired of all the drama too.

The rest of the evening Ralph was attentive to Ann. Ann told Ralph she felt a little dizzy and probably better go lay down herself. She stood up from the table and crashed down to the floor. Ralph jumped back in shock.

"Ann! Ann wake up!" He yelled as he bent down and started shaking her. "Somebody help her, what's wrong with her?"

Eva jumped up. Patsy followed behind her, thinking her Aunt she should have been a nurse as many bruises as she had to fix in this family.

"Everybody move! Give her some air!" Eva yelled fanning everybody back.

Ralph stood frozen. He didn't know what to do.

Grandma Ruth started fussing.

"Where's her momma? She needs to be here seeing about her instead of trying to hide her face in sanctified sand."

"Ralph help me get her up." Eva said lifting Ann off the floor. Ralph bent down to help her.

"Now wet that towel on the bar with some cold water and bring it to me." Eva directed ralph as she pointed to the bar. Ralph wet the towel, brought it back to her and Eva started wiping Ann's face. She started moaning a little.

"Ann, you okay?" Ralph asked with a worried look on his face. "I'm okay. I think it's just too hot in here for me. I need to get some air." Ann said. "I feel like I'm suffocating. I'm gonna go and sit out on the porch for just a minute." Ralph grabbed her jacket and wrapped it around her arms.

David was standing outside on the front porch smoking.

"Baby girl, what drama going on now?" He asked Ann as she came out of the door and sat in the chair. "Your crazy aunt in there acting up again? Her and your momma need to learn how to treat a man then they would keep a man. Ain't that right?" He looked over at Ann and winked before crushing his cigarette to the ground.

"Ann, you need me to go get something for you?" Ralph asked ignoring David's comment. Ann leaned over on his arm.

"I'm fine Ralph. I appreciate you being here for us."

Patsy felt sorry for Ralph because deep down inside she didn't really believe Ann would stay with him. Ann was just in a needy place right now. Once the baby came and she began her new "normal" life, she'd probably get bored with him and push him away.

Ralph, can you get me some ice chips please?" Ann sweetly asked Just as he went in the house Sandra and Lavon pulled up. Lavon blew the horn. Sandra jumped out waving.

"Hey, Ann!"

Ann laughed. "Hey, ole country girl. The whole neighborhood can hear you."

"The neighborhood needs to mind their business. Lavon, grab the baby and come on." Sandra said, jumping out of the car and leaving Lavon to take Solomon out of the baby seat.

She came up on the porch and hugged Ann. "Sis, you looking like you might be pregnant," she teased.

"You think?" Ann replied as she returned Sandra's hug.

"Young lady, that's all you see standing out here? Where's your respect for your elders? Just cause you got a baby doesn't make you grown enough to try and disrespect me." David said to Sandra as he pulled his second cigarette out of the pack.

"Mr. David, I was gonna speak to you I just wanted to give Ann a hug first. It ain't nothing personal." Sandra replied.

"Well, I was about to take it that way. That young man right there slept with you last night not me." David said, pointing to Lavon as he came up on the porch.

"Hey, Mr. David. You good?" He asked. "I saw you pointing at me." He asked trying to steady Solomon in his arms.

"I'm one-hundred, young buck. What about you?" I ain't seen you since Patsy lost her mind at that school dance," David said looking at him through a cloud of cigarette smoke.

Lavon smirked a little. "I'm good. Ann, how you been?"

"I been making it, Lavon. How about you?"

"Same thing. I been making it. Got a few things I need to get in order but I'm good," he told her.

"What dance you seen Lavon at?" Sandra asked David.

"Watch it little girl. You question him not me." David said throwing his cigarette butt to the ground. "I swear, all y'all need a lesson in manners."

"Sandra it ain't no big deal. I was just headed over to a friend's house and drove through a few weeks ago when they was having that dance at Ann's school. I just blowed at Mr. David." Lavon said looking at David for confirmation.

David just shook his head in agreement. Ann tried to ease the tension.

"San, you and Lavon better be careful before another one comes along." Ann said.

"Girl, don't speak that. Lavon and I ain't having no more babies until we get married. Let me take Solomon on in the house so your grandmomma can see him." Sandra said taking Solomon from his daddy. "Lavon, we gone talk about this dance later."

"Young blood you better get out while you still got time." David advised Lavon.

"It's all good. She just trippin' and I'm just doin what I gotta do for the time." Lavon said walking up the steps towards the door. Just then Grandma Ruth appeared at the door.

"Ann! Time for you to get back in this house before you and that baby get a cold from this night air. We about to eat in a few minutes." Grandma Ruth said standing at the door.

"Yes, ma'am. I was waiting on Ralph to bring me some water. What's he doin'?" Ann asked her grandmother.

"He's in here helping me. I'll send him out in a minute. He reminds me of your daddy so much." Grandma Ruth said as she closed the door.

"Ann, you probably need to go in. You don't want to get sick carrying that baby," Lavon said. Before Ann could answer David walked up, reached over, and rubbed Ann's stomach as he headed back into the house.

"That baby is going to be fine just like it's momma. She filling out real good."

Lavon reached over and roughly pushed his hand off of Ann's stomach. David laughed and stepped back with both hands up in the air.

"Hey, lil' man relax. I'm just showing her a little concern that's all."

"That's not cool. You shouldn't be touching her like that." Lavon said looking at David like he dared him to try it again.

"You act like you got some skin in this game youngblood. That surely ain't the case, is it?" David asked "Ann, you got some doubts about that baby's daddy?"

"Lavon just ignore my aunt's boyfriend. He gets like this sometimes. Aunt Eva! Aunt Eva come get David!" Ann yelled.

David laughed at her. "You know your aunt don't run me." He said. "Youngblood. Be careful. Stay in your place. Look to me like you already got plenty to keep you busy." David said patting Lavon on the shoulder as he walked into the house.

As he entered the door, Eva walked out with Ralph behind her. "Ann, what is David doin' out here aggravating you? I have told him not to tease with you. You pregnant and moody. Lord, he is like a child sometimes. Oh, hey Lavon, I didn't know you were out here."

"Yes, ma'am. Probably glad I was the way Mr. David was coming at me and Ann both. He was touching her stomach. I know how Sandra was about that when people did it to her. I got her though." Ralph stepped from behind Eva with the ice chips Ann had asked for earlier.

"I appreciate you for making sure Ann is okay but I'm here now," Ralph said. "Ann, you ready to come inside? Your grandmother is getting worried about you and all the food looks like it's done."

"I guess so. It's getting too crowded on this porch." Ann said reaching her hand out. Ralph reached down to help Ann get up out of the chair. "Thanks, Lavon. I appreciate you looking out for me."

"You know I got you, Ann. Guess I better go in and check on Solomon."

"I don't think I like your uncle. I thought he was cool before but after today I changed my mind." Ralph told Ann on their way back inside.

"He is just arrogant. Ignore him." Ann said trying to walk steady.

"Ann, I don't want you around him. Something ain't right about him." Ralph said.

"Ralph don't start bossing me around. You this baby's daddy, not mine just remember that." Ann said.

"Ann, what you got goin' on out there on that front porch?" Sandra asked as she fed Solomon a piece of sweet potato pie. "Lavon said your uncle was tripping with you. You know my baby daddy love you and Patsy like his own sisters he ain't gonna let nobody bother you."

"I guess everybody is hungry. Grandma can we eat now?" Ann asked sitting down at the kitchen table.

"You sure can. I wish my son-in-law was here to bless the food for old time sakes but since he not I guess I'll have to do it myself." She told Ann.

"You act like it's not another man up in here." David said to Grandma Ruth.

She glanced at him and bowed her head. "Dear heavenly father. We thank you for this gathering and we ask you to bless this food and the hands that prepared it. Amen."

She lifted her head and looked at David. "I just wasn't feeling like you could get a prayer through today David. You and Eva had too much going on earlier. Now pass me one of those turkey legs and sit down." Grandma Ruth said. "Ann, you eat up, you eating for two now."

"Grandma if you keep filling up my plate, I'm gonna be too big to fit through the front door." Ann said shoving a yeast roll in her mouth.

"Don't worry about that. It'll drop soon as you have that baby. You young, your body will snap right back into place and hopefully you'll wait till marriage for the next one."

"Well on that note I think I'll have some more collard greens." Eva said reaching over the table for the bowl of greens.

The rest of the meal was eaten with plenty of laughter going around. Ann joined in but in the back of her mind she felt a slight emptiness because all of her family was here except her own parents. Regardless of their personal issues they were still supposed to be here at this table, in this moment.

"Well Ms. Ruth, dinner was really good, but I better get this little boy to bed. Me and him both full and sleepy." Sandra said as she stood up and started gathering Solomon's things off the table and putting them in his diaper bag.

"Do you mind if we get a to-go plate for my mom, Ms. Ruth?"

"You and your momma welcome to it. Eva fix these children something to take with them." Eva got up and prepared the plates. "Here you go, love. You take care of that baby. Lavon, you try and keep your temper in check darling. Getting up in my man's face like you did earlier ain't the best choice you could make healthwise."

"Eva that is a child. Let that go." Grandma Ruth said.

"Momma he got a whole baby and almost a wife, he ain't no child. He wasn't acting like no child when he came at David. David still a little warm about it too." Eva said handing the plates to Sandra.

"Ms. Eva I was just looking out for Ann. I wasn't trying to get into it with Mr. David." Lavon tried to explain.

"Lavon, you and Sandra welcome to come back to my house anytime you want. I'm the only one paying bills up in here." Grandma Ruth said.

"Thank you, Ms. Ruth," Lavon said grabbing Solomon's diaper bag. He knew if he said something back to Ann's aunt again about the situation it would get worse.

"Goodnight, Ms. Eva. Ann. Patsy thanks for inviting us." Lavon said taking the plates from Sandra.

"Yeah, thanks for the invite, bestie. Call me if you need something." Sandra said. She grabbed Solomon's cup and headed out.

"Guess I better be heading that same way." Dustin said walking out behind them.

"Yeah. It's been a lot going on today and we ate way too much food." Patsy said.

She walked him to his car and kissed him goodnight.

"Good to see you," Dustin said holding her close to him. She could feel how good it was for him to see her.

"I can tell."

Dustin put his head down a little and smiled. "That's what you do to me."

Patsy didn't really know how to respond to that, so she just leaned into his chest and kissed him. "I better go pull Ralph outta there too. If you can't stay the night, then he can't." Patsy said patting Dustin on his chest. They both laughed.

"You right." Dustin said, slowly nodding his head up and down in agreement.

When Patsy made it back in the house, she could hear her Grandma Ruth already telling Ralph he had worn out his welcome too.

"Ralph glad to have you but it's time Ann got some rest. You can give her a call on tomorrow. You two already spent way too much time with each other." Grandma Ruth said.

Patsy giggled. Her grandmother sure didn't bite her tongue.

"Yes, ma'am. I was just about to go. I just wanted to make sure everything was good with Ann." Ralph said getting up to leave feeling the warmth of embarrassment spread all across his face.

"I guess it is getting late. I'll check on you later."

"Tomorrow is good. I'm done for tonight." Ann told him.

"That's cool. Good night, everybody." Ralph said on his way out the door. When he walked out Dustin was starting up his car.

"Ralph, you need a ride man?" Dustin asked as he turned on the car radio.

"Yeah, I would appreciate that. Thanks." Ralph said.

When Grandma Ruth closed the front door, Ann got up from the table. Patsy was standing in front of her, "Girl your face is all lit up." Ann grinned and said.

"You're imagining things. The only thing you see is a smile on my face." Patsy said as she reached up and wiped her face.

"What's the matter? Your boyfriend got you on fire and you need him to put it out?" Ann said poking at her.

"You need Jesus, Ann," Patsy said and walked off from her. She wasn't interested in discussing her private life with her little sister who had been careless enough to get herself pregnant.

18

THE NEXT MORNING, Nadeen woke with a bad feeling. She felt like she was just waiting on something to happen. She tried to shake it off by humming one of her favorite songs but it wasn't working. She was trying to focus on going into the church office and typing up the programs for Sunday when all of a sudden her phone rang. A voice whispered: "Don't answer that. You ain't got time to talk about Greater Trials mess today or about First Lady Champagne coming back looking like a call girl." Nadeen grabbed her purse and headed out the bedroom door. As she passed the girl's room, she thought about the fact that Ann wasn't there.

She wasn't there because she had let some boy make a fool of her and get her pregnant. She was at her Grandmother's house with her belly steady swelling while her momma was dealing with strange looks and church ladies gossiping behind her back.

Ann did this to get back at me. She did this to embarrass me at church, Nadeen thought. *Well, the embarrassment is going to be hers. She's the one that will have to deal with the consequences of being disobedient to her God-fearing mother.* Nadeen thought to herself without noticing she had made it to the church ten minutes earlier than usual due to speeding.

As she parked in the spot reserved for her at the church, she noticed other members pulling up also. This was unusual for this time of morning. Usually, it was just her at the church. As she stepped out of her car, Brother Everett, one of the members of the church executive board, came up to her.

"Sister Nadeen, I'm glad to see you. The Board Member's been trying to reach you about the meeting this morning." He said.

Nadeen was puzzled. "What meeting?" She asked. "The Special Call meeting First Lady Champagne called to tell us who she chose to replace Reverend Craig. You know she had gotten it down to three candidates she was looking at real close. She said she was gonna pray over it and let us know at the next meeting. Well, looks like her decision came earlier than expected.

"She called Elder Rogers late last night and told him she had made a decision and we was to meet her here around 10:00 am this morning to find out. I guess he thought she'd reached out to you too.

"No, Brother Everett, she didn't," Nadeen said biting her tongue from saying anything further about Champagne Porter.

"Well, it all worked out, didn't it? We need you to take notes at the meeting and type up something nice in the church bulletin for tomorrow welcoming our new pastor."

Now Nadeen thought she knew why she had that feeling in her stomach this morning. She was getting a warning from God about this meeting.

"Well, I didn't know about this meeting," Nadeen said. "It's still rather early so why are you here?" She asked him.

"I came to turn on the heat and get the meeting room set up in case you weren't gonna make the meeting on time but since you are here can you go ahead and take care of that?" He asked. "I'll be back with the other committee members."

Nadeen tried to hold the fake smile on her face because in her mind she was cussing him out for being so trifling.

He was already there he could have done that himself. She had other things to do. "Brother Everett I'll be glad to do that for you. Just let me finish typing up the bulletin for service tomorrow and I'll get everything set up for you." She said holding back the nails she wanted to spit into his face.

"I appreciate that, Sister Nadeen. Reverend Craig always said you was the most reliable person he had working in his office. I know you miss him."

Brother Everett said.

"I sure do. Greater Trials will never be the same without Reverend Craig." Nadeen said biting her tongue not to spit out the rest of the words floating around in her mouth. They were related to how glad she would be to get that sneaky Champagne Porter out of their church. She was an adulterer and a "pulpit trick" all rolled up into one tight red dress. She had been a thorn in the side of Greater Trials. Nadeen would be glad to see her leave town.

"All right. See you in a few hours Sister and thank you again for always taking care of things around here. I'm sure the new pastor will be glad to keep you as the church secretary." Brother Everett said and walked back to his car.

As Nadeen walked towards the church office she thought about his last statement. She had never considered that she wouldn't be church secretary anymore when they got a new pastor.

Reverend Craig had listened to Champagne before and tried to replace her. If it wasn't for them trying to put her out of the place God ordained her to be, she wouldn't have had to take care of Sister Haymer the way she did. She hated that she had to lead Sister Haymer back to her drug-using ways but it was Champagne's fault, not hers. Nadeen had only protected what was hers. She hoped she wouldn't have to do it again with this new pastor.

She called home when she finished typing up the church bulletin. She hoped Eva had Patsy and Josie home by now. She knew how she was about them being up in anybody's house too long, even her mommas. Patsy answered the phone.

"Patsy. Look I got a special call meeting here at the church this morning. You go ahead and get that house cleaned up and have dinner started before I get home."

"Yes, ma'am. What you want me to cook?"

"Patsy, just look in that deep freezer and find something. You'll know it when you see it," Nadeen said and hung up the phone.

Nadeen was setting the last glass out on the board table when Champagne Porter walked in the room. Nadeen had prepared sweet tea with lemons for the meeting just like Reverend Craig always liked.

"Sister Nadeen, the table looks so nice. I see you got my late husband's favorite drink. He loved that sweet tea almost as much as he loved me." She said flipping her hair back over her shoulder. Nadeen just smiled. It was all she could do to keep from stomping on Champagne at that moment.

In Nadeen's opinion, Champagne Porter was never meant to be a First Lady. She was too worldly with her low-cut dresses and tight skirts, even today she'd showed no decency in her dress. She looked like she was about to go out on a night on the town instead of a woman in mourning and here to take care of important church business for her dead husband.

"I guess you know I made a decision on who the new pastor of the church would be? I think the congregation will embrace him and make him feel right at home.

"I'll be here for a few more months to get the house sold and wrap up his estate then Daphne and I are leaving to make a fresh, new start. God knows we need it. Your pastor took real good care of me with that insurance policy he bought. God bless him."

"I'm sure he did. His first wife never wanted for anything bless her heart. She was truly a Saint." Nadeen said. She hoped Champagne got the hint.

The rest of the board members arrived. They had a hard time focusing on the words coming out of Champagne's mouth because of the breast creeping out of her dress. David even showed up. Nadeen wondered why he was there.

Guess he would use the church meeting as an excuse for the reason he'd been missing since last night. She started to call her sister and tell her he'd slithered his way to the meeting. He wasn't all the way saved. He was just playing games trying to look good for the church. She knew it was a grey-eyed wolf under that suit coat it was just a matter of time before everybody else knew it too.

She didn't understand why Reverend Craig even chose him to help with church business. She had meant to talk to him about her concerns in his selection before he died.

David walked up to Nadeen, "Your sister is crazy did you know that?" He whispered in her ear.

"I stayed out a little late with the boys last night and she lost her mind when I got home. Y'all just like your momma. Good and crazy. Oh, yeah, you better get those diapers ready. Looks like Ann is gonna pop that baby out earlier than expected." He whispered to Nadeen.

Nadeen cut him a look that let him know if they had not been in the presence of the Greater Trials Board Members, he would have got the cussing out from her that he was so desperately seeking. She tried the best she could to stay in the spirit, but some folks just made her get in the flesh cause they had to be handled that way. It was the only thing they understood. David was one of those people.

She hated that Eva was so tied to him.

"Brother David, I'm glad you managed to make it to the meeting though it looks like you were rushing." She told David as she gave him a look that let him know she didn't appreciate his tardiness.

"Hey, men been waiting on Women since God made Adam. I don't see nothing wrong with you waiting on us sometimes. We worth the wait too." He snapped back at her with a satisfied grin on his face.

"But you don't have the right to waste my time no matter what your personal idiotic beliefs might be." Champagne shot back at him.

"Okay. That's enough you two. Let's do what we came here to do and go on about the business of keeping Pastor Craig's vision alive for our church." Brother Everett interjected.

Champagne gave a strained smile, intertwined her hands together, and continued talking.

"Thank you for handling that Brother Everett. It's enough stress on me with my husband dying suddenly, I definitely don't need additional strife. Anyway, I won't be before you long. I want to, first of all, thank you for being so thoughtful and patient as I dealt with the passing of my beloved husband. He left a big decision for me but gentleman and Sister Nadeen, I think that I have come to the best choice for the legacy of this church to continue.

"I believe you all will be pleased with my choice. I spoke personally with each candidate and I listened to their plan for the growth of this ministry. I put all of this into consideration before I made my selection for the new pastor. I also asked him to come to this meeting today and I believe he has just arrived according to this text message I just received. She looked over at David and smiled.

"Brother David, could you please go and escort our new pastor and his family in please?" She asked David in a soft voice. David smiled and nodded his head. He got up from the chair, straightened his jacket, and went to meet the new head of Greater Trials MB Church.

While he was gone, Champagne informed the board she had a contract drawn up agreeing to pay the new pastor a six-figure salary the first year of his pastorship and the remaining salary would be determined by the board since she would no longer be the one to make decisions after today. She leaned forward so the board members could get a real good look at her breast and read the copies of the contract she'd passed out. When she finished reading it, she licked her lips, pushed her hair behind her ear, and asked each member to sign it prior to the pastor entering the room.

Each member signed the contract with their sweaty hands and secret desires poking out under the church board room table. *She is a customized deception from the pits of hell,* Nadeen thought to herself as she watched Champagne work the board members just the way she wanted. Nadeen now regretted advising Pastor Craig to make it an all-male board except for her. She believed the other women in the church were too messy and loose-lipped to keep church business confidential.

Just as the last member signed the contract, there was a knock on the door. David stepped in and whispered in Champagne's ear. She looked up and smiled at the board.

"Lady and Gentleman I would like for you to stand and greet our new pastor and his family." She said. As she finished speaking, he entered the room.

Nadeen steadied herself as she recognized the smile, the slim, muscular build just right for his navy-blue tailored suit and the familiar chiseled features of his face.

"Welcome our new pastor, a family member, and a brother who has come back home to us, Pastor Dewayne Ryan and Family!" She said.

The room erupted with cheers and handclaps. Everyone rushed to embrace them. Nadeen stood back unable to move. Her lover. Her past shameful secret had returned. Just when she was getting over that whole ugly scene with the fight, the shooting, and the cover-up about what really happened that night.

She looked across the room with her legs losing all their strength and saw a smirk on Champagne's face. She was looking at Nadeen with satisfaction on her face. Nadeen looked into her eyes and saw vengeance. She had known. She had known the truth all the long and she had known what this would do to Nadeen. Champagne hugged the new pastor and his family members one more time.

Nadeen couldn't speak. She tried to find the other door out of the room. She raced through her mind until she remembered. She eased back and turned towards the back of the room. She raced towards the side door and stepped into the hallway to catch her breath. She needed to get to her office and sit down. She walked as steady and swiftly as possible toward the office.

"Sister Nadeen, you not in a hurry to leave, are you?" She heard a voice say. She turned around to see Champagne with a satisfied grin on her face. She knew what she'd done. Nadeen was not going to allow her to see how much she was shaken.

"As a matter of fact, I am Champagne. I have a few things I need to take care of at my other job before the end of the day." Nadeen told her trying to maintain the smile on her face.

Champagne came directly up to her face.

"What you think about the new pastor? He has some wonderful ideas for the church. They will involve lots of changes, some of them immediate. I hope everyone adjusts well. Rumor has it you already pretty familiar with each other." As she looked directly into Nadeen's eyes, she thought back to her husband's last few moments on the earth in his study and the conversation they'd had before his shame killed him, that's right, shame. He couldn't resist his greed for laying between other women's thighs and he had a baby to prove it, and not just any baby, her little sister Daphne, who was living, breathing truth that he'd been unfaithful to his wife and to his God. He'd gotten everything he deserved and more for causing her daddy to leave and taking away Daphne's right to have one in him. Vengeance felt sweet, not bitter.

"I'm sure it won't be that big of a problem. He knew the vision Pastor Craig had for Greater Trials."

You best to get up out of my face before I snatch all of that new Brazilian human hair weave out of your head. Nadeen thought to herself as she strained her tension through her smile.

Champagne laughed a little under her breath because she

knew that at that very moment a church trustee was changing the nameplate on the door of the church secretary's office from Sister Simmons to Sister Haymer.

She told her first cousin she'd handle Nadeen Simmons for what she'd done to her. Champagne had also promised herself she was going to shake the foundation of her husband's church in revenge for what he'd put her mother through for so many years. That plan included pulling his head doorkeeper, Sister Nadeen Simmons, from her post.

Champagne reached out and hugged Nadeen. As she pulled her close, she whispered in her ear.

"I've got one more wonderful surprise for you Sister Nadeen. You take care of yourself and your precious church. I'll be sure to let Sister Haymer, know the good news. She'll be back real soon." She said and walked out the door.

Nadeen almost lost her breath. Her head was swirling and she thought she was actually going to faint. She had to get out of this place or out of this bad dream. *That's it*, she thought. *This is a horrible dream*. But the moment she felt a pat on her back she knew it wasn't.

"Isn't this great, Sister? Our very own Brother Ryan back as the pastor of our church. Reverend Craig would be pleased." Brother Everett said to her. Nadeen wanted him to get out of her face as quickly as possible.

She strained a smile on her face. "Brother Everett, I think he will make a fine Pastor. He'll bring the rest of Pastor Craig's vision to life."

"I hear he's going to be making a lot of changes, one of them will be immediate in the church administration."

"Brother Everett, I have to go. It's been a lot going on today. I need to be rested for service tomorrow. I'll be ushering at both so if you will excuse me." Nadeen said, slipping past him and heading for the door that led to the parking lot instead of her office. She just wanted to get out of the entire building and clear her head. Champagne Porter's vindictive skills had caught her off guard.

She needed time to strategize her next move. When Nadeen made it to her car she sat there for a few minutes in disbelief. She'd noticed Brother Ryan hadn't even really looked at her. He just quickly glanced at her face in the room.

"God, why?" Nadeen looked up towards the sky with both hands on her steering wheel and asked. "Why did you let this happen? Haven't I been a good servant? I have given of my money, time, and talents to this house for your Kingdom. Why would you bring such a test my way? You already took my pastor. What more must I sacrifice to show myself worthy of the Kingdom?" She cried out. She needed someone to hold her at that moment for the first time since her best friend died. Kenny's face came to her mind.

19

THE LAST THREE months had been difficult for Nadeen. Champagne Porter had made good on her promise to find them a new pastor and to make changes in the church administration. Sister Haymer became the new Church Secretary and Head Usher of Greater Trials.

David was put over the church finances.

Pastor Ryan asked her to stay on as the Sunday School Director for the Children's Church with a stipend for incentive. She'd wanted to leave but she couldn't give Champagne Porter the satisfaction of telling everyone she'd defeated her. This was a temporary setback. She'd get it all back. She had to; it was her destiny to be a leader in God's house. All she would have to do is give Pastor Ryan a little time to settle into his new position.

Once he realized how incompetent Sister Haymer was he'd come back begging for her to take the position back. If all else failed, she was still his weakness even if he wanted to pretend she wasn't.

Her doorbell rang and knocked her out of her state of daydreaming. It was Eva.

"You still in mourning over here?" She asked gently pushing the front door open.

"Ann might be in labor. Momma said she been complaining of her back hurting. For the last few days. She only eight months. It's too early for the baby to be trying to pop out. You ready to be a grandmomma or you still trying to be the Head Usher of Greater Trials again?"

"Ann is you and Momma's problem, not mine," Nadeen said. "She think she grown let her deal with it. I got other things to focus on right now."

"You are a piece of work. Momma really scarred you for life. Kenny told me to come by and pick up the new insurance cards so Ann can keep going to her doctor appointments."

"Can't this wait? I got other things to do than to try to find that card. He should have had it mailed to momma's house anyway."

"It's a lot of things my brother-in-law should have done and didn't," Eva said putting her hands on her hips.

"So, Ann goes and makes a mess of her life and everybody else's gotta be interrupted? Wait right here while I go check my mail." Nadeen said to her sister. She came back within a few minutes and pushed the card in her hand. "Here. If Ann had kept her legs closed, she wouldn't be in this situation." Nadeen shoved the card at Eva.

Look just give me the new insurance card and I'll leave you to your pity party." Eva said snatching the card from her sister's hand.

"Eva I'm still trying to understand the where? And how? Of what Ann did.

"Oh, you all of a sudden don't know how babies are made?" Eva said sarcastically.

"Don't play with me right now. I'm not in the mood. Between you and my disobedient daughter, I keep my blood pressure high." Nadeen said with her hands on her hips. "I'm so mad I could spit nails into both her and him. I taught her better, but she doesn't do what I tell her, she does what she wants to and now it's landed her in the role of a single, unwed mother who trust and believe is gonna end up with a broken heart."

"Sounds kinda like when God tells us what and how doesn't it? Yet we go and do what we want then have to deal with the consequences. The only difference is God will forgive but you, you want every chance you get to remind Ann of the sin she has committed as though you have none of your own," Eva said and walked off before her sister could respond back.

Eva's cellphone rang as soon as she got in the car. "Hello?" she answered in a frustrated voice still aggravated from her argument with Nadeen.

"Eva you better step on it getting back here. I don't think Ann's gonna make it keeping this baby in. She's having some contractions. This baby either coming early or the doctor and Ann got the weeks mixed up."

"She's not due for another month, momma. I told her to sit her butt down somewhere! You called Ralph and told him?"

"She called him and told him she was going to the hospital. I called Dr. River's office and got the answering service. I'm waiting on her to call back. We gonna take her to the ER to get checked out if the doctor don't call soon and these pains don't stop. You got that card from Nadeen yet?"

"Yeah, I got the card and her attitude. She might as well get over it cause this baby is coming whether she wants it here or not."

"She better enjoy her little pity party now cause I'm giving her back her responsibility after Ann have this baby. This girl is gonna need all of us to help her raise this child and it needs to start with her grandmother. Look, I need to go and rub her back in a warm bath. She in there getting louder and louder with all that moaning and groaning.

"I'm almost home."

"Good cause it's gonna take the both of us to get her to the car the way she's balling up. I told that little boy and his Momma to stay near their phone."

"David can help us with her once I locate him. I been calling him for hours."

"Eva, I don't know where I went wrong with you when it comes to men but now ain't the time for that conversation. I'll see you when you get here." Grandma Ruth said and hung up the phone.

Nadeen was halfway into her dream when her phone rang. She really didn't want to answer it, but it was her mother, so she picked it up.

"Yes, Momma. What is it?" She asked groggily.

"You need to stick that attitude back in your balled-up panties and get your sanctified self over to this hospital right now!" Grandma Ruth yelled at her. "This girl is being admitted. She's gonna have this baby tonight. Me and Eva have stood in for you long enough. It's time you stepped up." Her mother hollered through the phone.

Not now, Lord, Nadeen thought to herself. *I've had all I can take today, I'm just about to break.* She thought.

"I wasn't there when she made that baby so why do I have to be there now? Call that boy. He needs to be there to see what he gotta deal with for the rest of his life." Nadeen told her mother as she sat up in the bed and rubbed her eyes.

"Funny how you can pray for everybody else and go see about everybody else in the church but when your own daughter in need, you too shame to even be seen with her. You wake up Patsy and Josie and you get over to this hospital and I do mean right now because if I have to come to that house and get you, I'm going to let the whole neighborhood know what a terrible mother you really are!"

"Okay. I'm on my way, Momma," Nadeen said and hung up the phone. She crawled out of the bed and went across the hall to the bedroom where Josie and Patsy were sleeping. She turned on the light, "Patsy. Patsy get up. Your sister's about to bring forth the consequences of her actions. Get ready so you will learn your lesson now and not have to buy it." She said as she turned and headed back to her bedroom to get dressed.

"You want me to call daddy and tell him," Patsy asked as she tried to wake up and grasp that Ann was about to have her baby.

"Call him for what? If he cared so much, he would have been back home. You girls just won't listen to me when it comes to men. They always gotta show you first, one day you gonna listen to me when your heart is tired of believing in what you think is love. Just get Josie dressed so we can get up to that hospital before I have to choke your grandmother out for thinking I'm a child. I'm a grown woman. I do what I want to do when I want to do it."

Patsy let her mother keep venting as she got dressed, then gently changed Josie and got her dressed. When she came out of the door with Josie in her arms her mother was coming out with her purse, perfectly styled hair, and make-up laid on. You would have thought they were headed to church. *Maybe she wanted her new grandchild to meet her grandma looking her best.* Patsy smiled and thought to herself. As they opened the front door it began to gently rain, "Patsy grab the umbrella, looks like we got two storms coming tonight." Her mother said as she reached to take Josie from her arms.

20

KENNY WOKE THAT morning with an odd feeling that he couldn't seem to shake. It distracted him at work so much that he ended his shift early. He tried to sleep later that night but it wouldn't let go. He awoke at 4:00 am and tried praying but it was still there. Something was going on inside of him and he couldn't put his finger on it. As he sat on the couch thinking about his girls and Nadeen he had a thought that made him bend over. The thought seemed to turn into a voice, and it got louder and louder, it came faster and faster. *Go home. You need to go back today. Now is your time. Go back now.* Kenny began to cry. He began to release months of wanting to go but waiting to hear God's voice tell him he could.

He released months of being tired of seeking God's face for an answer, fasting and praying, praying, and crying. He had done all this for this moment right here in the stillness of his one-bedroom apartment.

He knew God was going to answer but he didn't know when. That's the reason he chose to pay month to month for his small apartment. He wanted to be ready to go when God said he could. He cried on that couch and thanked God for about fifteen minutes before he pulled himself together and went to his room to start packing. God had finally answered. He packed everything he had in three suitcases. He would leave the furniture. Maybe Sister Sara could use it or the church could give it to a needy family.

He was going home to take care of his family. He was going back to be the man he needed to be and to put his wife in her rightful place, which was by his side. She was the Queen and not the King and whatever he'd done to put her in his place on the throne he was ready to rectify and get along with the business of raising their three princesses.

He loaded up his truck at the first sign of daylight, slipped an envelope with a letter under the door of the apartment manager for a month in advance for any inconvenience his unplanned exit may have caused, and went back to take one final look at the place and make sure he had packed all the necessities.

He was going to call Sara and tell her the good news on his way down the highway. She would be glad for him he knew. As he finished checking the apartment out, Sara came thru the door. She was carrying a dish that smelled like fried chicken and waffles. Sara stood in the living room looking around at the missing pictures on the table and the furniture pushed out of the way. She wasn't sure what was happening.

She looked at Kenny confused.

"Brother Kenny, what happened in here? You been robbed or someone got into a fight in your place?" She asked as she sat the dish down on the coffee table. Kenny smiled real big at her and walked up to her to give her a hug. His arms felt so good to her.

He pulled back and looked her in the face, "Sister Sara, God told me this morning I could go home. Isn't that good news?" He asked her with the grin stuck on his face.

Sara hesitated a moment she had to pull herself together. "Brother Kenny." She spoke softly. "You sure it was God speaking to you? You sure he told you to go back into such a bad situation? I mean you have done so well here in Miami. You been so faithful to the church and you hadn't touched a drop of alcohol since you been here. I think you better slow down and make sure. You know the enemy is crafty. He can fool you."

"No Sister Sara. I know it was God. I heard his voice clearly speak to me. I been waiting for a long time to hear him. I know it was him and I know it's time to go. Now. Today." Kenny said.

"Brother Kenny you probably had a dream. They can seem real sometimes. Anyway, I just got off work and wanted us to enjoy some breakfast together before you headed to work. You can't just leave your job like this. You need to tell them and you need to tell Pastor." Sara said trying unsuccessfully to hold back the tears filling in her eyes. She could hear her heart beating.

This couldn't be happening. This is not the way it was supposed to be. Kenny held her in his arms and patted her on her back.

"Now Sister Sara don't you cry. I appreciate that breakfast and I know you're gonna miss me I'm gonna miss you too, but maybe now you can find that husband since you won't be taking care of me so much. I appreciate you so much and all you did to help prepare me for this day. You're going to be just fine here. You got a great job and a great church family." Kenny told her with a smile on his face. "My job and my place here was always temporary. God promised me that."

Sara wanted to tell him she loved him. She wanted to beg him to stay. She wanted to tell him he was making a mistake but she was crying too hard to get the words out. He held her for a few more minutes then he released her gently.

"You keep that breakfast. I'm too excited to eat. I better hit the road before it gets too late. I got a long drive tonight and I don't plan on making too many stops." He saw the tears in her eyes. "I'm sorry this happened so suddenly but I promise to check in on you. Your big brother wouldn't leave you all alone." Kenny said looking into her face. As he headed towards the door.

Sara followed him out the door with her head spinning in

disbelief. He just couldn't be going back home. He was supposed to stay there and become her King, her Boaz, not go back home and be a servant.

She felt the warm tears running down her face, but she couldn't stop them. She opened her mouth to speak, the dryness in her throat made it painful but she knew she had to try to stop him. Her future, their future, was on the line in this moment.

Sara wanted to tell him, stay and make a better life with her. She wanted to ask him why was he going back to a woman that didn't love or appreciate him? She couldn't see Kenny was a gift from God. A gift she had misused.

"Brother Kenny if it's the children, I think they understand why you had to leave. They can come and visit any time. I'll help you with them just please don't go back into that valley." Sara pleaded with him wiping the tears from her face. "That's all it is with your wife Brother Kenny. It's a deep valley!"

"It may be a valley, but it is a valley that Nadeen and I are in together but not alone. God is in that valley with us and today he is walking us out." Kenny said as he took his hand and gently wiped Sara's face.

Kenny looked at Sara standing there with tears running down her face. She looked so devastated. His heart hurt for her but it longed more for his home, his girls, and his wife whom he knew needed deliverance.

"I know you don't understand right now, but you have to trust God's plan. This may seem strange to others but remember that God's ways are not our ways, he does things differently to get his glory and he will get his glory out of this situation. I believe that.

"I know there is some young man here in this town on his knees right now praying for a good woman like you. Let me know when he finds you." Kenny said as he opened the door of his truck and got in.

Sara stood there feeling sick in the stomach as he closed the door and strapped on his seat belt. This just couldn't be happening.

"You will be just fine. You are a beautiful, intelligent, and God-fearing Woman. If I was single and twenty-plus years younger who knows but then again, I think it was always suppose to be Nadeen. She always had my heart from the moment I saw her beautiful brown eyes, tiny waist, and long beautiful black hair." He said with a look like he was daydreaming.

She watched his smile as he waved goodbye to her and drove off. She lost her strength and dropped to her knees right there in that parking lot. She was too hurt to be ashamed. She stayed there for about twenty minutes but it seemed like an hour.

She only got up when she heard a voice say, "You know some things you have to take by force. Get up and get yourself together. He is worth the fight." Sara got up from the parking lot, dusted off her throbbing knees, wiped away the tears from her eyes, and walked to her car with a new and stronger desire to figure out a way to become Mrs. Kenny Simmons, a title she valued since the other one didn't. With all the strength she had remaining she looked into that rearview mirror at what looked like liquid fire in her eyes and declared out loud.

"Kenny Simmons, I declare and decree that you are my husband. I will have you in my life and in my bed as my husband."

*　　*　　*

Kenny drove away listening to the gospel jazz CD Sara had given him a few weeks ago. It was relaxing to his soul and his mind. He could hear the smooth sounds of the music as his mind drifted back to her standing in the parking lot. Her question haunted him, "Why?" she asked. Why was he going back to a woman that didn't seem to love, honor or respect him? He rolled that question around in his mind as he headed down the highway back to that same woman. He decided then that he had to face the reason why in order to truly step into the new beginning God was preparing for him. He couldn't walk through this open door with the weight of his "Why?" wearing him down.

Kenny thought back. He went way back to his days of being a child growing up in a house where his father would slap his mother around every Friday night. He remembered the times she would be screaming and begging on the kitchen floor or in the bedroom. He wanted to stop his father but his mother always screamed at him to go to his room and close the door.

He had to hear her begging and crying for hours as the blows of his father's hand or belt whistled through the air. He cried himself to sleep many nights as a child. He promised himself he would never, ever do that to his wife.

Each Saturday morning after the fight, he would find his mother praying. She had built a small space in their living room with candles and her Bible. She would get down on her knees and pray that God would deliver her husband from the demons that made him do those things to her.

She prayed for him to be a good role model for Kenny. Kenny recalled how he would go into the living room and kneel next to her. He smelled the green rubbing alcohol and the medicated ointment she put on her wounds. She covered up on Sunday with long sleeves and a good makeup foundation. It was a good thing her hair was long. She knew just how to wear it so it fell in her face to hide the bruises.

Kenny's father was an elder in the church. He would come in the sanctuary smiling with his wife on his arm and even escort her to her chair. Only Kenny could see the hurt behind his mother's smile. It broke his heart. He hoped his hugs and his love would make her feel better every time it happened. He prayed it would stop.

Then, Kenny traveled back in his mind to a time that it did stop. He told himself back then that God didn't mind. He told himself that his daddy had to be stopped and that what happened to him was his just punishment for years of abusing his mother.

It was a cold December day; His father's parents had come to town and his mother had prepared a large meal. She'd invited all of her in-laws to come over and fellowship with them. Chris, one of his father's cousins, brought a woman with him. She was tall and dark chocolate, she had medium-length hair with light brown streaks that stopped right below her high cheekbones. She looked like a model from a magazine cover.

Her lipstick was burgundy and she had an amazing smile. Kenny remembered her because she was so captivating to him. He remembered she came in with a fur coat on and a red glass dish in her hand. She handed the dish to Kenny's father, which was strange anyway because usually his father just sat in his recliner and waited for Kenny's mother to call them to dinner. This day though, he saw his cousin Chris pull up in his car and he got up to open the door for them.

When Kenny's mother saw them coming down the hall, Kenny remembered the frown on her face and the grin on his daddy's as he handed her the dish from the woman, "Do something with this will you?" he said to Kenny's mother as he handed the dish to her and hurried off into the living room behind them. Kenny went with his mother to fix the table and help with filling the glasses with ice tea. When everyone was at the table, Kenny noticed his mother straining to smile, she barely ate anything.

She moved quietly getting up to get anything that the guest needed. When dinner was over, she stayed in the kitchen cleaning up and storing food. She kept herself busy while her in-laws all visited with each other and his older sister, Ernestine, who was supposed to be in the kitchen helping had managed to slip out and sit in the living room with everybody else.

As everyone was leaving, Kenny recalled his mother pulling the red glass dish out of the refrigerator that the woman brought. It had some type of potato casserole in it.

She'd told Kenny's cousin she would get it back to him as soon as she had a chance to clean it. He told her that would be fine he would pick it up later in the week.

His mother sat it on the top of the oven. Kenny went to the door to wave goodbye to everybody. When he got to the kitchen door he stopped for a minute, he watched his mother as she was mixing or breaking up something on the counter. It was crunchy and loud but she was grinding it with a weird-looking spoon. She was humming as she grounded it up. His father had gone to lay down and finish off the bottle of whiskey his cousin Chris had slipped him.

Kenny remembered that when his mother had finished grounding up what looked like sugar crystals, she gathered them all together in a bowl and poured it into the casserole in the red glass dish that the beautiful woman had brought. She stirred it up real good, put extra cheese on top of it, and put it back in the oven. She turned the oven on and cleaned her hands off on her apron. Kenny walked up to her and asked her what she was making.

She gave him a huge smile, the biggest he'd seen in a long time. She kissed him on the forehead and said, "I'm cooking your daddy something special. Something just for him to show him how I feel about him. It's a brand-new recipe."

Kenny loved when his mother invented new recipes, they were always good. She was a great cook. He remembered asking her if he could have some too when it was ready. She told him that this was only for husbands and she walked out the kitchen still humming. A few hours later he remembered his parents arguing. He heard his father slam the door as he left out the house.

He must have been gone for hours because when Kenny woke up it was late. He was headed to the kitchen to get some water when he heard his father unlock the front door. He came in and went straight to the kitchen. He turned on the light as Kenny tip-toed in a few minutes later for the glass of water. He remembered seeing his father fill his plate with the casserole from the red glass dish, microwave it till the cheese was hot and bubbly, then he sat down at the table. Just before he put the first bite in his mouth, he saw Kenny.

"Boy, what you doin' up this time of morning? Take your dusty behind to bed. Your momma so busy laying on her sorry behind she don't even know where her children at." He said to Kenny. "Go knock on that door and wake her up. Tell her to come fix me a glass of whiskey." Kenny didn't want to go get his momma but he knew he had better do what his father said, he knew his fists swung both ways in that house.

Kenny went to the bedroom door and called his mother. "Momma! Momma, daddy wants you to come and fix him something to drink!" He said through the door. He didn't hear anything so he knocked and said it again. The second time the bedroom door opened, his mother stepped out in her robe.

"Okay, baby. You go back to bed. No need to be up this late. I'm gonna take care of your daddy. You go on back to sleep." She said as she kissed his cheek and slowly walked to the kitchen.

Kenny remembered how it seemed she moved slower than ever down the hall that night. He also remembered that he didn't do what his momma told him to do. Instead of going back to bed, he turned back around and went towards the kitchen. He stood in the hallway and watched. He watched in fear and confusion but also in gratefulness as wicked as that sounded. He watched his mother standing over his father at the kitchen table with a smile on her face and a glass of whiskey in her hand.

His father was grabbing his throat and spitting onto his plate. At first, it looked like ketchup to Kenny, but why would ketchup be making his daddy make those gurgling noises? He remembered the sound of his daddy pushing the chair back across the floor. His mother stepped calmly back and watched him fall onto the very kitchen floor that he had beat her on so many times before.

Kenny couldn't move. He didn't understand what was going on but his mother wasn't moving to help his father so he didn't. The ketchup just kept coming out of his father's mouth and running down his chin. It had turned a dark red. Kenny remembered that because it was so much of it. His father was gasping and gurgling on the floor. His mother walked around her husband looking at him. She began to quote the Lord's Prayer over him. When she finished, she spoke, "You have done many disrespectful things to me over the years in this marriage Bobby and I have taken them. I have taken them because I believed that one day you would be delivered.

"I believed that you could be redeemed but sometimes a person is just destined to burn in hell and you Bobby Simmons are that person. I accepted that today when she came in my house, our house, the house where we raise our children, the house where you beat me because of your own demons, and I'm tired." She said slowly and peacefully to him as she watched him twist and turn on the floor holding his throat. "My children are tired. We have had enough and today when your weekend piece came into our home you crossed the line. Oh, you thought I didn't know about her? You thought that I didn't know half the beatings I was getting in this kitchen were because there were nights you couldn't layup with her? You didn't know that women talk? Gossip travels and it always finds its way to this house. Yes, I knew about her. I have known about her for the last few years. How could you do that to me and your own flesh and blood? Chris is your cousin. He ain't much better than you but he didn't deserve this betrayal from either one of you.

"Guess he was too busy running behind other short skirts to know you been slipping in his back door, but I knew. I knew but I never expected you to bring that nasty trick into our home.

"Your own daddy didn't teach you not to bring your dirt home? Everybody in town knows he got children across them railroad tracks but not one ever came to your momma's door, did they? That's cause they knew their place. Yours should have known hers. Anyway, none of that matters now because I'm going to give you the goodbye I should have given you years ago." She told her husband as he lay dying on the kitchen floor.

Kenny remembered his father reaching for her robe but she

stepped back, he remembered hearing him whisper, "I'm sorry. Help me please baby. I'm sorry."

"It's too late to be sorry. The only good thing you did for me was put my name on your life insurance policy and pay this house off after you get rolled out of this door which is about to happen in a few more minutes." His mother said.

"Baby, please. I'm dying." Those were the last words his Father spoke. His mother stood there looking at him for a few minutes dying then she looked towards the doorway and saw Kenny.

She walked over to him and squatted down to look him in the eyes, "Don't you ever disrespect your wife. You hear me? Don't you ever put your hands on her. The hands you used to place a ring on her finger, to hold her in your arms at night, and to praise the living God. Don't you ever lift those hands up against her and never bring your Babylonian whore into her house." Kenny didn't know what a Babylonian whore was but it sounded like somebody that would get you on the kitchen floor like his daddy. Her words sent chills through his body. "Yes, ma'am" was all he could say.

His mother went to the phone and called the police. Once she'd done that she stood at the front door looking out, waiting on them to come. Kenny sat on their stairs. When they arrived, the ambulance workers came in behind them. All the sirens must have woken his sister Ernestine up because she came down the hall rubbing her eyes.

"What's going on?" She asked. His momma turned to her and softly said "Your daddy has had a bad accident. He's dead." Ernestine was shocked. She followed the police into the kitchen and when she saw him on the floor she started screaming. The medics had to give her a sedative to calm her and put her to bed. Kenny remembered them lifting his daddy off of the kitchen floor and putting him on a stretcher as the blood ran from his mouth and hit the floor.

He also remembered one of the medics saying, "It looks like

little fine pieces of glass. Oh my god, he swallowed glass. It must have ripped his throat and his insides to shreds look at all the blood."

Kenny's mother came up to him, "Baby you try to lay down now while I talk to the police officers. I'll come in later to check on you and Ernestine."

Kenny went to bed knowing he carried a bad but necessary secret that he would never tell. His mother sat in the living room and gave the police officers a story that was going to tie up all loose ends and leave no doubt.

Kenny's mother forced out tears, when the officer asked her how did her husband come to eat glass, she told him it must have been in the casserole that the woman that came to their home earlier that day for dinner brought in the red glass dish.

She told the officer when she got up to check on the loud noises she heard in the kitchen, she found her husband on the floor bleeding and the dish was on the table. The police officer asked her if she knew the woman and she told him that she was the girlfriend of one of her husband's cousins, she gave them the address and they left to go and talk to her.

Six days later as they were rolling Bobby Simmons body out of Redemption Road AME church to the silver hearse waiting to take him to his final resting place, his cousin's girlfriend, his weekend piece, was sitting behind bars in disbelief charged with murder and professing her innocence as well as their three-year affair.

Kenny recalled his last thought as he watched them roll his father out of the church: "I'll never hit a woman with these hands or bring a Babylonian whore to our house." Kenny had watched his mother kill his father that night. Kenny's mother had left no loose ends when she cleaned the house and she'd left an impression on him about his hands, women, and faithfulness to your family. This impression was the reason he could never hit Nadeen. He would always see his own mother's face, her pain, and her tears, he would hear her voice begging his father to quit until one day she stopped him herself. He'd pushed that memory far back in his mind. Maybe that familiar spirit was what drew Kenny to Nadeen. What he thought was a warm feeling of love and belonging when he was with her in the beginning, was really that spirit his father had carried in his own bloodline. It knew it couldn't operate through Kenny so it drew him in through Nadeen.

It disguised itself just enough to the point he felt the comfort of being around it and being familiar with it, but he was not able to recognize it dressed up in a beautiful face, small waist, and hips shaped like a slim Coca-Cola bottle. There. He'd identified it. He'd identified the "Why?" of allowing his wife to abuse him verbally and physically without ever fighting back, the reason why no one would ever understand him going back home to her. He was thankful to God for showing him and he was thankful to Sister Sara for waking it up.

The reason had been sleeping for far too long.

21

NADEEN COULD BARELY see the lines on the highway in front of her, the rain was coming down so fast. The darkness along with the heavy sounds of the rain hitting the top of the car just put Nadeen into a deep and distant place in her mind. Ann about to have this baby was way too much for her after all that Champagne Porter had done to try and run her out of Greater Trials. She kept playing that picture back in her mind of Brother Ryan, now Pastor Ryan, stepping through that door with his family, Champagne grinning in satisfaction at what she knowingly had done and the promise of more devastation to come.

Nadeen wasn't paying attention to how fast she was driving.

"Momma, you okay? You going kinda fast in this rain." Patsy said trying to make sure she used a concerned tone."

"I got this. You just sit over there and ride," Nadeen told her, hitting the brakes to slow down just a little bit, the next thing they both felt was the car spinning, heading off the side of the highway on its way down an embankment full of large trees. The last thing Nadeen remembered before her head hit the steering wheel and blacked out was the sound of her girls screaming.

Nadeen felt the water all around her, it was up to her waist. It was hot on one side and cold on the other. She looked around but couldn't see in the darkness. Where was she?

She was scared. The water seemed to be rising around her. She turned to the left side and touched the hot water. Just as she tried to walk through it a wave came up the middle of where she was standing and came crashing down on her. It was lukewarm, it knocked her on her back as she gasped to breathe. When she swam back up to the surface, she turned to her right side, the water was cold.

She tried again to get out of the river but again the wave of lukewarm water came crashing down on her, knocking her under the wave again. This seemed vaguely familiar to her. It reminded her of the weird dream she'd been having a few weeks ago.

She called out for help. "Somebody for God's sake help me?" She yelled into the darkness. All of a sudden she saw a flash, as it flashed past her to the other side she heard it say, "Too late." She didn't understand what it was and why it said what it did. She called out again, "Hello? Can someone tell me where I am?" She yelled. Another form flashed past her, it whispered, "Spit her out." Nadeen began to feel dread spreading all over her. She saw the lukewarm wave of water coming towards her again about to come crashing down on her. Just before it hit her she heard a voice, it was a familiar voice, it yelled out into the darkness,

"Please give her another chance!" Nadeen turned to look behind her. The voice was coming from a form filled with light. Again it said, "Please give her another chance. I love her. I'll pray for her."

"She never prayed for you. Let her go. This is where she belongs." The voices hissed back.

"No. God shows us all Mercy and Grace. She is no different." The form responded in a sweet gentle voice.

"She is out of order. Rebellious and disobedient, she must go with us. We have no mercy nor grace." The voices replied releasing a chilling laugh as the waves crashed down on Nadeen again. This time they threw her onto the land. The form stepped closer toward her. Nadeen looked up at it and her heart began to beat rapidly, it was her friend Dhmonique.

Nadeen's mind was racing. How could she be looking at Dhmonique? She'd been dead for a long time now. How could this be her?

"Dhmonique? Dhmonique is that you?" She asked the form. The form nodded "yes" to her. "But how? How can it be you? You died." Nadeen said. The form smiled and then it spoke, "So did you." Nadeen heard voices of loud laughter in the darkness all around her.

It was at that moment Nadeen realized in disbelief where she was. "Dhmonique, am I in eternity? Am I dead?" She asked the form. The form nodded "yes" again to her question.

"Dhmonique, please help me. Get me out of here. I don't understand why am I in this water?" She asked the form. "He spit you out." The form said. Nadeen was confused by what the form said.

"He spit me out? What do you mean he spit me out?" She asked the form." The Father spit you out. You are not in the book." The form that looked like her friend spoke to her. Just as Nadeen was about to ask her what book she was talking about, something that felt like a hook grabbed her leg, she looked down and saw a strange creature dragging her back towards the water which had begun rapidly boiling.

She started screaming, "Dhmonique! Dhmonique, please help me! I'm sorry for everything! Please forgive me!" She yelled as the creature pulled her closer and closer to the boiling water. Nadeen could feel the heat getting closer.

"I forgave you years ago. You must get in order. You must break the generational curse." The voice spoke as she felt the water on her body begin to cause her skin to peel away. It was scalding. Nadeen screamed out "Father God please save me!" as the water began to fill her lungs. As she went deeper and deeper into the burning water, she heard her friend's voice crying out.

"Spare her, Father! Spare her!" and then she went deeper into the darkness of the boiling abyss.

*   *   *

Kenny had been driving for hours. When he hit the sign welcoming him back home, he shouted a loud "Thank you, Jesus!" He couldn't wait to see his girls. He knew he was going to have to face Nadeen's attitude but he was ready.

He was ready to do battle because God had sent him back to get things in order. He was in a hurry to get home but with the rain coming down like it was he decided to slow it down a little bit. As he passed the steep ravine, he noticed what looked like car lights shining from it. He stopped the truck and got out in the heavy rain. He could smell gas coming from the car. He moved a little closer to the edge to look down and could hear the sounds of a baby crying.

He ran back to his truck and got his cellphone to call for help. The sound of a child crying made his heart almost stop. It made him think of Josie. After he called for help, he started back towards the ravine. He was going to need a rope to go down the slope. He went to his truck, got out his rope, and tied it to the bar on the back of his truck. He wrapped the rest of it around his waist and began lowering himself down slowly towards the smoking car. He could see the car, but the mud and the trees made it hard for him to tell what color it was. It was laying on its side on top of a large tree. The tree had saved the car from dropping to the bottom of the ravine.

The baby in the backseat was crying louder and louder. When he reached the car, Kenny wiped the window to look in. He tried to open the back passenger door. He pulled and pulled until finally, it came open. He fell back onto the ground as he looked into the baby's face. It was Josie. She was bleeding and screaming.

"Please, God No! No, God! You didn't bring me back home to bury my family!" Kenny cried out. "Please God don't take them. Not now, Lord. Not now!" Kenny prayed in the rain. He looked in the front seat and saw Patsy knocked out with her head against the dashboard, wet glass in her hair. He already knew who the woman was on the driver's side. Nadeen was covered with glass and blood all over her face.

He reached out and shook Patsy's shoulder. "Patsy. Patsy baby wake up. It's your daddy. Wake up." He said firmly. Patsy moaned a little. He kept shaking her shoulder, "That's it, my girl. Come on. Wake up for me." He said trying to hide the fear in his own voice.

"Daddy! Daddy is that you?" Patsy said weakly. "Help us. Please help us, Daddy."

"It's me, baby. I'm going to get all of you out of here. Let me get Josie out and I'll come back for you Patsy. I promise! Let me check on your Momma." He said slowly moving around the car to prevent his feet from slipping. He made it to the driver's side of the car and reached through the broken window to touch Nadeen.

"Nadeen. Nadeen, baby wake up it's me."

He shook her but she didn't wake up. "Nadeen it's Kenny. You hear me? It's me. I'm back." He said shaking her more aggressively. Josie's cries began to increase. Kenny headed back towards her. "Nadeen hold on. Let me get Josie out and I'll be back for you and Patsy." He said slowly maneuvering his way back around to the back passenger door where Josie was screaming with all her might.

Kenny reached over Josie's car seat and managed to pop it out of the seat belt. He picked her gently up out of the car seat and pulled her from the car. He attached her to the rope, wrapped it tighter around his waist, and headed slowly back up the hill with her. When she recognized him, she cried out "Daddy!" Kenny's heart filled with gratefulness. He missed his baby. God had sent him back right on time.

The ambulance pulled up as he laid Josie down on the front seat of his truck.

"I've got to go back down there. The rest of my family is trapped down there. I have to get them out." Kenny told the EMR tech as he reached over to take Josie.

"I understand but it's too risky to go back for them." The EMR tech said as he strapped Josie down.

"It's worth it. "Kenny said as he tightened the rope around his waist and headed back down to get Nadeen and Patsy out of the car despite the yells from above telling him to come back.

He decided to get Patsy out next.

She'd passed out again. Kenny pried open the passenger side door and checked for her pulse. It was faint but it was there. "Thank God. Okay, Patsy." Kenny said as he reached around her to unlock her seatbelt.

"Daddy? Daddy, it's you?" She said softly.

"Yes, baby. It's me. It's your daddy." Kenny said.

"You came back. You said you would. You came back." Patsy kept saying to him as he lifted her out of the car.

"I never doubted that I would. I hope you didn't either." Kenny told her as he slowly began removing her from the car. He pulled her close to him and tied the rope around them both.

"Get us out of here," Patsy whispered with her eyes closed.

'I'm about to do that right now, baby girl." Kenny said walking backward up the muddy hill. "Just hold on to your daddy. I got you. I always got you."

As he reached the top of the hill with Patsy he saw the tow truck. It backed up and the driver dropped the hook down the muddy embankment.

Kenny untied Patsy and handed her to the EMR's.

"Daddy? Daddy where is Momma? She okay? Where's Momma?" Patsy asked still dazed. "I'm headed down to get her now, baby. She is fine don't worry about her." Kenny said trying to sound as confident as possible.

They tried to tell him to wait for help before going back down. "If that was your wife down there would you wait?" he said heading back down towards the car. When he reached the car, he grabbed the tow truck hook and attached it to the bumper of the car.

He went back to the driver's side. He looked at his wife. She looked so vulnerable and helpless. He hadn't seen her this way since they dated, she needed him back then. He bowed his head for a quick prayer.

"God, we had a deal. You promised me you would bring me back to them so that I could be the man you called me to be so that she could be set free. Don't do this to me please God. Please don't take her. Give us a chance God. Give us a chance to get it right. I believed what you told me!" He cried out into the dark with the rain falling on his face. When he finished, he put his hands in Nadeen's hair and stroked it.

"We about to get you out of here baby. I don't know where you at right now but I need you to come back." He said then he walked back to the tow hook and yanked on it. "Pull it up!" He shouted. "Get my wife out of here.!"

Kenny followed the car up the hill.

As they put Patsy in the ambulance, Kenny went around to the driver's side of the car where the EMR tech was removing Nadeen to put her on the stretcher. He touched her face.

"Wake up, baby." He said to her. Her face was colder than before. A voice said to him. "She's dead." Kenny squeezed her arm and whispered. "You are a God that keeps his promises. Your name is on the line right now you have to do what you said."

At that very moment, Kenny saw Nadeen's head move slightly. She groaned. It sounded like she was saying, "Let me go. I'm sorry. I'll break it Dhmonique! I promise I'll break it."

Kenny shook her again, "Nadeen, baby it's me." He said.

Suddenly she opened her eyes wide and gasped for air. She had a terrified look on her face. She started screaming and twisting trying to get loose from the straps that had her tied to the stretcher. Kenny tried to calm her. "Nadeen! calm down! It's okay. You're safe." Kenny said trying to comfort her.

Nadeen had a wild look in her eyes. She gripped his arm as she looked around. "Kenny? Where am I? Where is this place? Where are we, Kenny?"

You and the girls been in a car accident" He told her. She grabbed his arm tightly.

"The children okay? My babies alive?" She asked.

"They gone be fine Nadeen. All of you are gonna go to the hospital to get checked out and then we all going home." Kenny said.

Her sobs got louder and louder, in between each one she kept saying "Oh my Lord! What have I done? God, please don't spit me out! Please don't spit me out!" She cried out. Kenny figured she'd bumped her head and was not in her right mind.

She reached out for him; Kenny leaned down towards her. She wrapped her arms around his neck. "I'm so glad you came and got me." She cried out to him. "Thank you. Thank you for saving me." She said. "I'm sorry. I'm so sorry I made you leave. Please forgive me. I need you. I see that now." The words shocked him. This moment, as bad as it was, was the moment he had been asking God for, the moment that his wife would need him, would see him as a man that she could lean on. "I forgive you. I forgave you the moment I left. I had to so that God would forgive me and perform his promise." Kenny said as he bent down and kissed her gently on the lips.

He had so many emotions going on at that moment he didn't know how to handle them. In his mind, he said, "Thank you, Father."

The EMR worker told Nadeen they were going to take her to the hospital. She looked over to the worker and whispered. "Please let my husband go with me."

Kenny couldn't believe what he'd heard. Nadeen called him her husband. Got had kept his word and done just what he said he would.

"I'll be right behind the ambulance, baby," Kenny told her as she squeezed his hand. She looked into his face. "You promise?"

"I promise. I won't ever leave your side again, lady." He kissed her forehead and gently pulled his hand away. "Get my family to the hospital." He told the EMTs as he walked briskly to his truck. He tried calling Eva to tell her about the accident but she didn't answer the phone neither did his mother-in-law. He decided to try again once they got to the hospital.

* * *

As they sped to the hospital with half of his family he had no idea the other half, Ann, had gone into full labor. Eva and Grandma Ruth were both fussing because Nadeen hadn't made it yet and wasn't answering her phone.

Ann was having a hard time delivering the baby. She grabbed on to Eva's hand during each contraction and she kept moaning to Eva she was so sorry for the pain she had caused.

"I'm sorry Auntie. I'm sorry." She kept saying. Eva tried to comfort her and talk her through the birth.

"Baby, let's get this little doll into the world. You can't change the past. Let's just get ready for the future. I got you. Push baby girl." Eva told her.

It took hours for Ann to push her little girl into the world but finally, she arrived. She was beautiful. Her hair was thick, soft, black, and curly, she had almond-shaped eyes with a sharp-pointed nose. Ann noticed that her features looked a lot like her mother. What a relief in a way. *The less she looked like the father the better.* Ann thought to herself.

"Ann, she is beautiful. She is thick as a ham but she is a doll." Grandma Ruth said looking at her great-granddaughter. "What are you going to name her?"

The nurse placed the baby in her arms. Ann looked at her still in disbelief. She was whining but she wouldn't open her eyes.

Ann looked down at the beautiful little girl that had come out of her. "Her name is Merci Grandma. Merci with an 'I' not a 'Y' but the same meaning.

"That's a beautiful name. We all need mercy in our lives with or without an I." Grandma Ruth laughed and said.

"I'll go get her, Daddy," Eva said touching the baby's balled fist. She favors your momma to me already. Lord help us."

Ralph was in the waiting room with his mother sitting in the chair looking like a scared little boy. Eva burst into the waiting room.

"You got a big, fat beautiful baby girl, Ralph." She announced with her arms spread wide.

Ralph smiled. "Really? It's a girl?"

His mother patted his lap she didn't say a word.

"What's her name? Me and Ann went at it every day about a name. Can I go see her now?"

"Her name is Merci," Eva said.

"Good. That's what I wanted her name to be." Ralph said. "I knew she liked it, she just didn't want to let me know always trying to be so hard."

"You all can see her as soon as they clean her up. She's pretty mad about being here a few months early and all she had to go through to get here." Eva said with a big grin on her face.

"She won't open her eyes. Maybe if she hears her daddy's voice she will." Eva said to Ralph as she checked her cellphone for the time. "Lord looks like Kenny called me. I'll call and give him the good news as soon as I walk you two in to see the baby."

"I told Nadeen to get her butt to this hospital hours ago. Where is she at? I'm liable to break her neck when I see her." Grandma Ruth said as she walked into the waiting room.

"I'm gonna go downstairs and get me some coffee and a sandwich. They should have the baby ready by that time and you all can go on in." Grandma Ruth said.

"Come on, Daddy and Grandma let's go see this beautiful baby," Eva said putting her arms around Ralph's shoulders.

As Grandma Ruth stepped off of the elevator, she heard the

ambulance sirens. She went over to the glass door and looked. There were at least three ambulances and a truck.

She watched them pull out each person from the ambulance and wheel them in. They were covered with blood. There was a baby too. Grandma Ruth felt something crawl up her neck when she looked at the baby. She closed her eyes and opened them again to focus in on the body on the stretcher. She moved closer to the door and then she saw him come in. She knew him. She knew her son-in-law. She ran up to him in panic.

"Kenny? Kenny, what you doing here? Kenny, why do you have blood all over your shirt, baby?" She asked trying to catch her breath between each sentence. Kenny was as surprised to see her as she was him.

" Momma Ruth? Momma Ruth, what you doin' up here? I was trying to reach you and Eva to tell you Nadeen, Josie, and Patsy had been in an accident. The car went off the road into a deep ravine. God worked it out that I passed by. How'd you find out so fast?" He asked, confused. Grandma Ruth looked behind him and saw the EMTs bringing in the stretchers.

She couldn't believe what she was hearing or what she was seeing. Her grandbabies and Nadeen were covered with glass and blood. "Oh, Lord." She cried out grabbing Kenny by both arms to brace herself. "They dead? They alive? Is my child alive? Lord give her more time to change Lord. Give her more time." She said looking at Kenny's face for answers.

Just as she finished the EMTs brought them in. Grandma Ruth ran up to the stretcher with Josie on it first. "Lord, keep my babies." She said touching Josie all over her face. Next, she went to Patsy. "Patsy, baby, it's your grandma. You hear me?" She asked her trying to remove some of the glass from her hair. "Just blink if you do." Patsy blinked once.

When she got to Nadeen she put her hands together and prayed, "Lord don't take my child. She ain't ready and it ain't her fault it's mine." She said as a small tear ran down her face. Kenny went up to her and gently touched her shoulders.

"Momma Ruth you gotta let them get them to the back. They beat up pretty bad."

"Alright. Y'all tell that doctor he got me to deal with if he don't get it right." She warned the EMTs as they took them to the back.

"How did you find out about the accident?" He asked her.

"I didn't know. I was waiting on her to get here for the birth of the baby."

Kenny grabbed ahold of the desk to steady himself. His head was spinning.

"Ann had the baby? The baby wasn't due yet."

"She decided to come early." Grandma Ruth said.

Kenny looked even more surprised. "She? It's a girl?"

"Yes." She told him.

"Ann okay?" He asked.

"Yes. But now isn't the time to tell her about this accident."

"I agree. Is the boy here?" Kenny asked.

"Yes, him and his momma. He's been real good about watching after Ann."

"Glad to hear that. They got a long road ahead of them we have to be there for them both." Kenny said taking a deep breath. "It's been quite a night."

The doctor came up to Kenny and told him Patsy was going to need surgery. Her arm had been fractured. He paused a moment and looked seriously at Kenny as he spoke slowly.

"Mr. Simmons, I'm afraid your wife's vision has been damaged. The debris from the shattered glass went into her right eye. She may lose her sight."

Kenny was floored. "Can you save it?"

"I'll do my best. The rest is up to God. Your daughter also has some deep cuts to her face, but time will heal them.

He then told him Nadeen seemed to be delirious talking about drowning and having outbursts asking God and Dhmonique to forgive her.

"I know who God is but who is this Dhmonique?" the doctor asked.

"She was her best and only friend in this world. She passed a year before Josie was born. Nadeen took it pretty hard." Kenny told him.

"I can tell the way she was screaming her name. I had to give her a sedative to calm her down. Well, I'm going to go in and fix your daughter up. I'll talk with you after it's done. They all are truly blessed to be alive. They have all been given a second chance." The doctor said as he patted Kenny on the shoulder.

"We all have been," Kenny said giving the doctor a slight smile as he turned back to his mother-in-law. "Momma Ruth, I'm going to stay with them until Patsy is out of surgery and I know the other two are stable then I'll come up and see my daughter and my new grandbaby. By the way, what's the baby's name?"

"She named her Merci, with an I." Grandma Ruth said.

Kenny could barely speak." What a beautiful name. My next generation. My next chance to leave something good in this world is named Merci. I thank God."

Grandma Ruth hugged him. "Glad to have you back home, son. God sent you right on time. I won't tell Ann you're here. I want her to be surprised."

"I'm glad to be back," Kenny said as he hugged her back and softly kissed the top of her head.

* * *

Eva wondered what was taking her mother so long to come back from the sandwich shop downstairs. The nurse had just told them the baby was clean and ready for visitors.

"Ralph you and your momma go ahead. I'm going to try and reach David again." Eva said as she pulled out her cellphone and walked down to the other end of the hall. She called David's phone again and the greeting said his mailbox was full.

"His ear is gonna be full when I get him on this phone," Eva said heading back up the hall to Ann's room. "And what is taking Momma so long?"

She waited around for her mother a little while longer and then decided to head back to the room. *She probably got to talking with somebody*, Eva thought. As she headed back towards Ann's room, she saw Ralph's mother come walking out of the room at a fast pace down the hall. Ralph was walking slowly behind his mother with his head down.

When she came upon Eva she got right in her face. "How dare you and your family put me and my son through this knowing that baby wasn't his!" She shouted at Eva.

Eva was caught off guard.

"What do you mean the baby isn't his?" She shouted back at Ralph's mother. "Ann said that was his baby and he did too. Why do you think it's not his baby? She got a momma. Maybe she looks more like her." Eva said to Ralph's mother tilting her head to the right.

Ralph's mother held her purse clutched in front of her. "That bastard child in there is no more my son's baby than it is the Pope's!" She said and grabbed Ralph by the arm.

"Y'all better go take a closer look at that baby and look for her real daddy," She told Eva. Then she turned to her son. "Come on, boy. Leave this dysfunctional family alone." She told Ralph and headed towards the elevator. Eva was stunned. *What was going on?* She thought to herself. *Ann wouldn't lie about the father of her baby. She wasn't sleeping around with different boys. No way she'd done that but then again, Sandra's boyfriend, Lavon, was acting a little weird about her at the birthday dinner and Patsy did say he had been at Ann's school on the night of the dance. Ann was going to have some big explaining to do if she had fooled around with Patsy's friend's boyfriend.*

She headed to the room to ask Ann about what just happened. She opened the door and didn't see her. The baby was inside the incubator. She was so beautiful. She was caramel brown. Her eyes were almond-shaped like Nadeen's and her lips a pretty cherry pink color. Eva picked her up. It tickled her how much Merci looked like her grandmomma. *That's just what Nadeen gets for being so mean,* Eva thought to herself.

Merci squirmed and began to whine a little bit as she stuck her balled-up fingers in her little mouth. "Niece, your baby is getting hungry." She yelled into the bathroom.

"Okay. I'll get her Aunt Eva," Ann responded back.

Eva checked the baby's diaper it was soaking wet. Eva put her back in the incubator and started to change her. As she took the diaper off, she noticed the mark on her belly next to her navel. It was a strange shape. It was like a crescent moon almost.

Ann came out of the bathroom just as her aunt was finishing up changing the baby's diaper. She walked slowly back to the bed with a funny look on her face. Eva laughed at her.

"Girl, you might as well get that shocked look off your face. This is your baby girl." She told Ann as she picked the baby back up and rocked her gently in her arms.

"Ann, what is going on with you and Ralph's momma? She saying this baby ain't Ralph's and I know better than that. You aren't out like that. She must think every baby has to look like their daddy." Eva said gently rocking Merci.

Ann sat on the bed looking at her Aunt. Her Aunt Eva was her heart. She loved her so much. She didn't know how to tell her that Ralph wasn't the daddy but she knew she had to say the words. "Ralph is not the baby's daddy." She heard her voice say. Eva stopped rocking the baby. She looked at Ann as though she had just grown a unicorn horn out of the center of her forehead.

"Ann, you been sleeping around?" Eva asked her in disbelief.

Ann put her head down. "Is this Sandra's boyfriend's baby? Lord if it is you are going to have a huge mess on your hands."

"No ma'am. I only been with one person." She said looking down at her hands as she rubbed them. They were sweaty.

"Why would Ralph let you blame this baby on him if he isn't the daddy?" Eva asked twisting left to right with the baby.

"He loves me, Aunt Eva. He did it for me. He loves me and that baby. He wants to be with me and I know I can love him. He's a nice guy." Ann said twisting her bed sheet in knots.

Eva walked closer to her bedside. "Ann who is the daddy of this baby?"

Ann kept her head down unable to speak or look her Aunt in the eye. Eva asked her twice but she didn't respond. The third time she asked her the baby opened her eyes. Eva looked into those beautiful almond-shaped eyes, dark grey eyes, and her thoughts became blurry, not making sense. Her vision was off. She stared into the baby's eyes. She stared for a few more minutes and then she got sick inside her stomach. Her knees got weak.

Her mind told her what she could not say. She looked up at her niece and Ann's eyes said the terrible words she could not speak.

"Ann?" Eva spoke with her voice trembling and her mouth dry. "Ann? Answer me. Who is the father of this baby?" Eva looked again into the baby's eyes through the tears filling up in her own. She knew those sneaky grey-colored eyes. Her mind rushed back to where she had seen the crescent-shaped moon birthmark on his back. Her hands became shaky.

Ann grabbed her daughter. Eva dropped to the floor and let out a scream worse than any Ann had ever heard. "Ann! Ann, please tell me it's not true! Please tell me! No, Ann! No! This is not David's baby! Tell me this isn't David's baby!"

The nurses rushed in. "Miss Simmons is everything okay in here?" They looked at her and then Eva on the floor. "Please leave.

Please. It's private." Ann said as the tears gushed out and she almost choked on her words.

"Call us if you need anything." The nurses said as they slowly backed out of the room.

Grandma Ruth came into the room next and saw Eva on the floor. Ann saw the look on her grandmother's face.

"Eva, what in God's name is wrong with you?" She asked. She went over to her daughter and put her arms around her shoulder. "Eva, what happened? Tell me what's wrong?" She pleaded gently shaking her.

"David! David! How could you?" Eva couldn't stop screaming his name long enough to answer her mother.

"Ann, what's wrong? What is she talking about? Why is she screaming about your uncle David? What did he do this time?" She asked her granddaughter who couldn't bring herself to open her eyes and look at her grandmother. She couldn't say it to her.

"Eva, get up off this floor and tell me what's going on before they call security in here." Grandma Ruth said trying to pull her daughter up. She stood in front of her and lifted her face. It was full of an agony she hadn't seen in all her years on earth.

"Momma. Momma. That baby is David's." Eva said barely able to get the words out.

"Whose baby, child? Whose baby is David's?"

Ann exploded in tears. "I didn't. I'm sorry. I'm sorry Aunt Eva. Grandma, I didn't mean for it to happen."

In that moment, Grandma Ruth felt her head spinning as she began piecing the scene before her together. A scene of two lives ripped apart by the pain of a little girl being born who was innocent of the sins of her mother and father and the devastation planted in her aunt by their deception.

"Oh, merciful Father, please step in right now. This family needs you. Ann, you know this is gonna almost kill your momma. Jesus what have you allowed to come upon my family?" She cried out as she held herself to keep from joining her daughter on the floor, on her knees in disbelief.

Eva was beyond reach. She couldn't even hear her mother's prayers for the screaming in her head. She was falling down a dark pit calling her lover's name but no matter how loud she called his name he wouldn't hear it.

*   *   *

He was headed out of the country on a private jet that had been reserved earlier in the week for him and his secret lover. As he reached over to pour her another glass of wine, Champagne Porter, the Ex-First Lady of Greater Trials, laid back in the arms of David, the ex-church financial officer, the man she truly loved and headed back to the islands. Neither she nor her sister, Daphne, would ever have to see the members of Greater Trials MB church again.

Turn the page for a sneak peek at the final book in this series...

JOSIE'S WAYS OF GRACE

SUNDAY MORNING

"Everybody needs to be headed to the car before I get there!" Josie yelled through the house as she slipped on her gold Louboutin shoes and her wrap dress. She could hear the sounds of shoes tapping across her new wooden floor as they scurried towards the front door. She had to laugh just a little bit. Her five-year-old twin boys, Xander and Xavier, reminded her of the times she and her sisters would rush out of the house on Sunday morning to try and make it to the car before their mother, Nadeen, so they wouldn't be left for church or much worse. As she came out of her bedroom door, she saw Mason standing in the living room smiling at the boys as they ran past him and slung the front door open.

It was such a beautiful sight to see them headed down the stairs together. "I believe if they had the keys, they'd drive off right now and leave us both," Mason said. They both laughed.

"You probably right about that," Josie responded. She walked out onto the front porch and Mason followed. "I'll go ahead and drive so I don't have to get out with my robe on in the church parking lot, Mason." Josie said.

Mason looked at his beautiful wife, her skin was a smooth

polished mahogany brown, with full lips and the remnant of the scar on the side of her mouth and under chin from a time not so long ago that she had experienced a childhood trauma she never talked about. When he first met her, it was her beautiful face and Asian-looking eyes that got his attention. He hardly even noticed the scars—she wore makeup constantly to try to cover them up.

He walked up to her and pulled her close to him. She smiled looking up at him. "You look good enough for me to miss church this morning." He told her as he reached down and kissed her. Josie returned the kiss.

"Well, I'm afraid we won't be giving in to fleshly temptations this morning, husband. And not this afternoon either. Remember we have to attend our church member's book signing."

"I hate that." Mason grinned as he patted her on her behind and she released herself from his arms. "You wearing what you got on to the book signing?" He asked her.

"No. I want to look cute but casual. It'll only take me a few minutes to come back home and get my clothes on and pin up my hair."

Mason patted her on the hand she wore her wedding band on. He'd worked three jobs to come up with the money to get that ring. He wanted it to reflect all the love he had inside for her and just how hard he was willing to work to make her happy. The square diamond glared in the sunshine surrounded by a diamond frame all shaped inside of the pure white gold ring guard. He was proud of it himself. They'd married when Josie was nineteen.

Both of their parents thought they were too young but Mason told them it was better to marry than to burn and because he loved Josie he didn't want to wait. So, despite the advice of their parents, they got married in a beautiful church ceremony that her father, Kenny, spared no cost on since she was his last baby girl at home. Her mother, Nadeen, had a dress that turned almost as many heads as Josie's when she entered the church sanctuary. Of course, they were married at Greater Trials MB Church. Her mother had insisted she wouldn't have it any other way. She had raised her girls up in Greater Trials and this was where she would give them away one by one. Two years after they were married, Mason and Josie got the news she was pregnant with twins. They were elated. They both believed that God was enhancing their joy and happiness and that life could only get better.

Josie looked down at the ring. "It's just about time for an upgrade don't you think? I have given you two beautiful boys that almost destroyed my figure so I think I deserve it." Josie said with a smile on her face. Mason pulled her hand to him and kissed the ring.

"And I am so grateful every day for you and them. You, my Queen, can have anything you want." He said.

"Momma, can we go see Grandma Na-Na today after church?" The twins shouted from the front porch breaking the spell of the moment between Josie and Mason. They loved Nadeen. She spoiled them rotten. When Xander and Xavier were born she was ecstatic. She asked to pray over the boys as soon as they were rolled back into Josie's hospital room. She also recalled her mother whispering to her, "I'm so glad you did everything in the right order unlike your sister Ann." Josie didn't respond to the comment. She didn't want to spoil the beautiful moment in front of them. Her mother had changed in many ways but there were still some places where she needed a great deliverance.

She recalled her father hugging her mother around her arms and just beaming with pride as he looked at her. He was the only one that was paying attention to Josie at that moment. They made eye contact and the message transferred was clear. He loved his little girl. She would always be his little baby girl even though now she had her own babies to love and her own husband to help her love them and raise them.

"Momma!" She heard the twins yell in unison. "Momma! We wanna go see Grandma!"

"It depends on how you act in service today. Now get in the backseat of that car. I won't repeat myself again." Josie yelled.

"You make me want to jump in my car the way you said that," Mason said.

"Boy, bye. You better come on too or get left." Josie said walking out the door while digging out her keys from her purse.

"Grandma gonna have us some peppermint at church," Xavier said pulling on the headrest in the car.

"I remember a time when eating anything in the sanctuary got you tore out of the frame by my momma, honey. Times sure have changed." Josie told her boys.

"Grandma gonna be at the door of the church waiting to kiss us ain't that right momma," Xander asked. "You absolutely right you sweet boy. She runs all around that sanctuary but she will stop everything for you two boys. She loves you both." Josie told them

"And we love her too." They said in unison. Josie had been daydreaming a little while driving and drifted mentally out of the car for a few minutes as she remembered her mother, church, and her childhood. Her mother was different back then. She was a person you didn't cross in the sanctuary or at home. God had truly changed her in many ways. Josie remembered the many cries and screams of her sisters Ann and Patsy and the many times she laid on Ann as she cried not completely understanding what had made her big sister so sad.

Nadeen still poured herself into church like it was a paying job. She would tell them the reward she was gonna get from Jesus had more zeroes on it than a paper check from the bank cause she was making deposits constantly.

Josie thought she was trying to make up for all the bad deposits she'd made into their lives. She'd put things in them they had to fight to hide. Her oldest sister, Patsy, had gone off to New York to work at a university and hardly ever came home; she said she was still trying to recover mentally and emotionally. Ann, her middle sister, had married Ralph, her junior high school sweetheart, and was so turned off by anything dealing with church that she hadn't set foot in one since the day she got married and she didn't want to do it then, but Nadeen put her foot down and told her she would not allow her to keep putting mud on her good name up in Greater Trials.

They all knew what that meant. Nadeen was trying to give Ann a subtle hint that the scandal attached to her first grandchild had been quite enough for her to have to fight her way through. Ann's actions had caused Nadeen's image to be slightly scarred and cost her sister, Eva, two years in a mental hospital out of state. Ann was carrying so much guilt from the pain and the shame she believed she'd caused that she agreed to marry Ralph at Greater Trials. She'd told her sisters on her wedding day to take a good look at her on her way back down the aisle cause it was the last time they'd see her in Greater Trials or any other church for that matter.

Josie had to say that Ann had so far kept that promise. As for Josie herself, she was battling a monster so big and so familiar she couldn't seem to win. No matter what weapons she had available to her she couldn't or honestly didn't seem to want to win the war inside of her flesh. She never won the battle. She was always willingly going onto the battlefield and loved every second of it only feeling the guilt once it was done.

She kept it a secret, not even telling Jesus in prayer yet she knew that he already knew and he already saw. She blamed her mother for the battle because it seemed to come naturally and the only way she could be this comfortable with it was if it was 'rooted' deep inside of her.

She wished she could cut it out but she couldn't. She had a good husband and two wonderful twin boys yet she had a desire inside to live on the edge.

She felt like she had her foot on the gas pedal of a fast-moving car and she wasn't able to put her feet on the breaks to stop it as it went around steep and dangerous curves that she knew eventually would cause death or serious injury to her marriage if she didn't pump the breaks on it.

"Baby you just drove over the curb." She heard Mason say.

Josie looked at him, "What?"

Mason smiled at her "You just drove over the curb in the parking lot. That daydreaming is getting kinda dangerous."

"I wasn't daydreaming." Josie lied. Mason gave her a look like 'Really Josie?' and opened the passenger door of the car.

"Alright boys let's unload so your momma can go get ready. You know how she does it." Mason said. "You're pretty momma." The boys said one after the other. They each reached over from the back seat and kissed her on the jaw. Josie's heart swelled with joy. *'This is so wonderful why can't it be enough for me? Why?'* she thought. As she reached for her purse on the floor she looked up at Mason. "Darn. I left the gift for First Lady. Mason, I gotta go back and get it. Here, take my choir robe in. I'll be back before they get to the last offering."

"Momma, you coming in to see Grandma?" Xander asked. "Soon as I get back. Momma left something important gotta go home and get it." She told him. Xander reached up through the car window and hugged her neck again. Josie kissed him. "Bye baby. See you in about an hour or so."

"Come on boys. Let's go on in and help set up for Sunday school." Josie watched him walk towards the front doors of the church. All of them holding hands. It was such a beautiful picture. The twins were the reason her mother changed her church membership from Greater Trials to their new church home, Mt. Transformation, even though it was twenty minutes out of her way. It was Mason's home church and Josie had decided it was only right to follow her husband. Nadeen was so in love with her grandboys she'd do anything for them so when she came to visit with them one Sunday, she ended up joining the next.

As she turned out of the parking lot and pass the church sign she read it and thought Mt. Transformation Church it wasn't living up to its name in her life. She hadn't been transformed she'd only been cloaked. Cloaked with deceit that one day was going to become transparent if the Lord didn't do something to stop it. It had to be him because her own spirit wasn't willing and her flesh was weak. She drove home with a belly full of dread and desire. She knew what she was driving into.

In her mind, she knew she should be ashamed of this thing but her body knew something else it knew that it loved this thing. It enjoyed this thing. This thing gave her excitement. It explained things to her, helped her to see clearly as to why her own mother had been drawn into this abyss. Why it was so hard for her to break free? Josie had seen for herself the devastation it could cause, the way it swept through a family and viciously destroyed everything within and without yet she was wrapped up in it. She parked the car in the front yard and begin to see pictures in her mind of the times she'd allowed her body to give in.

ABOUT THE AUTHOR

Felicia Kelly Brookins is a native of Meridian, Mississippi, and a four-time Award-Winning Author of her first Christian Fiction Novel, *Sister Nadeen's Ways* available on Amazon, Walmart.com, Barnes & Noble, and Books-A-Million websites.

She is also the Founder of Inspired Resources, LLC, Write The Vision: Aspiring Authors and Writer's Workshop established in 2015. In the Spring of 2020, she debuted her first virtual literary platform, Prison To Pens which highlights the restorative and rehabilitative power of writing for previously incarcerated individuals. The event has since been well received. She has been featured on several conversational, interview, and literary podcasts.

"Setting the Emotional, Spiritual and Mental captive free, even if that includes me."

CPSIA information can be obtained
at www.ICGtesting.com
Printed in the USA
LVHW041541010322
712306LV00009B/747